Olivia snuggled up closer to Xander, loving the fact she could.

"I was thinking about the accident," Xander said, "and wondering when the last time was that I told you how much you mean to me. It frightened me to think I might have died without ever telling you again. And I wanted to thank you."

"Thank me? Why? I'm still your wife."

She gasped. Would he pick up on the slip she'd made referring to herself as *still* being his wife?

"You've been so patient with me since I was released from the hospital. I appreciate it."

He leaned closer until his lips touched hers. Olivia felt her body unfurl with response to his touch. She couldn't help it—she kissed him back. Their lips melding to one another as if they'd never been apart. But doing this was perpetuating another lie.

With a groan of regret, Olivia gently pulled away.

"If that's how you show your appreciation, remind me to do more for you," she said, injecting a note of flippancy she was far from feeling.

Somehow she had to get them back to where they once had been.

THE WIFE HE COULDN'T FORGET

BY
YVONNE LINDSAY

Published in Great Britain 2015
by Mills & Boon, an imprint of Harlequin (UK) Limited,
Eton House, 18-24 Paradise Road, Richmond, Surrey, TW9 1SR

© 2015 Dolce Vita Trust

ISBN: 978-0-263-25266-8

51-0615

A typical Piscean, *USA TODAY* bestselling author **Yvonne Lindsay** has always preferred her imagination to the real world. Married to her blind date hero and with two adult children, she spends her days crafting the stories of her heart, and in her spare time she can be found with her nose in a book reliving the power of love, or knitting socks and daydreaming. Contact her via her website: www.yvonnelindsay.com.

This story is dedicated to my fabulous readers,
whose continued support I cherish.

One

She hated hospitals.

Olivia swallowed hard against the acrid taste that settled on her tongue and the fearful memories that whispered through her mind as she entered the main doors and reluctantly scoured the directory for the department she needed.

Needed, ha, now there was a term. The last thing she needed was to reconnect with her estranged husband, even if he'd apparently been asking for her. Xander had made his choices when he left her two years ago, and she'd managed just fine, thank you, since then. Fine. Yeah, a great acronym for freaked out, insecure, neurotic and emotional. That probably summed it up nicely. She didn't really need to even be here, and yet she was.

The elevator pinged, and its doors slid open in front of her. She fought the urge to turn tail and run. Instead, she deliberately placed one foot in front of the other, entering the car and pressing the button for the floor she needed.

Damn, there was that word again. *Need.* Four measly

letters with a wealth of meaning. It was right up there
with *want*. On its own insignificant, but when placed
in the context of a relationship where two people were
heading in distinctly different directions it had all the
power in the world to hurt. She'd overcome that hurt.
The pain of abandonment. The losses that had almost
overwhelmed her completely. At least she'd thought she
had, right up until the phone call that had jarred her from
sleep this morning.

Olivia gripped the strap of her handbag just that little
bit tighter. She didn't have to see Xander if she didn't
want to—even if he had apparently woken from a six-
week coma last night demanding to see her. Demanding, yes, that would be Xander. Nothing as subtle as a
politely worded request. She sighed and stepped forward
as the doors opened at her floor, then halted at the reception area.

"Can I help you?" the harried nurse behind the counter asked her, juggling an armful of files.

"Dr. Thomas, is he available? He's expecting me."

"Oh, you're Mrs. Jackson? Sure, follow me."

The nurse showed her into a blandly decorated private waiting room, then left, saying the doctor would be
with her shortly.

Unable to sit, Olivia paced. Three steps forward. Three
steps back. And again. They really ought to make these
rooms bigger, she thought in frustration. The click of
the door opening behind her made her spin around. This
was the doctor, she assumed, although he looked far too
young to be a neurological specialist.

"Mrs. Jackson, thank you for coming."

She nodded and took his proffered hand, noting the
contrast between them—his clean, warm and dry, hers
paint stained and so cold she'd begun to wonder if she'd

lost all circulation since she'd received the news about Xander.

"You said Xander had been in an accident?"

"Yes, he lost control of his car on a wet road. Hit a power pole. His physical injuries have healed as well as could have been expected. Now he's out of the coma, he's been moved from the high-dependency unit and onto a general ward."

"And his accident? I was told it happened six weeks ago? That's a long time to be in a coma, isn't it?"

"Yes, it is. He'd been showing signs of awareness these past few days, and his nerve responses were promising. Then last night he woke fully, asking for you. It caught the staff by surprise. Only his mother was listed as next of kin."

Olivia sank into a chair. Xander? Asking for *her*? On the day he'd left her he'd said they had nothing to say to each other anymore. Were they talking about the same man?

"I…I don't understand," she finally managed.

"His other injuries aside, Mr. Jackson is suffering from post-traumatic amnesia. It's not unusual after a brain injury—in fact, studies show that less than 3 percent of patients experience no memory loss."

"And he's not in that 3 percent."

The doctor shook his head. "Post-traumatic amnesia is a phase people go through following a significant brain injury, when they are confused, disoriented and have trouble with their memory, especially short-term memory loss. Although, Mr. Jackson's case is a little more unusual with some long-term memory loss evident. I take it you were unaware of his accident?"

"I rarely see anyone who is in regular contact with him and I was never particularly close with his mother. I'm not surprised no one told me. I haven't seen Xander since he walked out on our marriage two years ago. We're just waiting for a court date to complete our divorce."

Olivia shuddered. Even now she couldn't keep the bitterness from her voice.

"Ah, I see. That makes things problematic then."

"Problematic?"

"For his release."

"I don't understand." Olivia furrowed her brow as she tried to make sense of the doctor's words.

"He lives alone, does he not?"

"As far as I know."

"He believes he's coming home to you."

Shock held her rigid in her chair. "H-he does?"

"He believes you are still together. It's why he's asking for you. His first words when he woke up were, "Tell my wife I'm okay.""

Dr. Thomas began to explain the nature of Xander's injuries, but his words about loss of physical form due to the length of his coma and difficulties with short-term memory on top of the longer-term memory loss barely filtered through. All she could think of was that after all this time, her estranged husband wanted her.

"Excuse me," she interrupted the doctor. "But just how much *does* Xander remember?"

"As far as we can tell, his most recent clear memory is from about six years ago."

"But that was just after we married," she blurted.

That meant he remembered nothing of them finishing renovations on their late 1800s home overlooking Cheltenham Beach, nothing of the birth of their son five years ago.

Nothing of Parker's death just after he turned three.

She struggled to form the words she needed to ask her next question.

"Can he...does he...will he remember?"

The doctor shrugged. "It's possible. It's also possible he may never remember those lost years or that he may only regain parts of them."

She sat silently for a moment, letting the doctor's words sink in; then she drew in a deep breath. She had to do this. "Can I see him now?"

"Certainly. Come with me."

He led Olivia to a large room on the ward. There were four beds, but only one, near the window, was occupied. She steeled herself to move forward. To look at the man she'd once pledged her life to. The man she'd loved more than life itself and who she'd believed loved her equally in return. Her heart caught as she gazed on his all-too-familiar face, and she felt that same tug anew when she saw the similarities to Parker. They'd been like peas in a pod. She rubbed absently at the ache in the center of her chest, as if the motion could relieve the gaping hole there.

"He's sleeping naturally, but he'll probably wake soon," the doctor said at her side after a cursory glance at Xander's notes. "You can sit with him."

"Th-thank you," she replied automatically, lowering herself onto the seat at his bedside, her back to the window and the sunshine that sparkled on the harbor in the distance.

Olivia let her eyes drift over the still figure lying under the light covers. She started at his feet, skimming over the length of his legs and his hips before drifting over his torso and to his face. He'd lost weight and muscle mass—his usually powerful frame now leaner, softer. A light beard covered his normally clean-shaven jaw, and his hair was in dire need of a cut.

She couldn't help it. She ached for him. He would hate being this vulnerable and exposed. Xander was a man used to action, to decisiveness. To acting rather than being acted on. Lying helpless in a hospital bed like this would normally drive him nuts. Olivia started in shock as Xander's eyes opened and irises of piercing gray met hers. Recognition dawned in Xander's gaze, and her heart wrenched as he smiled at her, his eyes shining in genuine delight. She felt the connection between them as if it were a tangible thing—as if it had never been stretched to the breaking point by circumstances beyond both of their control. Her lips automatically curved in response.

How long had it been since she'd seen his smile? Far, far too long. And she'd missed it. She'd missed him. For two awful, lonely years Olivia had tried to fool herself that you could fall out of love with someone just as easily as you had fallen in love with him, if you tried hard enough. But she'd been lying to herself. You couldn't flip a switch on love, and you couldn't simply shove your head in a hole in the ground and pretend someone hadn't been the biggest part of your life from the day you'd met him.

She loved him still.

"Livvy?" Xander's voice cracked a little, as if it was rusty and disused.

"It's me," she replied shakily. "I'm here."

Tears burned in her eyes. Her throat choked up, and she reached out to take his hand. The tears spilled down her cheeks as she felt his fingers close tight around hers. He sighed, and his eyes slid closed again. A few seconds passed before he croaked one word.

"Good."

She fought back the sob that billowed from deep inside. On the other side of the bed Dr. Thomas cleared his throat.

"Xander?"

"Don't worry—he's sleeping again. One of the nurses will be by soon to do observations. He'll probably wake again then. Now, if you'll excuse me...?"

"Oh, yes, sure. Thank you."

She barely noticed the doctor leave, or one of the other patients shuffling into the room with his walker and a physical therapist hovering beside him. No, her concentration was fixed solely on the man in the bed in front of her and on the steady, even breaths that raised his chest and lowered it again.

Her thoughts scattered to and fro, finally settling on the realization that Xander could have died in the accident that had stolen his memory and she might never have known about it. That she might never have had another opportunity to beg him for one more chance. It opened a whole new cavern of hurt inside her until she slammed it closed. He hadn't died, she reminded herself. He'd lived. And he'd forgotten that he'd ever ended things between them.

Xander's fingers were still locked around hers. As if she was his anchor. As if he truly wanted her to be there with him. She leaned forward and gently lifted his hand up against her cheek. He was warm, alive. Hers? She hoped so. In fact she wanted him as deeply and as strongly right now as she had ever wanted him. A tiny kernel of hope germinated deep inside Olivia's mind. Could his loss of memory allow them that second chance he'd so adamantly refused?

Right here, right now, she knew that she'd do anything to have him back.

Anything.

Including pretending the problems in their past had never happened? she asked herself. The resounding answer should have shocked her, but it didn't.

Yes. She'd do even that.

Two

Olivia let herself in the house and closed the door, leaning back against it with a sigh as she tried to release the tension that now gripped her body. It didn't make a difference. Her shoulders were still tight and felt as if they were sitting up around her ears, and the nagging headache that had begun on the drive home from the hospital grew even more persistent.

What on earth had she done?

Was it lying to allow Xander to continue to believe they were still happily married? How could it be a lie when it was what he believed and when it was what she'd never stopped wanting?

You couldn't turn back the clock. You couldn't undo what was done five minutes ago any more than you could undo what happened in the past two years. But you could make a fresh start, and that's what they were going to do, she argued with herself.

It might not be completely ethical to take advantage of his amnesia this way, and she knew that she was running a risk—a huge risk—by doing so. At any moment his memory could return and, with it, Xander's refusal to talk through their problems or lean on her for help of any kind. Yet if there was a chance, any chance that they could be happy again, she had to take it.

She pushed off the door and walked down the hall toward the large entertainer's kitchen they'd had so much fun renovating after they'd moved into the two-story late nineteenth-century home a week after their marriage. She automatically went through the motions, putting the kettle on and boiling water for a pot of chamomile tea. Hopefully that would soothe the headache.

But what would soothe the niggling guilt that plucked at her heart over her decision?

Was she just doing this to resolve her own regrets? Wrapped in her grief over Parker's death and filled with recriminations and remorse, hadn't she found it easier to let Xander go rather than fight for their marriage—hell, fight for *him*? She'd accused him of locking her out of his feelings, but hadn't she done exactly the same thing? And when he'd left, hadn't she let him go? Then, when she'd opened her eyes to what she was letting slip from her life, it was too late. He hadn't wanted to even discuss reconciliation or counseling. It was as if he'd wiped his slate clean—and wiped his life with her right along with it.

It had hurt then and it hurt now, but time and distance had given her some perspective. Had opened her eyes to her own contribution to the demise of their marriage. Mistakes she wouldn't make again.

The kettle began to whistle, momentarily distracting her from her thoughts. Olivia poured the boiling water into the teapot and took her favorite china cup and saucer from the glass-fronted cupboard where she displayed her antique china collection. After putting the tea things on a tray, she carried everything outside. She set the tray

down on a table on her paved patio and sank into one of
the wood-and-canvas deck chairs. The fabric creaked
a little as she shifted into a more comfortable position.

Bathed in the evening summer sun, Olivia closed her
eyes and took a moment to relax and listen and let the
sounds of her surroundings soak in. Behind the background hum of traffic she could hear the noises of children playing in their backyards. The sound, always
bittersweet, was a strong reminder that even after tragedy, other people's lives still carried on. She opened her
eyes, surprised to feel the sting of tears once more, and
shifted her focus to pouring her tea into her cup. The
delicate aroma of the chamomile wafted up toward her.
There was something incredibly calming about the ritual
of making tea. It was one of the habits she'd developed
to ground herself when she'd felt as though she was losing everything—including her mind.

She lifted her cup, taking a long sip of the hot brew
and savoring the flavor on her tongue as she thought
again about her decision back at the hospital. The risk
she was taking loomed large in her mind. So many things
could go wrong. But it was still early days. Xander had a
long road to recovery ahead, and it would be many days
yet, if not weeks, before he was released from hospital.
He had yet to walk unaided, and a physical therapy program would need to be undertaken before he could come
home again.

Home.

A shiver ran through her. It wasn't the home he'd lived
in for the past two years, but it was the home they'd
bought together and spent the first year of their marriage
enthusiastically renovating. Thank goodness she'd chosen to live with her memories here rather than sell the
property and move on. In fact, the decision to stay had
very definitely formed a part of her recovery from her

grief at Parker's death followed so swiftly by Xander's desertion of her, as well.

She'd found acceptance, of a sort, in her heart and in her mind that her marriage was over, but her love for Xander remained unresolved. A spark of excitement lit within her. This would be their new beginning. After his release from hospital, they'd cocoon themselves back into their life together, the way they had when they'd first married. And if he regained his memory, it would be with new happier memories to overlay the bitterness that had transpired between them before their separation.

Of course, if he regained his memory before coming home with her, it was likely they'd never get the chance to rebuild their marriage on stronger ground. She had to take the risk. She just had to. And she'd cope with Xander's real world later. The world in which he worked and socialized was not hers anymore. Keeping his distance from his friends and colleagues would be easy enough, initially—after all, it's not as if his bedside cabinet had been inundated with cards or flowers. Just a card signed by his team at the investment bank where he worked. Until he was strong enough to return to his office anyway. By then… Well, she'd cross that bridge when they got there.

Xander's doctors had categorically stated he was in no condition to return to work for at least another four weeks, possibly even longer depending on how his therapy progressed. It should be easy enough to fend Xander's colleagues off at the border, so to speak, Olivia thought as she sipped her tea and gazed out at the harbor in the distance. After all, with Xander in the high-dependency unit at the hospital, and with family-only visitation—which she understood equated to the occasional rare visit from his mother who lived several hours north of the city—it wasn't as if they'd be up-to-date beyond the minimal status provided by the hospital. She'd call one of his partners in the next few days and continue to discourage visitors at the same time.

She felt a pang of guilt. His friends had a right to know how he was, and no doubt they'd want to visit him. But a careless word could raise more questions than she was comfortable answering. She daren't take the risk.

It was at least two years late, but Xander's amnesia was offering her another chance, and she was going to fight for him now. She just had to hope that she could successfully rebuild the love they'd shared. The fact that he woke today, obviously still in love with her, was heartening. Hopefully, they would have the rest of their lives to get it right this time.

Xander looked at the door to the hospital room for what felt like the hundredth time that morning. Olivia should be here by now. After a heated debate with Dr. Thomas about whether or not he'd go to a rehab center—a debate Xander had won with his emphatic refusal to go—the doctor had finally relented and said he could go home tomorrow, or maybe even later today. He'd used the mobile phone Olivia had left with him—his had apparently been pulverized in the accident and his laptop, as well, had been smashed beyond repair—to call the house and get her to bring him some clothes. He'd missed her, and she wasn't answering her mobile phone, either.

He'd go home in his pajamas if he had to. He couldn't wait to get out of here and back to their house. He liked to kid himself he could even see its green corrugated iron roof from the hospital window. It gave him a connection to Olivia in the times she wasn't here.

It had been three weeks, but, God, he still remembered that first sight of her when he'd fully woken. The worry on her exquisitely beautiful face, the urge to tell her that everything would be all right. Sleep had claimed him before he could do anything more than smile at her. This damn head injury had a lot to answer for, he cursed inwardly. Not only had it stolen the past six years from his memory but it had left him as weak as a kitten. Not even capable of forming proper sentences on occasion. Each of the therapists he'd seen had told him he was doing great, that his recovery was progressing well, but it wasn't enough. It would never be enough until he could remember again and be the man he was before his crash.

He couldn't wait to be home. Maybe being around his own familiar things in his own environment would hasten the healing process. He looked out the window and cracked a wry smile at his reflection in the glass. At least one thing hadn't changed. His levels of impatience were right up there where he always remembered them being.

Xander caught a sense of someone in the doorway to his shared room. He turned and felt the smile on his face widen as he saw Olivia standing there. Warmth spread through his body. A sense of rightness that was missing when she wasn't with him.

"You're looking happy," Olivia remarked as she came over and kissed him on the cheek.

Her touch was as light as a butterfly. Even so, it awakened a hunger for more from her. He might not be at his physical peak, but the demands of his body still simmered beneath the surface. They'd always had a very intense and physically satisfying relationship, one he couldn't wait to resume. He laughed inwardly at himself. There was that impatience again. One thing at a time, he told himself.

He swung his legs over the edge of the bed. "I might be able to come home today. I tried to call you—"

"Today? Really?"

Was he imagining things or did the smile on her face look a little forced? Xander rejected the thought immediately. Of course she was as genuinely excited as he was. Why wouldn't she be?

"Dr. Thomas just wants to run some final tests this morning. Provided he's happy I should be able to leave here later this afternoon."

"Well, that's great news," Olivia said. "I'll shoot back home and get some things for you."

Xander reached out and caught her hand in his. "In such a hurry to leave me? You just got here. Don't go yet."

Her fingers curled around his, and he turned her hand over before lifting it to place a kiss on her knuckles. He felt the light tremor go through her as his lips lingered on her skin and her fingers tightened, saw the way her pupils dilated and her cheeks flushed ever so slightly.

"I miss you when you're not here," he said simply, then examined the hand he held more closely. Her nails were short and practical, and even though she'd scrubbed at them, he could still see traces of paint embedded in her skin. It made him smile. "I see you're still painting. Good to know some things haven't changed."

She bit her lower lip and turned her head, but not before he saw the emotion reflected in her eyes.

"Livvy?"

"Hmm?"

"Are you okay?"

"Sure, I'm fine. I'm just worried I'm going to have to cart you home in those," she said lightly as she tugged her hand free and pointed at his striped pajamas with a disparaging look on her face. "And yes, I'm still painting. It's in my blood. Always has been, always will be."

He laughed, like she wanted him to, at the line he'd heard her say so many times. He saw the strain around her eyes lift a little.

"Fine, you better go then, but come straight back, okay?"

"Of course. I'll be as quick as I can," she said, bending down to kiss him on the forehead.

Xander leaned back against his pillows and watched her departing back. He couldn't quite put his finger on it, but something wasn't right. They'd talked about him going home for days. Now that the time was finally here, was she afraid? He mulled the idea over in his head. It was possible. He'd been through a lot, and maybe she was worried about how he would cope on his reentry into the real world. She was such a worrier, always had been. He guessed that came with the territory of being the eldest out of four kids growing up on a farm without their mother. His Livvy was used to micromanaging everything around her so that nothing would go wrong.

When he'd married her, he'd silently promised himself that he would never be a burden to her—that he would never make himself one more responsibility she had to shoulder. Even now, he was determined to make certain that his recovery didn't weigh her down. He'd do whatever it took to ensure that the rest of his recuperation went smoothly so that the worry would disappear from her eyes once and for all.

"Nothing will go wrong," he said aloud, earning a look from the guy in the bed opposite his.

Olivia hastened to the car parking building and got into her car. Her hand shook slightly as she pressed the ignition, and she took a moment before putting on her seat belt and putting the car in gear.

He was coming home. It was what she wanted, so why on earth had she run like a startled rabbit the minute he'd told her? She knew why. It meant she would have to stop putting her head in the sand about the life he'd created when he'd left her. It meant taking the set of keys that she'd been given, among the personal effects the hospital had held since his accident—ruined blood-stained clothing included—and going to his apartment to get his things.

She knew she should have done it before now. Should have gathered together what he would expect to find at their home. His wardrobe, his toiletries. Those were pretty much all he'd taken with him when he'd left. There was nothing for it but to steel herself to invade the new home he'd created. At least she knew where he lived. That was about the only thing the legal separation documents had been any good for, she thought grimly as she drove the short distance from Auckland City Hospital to the apartment block in Parnell where Xander had taken a lease.

She parked in one of the two spaces allocated to his apartment and rode the elevator to the top floor. Letting herself in through the door at the end of the corridor, she steeled herself for what she would find on the other side. As she stepped through the entrance hall she found herself strangely disappointed.

It was as if she'd stepped into a decorator's catalogue shoot. Everything perfectly matched and aligned—and totally lacking any character. It certainly didn't look as though anyone actually lived here. There was none of his personality or his love of old things, no warmth or welcome. She walked through the living room and toward a hallway she hoped would lead to his bedroom. It did, and she was surprised to discover the bedroom was in the same pristine, sterile condition. Not so much as a stray sock poking out from the simple valance that skirted the king-size bed. It wasn't like the Xander she'd known at all—a man who was meticulous in all things except what she teasingly referred to as his *floor-drobe*. Maybe he had a cleaning service come through. Or maybe, the thought chilled her, he really had changed this much.

Anyway, she was wasting time. She needed to get his things and take them back to her house on the other side of the harbor bridge and then get back to the hospital again before he began to think she wasn't coming to take him home after all.

In the spare room closet Olivia found a large suitcase, and she quickly grabbed underwear, socks and clothing from the walk-in wardrobe in Xander's bedroom. From the bathroom she grabbed shower gel, cologne and his shaving kit. She wondered briefly if he remembered how to use it. It had been a while since he'd shaved properly. Only last week she'd teased him about the furry growth that ringed his jaw. Privately, she found she quite liked it. It made him seem a bit softer, more approachable than the cold stranger who'd stalked so emphatically out of her life.

She shook her head as if she could rid herself of the memory just as easily and wheeled the case to the front door. Should she check the refrigerator? She cringed a little at the idea of finding nine-week-old leavings rotting inside, but she figured she would have to do it sometime. She poked around in the drawers until she found a plastic garbage bag and then, holding her breath, opened the shiny stainless-steel door of the fridge.

Empty. *How odd*, she thought as she let the door close again. Not even a half bottle of wine stood in the door. If she hadn't taken Xander's things from his bedroom and en suite herself, she would hardly have believed he even lived here. She pulled open a pantry door and was relieved to see neatly labeled containers and a box of his favorite cereal stacked on the shelves. Okay, so maybe whoever had made the apartment look so spick-and-span had cleaned out the fridge, as well. She made a mental note to try and find out from somewhere, perhaps among his personal papers, if he had a cleaning service. If so, she'd need to put their visits on hold indefinitely.

She looked around the open-plan living room and dining area to see where he might keep his personal files and records. There was nothing to suggest a desk or office space in here. Maybe there was another bedroom? Olivia went back down the hall that led to Xander's bedroom, and spied another door. She opened it, stepped inside and immediately came to a halt.

Her heart thumped erratically in her chest as her eyes fixed on the photo on the desk in what was obviously Xander's home office. She recognized the frame as one she'd bought for him for his first Father's Day and in it was the last photo they'd taken of Parker before he died.

Three

Her hand went to her throat as if she could somehow hold back the sob that rose from the deepest recesses of her grief. She hadn't even realized Xander had taken the picture with him when he'd left. He must have hidden it away when, after the funeral, she'd packed up Parker's room and shoved all the boxes in the attic, along with his albums and the framed photos they'd had scattered around the house.

It had hurt too much to see the constant reminders of his all-too-short life.

If only…

Those two words had driven her almost insane. If only Xander hadn't left the gate open, or hadn't thrown the ball quite so vigorously for Bozo, their dog. If only Bozo hadn't run out into the street in pursuit of the ball and—even now, she gasped against the pain from the memory—if only Parker hadn't run out into the street after him. If only she hadn't told Parker to run outside and play with Daddy in the first place, instead of staying safely in the studio with her that day.

Racked with her own guilt and her anger at the world in general and Xander in particular, she'd done the only thing she could to alleviate the searing pain. She'd packed up Parker's short life and hidden it, telling herself she'd look at his things again when she was able. Every piece of clothing, every toy, every photo—hidden away.

All except this one. She reached out a finger and traced the cheeks of her little boy, locked behind the glass. A child forever—never to grow up and go to school, play a sport or meet girls. Never to stretch his wings, push his boundaries or be grounded for some misdemeanor or another.

Her hand dropped back to her side. She stood like that for several minutes before shaking herself loose from the memories and trying to remember why she'd come in here in the first place. Yes, the cleaning service, that was it. Olivia rifled through Xander's filing system—as linear and exact as she remembered—and found the number she was looking for. A quick phone call to suspend services until further notice was all that was required, and then she was on her way.

Before she left the room, though, she lifted the photo from Xander's desk and shoved it in a drawer. It hurt to shut her baby away like that, but if she had to come back here again, she couldn't bear to see the stark reminder of all they'd lost.

Thankfully traffic through the city to the harbor bridge approach was lighter than usual and she made the trip home in good time. She dragged the suitcase up the flight of stairs and into the guest bedroom, and quickly unpacked and hung up Xander's shirts and trousers and a few suits, still in their drycleaner bags, in the closet and shoved his underwear, socks and T-shirts into the small chest of drawers. She put his toiletries in the bathroom across the hall. It wouldn't be a lie to tell him she'd moved his things in there so he could recuperate in his own space. She just wouldn't mention that she'd moved them from across town rather than from down the hall.

Before leaving the house again, she folded a set of clothes and a belt into a small overnight bag for him and then flew out the door. She was jittery with emotional exhaustion and lack of food by the time she got back to the hospital. Xander was standing at the window when, slightly out of breath, she finally arrived.

"I was beginning to think you'd changed your mind about taking me home," he said lightly when she approached him.

Even though his words were teasing, she could hear the underlying censure beneath them. And she understood it; really she did. Under normal circumstances she would have been back here much earlier. But their circumstances were far from normal, even though he didn't know that yet.

"Traffic was a bitch," she said as breezily as she could. "So, are we good to go? I have some clothes for you here, although I'm thinking you'll find everything on the big side for you now. We might need to get you a whole new wardrobe."

Her attempt at deflection seemed to work. "And I know how much you love shopping," he said with a laugh.

She felt her heart skip a beat. He'd always teased her about her shopping style. While she liked getting new things, she hated crowded stores. She had the tendency to decide what she wanted before she left the house and, with no dillydallying, get in, get the product and get right back out again as quickly as possible. No window-shopping or store browsing for her. Unless it was an art supply store, that was.

Olivia told herself it was ridiculous to be surprised that he'd remember that. After all, he hadn't lost all his memory, just the past six years. She forced a laugh and handed him the bag of his things.

"Here you go. Will you need a hand to get dressed?"

He'd had issues with balance and coordination since awakening from his coma. Physical therapy was helping him regain his equilibrium and motor skills, but he still had some way to go.

"I think I can manage," he said with the quiet dignity she had always loved so much about him.

"Just call me if you need me."

Xander looked her straight in the eye and gave her a half smile. "Sure."

She smiled back, feeling a pang deep inside. She knew he wouldn't call her. He was nothing if not independent—and stubborn. Yes, there'd been a time, early in their marriage, when they'd each been the center of the other's world. But that had all changed.

He was so lucky he didn't remember, she thought fiercely. Lucky that he was still locked in the best of their marriage and couldn't remember the worst of them both.

Xander took the bag through to the shared bathroom and closed the door behind him. A tremor ran through his body as he allowed the relief he'd felt when he'd seen Olivia return run through him. Ever since she'd left earlier today he'd been tense and uncomfortable, so much so the nurse preparing his discharge papers had remarked on the spike in his blood pressure.

He couldn't understand it. Olivia was his wife. So why had he suddenly developed this deeply unsettled sensation that things weren't what they should be between them? He shoved off his pajamas and stepped into the shower stall, hissing a little as the water warmed up to a decent temperature. He couldn't wait to be out of here. Even with Olivia's daily visits to break the monotony of sleep, eat, therapy, eat, sleep, over and over again, he wanted to be *home*.

Xander roughly toweled himself off, swearing under his breath as he lost his balance and had to put a hand on the wall to steady himself. His body's slow response to recovery was another thing driving him crazy. It was as if the messages just weren't getting through from his brain to his muscles.

He looked down at his body. Muscles? Well, he remembered having muscles. Now his build was definitely leaner, another thing he needed to work on. He pulled on his clothing and cinched his belt in tight. Olivia had been right. His clothes looked as if they belonged to another man entirely. He couldn't remember buying them, so they had to be something from his lost years, as he now called them.

A light tap at the door caught his attention.

"Xander? Are you okay in there?" Olivia asked from outside.

"Sure, I'll be right out."

He looked at his reflection in the small mirror and rubbed his hand around his jaw, ruffling the beard that had grown during his stay here. He looked like a stranger to himself. Maybe that was part of Olivia's reticence. The beard would have to go when he got home. Xander gathered his things off the floor and shoved them in the bag Olivia had brought and opened the bathroom door.

"I'm ready," he said.

"Let's go then," she answered with that beautiful smile of hers that always did crazy things to his equilibrium.

Had he ever told her how much he loved her smile, or how much he loved to hear her laugh? He couldn't quite remember. Another thing he would have to address in due course.

They stopped at the nurses' station to say goodbye

and collect his discharge papers, and then they began the walk down the corridor toward the elevator. It irked him that Olivia had to slow her steps to match his. It bothered him even more that by the time they reached her car he was exhausted. He dropped into the passenger seat with an audible sigh of relief.

"I'm sorry—I should have gotten you to wait at the front entrance and driven round to get you," Olivia apologized as she got in beside him.

"It's okay. I've had plenty of time to rest. Now it's time to really get better."

"You say that like you haven't been working hard already." She sighed and rested one hand on his thigh. The warmth of her skin penetrated the fabric of his trousers, and he felt her hand as if it were an imprint on him. "Xander, you've come a long way in a very short time. You've had to relearn some things that you took for granted before. Cut yourself some slack, huh? It's going to take time."

He grunted in response. Time. Seemed he had all too much of it. He put his head back against the headrest as Olivia drove them home, taking solace in the things he recognized and ignoring his surprise at the things that had changed from what he remembered. Auckland was a busy, ever-changing, ever-growing city, but it still disturbed him to see the occasional gaping hole where, in his mind at least, a building used to stand.

"Did the school mind about you taking time off to spend with me?" he asked.

"I don't work at the school anymore," Olivia replied. "I stopped before—"

"Before what?" he prompted.

"Before they drove me completely mad," she said with a laugh that came out a bit forced. "Seriously, I quit there just over five years ago, but I've been doing really well with my paintings since. You'd be proud. I've had several shows, and I'm actually doing quite well out of it."

"But it was never about the money, right?" he said, parroting something Olivia had frequently said to him whenever he'd teased her about not producing a more commercial style of work.

"Of course not," she answered, and this time her smile was genuine.

By the time they arrived at the house he felt about a hundred years old, not that he'd admit it to Olivia, who, to his chagrin, had to help him from the car and up the front stairs to the house.

As she inserted a key into the lock and swung the door open he couldn't help but twist his lips into a rueful smile.

"Seems like not that long ago I was carrying you across that threshold. Now you're more likely to have to carry me."

He regretted his attempt at humor the moment he saw the concern and fear on her face.

"Are you okay?" she said, slipping an arm around his back and tucking herself under his arm so she supported his weight. "You should rest downstairs for a while before tackling the stairs to the bedroom. Or maybe I should just get a bed set up down here for you until you're stronger."

"No," he said with grim determination as they entered the hall. "I'm sleeping upstairs tonight. I'll manage okay."

She guided him into the sitting room and onto one of the sofas.

"Cup of coffee?"

"Yeah, thanks."

While she was gone he looked around, taking in the changes from what he remembered. French doors opened out onto a wooden veranda—they were new, he noted. There'd been a sash window there before and—he looked down at the highly polished floorboards—there'd been some ancient and hideous floral carpet tacked onto the floor. Seems they'd done quite a bit of work around the place.

Xander levered himself to his feet and walked around the room, trailing his hand over the furniture and the top of the ornate mantel over the fireplace, which was flanked by wingback chairs. Had they sat here on a winter's evening, enjoying the warmth of the fire? He shook his head in frustration. He didn't know. He sat in one of the chairs to see if it triggered anything, but his mind remained an impenetrable blank.

"Here you are," Olivia said brightly as she came back into the room. "Oh, you've found your chair. Would you like the papers?"

"No, thanks. Just the coffee."

"Still struggling with concentration?"

He nodded and accepted the mug she handed him. His fingers curled around the handle with familiarity and he stared for a while at the mug. This, he knew. He'd bought it at the Pearl Harbor memorial when they went to Hawaii for their honeymoon. He took a sip and leaned back in the chair.

"That's good—so much better than the stuff they serve in the hospital." He sighed happily and looked around the room again. "I guess we did it all, huh? Our plans for the house?"

Olivia nodded. "It wasn't easy, but we completed it in just over a year. We…um…we got impatient to finish and hired contractors to handle a lot of it. I wish you could remember haggling for those French doors. It was a sight worth seeing."

He must have pulled a face because she was on her knees at his side in a minute. She reached up to cup his cheek with one hand and turned his face to hers.

"Xander, don't worry. It'll come back in its own good

time. And if it doesn't, then we'll fill that clever mind of yours with new memories, okay?"

Was it his imagination or did she sound more emphatic about the new memories than him remembering his old ones? No, he was just being oversensitive. And overtired, he thought as he felt another wave of exhaustion sweep through him. It was one thing to feel relatively strong while in the hospital, when there were so many people in worse condition he could compare himself with. Quite another to feel the same in your home environment, where you were used to being strong and capable.

He turned his face into her palm and kissed her hand. "Thanks," he said simply.

She pulled away, a worried frown creasing her brow. "We'll get through this, Xander."

"I know we will."

She got up and smoothed her hands down her jeans. "I'll go and start dinner for us, okay? We should probably eat early tonight."

He must have fallen asleep when she left the room because before he knew it he was awoken with another of those featherlight kisses on his forehead.

"I made spaghetti Bolognese, your favorite."

She helped him stand and they walked arm in arm into the dining room. It looked vastly different from the drop-cloth-covered space he remembered. He looked up at the antique painted glass and polished brass library lamp that was suspended from the ceiling.

"I see you got your way on the prisms," he commented as he took his seat.

"Not without a battle. I had to concede to the ugliest partner desk in all history for the study upstairs to get this," she said with a laugh.

He smiled in response. There it was. The laugh he felt had been missing from his life for so long. Odd, when it had only been nine weeks since his accident. It felt so much longer.

After dinner Xander propped himself against the kitchen counter while Olivia cleaned up. He tried to help, but after a plate slipped from his fingers and shattered on the tile floor, he retreated in exasperation to the sidelines to watch.

"Stop pushing yourself," Olivia admonished as she swept up the last of the splinters of china on the floor with a dustpan and brush.

"I can't help it. I want to be my old self again."

She straightened up from depositing the mess in the kitchen trash bin. "You are your old self—don't worry so much."

"With Swiss cheese for brains," he grumbled.

"Like I said before, we can plug those holes with new memories, Xander. We don't have to live in the past."

Her words had a poignant ring to them, and he felt as if she wanted to say more. Instead, she continued tidying up. When she was done, she looked at him with a weary smile. Instantly he felt guilty. She'd been doing a lot of driving back and forth from here to the hospital and helping when she could with his physical therapy. And he knew that when she was painting, she'd often work late into the night without eating or taking a break. Why hadn't he noticed the bluish bruises of exhaustion under her eyes? Silently he cursed his weakness and his part in putting those marks there.

"I don't know about you, but I'm ready for an early night," Olivia said with a barely stifled yawn.

"I thought you'd never ask," he teased.

Together, they ascended to the next floor, too slowly for Xander's liking but an unfortunate necessity as his tiredness played havoc with his coordination.

"Did we change bedrooms?" he asked as Olivia led him to the guest room at the top of the stairs.

"No," she answered, a little breathlessly. "I thought you'd be more comfortable in here. I've become a restless sleeper, and I don't want to disturb you."

"Livvy, I've been sleeping too long without you already. I'm home now. We're sleeping in the same bed."

Four

Sleep in the same bed?

Olivia froze in the doorway of the guest bedroom and watched as Xander made his way carefully down the hall to the master suite. She followed, then halted again as she watched Xander strip off his clothes and tumble, naked, into the side of the bed that had always been his. He was asleep in seconds. She watched him for a full five minutes, unsure of what to do. In the end, she grabbed her nightgown from under her pillow and slipped into the en suite bathroom to get ready for bed. By the time she'd washed her face and brushed her teeth her heart was pounding a million miles a minute.

He'd done so many things automatically in the few short hours since they'd returned to the house. It had been reassuring and frightening at the same time. It showed the damage from his injury hadn't destroyed everything in his mind, but it certainly raised questions, for her at least, about how long she'd have before he might remember everything.

Olivia gingerly slid under the bedsheets, trying not to disturb Xander, and rolled onto her side—taking care to stay well clear of him—so she could watch him sleep. She listened to one long deep breath after another, finding it hard to believe he was actually here. His breathing pattern changed, and he suddenly rolled over to face her.

"What are you doing all the way over there on the edge? I've missed you next to me long enough already." His voice was thick with sleep; he reached an arm around her to pull her toward him and snuggled her into his bare chest. "You *can* touch me. I'm not made of spun glass, you know."

And with that, he was asleep again.

Olivia could barely draw a breath. Every cell in her body urged her to allow her body to sink into his, to let herself soak up his warmth, his comfort. He felt so familiar and yet different at the same time. But the steady heartbeat beneath her ear was the same. And, right now, that heart beat for her. How could she not simply relish the moment, take pleasure in it, accept it for what it was worth?

Gold. Spun gold. Jewels beyond compare.

How many achingly lonely nights had she lain here in this very bed since he left her? Made futile wish after wish that they could lie here together, just like this, again? Far, far too many. And now, here he was. All her dreams come true, on the surface at least.

They said you couldn't turn back time, but isn't that effectively what his accident had done?

She sighed and relaxed a little. The moment she did so her mind began to work overtime. If his memory came back, would he forgive her this deception? Could he? She'd basically kidnapped him from the life he'd been leading before the accident. Brought him here to resume a life he'd chosen to leave behind.

She'd never been a deceitful person, and now it felt as if a giant weight hovered above her, held back by nothing more than a slowly fraying thread. One wrong step and she would be crushed; she knew it. Doing this, bringing him home, acting as if nothing bad had ever happened to them? It was all a lie. She felt it was worth telling—would he feel the same way? Only time would tell.

Olivia drew in a deep breath through her nose, her senses responding to the familiar scent of the man she'd already lost once in her life. She wasn't prepared to lose him again. She had to fight with all her might this time. Somehow she had to make this work.

She shifted a little and felt Xander's arm close more tightly around her, as if now he had her in his arms he wouldn't let her go, either. It gave her hope. Tentative, fragile hope, but hope nonetheless. If, in his subconscious mind, he could hold her like this, then maybe, just maybe, he could love her again, too.

Olivia woke to an empty bed in the morning and the sight of Xander standing naked in front of their wardrobe with the doors spread wide-open.

"Xander?" she asked sleepily. "You okay?"

"Where are my clothes?" he asked, still searching through the rails and the built-in drawers.

"I put them in the spare room when I thought you'd be convalescing there."

He made a sound of disgust. "Convalescing is for invalids. I'm not an invalid."

Olivia sat up and dropped her legs over the edge of the bed. "I know you're not," she said patiently. "But you aren't at full strength, either. What is it that you want? I'll see if I can find it for you."

At least she hoped she'd be able to find it for him. She hadn't brought everything of his from the apartment.

What if he had something he particularly wanted to wear and she'd left it behind? Now he was home it would be a lot harder to go back to his apartment and get more of his things. She castigated herself for not thinking about that sooner.

"I want my old uni sweatshirt and a pair of Levi's," Xander said, turning around.

Olivia's eyes raked his body. He'd lost definition, but he was still an incredibly fine figure of a man. There was a scar on his abdomen, pink and thin, where his spleen had been removed after the crash. The sight of it made something tug hard deep inside her. He could so easily have died in that accident and she wouldn't have this chance with him. It was frightening. She already knew how fragile life could be. How quickly it could be stolen from you.

Her gaze lingered on his chest where she'd pillowed her head for most the night. Beneath her stare she saw his nipples tighten and felt a corresponding response in her own. She sighed softly. It had been so very long since they'd been intimate and yet her body still responded to him as if they'd never been apart. And his, too, by the looks of things.

"Why don't you grab your shower and I'll go get your clothes," she suggested, pushing herself up to stand and heading for the spare room.

The sheer need that pulled at her right now was more than she could take. She had to put some distance between them before she did something crazy—like drag him back to bed and slake two years of hunger. As if he read her mind, he spoke.

"Why don't you grab it with me?" Xander said with a smile that make her muscles tighten.

"I'm not sure you've been cleared for that just yet," she said as lightly as she could.

Before he could respond, she headed into the hallway and hesitated, waiting until she heard the en suite door close and the shower start. Then she went to the narrow spiral wooden staircase that led to the attic. Her foot faltered on the first step, and she had to mentally gird herself to keep putting one foot on each step after another.

Somewhere along the line, the attic had become the repository for the things she didn't want to face. But right now she had no choice. She closed her eyes before pushing open the narrow door that led into the storage area lit only by two small diamond-shaped multipaned windows set in at each end. Another deep breath and she stepped inside.

Keeping her line of sight directly where she had stored the large plastic box of clothing that Xander had left behind, she traversed the bare wooden floor and quickly unsnapped the lid, digging through the items until she found the jeans and sweatshirt he'd been talking about.

She dragged the fabric to her nose and inhaled deeply, worried there might be a mustiness about them that would give away where they'd been stored, but it seemed the lavender she'd layered in with his clothing had done its job. There was just a faint drift of the scent of the dried flowers clinging to the clothing. With a satisfied nod, Olivia jammed the lid back on the storage box and fled down the stairs. She'd have to come back later and get the rest of Xander's clothes. She certainly couldn't just take a box down to their bedroom right now because she didn't want to invent explanations for why his things were stored away, either.

In her bedroom—*their* bedroom, she corrected herself—Olivia laid the jeans and sweatshirt on the bed and was getting her own clothing together when Xander came out of the en suite wrapped in a towel, a bloom of steam following him.

"I see we got the hot water problems fixed," he said, coming toward her.

"Yeah, we ended up installing a small hot water heater just for our bathroom." Olivia nodded. "Did you leave any for me?"

"I invited you to share," Xander said with a wink.

She huffed a small laugh, but even so her heart twinged just a little. He sounded so like his old self. The self he'd been before they realized they were expecting a baby and would be dropping to one income for a while. While they'd never been exactly poor, and her income as a high school art teacher had mostly been used to provide the extras they needed for the renovations, it had still been a daunting prospect. Of course, since then, Xander's star had risen to dizzying heights with the investment banking firm he now was a partner in. And with that meteoric rise, his income had hit stratospheric levels, too.

"Hey," Xander said as he walked over to the bed and picked up his clothes. "You expecting me to go commando?"

"Oh, heavens, I didn't think. Hang on a sec."

Olivia shot into the guest bedroom and grabbed a pair of the designer boxer briefs she'd brought back from his apartment. She tossed them at him as she came back in the door.

"There you are. I'll grab my shower quickly. Then I'll get some breakfast together for us, okay?"

Xander caught the briefs she'd thrown at him and nodded. "Yeah, sounds good."

The bathroom door closed behind her, and he sat down on the edge of the bed, suddenly feeling weak again. Damn, but this was getting old, he thought in exasperation as he pulled on his boxers and stood up to slide on his jeans. They dropped an indecent distance on his hips.

He stepped over to the chest of drawers and opened the one where he kept his belts. He was surprised to find the drawer filled with Olivia's lingerie instead. Maybe he'd misjudged, he thought, opening another drawer and then another—discovering that the entire bureau was filled with her things. That wasn't right, was it? It was as if he didn't share a room with her anymore. She said she'd moved his clothes to the guest room, but it seemed odd that she'd have moved everything. And shouldn't there be empty spaces left behind where his things had been?

Xander spied the pair of trousers he'd worn yesterday, lying on the floor. He picked them up and tugged the belt free from its loops. As he fed the belt through his Levi's he wondered what else he'd forgotten. What else was so completely out of sync in this world he'd woken up to? Even Olivia was different from how he remembered her. There was a wariness there he'd never known her to have before. As if she now guarded her words, not to mention herself, very carefully.

Olivia came through from the bathroom, and his nostrils flared as he picked up the gentle waft of scent that came through with her. A tingling began deep in his gut. She always had that effect on him. Had right from the first moment he'd laid eyes on her. So how was it that he could remember that day as if it was yesterday, yet his brain had switched off an entire chunk of their life together?

They went downstairs—Olivia tucked under his shoulder with her arm around his back, he with one hand on the rail and taking one step at a time. His balance and coordination were still not quite there, and he fought to suppress his irritation at being so ridiculously helpless and having to depend on his wife to do such a simple thing. He normally flew down these stairs, didn't he?

"What would you like for breakfast?" Olivia asked when they reached the kitchen.

"Anything but hospital food," he replied with a smile. "How about your homemade muesli?"

She looked startled at his request. "I haven't made that in years, but I have store-bought."

He shook his head. "No, it's okay. I'll just have some toast. I can get that myself."

Olivia gently pushed him onto a stool by the counter. "Oh no you won't. Your first morning home, I'm making you a nice breakfast. How about scrambled eggs and smoked salmon?"

His mouth watered. "That sounds much better. Thanks."

He watched her as she moved around the kitchen, envying how she knew where everything was. None of it was familiar to him. The kitchen was different to the poorly fitted cupboards and temperamental old stove that had been here when they'd bought the property in a deceased estate auction. The place had been like a time capsule. The same family had owned it since it had been built. The last of the family line, an elderly spinster, had lived only on the ground floor in her later years, and nothing had been done to modernize the property since the early 1960s.

The aroma of coffee began to fill the room. Feeling uncharacteristically useless, Xander rose to get a couple of mugs from the glass-fronted cupboard. At least he could see where they were kept, he thought grimly. Automatically he put a heaping spoon of sugar in each mug.

"Oh, no sugar for me," Olivia said, whipping one of the mugs away and pouring the sugar back in the bowl before putting the mug back down again.

"Since when?"

"A couple of years ago, at least."

Just how many of the nuances of their day-to-day life did he need to relearn, he thought as he picked up the mugs and moved toward the coffee machine. She must have seen the look that crossed his face at the news.

"It's okay, Xander. Whether I take sugar or not isn't the end of the world."

"It might not be, but what about important stuff? The things we've done together, the plans we've made in the past few years? What if I never remember? Hell, I don't even remember the accident that caused me to lose my memory, let alone what car I was driving."

His voice had risen to a shout, and Olivia's face, always a window to her emotions, crumpled into a worried frown—her eyes reflecting her distress.

"Xander, none of those things are important. What's important is that you're alive and that you're *here. With me.*"

She closed the distance between them and slid her arms around his waist, laying her head on his shoulder and squeezing him tight as if she would never let him go. He closed his eyes and took in a deep breath, trying hard to put a lid on the anger that had boiled up within him at something so simple, so stupid, as misremembering whether or not his wife took sugar in her coffee.

"I'm sorry," he said, pressing a kiss on the top of her head. "I just feel so bloody lost right now."

"But you're not lost," Olivia affirmed with another squeeze of her arms. "You're here with me. Right where you belong."

The words made sense, but Xander struggled with accepting them. Right now he didn't feel as if he belonged here at all. And the idea was beginning to scare him.

Five

Olivia could feel him mentally withdrawing from her and it made her want to hold on to him all the harder. The medical team had warned her that Xander would experience mood swings. It was all part and parcel of what he'd been through and what his brain was doing to heal itself. She gave him one more squeeze and then let him go.

"Shall we eat breakfast out on the patio?" she asked as brightly as she could. "Why don't you pour our coffees, and then maybe you could set the table out there for me while I finish making breakfast."

Without waiting for a response, she busied herself getting place mats and cutlery and putting them on a large wooden tray with raised edges so that if he faltered nothing would slide off. She couldn't mollycoddle him all the time, but no one said she couldn't try to make things easier for him, either. She went ahead and opened the doors that led onto the patio, ensuring that the way was clear for him with nothing to trip over.

"There, I'll be out in a minute or two," she said after

he'd filled both mugs with coffee. He seemed to hesitate. "Something the matter, Xander?"

"I didn't notice yesterday if you still take milk or not."

His voice was flat, with an air of defeat she'd never heard from him before. Not even after Parker died.

"I do, thanks."

She turned around to the stove and poured the beaten eggs into the pan rather than let him see the pity that she knew would be on her face. As she stirred the egg in the pan, she listened, feeling her entire body relax when he picked up the tray and slowly began to move out of the kitchen. When the eggs were almost done, she sprinkled in some chopped chives from her herb garden and stirred the egg mixture one last time before loading the steaming mix onto warmed plates. She garnished the egg with some dots of sour cream, another sprinkle of chives and some cracked pepper, then added the smoked salmon shavings on the side. Satisfied the meal looked suitably appealing, she carried the plates out to the patio.

Xander was standing on the edge of the pavers, staring at the cherry blossom tree he'd planted when they moved in.

"It's grown, hasn't it?" Olivia remarked as she put the plates down on the table. "The tree. Do you remember the day we planted it?"

"Yeah, I do. It was a good day," he said simply.

His words didn't do justice to the fun they'd had completing the raised brick bed and then filling it with barrow loads of the soil and compost that had been delivered. After they'd planted the tree, they'd celebrated with a bottle of imported champagne and a picnic on the grass. Then, later, made love long into the night.

"Come and have breakfast before it gets cold," Olivia said, her voice suddenly thick with emotion.

They'd made so many plans for the garden that day,

some of which they'd undertaken before their marriage fell apart. She hadn't had the time or the energy to tackle the jobs they'd left undone on her own. In fact, she'd even debated keeping the house at all. Together with the separate one-bedroom cottage on the other side of the patio, where she had her studio, the property was far too big for one person alone.

But now he was home again, the place already felt better. As if a missing link had been slotted back in where it belonged. She pasted a smile on her face and took a sip of her coffee.

Xander desultorily applied himself to his plate of eggs.

"Is it not to your liking?" Olivia asked.

"It's good," he replied, taking another bite. "I don't feel hungry anymore, that's all."

"Are you hurting? They said you'd have headaches. Do you want me to get your painkillers?"

"Livvy, please! Stop fussing," he snapped before throwing down his fork and pushing up from his seat.

Olivia watched as he walked past the garden and out onto the lawn. His body was rigid, and he stood with his hands on his hips, feet braced slightly apart, as if he was challenging some invisible force in front of him.

She stared down at her plate and pushed her breakfast around with her fork, her own appetite also dwindling as the enormity of what she'd done began to hit home. He wasn't a man to be pushed or manipulated; she'd learned that years ago. She'd made decisions before that had angered him. Like the day she brought Bozo home from the pound without discussing it with him first. And the day she stopped taking her birth control.

A shadow hovered over her, blocking the light. Xander's hand, warm and strong and achingly familiar, settled on her shoulder.

"I'm sorry. I shouldn't have reacted like that."

She placed a hand on top of his. "It's okay. I guess I am fussing. I'll try to keep a lid on it. It's just that I love you so much, Xander. Hearing about your accident terrified me. Thinking that I could have lost you…" Her voice choked up again.

"Oh, Livvy. What are we going to do?" he said wearily, wiping a stray tear from her cheek with his thumb.

She shook her head slightly. "I don't know. Just take one day at a time, I guess."

"Yeah." He nodded. "I guess that's all we can do."

He sat back down at the table and finished his breakfast. Afterward, he looked weary, as if every muscle in his body was dragging. Olivia gestured to the hammock she'd only recently strung up beneath the covered rafters.

"You want to test-drive the hammock for me while I tidy up?"

"Still fussing, Livvy," he said, but it came with a smile. "But yeah, that sounds like a good idea."

She gave him a small smile in return and gathered up their things to load the tray he'd brought out earlier.

"Do you want another coffee?" she asked.

"Maybe later, okay?"

She nodded and went back inside. After she'd stacked the dishwasher she intended to tackle the hand washing, but all of a sudden she was overwhelmed with the enormity of the road ahead. She closed her eyes and gripped the front of the countertop until her fingers ached and turned white. For a moment there, outside, when he was staring at the garden, she'd been afraid he'd remember that fateful day when he'd been playing with Bozo and Parker in the yard. She still remembered his shout at Parker to stop. There'd been something in his voice that had made her drop her paintbrush, leaving it to splatter on the floor as she'd turned and run outside in time to hear the sickening screech of tires.

A shudder ran through her body, and she pushed the memory aside. She'd dealt with all of that. Dealt with it and put it away in a filing cabinet in her mind and locked the drawers as effectively as she'd taped the boxes of Parker's things closed before hiding them in the darkest recess of the attic.

Olivia opened her eyes and applied herself to scrubbing her cast-iron pan clean and wiping the stove top and the benches down until they gleamed. She cast a glance outside to where Xander lay in the hammock, asleep. Maybe now would be a good time to bring his clothes down from the attic and filter them in among the items she'd brought from his apartment. *And* put the whole lot back in their bedroom where he believed they belonged.

And they did belong there, she affirmed silently. Just as he belonged here, with her.

Mindful that she might not have much time, Olivia moved quickly. This time she managed to avoid looking at the boxes of Parker's things altogether, right up until she turned around with the storage box and headed back to the door. She had to pass the shadowy nook where she'd put her child's entire history. If only it could be as easy to put away the pain that crept out whenever she least expected it and attacked her heart and soul with rabid teeth.

The all-too-familiar burn of tears stung at the back of her eyes, and Olivia forced herself to keep moving toward the stairs. She wouldn't cry. *Not now. Not now. Not now*, she repeated down each step on the spiral staircase. In her bedroom—*their* bedroom, she corrected herself again—she shoved her things to her side of the wardrobe and, after grabbing a few extra hangers, she shook out and hung up the clothes that had been packed in the box. Then she went to the spare room and transferred all the things she'd put in there to the bedroom, clearing the bureau drawers that she'd taken over and putting his clothing away.

It didn't look as though he had much. Certainly not as much as she'd left behind at the apartment. Would he notice? Probably. She *was* talking about Xander, after all. A man who was precise and who took planning to exceptional levels. Detail was his middle name. It was part of why he was so good at what he did and why he'd rocketed through the company ranks. She doubted she'd be able to sneak another visit to his apartment now he was home, not for a while anyway. And if she did that, it would only cause more problems when he discovered she'd added more clothing to his existing wardrobe. No, she'd just have to stick with what she'd already done.

And hope like crazy that it would be enough.

Xander woke abruptly. At first confused as to his surroundings, he let his body relax when he realized he was home, lying in the hammock in the garden. He let his gaze drift around him, taking in the familiar and cataloguing the changes that they'd obviously made over time. They'd done a good job, he had to admit—if only he could remember actually doing any of it, then maybe he'd feel less like a stranger in his own home and more as if he belonged here.

Carefully, he levered himself to a sitting position and lowered his legs to the ground. He wondered where Olivia had got to. He couldn't see her through the kitchen window. He got up and shuffled a few steps forward. Then, as if his brain had taken a little longer to wake up and join the rest of him, he moved with more confidence.

"Livvy?" he called as he went back inside the house.

The creak of floorboards sounded overhead, followed by her rapid footsteps on the stairs.

"Xander? Are you okay?" she called before she reached the hallway where he stood.

He watched as she did a quick inventory of him and suppressed the surge of irritation that she'd immediately jump to the conclusion there was something wrong. It wasn't fair of him to be annoyed with her, he told himself. This was all as new and as intimidating for her as it was for him.

"I'm fine," he said calmly. "Just wondering what you were up to."

"I put your things back in our bedroom," she said breathlessly. "It took me a little longer than I expected. Sorry."

"Don't apologize. You don't have to be at my beck and call."

Some of his irritation leaked out into the tone of his voice, and he wished the words back almost immediately as he saw their impact on her face and in her expressive eyes.

"I might want to be at your beck and call, Xander. Have you considered that? It…it's been a while since I've had you here."

He felt like a fool. Once again he'd hurt her and all because she cared. He reached out and grabbed her hand before tugging her toward him. He felt the resistance in her body and looped his arms around her, pulling her even closer.

"I guess when we promised the 'in sickness and in health' thing we didn't think it would ever really apply to us," he said, pressing a kiss to the top of her head.

He felt her body stiffen, then begin to relax until she was resting against him, her head tucked into his shoulder and her breath a soft caress on his throat. His arms tightened, trying to say with a physical touch what he couldn't seem to say with words. After a few minutes, Olivia pulled away.

"What did you want to do today? Go for a drive maybe?" she asked. "We may as well make the most of it today because your physical therapist will begin home visits tomorrow."

She smoothed her hands down her jeans, making him wonder what she was nervous about. The action had always been her "tell" when something made her uncomfortable. Had it been their embrace? Surely not. They'd always been a physically demonstrative couple. In private anyway. Memories of just how demonstrative they'd been filled his mind and teased his libido into life. Good to know not everything was faulty, he thought cynically.

But even though that part of his body appeared to be in working order, it was as though there was some kind of a barrier between him and Olivia right now.

"Xander?" she prompted, and he realized he must have looked as if he'd zoned out for a while—and probably had.

"You know, I'd like to stay home today. I tire all too damn easily for my liking. How about you show me what you've been working on in your studio lately?"

Her face brightened. "Sure. Come with me."

She slid an arm around his waist—apparently more comfortable with aiding him than accepting physical comfort from him, he noted—and they walked outside and across to the small cottage on the property.

The cottage was one of the reasons they'd bought the property in the first place. He knew that it was Olivia's dream to give up teaching and paint full-time, and if he had it in his power to help her achieve that dream, well he'd been prepared to do whatever he could to see her do it.

Stepping over the threshold and into what was originally an open-plan living/dining area but was now the main part of Olivia's studio almost made him feel as if he were trespassing. This was very much her space, and she'd made it so right from the start.

He could understand it in some ways. In her childhood, she'd never had a space to call her own. Instead she'd been too busy caring for her siblings, supporting her father where she could, right up until she'd graduated high school and come to Auckland for her degree. Even then she'd lived in a shared-flat situation with ten students in a dilapidated old house.

"You've made some changes," he commented as they stepped inside.

"Not recent—" she started, then sighed. "Oh, I'm sorry. That was insensitive of me."

"Not insensitive," he said, looking around at the canvases she had stacked on the walls. "Don't worry about it."

He walked over to the paintings and gestured toward them. "Can I look?"

"Of course you can. I'm doing this harbor series for a gallery showing a bit closer to Christmas."

"Your style has changed," he commented. "Matured, I think."

"I'll take that as a compliment," Olivia said from behind him as he lifted one canvas and held it at arm's length.

"It's meant as one. You've always been talented, Livvy, but these…they're something else. It's like you've transformed from a very hungry caterpillar into a butterfly."

"That's a beautiful thing to say, thank you."

"I mean it. No wonder you gave up teaching."

She ducked her head, her hair—loose today—fell forward, obscuring the blush he caught a hint of as it bloomed across her cheeks.

* * *

Olivia kept her face hidden so he wouldn't see her sudden change of expression. She'd given up teaching six weeks before Parker was born. It had nothing to do with her art. Keeping up this facade was as difficult as it was emotionally draining.

"Do you miss it? The teaching?" Xander asked, oblivious to the turmoil that occupied her mind. He gave a snort of irritation. "I feel like I should know all this. I'm sorry if we're going over old ground."

She lifted her head and looked him straight in the eye. "Don't apologize, Xander. You don't need to. You didn't ask for this to happen—neither of us did. We both have some adjusting to do."

Not least of which was his casual reference to Parker's favorite book. When Xander had likened her improvement in her painting to that of a very hungry caterpillar morphing into a butterfly, she'd wondered if he recognized the reference. Wondered if, deep down inside that clever mind of his, he still could recite, verbatim, the book he'd read to Parker every night.

Six

"Is this what you're working on right now?" Xander asked, coming to a halt in his traverse of her studio to stand in front of a large canvas she had on her easel.

It was a broad watercolor of Cheltenham Beach, only a block down the hill from their house. A place where she usually took daily walks to blow away the cobwebs of the past that continued to stubbornly cling to the recesses of her mind.

"It is. I'm nearly done," she replied, watching him as he stared at the picture.

Would he remember the times they'd taken Bozo for a run on the white sand, laughing as he'd chased seagulls—his short legs and long hairy body no match for the svelte grace of the birds? Or when they'd taken Parker to the beach for his first swim in the sea? Their son had been such a water baby. Crawling flat out on his pudgy hands and chubby little knees to get back to the water every chance he could. In the end they'd had to bundle him into his stroller and take him home, amid much protesting.

Her heart gave a sharp twist. This was going to shred her into tiny pieces—this wondering, the waiting, the fear that he'd remember and the hope that he might not. But was that entirely fair—to hope that he would never recall the past? He'd been a loving father and a good, if initially reluctant, dad. Was it fair that he shouldn't remember all that he'd been to Parker and the love that had been returned from child to father?

"I like it," Xander said, interrupting her thoughts. "Do you have to sell it? It would be perfect over the mantel in the sitting room, don't you think?"

She'd thought that very thing. And there it was. The synchronicity she and Xander had shared from the day they'd met. Just when had they lost it so completely? she wondered.

"I don't have to sell it," she said carefully. "But it's the focal point of the collection."

"Maybe I'll need to buy it myself," Xander said with a wink that reminded her all too much of the reasons she'd fallen in love with him in the first place.

She laughed. "I hope you have deep pockets. It'll command a good price."

"Maybe I have an 'in' with the artist," he said suggestively. "We might be able to come to reciprocal agreement."

Her body tightened on a wave of desire so sharp and bittersweet she almost cried out. It had been so long since they'd bantered like this. So long since it had led to its inevitable satisfying and deeply physical conclusion.

"We'll have to see about that," she said noncommittally and stepped away just when Xander would have reached for her. "I was thinking of baking cheese scones for lunch. You keen?"

"I shouldn't be hungry after that breakfast, but I am,"

Xander conceded but not before she saw the hint of regret in his eyes.

Had he wanted her in that moment when they were teasing? She'd certainly wanted him. She wished she had the courage to act on it. The doctors hadn't said outright that they shouldn't resume normal marital relations. Thing was, theirs was no longer a normal marriage. She'd be taking even greater advantage of him, wouldn't she, if she gave in to the fierce physical pull between them?

Of course she would, she told herself. No matter how much she might wish it to the contrary, it would be lying to him. *Like you are already?* that cynical voice in the back of her mind intruded. *How much worse would it be?*

She shook her head slightly, as if she could rid herself of the temptation that way.

"Come on," Olivia said firmly, slipping her arm around Xander's waist in a totally nonsexual way and turning him away from the painting. "You can do battle with the coffee machine for me while I whip up those scones. We can discuss the painting later."

Two weeks later saw them settled into a more comfortable routine. The physical therapist came to the house twice a week, putting Xander through his paces and working with him to improve his balance and coordination. In between his visits, Olivia helped him through his exercises. She realized, with regular home-cooked meals and the physical exercise, he was slowly returning to normal. Physically, at least.

Mentally, he was still adrift in the past and none too pleased about it. He'd taken to spending a bit of time in his office upstairs each day, familiarizing himself with his client backgrounds all over again. Olivia was thankful he was nowhere near ready to return to work yet, but eventually he would be. She wouldn't be able to cocoon him within their home forever.

It occurred to her that at some point in time, if his memory didn't show any signs of returning, she'd have to tell him they'd had a child. It was too risky not to. Someone at his office could just as easily raise the subject when he returned to work, and she needed to head that train wreck off at the pass if she could. But now wasn't the time. He had enough to cope with, relearning everything in their current world.

Olivia picked up her palette, squeezed some colors onto the board and selected a brush to work with. She tried to force her mind to the small canvas she'd started this morning when Xander had been with the therapist, but her mind continued to drift back to her husband. To the man she loved.

She'd never struggled to focus on her work before. On the contrary, in the two years since Xander had left her, it had been an escape she'd sought with grateful abandon. Even before their separation, she'd guarded her alone time with a single-minded purpose and actively discouraged him from sharing her creative space. But now the gift of his return to her life made her want to spend every moment she could with him.

She put down her brush and palette and took them over to the small kitchen to clean. It was useless to keep trying to work today when all she wanted was to be near him. After she'd tidied up she walked across her studio to the bedroom on the other side. It was a large room, longer than it was wide. Its southerly aspect didn't allow for the best of light, which had made it useless to her as a work space, but it would work well for Xander as an office. He could even access it through a separate door so as not to disturb her when she was working, if he wanted to. And if they relocated his things down here, she'd be able to be near him as she felt she needed to be.

She tried to kid herself that this new overwhelming need to keep an eye on him was nothing more than that of a concerned wife for her recuperating husband, but in all honesty the need was pure selfishness on her part. Sure, she would worry less about him possibly losing his balance on the stairs if he was here in the single-level dwelling with her while she worked. But worry wasn't the only thing that drove her to consider the change. No, it was much more than that. It had more to do with grabbing this second chance at happiness and holding it close. Nurturing it. Feeding it. And never letting him go again.

Fired up by her decision, she went into the main house and straight up the stairs to the room Xander had set up as his office when they'd moved in. The door was open. When she noticed Xander, she hesitated in the doorway, her hand ready to knock gently on the frame.

He was slumped in his chair, his elbows on his desk and his head resting in his hands.

"Xander?" Olivia flew to his side. "Are you okay?"

"Just another of these damn headaches," he said.

"I'll get your pills."

Less than a minute later she was back at his side with the bottle of heavy-duty painkillers the hospital had prescribed and a glass of water to knock them back with.

"Here," she said, spilling the tablets into the palm of his hand. "Take these and I'll help you to our room. You've been pushing yourself again, haven't you?"

He'd already had a therapy session that morning and, for the past two hours after lunch, had been up here in his office. It was more than his tired body and damaged brain could handle—that much was obvious to her if not to her stubborn husband.

"Maybe," Xander grunted.

His admission told her more than he probably wanted to admit, which, in itself, worried her even more. He grew paler as she helped him to his feet and for once he made no pretense about not needing her support as they slowly made their way across the hall to their bedroom.

Xander lay down on the bed with a groan, and Olivia hastened to draw the drapes and cast the room into soft half light. She brushed a light kiss on his forehead and turned to leave the room. But Xander had a different idea.

"Come lie with me, Livvy, please?"

It was the "please" that did it for her. Carefully, she eased her body on the bed next to him and curled to face him—one hand lifting to gently tousle his hair and massage his scalp. Beneath her fingertips she felt the scar tissue that had formed as he'd healed during his coma. It both shocked and frightened her, and she started to pull her hand away.

"Don't stop. That feels great," Xander protested.

It felt ridiculously good to her to be needed by him. Most of the time since he'd been home he'd fought for independence—begrudgingly accepting her help only when he had to or when she insisted. But here, now? Well, it made her decision to bring him home all the sweeter. To be able to fill a need for him, in the home they'd created together rather than know he was alone in that barren and soulless apartment he'd been living in, gave her a stronger sense of purpose than she'd felt in a long time.

The first thing Olivia became aware of when she woke was Xander's face immediately in front of hers. His eyes were open, and his face so serious, so still, that for a split second she was afraid he'd remembered. But then his eyes warmed and he gave her that special half smile of his.

"Livvy?" he asked, lifting a hand to push a hank of hair off her face.

"Mm-mmm?"

"I love you."

Her eyes widened and her heart went into overdrive. How long had it been since she'd heard those precious words from Xander's lips? Far too long.

She turned her head so she could place a kiss in his palm. "I love you, too."

She snuggled up closer to him, loving the fact she could.

"I mean it," he said. "I was thinking about the accident and wondering when the last time was that I told you how much you mean to me. It frightened me to think it might have been a very long time ago, and that I might have died without ever telling you again."

She was lost for words.

Xander continued. "And I wanted to thank you."

"Thank me? Why? I'm still your wife." She gasped in a sharp breath. Would he pick up on the slip she'd made, referring to herself as *still* being his wife?

"You've been so patient with me since I was released from the hospital. I appreciate it."

He leaned in a little closer until his lips touched hers in the sweetest of kisses. Olivia felt her body unfurl with response to his touch—her senses coming to aching life. She couldn't help it; she kissed him back. Their lips melded to each other as if they had never been apart at all, their tongues—at first tentative, then more hungrily—meeting, touching and tasting. Rediscovering the joy of each other.

Xander's hands skimmed her body, lingering on the curve of her waist, touching the swell of her breasts. Her skin grew tight, her nipples aching points of need pressing against the thin fabric of her bra. He palmed them, and fire licked along her veins. And with it an awareness that doing this with him was perpetuating another lie.

With a groan of regret, Olivia caught at his hands and gently eased them from her aching body. She wriggled away from him and swung herself into an upright position. Drawing in a deep breath, she cast a smile at him across her shoulder.

"If that's how you show your appreciation, remind me to do more for you," she said, injecting a note of flippancy into her voice that she was far from feeling.

"Come back," he urged.

She looked at him, took in the languorous look in his eyes, the fire behind them that burned just for her. Even in their darkest days, they'd still had this physical connection between them. A spark that wouldn't be doused. A need that only each other could fulfill.

"I wish I could, but I've got work to do," she said, getting to her feet and straightening her clothing. "You stay in bed though. You're still a bit too pale for my liking. How's the head?"

"It's fine," Xander replied, also getting up.

As Olivia went to leave the room, he stepped in front of her. "Livvy, stop. You won't break me if we make love."

"I know, and I…I want to—don't get me wrong. I just think it's too soon for you, and on top of your headache, as well—" She broke off as the phone rang.

Grateful beyond belief for the interruption, she dived for the phone next to the bed.

"It's the gallery," she whispered to Xander, covering the mouthpiece once she identified who it was. "I'll be a while."

He gave her a piercing look, one that reminded her all too much of the determined man he'd been, and then turned and left the room. Olivia sagged back onto the edge of the bed, her pulse still beating erratically, her mind only half engaged with the gallery owner's conversation. She must have said all the right things in all the right places because the twenty-minute call seemed to satisfy the gallery owner's queries.

After replacing the phone on the bedside table, Olivia reached out and smoothed the covers of the bed. The indentations of where they'd been lying together were easily erased. If only it was as easy to erase the demand that beat like an insistent drum through her body. Sure, she could have given in to him, but the sense of right and wrong that had made her pull away still reared up in the back of her mind.

It would be unfair to make love with him when he didn't know about their past—about the problems that had driven them apart two years ago. She'd been a fool to think she could live in a make-believe world where the past never happened and everything was still perfect between them. She did love him, deeply, and that was more than half the problem. If she didn't, she would have been able to take advantage of his overture to make love, would have been able to lose herself in his skillful touch and the delirium of his possession without guilt holding her back.

She'd been nuts to think she could just bring him home from hospital and keep him at arm's length and not have to face a situation like this. He'd always had a high sex drive, and hers had mirrored his. It had been a long time since they'd found their special brand of perfection together.

Not for the first time, she felt strong misgivings about what she'd undertaken. She'd wanted to give their marriage a second chance. But once he knew what she'd done, how she'd used him and taken advantage of his injuries, where would that leave her?

Where would that leave either of them?

Seven

As she exited the bedroom she heard Xander back in his office. She crossed the hall and leaned against the doorjamb.

"You're supposed to be taking it easy," she said.

He swiveled around in his chair to face her. "I need to do something. Aside from the memory loss, I've started feeling better. I'm bored. With you working on your paintings, I was thinking about calling the office and seeing if I could go in for a few hours a week. Ease in gently, y'know?"

A fist of ice formed around Olivia's heart. If he did that, it wouldn't be long before he'd learn about her deception. And what chance would she have with him after that?

"You haven't been cleared by the doctor yet. Why don't you give it another week or two? See what he says when you go for your checkup?

"Look, I know I need to be working, but there's no reason why you can't be familiarizing yourself with the markets and what's been happening while I'm painting. Why don't we relocate your office to the bedroom off the studio? That way you can work and I won't have to worry about you. We can keep the single bed that's in there so that if you get another headache, or simply need to rest, you can just lie down."

"And you can keep hovering over me like a mother hen?" he asked with a raised brow.

She pulled a face. "If you want to call it that. I prefer to think of it as caring. Besides, at least that way you won't be bored and we can keep an eye on each other."

He inclined his head. "Okay, when you put it that way. You always lose track of time when you're painting, anyway. I'll be able to make sure *you* keep to *your* breaks."

"So, is it a deal?"

He stood up and brushed her lips with his. "It's a deal."

"Let's go and work out where we'll put everything," she said, turning to leave the room.

He followed close behind, and she hesitated to allow him to catch up so she could walk down the stairs with him. Yes, he was getting stronger every day, but she still worried.

"Y'know, I'm kind of surprised you're willing to give up your space to me," Xander commented as they hit the ground floor and started toward the doors that led out to the cottage.

"Why's that?" Olivia asked, although she had an idea she knew where this was heading.

"You've always protected your work space. I don't remember you ever suggesting we share it before."

She shrugged. "A lot can change in a few years. Would you rather not move your office down here? We don't have to."

"No, I'd prefer it. We can always use an extra bedroom upstairs for when we have those kids we've obviously kept putting off having."

Olivia stumbled as weakness flooded her body at his words. They hadn't put off having kids. Would things have been better if they had? Would they have been spared all that suffering if she'd stuck with the five-year plan Xander had painstakingly created for them? He hadn't thought they were ready to be parents—but she'd wanted a baby so badly. She could never regret the time they'd had with Parker, but if they'd waited…if she'd been a few years older, a few years wiser when she became a mother, would she have made better decisions? Would it have changed anything if Xander had been given more time to adjust and prepare himself to become a father?

She'd taken the decision out of their hands when she'd gone off her birth control pills without telling him. He'd been angry at first, when she'd told him she was pregnant, but he'd eventually warmed to the idea. Although she'd always suspected that in many ways he held a bit of himself back. As if he was afraid to love Parker too much.

She'd even accused him of loving their son less, in those immediate dark days after Parker had died.

"Hey, you okay?" Xander said, putting a hand to her elbow. "I thought I was supposed to be the clumsy one."

"I'm okay," she insisted, focusing on her every step even as her mind whirled in circles.

"About those kids?" Xander started. "I think we should do something about that as soon as we can. Life's too short and too precious to waste. If my car wreck has taught me nothing else, it has taught me that. I'd like us to start trying."

Outside the cottage Olivia hesitated. "Are you sure about that, Xander? You've only just begun your recovery. Do you really think having children right away is a good idea?"

She didn't even know if she wanted another baby, ever. Was her heart strong enough to take that risk? Loving Xander was one thing, and she'd lost him figuratively the day he'd left their home and she'd almost lost him literally in the wreck that had stolen his memories.

"Aren't you the one who usually accuses me of putting things off too long? Why the change of heart? Talk to me, Livvy."

"Xander, can't we just wait until you're better? You've never wanted to rush into this before."

"But what if I never get *better*? What if my memory doesn't return and those years stay locked away forever?"

There was a part of her that wanted that to happen. But Olivia knew that wouldn't be fair to him or to her. If they were to truly make this marriage work, there couldn't be any secrets between them. Even so, she couldn't bring herself to raise the subject of their separation or the tragedy that had triggered it with him just yet. Not when she was still unsure how he would react.

She'd learned as a child that it was best not to face the pain of loss—it was far better to tuck it away where it couldn't be felt. Her father had taught her that. After her mother had died, her dad had told Olivia that looking after "the wee ones," as he'd called her siblings, was up to her now. And then he'd thrown himself into his farm work with a single-mindedness that didn't allow for grieving.

Whenever Olivia had felt the overwhelming loss of her mother, she'd just buttoned it down and turned to the work she had at hand—whether it was her schoolwork or helping her siblings with theirs. And there were always chores to do around the farm and the house. Following her father's staunch example, she'd never allowed herself time to think about her loss or the pain she felt. And that's exactly how she'd coped after Parker's death.

"Livvy?" Xander prompted.

"We'll cross that bridge when we get there," she said stoically. "Right now the things that matter are getting you strong again and being happy together. And if having you here, sharing my space, means I can stop you from reaching the breaking point like you did earlier today, then that's all to the good."

"And vice versa," he reiterated, lifting a finger to trace the circles she knew were under her eyes. "You work too hard yourself."

She cracked a wry smile. "Pot, meet kettle."

Xander laughed, and Olivia felt some of the weight that had settled in her heart ease a little. They'd discuss the issue of children later. Much later. Which reminded her, she needed to go back on the Pill.

Inside the cottage they debated the best way to set up the bedroom to serve Xander's needs. She'd have to contact a contractor to run the separate phone line Xander had to his office upstairs, to the cottage, as well. The Wi-Fi proved patchy, so that was another thing to be looked into. Privately she was relieved that his access to the internet would be a little restricted here initially. What if he took it into his head to do a search on himself or her? There was bound to be some archived newspaper article that would spring up with the details of the speeding driver who had killed their son and their pet with one careless act. Again Olivia accepted that she'd have to tell him about that dreadful day at some stage, but as long as she could put it off, she would.

"How are we going to get my desk in here?" Xander asked as they surveyed the space. "I'd like it under the window, but I doubt we'll be able to manhandle it between the two of us."

"Wouldn't you rather get a new desk?" Olivia asked hopefully.

She hated the behemoth he'd insisted on installing upstairs in the early days of their marriage. It had been their only bone of contention back then.

"Don't think I don't remember how much you dislike my desk. But I love it, and if I'm moving in here, it's moving with me," Xander said with mock severity.

Olivia sighed theatrically. "Well, if you insist. Mrs. Ackerman next door has a couple of university students boarding with her. They might like to earn a few extra dollars manhandling it down the stairs and into here. With any luck, they might even drop it."

She added the last with a giggle that saw Xander reach for her and wrap her tightly in his arms. "I've missed that sound," he said before tickling her. "But I'm afraid I'm going to have to punish you for that comment."

By the time she'd managed to extricate herself from his hold she was weak with laughter and it felt good. She could almost believe that everything was going to be okay after all.

The next morning, Xander moped around the house at a complete loss for what to do with himself that he knew was at odds with his old self. Olivia had gone out to do some shopping while he was busy with the physical therapist. She'd been gone several hours now. Since he was alone in the house, he decided to use the time for some exploring. He went through each room, starting downstairs, poking through the kitchen cupboards and then examining every item in the living room, dining room and formal lounge. Some things spoke to him; others held their silence. No matter what, he felt as if something vital was missing, and he hated it. He wanted his life back. Hell, he wanted himself back.

On a more positive note, the weakness that had plagued him since awakening from the coma was receding, and his physical therapist was extremely pleased with his progress to date. Olivia had suggested turning the tool room, which only had access from outside on the ground floor, into a home gym. With his physical therapist's suggestions it had been outfitted so that he could keep up his program every single day without fail.

Pushing himself felt good but wasn't without its own problems. It often left him shaking and struggling to stay upright under the weight of yet another of those wretched headaches.

He picked up a silver-framed photo that had been taken of him and Olivia on their wedding day, and he felt a strong tug of desire as he studied her face and the creamy curve of her shoulders, exposed by the strapless figure-hugging beaded gown she'd worn. At least that continued to remain the same, he thought as he replaced the picture on its shelf. The bond between them was as strong as ever. She'd been of immeasurable support to him, even if she was still shy about making love. Those barriers would come down eventually. Their relationship had always been too well-founded and their attraction too strong to allow something like his brain injury to keep them apart for very long.

The sound of footsteps coming up the front path caught his attention. A visitor? They'd had no one since he'd come home from hospital. He'd had little to no contact with anyone else, even his mother, who lived in the far north. He'd called her once, to tell her he'd been released from hospital, but their conversation had been as short as it always was. He was fine, she was fine—end of conversation. The prospect of a fresh face was instantly appealing, and he was at the front door and ready to open it before the doorbell could even be rung. He felt his face drop as he recognized the uniform of the courier standing with his finger poised to press the bell.

"Package for Mrs. Olivia Jackson. Could you sign for me, please?"

The courier handed his electronic device and stylus over to Xander for his signature, then passed Xander the large flat envelope he'd had tucked under his arm. With a cheery "Thanks" and a wave, he was gone.

Xander slowly closed the front door and turned the envelope over in his hands. "Oxford Clement & Gurney" was printed on the envelope. Family law specialists. A frown furrowed his brow as he stared at the black print on the white background. He repeated the name of the firm out loud, knowing that there was something about it that was familiar. But no matter how hard he reached for the key in his mind to open that particular door, it remained firmly closed and out of reach.

Family law specialists—what on earth would Olivia be needing them for? The envelope was poorly sealed, just a slip of tape holding it down in the center of the flap. One small tug would be all it took to open it and check the contents inside. Maybe he'd find something that would fill in some of the gaps in his Swiss cheese for brains. But what if he didn't like what he discovered? And how would he explain to Olivia that he'd been prying in her personal mail? There was no question it was addressed to her and not to him.

Maybe something had been going wrong in their marriage before his accident. Maybe things weren't as he remembered and that was why Olivia remained cagey about the past six years. He hadn't pressed her too hard for any of it, and he now wondered if that wasn't in self-preservation. Were there things he really didn't want to know? Things he was actively suppressing?

The doctors said there was no permanent damage to his brain from the accident and only time would tell if the amnesia would be permanent or not. It was vague and frustrating as hell to know that he had no timeline to full recovery. But perhaps he didn't want to remember. If things hadn't been good between him and Olivia, to the extent that she'd been talking to lawyers, then could he have chosen to forget?

Even as he chewed the thoughts over and over in his mind, he couldn't believe that could be true. Or was it simply that he didn't *want* to believe? Without his memory, without her, what did he have left?

"Argh!" he exclaimed and tossed the envelope onto the hall table in disgust. "It's in there somewhere—I know it is," he raged.

He went through to the kitchen, poured himself a glass of cold water and downed it quickly. His hand shook as he put the glass back down on the counter and grimaced against the all-too-familiar shooting pain in his temple that was the precursor to another headache. He reached for the painkillers Olivia kept on the counter for convenience's sake and quickly threw a couple of them down with another drink of water, then went and lay down on one of the large couches in the sitting room. He'd learned the hard way that the only thing that would rid him of the headache was painkillers and sleep. With any luck, when he awoke, Olivia would be back home with some answers for him about the envelope that had arrived.

Eight

Olivia came in through the back door and was surprised to find the house silent. Had Xander gone out for a walk by himself? Fear clutched at her throat. They'd discussed this and agreed that he wouldn't go out on his own just yet. Even his physical therapist had agreed it probably wasn't a great idea until he was a bit stronger, at least not without a stick and Xander had flat-out refused to use one of those.

"Livvy? I'm in the sitting room," he called out. Olivia felt her entire body sag in relief.

"Coming," she answered, putting down the few extra grocery items she'd bought to cook a special dinner with before going to find him.

He was reclining on the largest of the couches in the sitting room, late-afternoon sunlight spilling over him and, no doubt, responsible for the flush on his cheeks. Even so, she automatically put a hand to his forehead to check for fever. Xander's hand closed around hers.

"Still expecting the worst, Livvy? I'm just a little

warm from the sun. That's all." He sat up and tugged her into his lap. Catching her chin between his fingers, he turned her face for a kiss. "Now, that's the proper way to say hello to your husband," he chided gently.

Her lips pulled into a smile and she kissed him again. "If you say so, husband. So, have you been behaving while I've been gone? No wild parties? No undesirable behavior?"

"All of the above," he answered with a cheeky grin. "I wish."

His expression changed under her watchful gaze. "What is it? Did something happen? Did you hurt yourself?"

He rolled his eyes at her. "No, I did not. But there was a delivery for you. An envelope from some law firm in town."

Olivia stiffened and got up from his lap, her movements jerky and tight. "An envelope?"

She turned away from him and closed her eyes. Hoping against hope that the thing hadn't triggered any memories for him.

"I left it on the hall table." He rubbed at his eyes. "Man, I feel so groggy after these naps. They're going to have to stop."

"Did you have a headache?"

"Yeah."

"Then you know the naps are the only thing to really get rid of them. Maybe it's the painkillers that leave you feeling dopey. We can talk to the doctor about it if you like, maybe ask about lowering the dosage?"

"Good idea."

He got up from the couch and walked through to the kitchen. She heard him pour water into a glass. While he was there, she quickly went into the hall and retrieved the envelope.

"I'm just going upstairs to have a quick shower and get changed," she called out. "I'll be back down in a few minutes."

Without waiting for a response she flew up the stairs and into the bedroom. She grabbed some jeans and a long-sleeved T-shirt and carried them and the envelope into the bathroom, where she closed and locked the door. She turned on the shower, then sat down on the closed toilet seat and tugged open the envelope, allowing the contents to slide into her lap. Her heart hammered an erratic beat as a quick scan of the letter from her lawyer confirmed that the two-year separation that was required under New Zealand law before a couple's marriage could be dissolved had passed. Also enclosed was a joint application for a dissolution order for her signature. It had already been signed in advance by Xander.

Olivia looked at the date he'd signed the paper. It was the same date he'd crashed his car. That meant the document had been lying around somewhere, waiting to be actioned. A shiver ran down her spine. What would have happened if it had been sent to her more promptly? If she'd received it before Xander had woken from his coma and asked for her? She'd probably have signed it and returned it to her lawyer and it would have been duly processed through the court.

She reread the cover letter more carefully. In it, her lawyer apologized for the delay in getting the documentation to her. Apparently a changeover in staff had meant it was overlooked. Just like that, her life could have been so drastically different. She and Xander could already be divorced, rather than still very much married.

Bile rose in her throat, and she swallowed hard against the bitterness. She had to put a stop to the divorce proceedings somehow, but how? She couldn't instruct Xander's lawyers for him. How on earth was she going to get around this? Not signing the papers was a start. She shoved them roughly back into the envelope and folded it in half as if making it smaller would diminish the importance of its contents, too.

She'd have to hide it somewhere where Xander would never think to look. She opened the drawer on the bathroom vanity where she kept her sanitary items and slid it into the bottom. There they'd be safe and he certainly wouldn't accidentally come across them.

She quickly shed her clothing and dipped under the spray of the shower before snapping the faucet off and drying and dressing to go downstairs.

"Good shower?" Xander asked as she came into the kitchen. "I started scrubbing the potatoes, by the way. Earning my keep."

"Thanks," she answered as breezily as she could manage given how she'd rushed through everything. "Good to see you have your uses."

And so it began anew, the teasing. The easy banter that had been one of the threads that had bound them together through the days before they'd become parents. Before everything had become so serious. Before they'd been driven apart.

A light spring rain meant they couldn't eat outside tonight, so Olivia laid the table in the dining room, setting it with their best cutlery and the crystal candleholders they'd received as a wedding gift from her father. Her fingers lingered on them, remembering how they'd originally been a gift to her parents for their wedding and, in particular, remembering the words her father had shared with her when he given them.

"I know your mum would have wanted you to have these, and I hope you and Xander can be as happy together as your mother and I were. We didn't have as long as we should have had, and I regret not telling her every single day that I loved her, but you can't turn back time. Don't leave love unsaid between you and Xander, Olivia. Tell him, every single day."

Recalling his words brought tears to her eyes as she leaned forward and lit the candles. She'd gotten out of the habit of telling Xander she'd loved him, long before Parker had died. She'd been so absorbed in her work at the high school and their renovations on the house. Then her pregnancy and subsequently their new baby. Loving Xander had never stopped, but telling him had.

"I'm sorry, Dad," she whispered as she blew out the match she'd been using. "I let us all down, but I'm not going to do that again. This time I *will* make it work. I promise."

And, later that night, when they went to bed, she curled up against Xander's back and whispered to him in the darkness.

"I love you."

His response was blurred with weariness as he mumbled the same words in return, but it was enough—for now.

The rain had cleared by morning. After breakfast, Olivia suggested they go for a walk on the beach. With Xander's balance and strength improving daily and his coordination almost back to normal, she was sure they'd be able to tackle the softer sand areas. If it proved too much, at least they were only a block away from home. Worst-case scenario, she'd leave him on a bench seat, get the car and pick him up. Not that he'd admit defeat or even let her consider doing something like that, she thought to herself as she finished stacking the dishwasher.

"Ready?" she asked as she straightened from her task.

Olivia looked at Xander, who was leaning up against the counter, watching her.

"Never more so," he said. "It'll be good to get out. Home is great, but I think I'm beginning to suffer a bit of cabin fever."

She'd expected as much, and dreaded it. Living as they had, cocooned together on their property, had been remarkably simple. Her brief weekly updates to Xander's boss, and her reiteration that he wasn't up to visitors or calls just yet, had meant his colleagues hadn't called to talk to him. And with Xander not being cleared to drive yet, his independence had been severely curtailed. Making it all the easier to keep up the pretense that their marriage was in healthy working order.

But was it a pretense? It didn't feel like it. Not when they spent their nights wrapped in each other's arms, their days either in the cottage together or with her painting while he did his physical therapy. She knew this was an idyll that couldn't last forever. Real life would have to intrude eventually, even more quickly if, or when, he began to recall the years he'd lost. She'd have to talk to him soon. She'd have to find a way to present the truth without all the ugliness or the pain or the accusations.

The downhill walk to the beach was a gentle one, the last few hundred meters on level ground. Getting back up the hill toward the house might be another story, but she decided to tackle that when it was time. A bit of an example of how she lived everything in her life right now, she realized.

A brisk breeze blew along the beach, so there weren't too many people about. Just a few hardy souls like themselves, wrapped in light jackets and enjoying the fresh air.

"I forgot how good it feels to be out on the beach,"

Xander commented as they strolled slowly along, arm in arm. "Although I miss running along here like I used to."

His eyes were wistful as he watched a guy power along the beach with long graceful strides, his leashed dog running right alongside him, tongue lolling in its mouth.

"You'll get that back, I'm sure," Olivia said with a squeeze of his arm.

"We should get a dog," Xander said, his eyes on the retreating figure of the runner. "In fact, didn't we have a dog?"

Olivia felt a chill go through her that had nothing to do with the wind that tugged like a mischievous child at her hair. And here it was, the moment she'd been dreading. Having to tell him the truth, or at least a part of the truth about a returning memory from the time he'd lost.

She took a deep breath before answering. "Yes, we did have a dog."

"Bozo?"

"You weren't too impressed with the name, but that's what he came home from the pound with."

A smile spread across Xander's handsome face, and his gray eyes glinted with satisfaction. "I remember him. But what happened? He was young, wasn't he?"

Yes, he was young. Only a year older than their son had been when they'd both been hit by the speeding driver.

"Yeah, he was just a puppy when I brought him home. He was only four when he died."

She held her breath, fearfully wondering if he would press her for more details and praying that he wouldn't at the same time. Her prayers were answered.

"We should get another dog. It'll be good for me, get me out of the house to exercise regularly—and you, too," he said with a wink as he hugged her in close to his body. "I know you—when you're working on your paintings nothing else exists, right? You neglect yourself when you're working."

Olivia swallowed against the lump in her throat. She'd been working the day Parker had died. She'd sent him out of the studio because he was playing havoc with her concentration. If she'd only allowed him to play around her, he would still be alive today.

She'd found it hard to get beyond that guilt. In fact, she doubted she ever would completely. Logically she knew it was a combination of events that led to tragedy that day, and that no single action was at fault, but it didn't stop her wondering how things could have been different.

"Speaking of neglecting yourself. How are you doing? Not too tired? Maybe we should head back," she said, turning the subject back to Xander. It was far easier than allowing the focus to be on her.

When Xander agreed to turn back she was surprised. It wasn't like him to concede anything—and it worried her. Back at the house she went to make them coffee while he rested in the hammock on the patio. When she came out again, he was asleep. He'd pushed himself too hard on the sand, she thought as she settled down at the table and watched him. He was still a little pale, but his cheekbones were less prominent than they'd been when he'd come home from the hospital, his shoulders a little heavier.

Slowly, he was gaining weight and condition again, but he still had a long way to go. The body's ability to heal never failed to amaze her. It was his mind that remained an unknown. The sense that she was living on borrowed time bore down on her. She just knew she'd have to find a way to tell him the truth soon.

It was the small hours of the next morning when Olivia woke in her bed with a sense that something was very wrong. She reached out for Xander and only felt the space where he should have been sleeping. In the gloom, she could see their bedroom door was open. She quickly got up from the bed and flew to the door. She could hear Xander, his voice indistinct as he muttered something over and over again.

Where was he? She followed the sound, feeling her heart pound in her chest as she realized he was in the bedroom that had been Parker's. What had driven him there? At the doorway she hesitated, wondering what she should do. Turn on the light? Wake Xander? But if she did that, it might leave him asking questions she had no wish to answer right now.

Cautiously she stepped into the room.

"Xander?" she said softly and placed a hand on his arm.

He muttered something under his breath, and she strained to hear it—her blood running cold in her veins as she made out the words.

"Something's not right. Something's missing."

His head swiveled from side to side. Even though his eyes were open, she knew he was still asleep.

"Everything's all right, Xander. Come back to bed," she urged gently and took his hand to lead him back to their room.

At first he resisted, repeating the words again, but then she felt his body ease and he followed her back down the hall and into their bed. She lay on the mattress, tension holding her body in its grip as Xander slid deeply back into a restful sleep. She didn't know how long it was before she managed to drift off herself. All she did know was that the writing was on the wall.

While his conscious memory was fractured and had wiped the slate clean of all memories of their son, his subconscious was another matter entirely. Deep down he knew something was out of sync with their life, which begged the question: How much longer did she have before he realized exactly what it was?

Nine

Xander watched through the studio's French doors as Olivia worked, lost in concentration and in the composition of another piece for her exhibition. He loved observing her when she was unaware of his scrutiny. It gave him a chance to see her as she really was and not the face she projected to him each morning and through each day.

Something was obviously worrying her—deeply, he suspected—but she was a master at hiding how she felt about things. When they'd first met, he'd actually admired that about her, had recognized her resilience and strength and found them incredibly appealing. Olivia never showed weakness or dependency, but he'd learned that in itself wasn't necessarily a good thing. He knew she had to feel weakness at times—she just refused to show it. Refused to let him help. Marriage was about sharing those loads. Meeting problems head-on, together.

So what was playing on her mind now and how on earth would he get her to share it with him? Was it something to do with the envelope that had been delivered from those lawyers a couple of weeks ago? The envelope that had magically disappeared and that she hadn't discussed at all? He'd searched the name of the firm online and discovered that they were specialists in divorce and relationship property laws. The knowledge had left him with more questions than answers.

Was there something wrong in their marriage that she couldn't bring herself to discuss? Was this existence they now shared just some facade for a crueler reality? Somehow he had to find out. From the moment he'd seen her at his bedside at the hospital, he'd been assailed with a complex mix of disconnection and rightness. Logically he knew a lot of it could be put down to the head injury he'd sustained and the amnesia, but a little voice kept telling him that there was more he should know. Something vitally important.

But if it was so important, why then was Olivia holding back? He could sense it in her. The words that she bit off on occasion, the sudden sad expression in her eyes when she thought he wasn't looking. Even the furrows in her brow, such as she had right now, implied she was worried about something.

He would give her another few days and then he'd push her to find out what it was. Maybe the missing information was the key to his memory; maybe it wasn't. One thing he knew for certain, he'd be stuck in this limbo forever if he didn't get to the bottom of it.

He moved toward the studio doors. Olivia must have seen him because she turned to face him, her features composed in a welcoming smile that didn't quite reach those beautiful blue eyes of hers. She had some paint in her hair, another proof of her distraction. Sure, she was never immaculately tidy and controlled when she worked, but today she looked pressured, distracted even. Until she put on her face for him, that was.

"It's getting late," Xander said as Olivia put down her brush. "You should call it a day."

"I'm inclined to agree with you," she admitted, stretching out her shoulders and shaking out her hands. "Nothing's going right today."

"Clean up and come inside the house. I have a surprise for you."

"A surprise?"

Her eyes sparkled with interest, and he smiled in response.

"Don't get your hopes up too high. It's nothing spectacular. I'll see you back at the house. Five minutes, no more," he cautioned.

"I'll be there," she promised.

True to her word, on his allotted deadline he heard the back door open and then her footsteps coming toward the kitchen.

"Something smells amazing," she said, coming into the room. "Did you cook for me?"

"I did," he said, bending down to lift the dish he'd made from the oven.

"Oh my, did you make your moussaka?" she asked, coming closer and inhaling deeply. "I haven't had that since—"

And there it was again. That sudden halt in her train of thought. The words she left unspoken. He wondered what she'd have continued to say if she'd left herself unchecked.

"Since?" he prompted.

"Since you made it last, which was a while ago," she replied smoothly. "I'm looking forward to it. Shall I set the table?"

"All done."

"Wow, you're organized tonight."

"You were busy, and I didn't have anything else ur-

gently claiming my attention," he joked. "Come on—
we're eating in the dining room."

Carrying the dish, he led the way to the room he'd
prepared with fresh-cut spring flowers and their best
crockery and cutlery. A bottle of sparkling wine chilled
in an ice bucket and tall crystal flutes reflected the glint
of the light from above.

"Are we celebrating?" she asked.

"I've been home a month, I thought it appropriate."

"I feel like I should change," Olivia said, plucking at
her paint-spattered shirt and jeans. "You've gone to so
much bother."

"It wasn't a bother and—" he let his gaze sweep her
body "—you look perfect to me."

A flush rose on her throat and her cheeks. "Thank
you," she said quietly.

Xander put the dish on the table and took a step toward her. He raised one hand, cupped her jaw and tilted
her face to meet his. "I mean it. You're perfect for me."

Then he kissed her. It started out gentle but swiftly
deepened into something much more intense. His arms
closed around her, and her body molded to his, igniting
a sense of rightness that swept over him like a drenching wave. Needs that had been suppressed for weeks un-
furled, sending hunger hurtling through his veins that had
nothing to do with the meal waiting on the table for them
and everything to do with this woman here in his arms.

Xander wanted nothing more than to push all the ac-
coutrements from the table and lay Olivia on its surface.
To feast on her and slake the appetite that demanded sa-
tiation. But he wanted their first time back together since
his accident to be special, and he'd been planning this all
day long. He was nothing if not a planner, and he knew
that the long-term satisfaction gained would be all the
sweeter for not rushing a single moment.

Slowly, gently, he eased back on the passion—loosening his hold on her and taking her lips now in tiny sipping kisses. After a few seconds he rested his forehead on hers. His breath was as unsteady as his hands, and desire for her still clamored from deep within his body.

"Now we've had our appetizer, perhaps we should move to the main course," he suggested, aiming for a light note that—judging by the languorous look in Olivia's eyes—he may have missed entirely.

"If you still cook as good as you kiss, dinner is going to be wonderful," Olivia said dreamily.

"Still?"

There was that hint of something he was missing again. They'd always taken turns cooking and often cooked together. But something in the way she said it made it sound as though she hadn't eaten his cooking in a long time.

"Oh, you know," she said with a flutter of her hand and stepped away from him, her gaze averted. "You've forgotten a lot of things—what if cooking is one of them?"

As an attempt at humor it fell decidedly flat, but Xander chose not to pursue it right now. Instead he tucked it away in the back of his mind, along with the other inconsistencies, to be examined another time. Tonight was meant to be a celebration, and he wasn't going to spoil that for any reason.

"I'm pretty sure you're safe from food poisoning," he said with a smile and held out her chair.

Once she was seated, he opened the sparkling wine and poured them each a glass. After taking his seat, he raised his crystal flute and held it toward Olivia.

"To new beginnings," he said.

She lifted her glass and quietly repeated the toast before clinking her flute against his. He watched her over the rim of his glass as they drank, taking in the shape of her brows, the feminine slant of her eyes and the neat straight line of her nose. Her features were exquisite, dainty, until you reached the ripe fullness of her mouth, which hinted strongly at her own appetites. Her lips glistened with a little moisture from her wine, and he ached to lean forward and taste them again. He reminded himself anew that the best things in life were to be savored, not rushed.

The meal proved he'd forgotten none of his prowess in the kitchen. After dinner they took the rest of the bottle of wine into the sitting room and watched a movie together, sipping slowly of the wine and of each other's lips. When Xander suggested they go upstairs, she didn't hesitate. As he rose from the sofa, where she'd been curled up against him, and held out his hand, she took it and allowed him to pull her upright.

He led her upstairs and into their bedroom. Filtered light from the street lamp outside drifted through the windows, limning the large iron bed frame and the furniture around the room and creating a surreal atmosphere. In some ways this *did* feel surreal. Knowing that they were going to make love again. To be what they'd promised one another they'd always be when they made their wedding vows.

Olivia's fingers went to the buttons on his shirt, and she made quick work of them before pushing the fabric aside and pressing her palms against his chest. Her palms felt cool to the touch; beneath them his skin burned in response, as his entire body now burned for more of her touch. Or, more simply, more of her.

A shudder went through him as her hands skimmed down over his ribs, across his belly and then lower, to the buckle of his belt. He shifted, taking her hands in his and lifting them to his mouth to kiss her fingertips.

"You first," he said, his voice rough with the strain of

forcing himself to take it slow. "I want to see you again. All of you."

Her delicious lips curved into a smile, and she inclined her head ever so slightly. It was enough to make his already aching flesh throb with need. She slowly unfastened each button of her shirt. When the last one was undone, she shrugged her shoulders back and allowed the garment to slide from her body. His eyes feasted on the sight of her. Her breasts were full and lush, pressing against the lace cups that bound them, swelling and falling with each breath she took. Olivia reached behind her, and he swallowed hard as, with the hooks undone, she slid down first one strap, then the other, before pulling the bra away.

He'd told himself he could wait, but he'd lied. He had to touch her again. Had to familiarize himself with the curves and hollows of her body. A body that had been imprinted on his mind and his soul over and over but that now seemed strangely different. He reached out to touch her—to cup her breasts in his hands and test the weight of them, to brush his thumb across the eager points of her nipples. And then, finally, to bend his head and take one of those taut tips with his mouth. She moaned as he swirled his tongue around her. First one side and then the other. Her fingers tangled in his hair and held him to her as if the very beat of her heart depended on it.

He made short work of the fastenings on her jeans and slid the zipper down before shoving the aged denim off her hips and down her legs. Xander slid one arm around her waist while the other dipped low, over her hips and to the waistband of her panties. Everything about Olivia felt familiar and yet different at the same time. There was a softness about her that he didn't remember. Her hips, once angular, were now more gently rounded, and her breasts seemed fuller and more sensitive than he remembered, too.

It was crazy, he thought. He knew her like he knew the back of his hand. She was still the same Olivia he'd fallen in love with and married and made a home with. She was the same Olivia who'd rushed to his bedside when he'd woken from his coma and the same woman who'd brought him home and cared for him this past month. And yet she was slightly altered, as well.

His fingers hooked under the elastic of her panties and tangled in the neat thatch of hair at the apex of her thighs. His long fingers stroked her, delving deeper with each touch until he groaned into the curve of her neck at the heat and moisture at his fingertips.

"You're so wet," he said against her skin, letting his teeth graze the tender skin of her throat.

"For you, Xander. Always for you," she murmured.

He felt a ripple run through her as he stroked a little deeper, the base of his palm pressing against her clitoris while he slid one finger inside her. The heat of her body threatened to consume him, to render him senseless with reciprocal need. He gently withdrew from her body and lifted her into his arms, ignoring her protest as he walked the few short steps to the bed and laid her down on the covers.

"You shouldn't have done that—you might have hurt yourself," she admonished in a husky voice that tried but failed to sound scolding.

"What? And miss doing this?" He wedged one knee between her legs and eased them apart, settling himself between them with the familiarity of the years of their love. He pressed his jean-clad groin against her and was rewarded with a moan from his wife.

"We're still wearing too many clothes," she pointed

out, her fingers drifting across his shoulders before tugging playfully at his hair.

"I'm getting to that," he answered, shifting lower on the bed and pressing a line of wet kisses down her torso as he did so. "One." Kiss. "Thing." Kiss. "At." Kiss. "A." Kiss. "Time."

With the last kiss he tugged her panties to one side and traced his tongue from her belly button to her center and slid his hands beneath her buttocks to tilt her toward him. As his mouth closed over her, his tongue flicking her sensitive bud, he heard her sigh. There was a wealth of longing in her voice when she spoke.

"I've missed this. I've missed you, so much."

And then she was incapable of speech or coherent thought, he judged from the sounds coming from her mouth. All she was capable of was feeling the pleasure he gave her. And he made sure, with every lick and nibble and touch, that it was worth every second.

She was still trembling with the force of her orgasm when he slid her panties off completely and shucked his clothes. He quickly reached into the bedside table drawer, grabbed a condom and sheathed himself. Settling back between Olivia's legs and into her welcoming embrace felt more like coming home than anything he'd felt before. The rhythm of their lovemaking had often been frenetic in the past, but, tonight at least, he wanted to take it slow. To truly live and love in each special moment. He positioned the blunt throbbing head of his penis at her entrance and slowly pressed forward, taking her gasp in his mouth in a kiss as he slid in all the way. Her inner muscles tightened around him, and he allowed himself to simply *feel*. Feel without pain. Feel without emptiness. Feel without frustration or loss.

Loss?

She squeezed again, and he stopped thinking and gave

himself over to the moment, to the beauty of making love with the woman he loved more than life itself. And moments after he'd slowly brought her to the brink of climax again, he pushed them over the edge and took them both on that wondrous journey together.

Later, as he drifted to sleep, his wife curled in his arms with her hair spread across his shoulder, he knew that everything had finally started to fall back into place in his world again. He might not remember everything, but he remembered this and he never wanted to let go of it—or of her.

Olivia woke before dawn with a sense that all was well with her world again. She'd slept better than she had in months, maybe even since before Parker had died. Xander slept deeply beside her, and she gazed at his profile in the slowly lightening room. She would never have believed it was possible to love a person as much as she loved him and she never wanted to lose him again.

That meant she had to talk to him. Had to tell him about Parker and his death; about their separation. But how on earth was she to start talking about something so horrible when they'd just reaffirmed everything about their love in the most perfect way possible? She didn't want the darkness of their loss and the cruel words they'd thrown at each other to taint the beautiful night they'd shared. Maybe they should take another day, or even a week.

It wasn't going to be easy telling him, whether he remembered eventually or not. But he deserved to know what had happened. Objectively and without emotion or harsh words clogging everything. It also meant facing up to the full truth about her contribution to the slow and steady breakdown of their marriage.

How did she explain why she'd taken decisions they

should have made together and made them herself? Decisions like getting Bozo—like stopping her birth control pills before they'd even really discussed when they'd have a family. They'd been in no way emotionally ready to be parents, but she'd forced the issue because she'd had an agenda and nothing and no one would sway her from it.

Looking back, she could understand why she'd behaved that way, but it didn't make it right. She'd had to become a mother at only twelve years old, caring for her three younger siblings—aged ten, eight and six—when their mother died. Waking them each morning, feeding them breakfast, packing their lunches and making sure they all got on the school bus on time. Then, at the end of each day, making sure everyone's homework was completed and a hearty meal was prepared and on the table when her father came in from the farm.

She'd hoped that taking care of everything would make him happy and proud of her. But it never seemed to work. She did everything she could to try and put some of the sparkle back in her father's dull blue eyes, but it seemed that no matter how hard she tried, no matter what she did, his grief over her mother's death locked his joy in life and his children in a frozen slab.

She became even more organized, more controlling of what happened around her, especially when it came to taking care of her family. And that didn't let up, not even when she went to university or began teaching. No, she continued to supervise and encourage her siblings' career aspirations, pushed them to apply for student loans and to enter university while working part-time jobs to help cover their living expenses just as she had. It was only after the youngest of them had graduated, and Olivia was teaching full-time at an Auckland high school, that she began to relax—and then she'd met Xander.

There'd been an aloofness, a self-sufficiency about

him that had appealed to her. While in some ways it had reminded her of her father and how he kept himself emotionally detached from his children, it also meant Xander wouldn't need her as much as her siblings had needed her. For the first time in years, she could focus on herself. She could be independent, to a point, and do what she'd always wanted to do. Paint and create her own family on her own terms. And she had done all that—but she'd forgotten the vital ingredient to a truly happy marriage. Making those big decisions as a couple, not as a pair of individuals.

She had a lot to make up to Xander for. Caring for him once he'd been released from the hospital had been a start. Repairing their marriage was next.

Xander's hand skimmed the curve of her buttocks even as he slept, and she smiled and closed her eyes again. She had plenty of time to work out when she would tell him everything. For now, she'd just revel in the moment.

Ten

When Olivia woke again, the sun was streaming into their bedroom windows. The space beside her in the bed was empty, and she could hear the shower running. A smile of deep satisfaction spread across her face as she stretched and relished the sensation of her naked skin against the sheets. Everything was going to be okay; she just knew it.

A perturbing memory flickered on the periphery of her mind. The condom Xander had used last night—she'd completely forgotten about them being in his bedside drawers. After Parker's birth, Xander had taken control of that side of things. They hadn't discussed it, but she suspected it was mostly because he didn't want to be hijacked into parenthood again. She'd had no objections. But how old would those condoms have been? And was the fact he'd reached for one so automatically an indicator that windows on the past were subconsciously opening for him again?

She leaned over the bed, slid open the drawer and

squinted a little as she tried to make out the date printed on the box. As she read the numbers her stomach somersaulted. Expired. Well and truly. She quickly put the box back in the drawer and closed it, her nerves jangling. Surely they'd still be safe, but just in case, she'd buy some more and replace the expired box.

Olivia grabbed her robe and shrugged it on. *A big breakfast*, she thought. Maybe pancakes made from scratch with maple syrup and bacon. She did a mental inventory of the contents of the refrigerator and her pantry as she made her way downstairs. After using the downstairs bathroom to quickly freshen up, she went into the kitchen and began whipping up the pancake batter.

She'd just put bacon on the grill when Xander came into the kitchen. She looked up and drank in the sight of him.

"Well, you look better than you have in a while," she said with a smile before crossing the kitchen to plant a kiss on his chin.

"I think we both know the reason for that," he said, playfully tugging on the sash of her robe and sliding his hands inside to cup her breasts.

Instantly her body caught flame. How had she survived without him all this time? she thought as he bent his head and kissed her thoroughly. Her body mourned the loss of his touch when he pulled away and straightened her robe.

"You hungry?" she asked. "I'm making pancakes."

"I'm always hungry around you," he said. "Are we eating in here or outside?"

"It's a beautiful day—why don't we eat on the patio?"

"I'll set the table."

While Olivia ladled batter into the heavy skillet she had on the stove top, Xander gathered up place mats, cutlery and condiments, and took them outside. She was humming with what she knew was a ridiculous smile on her face when the phone rang. After checking quickly on the bacon, she reached for the handset and answered the phone.

"Mrs. Jackson? It's Peter Clement here."

Olivia's joyful mood bubble burst instantly. Her lawyer. The one representing her in the divorce proceedings Xander had brought against her.

"Could you hold the line a moment?" she asked. Muting the phone, she popped her head out the back door. "Xander, could you keep an eye on the bacon for me and finish making the pancakes? I just have a call I need to take."

"Sure," he said, moving with his still-careful gait toward the house.

As soon as he was in the kitchen, Olivia went upstairs to their bedroom and sat on the bed.

"Sorry to keep you waiting."

"No problem," the lawyer said smoothly. "I've had a call from your husband's lawyers following up on the dissolution order I forwarded to you for your signature the other week. Did you receive it okay?"

"Y-yes, yes, I did. But there's been a change in circumstances."

"A change?" the lawyer pressed.

"Xander is back home with me. We…uh…I think it's safe to say we're no longer separated."

There was a long silence at the end of the phone before Olivia heard a faint sigh, followed by, "I see."

"Can we halt the divorce proceedings?"

"Is this something your husband is agreeable to?"

"Yes, of course." She crossed her fingers tight and prayed it wasn't a lie. It couldn't be. Not now. Not after last night.

"And has he instructed his lawyers in that regard?"

"Um, not yet. You see, he's been in an accident and unable to communicate with them—up until now, that is," she amended quickly. "But I'm sure he'll be in touch soon."

"This is quite irregular, Mrs. Jackson. Your husband has already signed the forms—"

A sound from behind her made her turn around quickly. Xander stood in the doorway. How long had he been there? How much had he heard? Too much, judging by the look on his face.

"Mr. Clement, I have to go. I'll call you later and confirm everything."

Before he could reply, she disconnected the call and dropped the phone onto the tangled sheets of the bed in which they'd made such sweet love last night. Her stomach lurched uncomfortably under Xander's gaze, and she reached out a hand toward him.

"Xander?"

"You mind telling me what that was about?" His voice was cold, distant and too much like that of the man who had left her two years ago.

"It…it's complicated."

She stood up, tugging the edges of her robe closer together—her hands fisting in the silky fabric.

"Then find simple words to explain. I'm sure I'll grasp them eventually even with my brain injury."

Sarcasm dripped from his every word, and she was suddenly reminded of the piercing intelligence he'd always exhibited, which she'd ridiculously assumed was impaired with his amnesia.

"Don't be like that," she implored. "Please."

"Then tell me, how should I be? Are you telling me I didn't overhear you instructing your lawyer to halt divorce proceedings? I'm assuming those would be *our* divorce proceedings?"

She quivered under the force of his slate-gray glare. "Y-yes," she admitted reluctantly.

"Divorce proceedings that obviously started before my accident."

She nodded, her throat squeezing closed on all the words she should have said long before now. She'd been an idiot. She'd had ample opportunity to be honest with him, and she'd held back the truth at every turn. Putting her own needs and desires, her own wish for a second chance, first before everything else. Including the man she loved. A sob rose from deep inside. Had she ruined everything?

Xander pushed a hand through his hair and strode across to the window, looking out at the Auckland harbor and the city's high-rises. That was his world—the one he had chosen. Not the enclosed space of this house they'd bought and renovated together, not the confines of the land surrounding it. This was supposed to be his sanctuary, not his prison, and she'd made it that by withholding their separation from him.

"How long had we been apart?" he demanded harshly, not even looking at her.

"Just over two years."

He abruptly turned around to face her, but she couldn't make out his features as he stood silhouetted against the window.

"And you brought me back here as if nothing had ever happened."

"Xander, I love you. I've always loved you. Of course I brought you home."

"But it's not my home anymore, is it?" he asked, his face tightening into a sharp mask of distrust. "That's why you didn't have all my clothes, why I didn't recognize everything...I can't believe you thought you could pull something like that off. What *were* you thinking?"

"I was thinking we deserved a second chance at making our marriage work," she said with a betraying wobble in her voice. "We still love one another, Xander. This past month has proven that to me as much as to you, hasn't it? Haven't we been great together? Wasn't last night—?"

"Don't," he said, slicing the air in front of him with the flat of his hand. "Don't bring last night into this. Do you have any idea how I feel right now?"

She shook her head again, unable to speak.

"I'm lost. I feel about as adrift as I did when I woke up at the hospital and found myself surrounded by people I didn't know and too weak to move myself without assistance. Except it's worse somehow because I should have been able to trust you."

Olivia moaned softly as the pain of his words struck home. He was right. She'd owed him the truth from the start.

"Why were we separated?" he asked, coming to stand in front of her.

Olivia's legs trembled, and she struggled to form the words in her mind into a sentence.

"We had begun to grow apart. I guess the gloss of our first year of marriage wore off pretty quickly. A lot of that is my fault. I made decisions about us that I should have included you in. Getting the dog was one of them."

She took in a deep breath, preparing to tell him about Parker, but an icy-cold fist clutched her heart and she couldn't push the words from inside her. Not yet, anyway. "We both got caught up in our separate lives and forgot how to be a couple. You spent a lot of time at work—initially, before you made partner, you put the time in so you could show them how good you were at your job. After that, you were proving you were worthy of the honor.

"I...I was unreasonable about it. I resented the additional hours you spent there, even though I knew you were doing it for us. We wanted to finish the house off quickly, and it was a juggle for us both. I was still teaching during the day and painting at night. When you were home, you expected me to be with you, but I had my own work to do, as well. We allowed ourselves to be at cross-purposes for too long, and we forgot how to be a couple."

What she said wasn't a lie, but it wasn't the whole truth, either. Their marriage hadn't been perfect before Parker had been born, but she'd ignored the cracks that had begun to show—plastering them up with her own optimism that as long as she stuck to her plan, everything would be okay.

But it wasn't okay. Not then and not now. Their marriage hadn't truly ended until they'd lost Parker—but the problems that had been in place all along were the reason why they hadn't been able to pull together after the death of their son. They'd gotten too used to going on their separate paths to find their way back to each other even in their time of greatest need.

"You don't exactly paint me in a very good light," Xander said. "I don't like the sound of who I was."

She stepped closer to him and laid one hand on his arm, taking heart when he didn't immediately shake her off. "Xander, it went both ways. I wasn't the easiest person to live with, either. We both had a lot of learning to do. We met, fell in love and got married so fast. Maybe we never really learned to be a couple like we should have. But I still love you. I've always loved you. Can you blame me for wanting to give us another chance?"

Xander looked at her and felt as if she'd become a stranger. She'd withheld something as important as their separation from him. A separation that had been on the brink of becoming permanent, according to the conversation he'd overheard.

And worse than the doubt and suspicion were the questions that now filled his mind. Why had he left her? Was there more to it than the growing apart? Was she keeping something else from him?

One thing she said, though, pushed past his anger and confusion to resonate inside him. She loved him; and he knew he loved her. Maybe that's why her betrayal in keeping the truth from him made him so angry. Was this the reason behind the disconnect he'd been feeling all this time?

Her fingers tightened on his arm. "Xander? Please, say something."

"I need to think."

He pulled away and left the room. Thundered down the stairs and out the front door. He vaguely heard Olivia's voice crying out behind him, but he daren't stop. He needed space and he needed time to himself. He powered down the hill, anger giving him a strength, coordination and speed he'd been lacking the past few weeks. His footsteps grew faster, until he broke into a jog. It wasn't long before a light sweat built up on his body and his lungs and muscles were screaming, reminding him that he was horribly out of condition and that if he kept this up, he'd likely be on bed rest again before he knew it.

He forced himself to slow down, to measure his pace. Automatically he went toward the beach. Seagulls wheeled and screamed on the air currents that swirled above the sandy shoreline, and he looked up, envying them the simplicity of their lives. But how had his own life grown so complicated? At what point had the marriage he'd entered into with Olivia become the broken thing she'd described to him just now?

He shook his head and began to walk along the beach, unheedful of the small waves that rushed up on the sand, drenching his sneaker-clad feet and the bottom of his jeans. The sand sucked at his feet, making walking difficult, but still he pushed on.

Why the hell couldn't he remember anything? The man she'd described, the driven creature who worked long hours and then expected her attention when he got home—that wasn't him. That wasn't who he remembered being, anyway. When and why had things changed so dramatically?

He remembered meeting Olivia at a fundraiser at an inner-city art gallery. He'd been drawn first to her beauty—her long red hair, porcelain-perfect skin and wide sparkling blue eyes had made his physical receptors stand up and take immediate notice. But it had been talking to her that had begun to win his guarded heart. He'd known he wanted her in his life right from that very first conversation, and it had been readily apparent that she felt the same way.

They'd spent that entire first weekend together. When they'd made love it hadn't felt too soon—it had felt perfect in every way. Six months later they were married and home owners and beginning to renovate the house he'd just fled from. Six years later they were separated and on the point of divorce. What on earth had happened in between?

He stopped walking and raised both hands to his head—squeezing hard on both sides as he tried to force his brain to remember. Nothing. Another wave came and sloshed over his feet, further drenching his jeans. He let his hands drop to his sides. He continued to the end of the beach and dropped down into a park bench on the edge of the strand.

Runners jogged by. Walkers walked. Dogs chased seagulls and sticks. Life went on. *His* life went on, even if he didn't remember it. There had to be something. Some way to trigger the things he'd lost, to remember the person he'd been. After ten minutes of staring at the sea a thought occurred to him. If he hadn't been living here in Devonport, with Olivia, where had he been living? Surely he had another home. A place filled with more recent memories that would trigger something in his uncooperative brain perhaps?

Olivia had to know where it was. The clothes she'd haphazardly shoved into their shared wardrobe had been a mixture of casual wear that he'd worn years ago and new items as foreign to him as pretty much everything else had become since coming home from the hospital. That meant she had to have picked up some things from where he lived. Which meant she could take him there.

He levered himself upright, his legs feeling decidedly overworked and unsteady as he turned and headed back on the paved path at the top of the strand and toward home. *Home?* No, he couldn't call it that. Not now. Maybe not ever again. Until he knew exactly why they were apart, exactly what his life had been like, he wondered if he'd ever belong anywhere ever again.

Eleven

Olivia clutched the now-cold mug of coffee she'd poured before sitting at the kitchen table. The breakfast she'd been cooking before the phone call from the lawyer had dried up in the warming oven. Xander had obviously finished cooking it, as she'd asked, and plated up their meals before coming to tell her it was ready. Before overhearing the conversation she'd have done anything to avoid sharing with him today. She'd finally had to throw the breakfast away, but she'd attempted to salvage the coffee. She'd even tried to drink it, but her stomach had protested—tying in knots as she wondered where Xander was.

She'd been frozen here since he'd left the house, alternately staring at the mug and then the clock on the wall as she worried herself sick about him. He'd been gone well over an hour. Unshed tears burned in her eyes. Where was he?

Maybe she should have run after him, wearing nothing but her robe, instead of remaining rooted to the bedroom floor until the front door had slammed closed. But she hadn't. Instead she'd showered quickly and dressed, then debated getting in the car and driving around looking for him. In the end she'd decided that would be a futile exercise. She simply had to wait for him to come back. *If* he came back.

A sound at the front door made her shoot up from her chair, unheeding as it tipped over behind her and bounced on the tiled floor.

"Xander? Are you okay? I've been worried sick—"

"I'm going upstairs to get changed. Then you're going to take me to where I've been living," he said bluntly.

"To where—?" Her throat closed up tight again.

He meant to his apartment. She couldn't refuse him as much as she wanted to.

"To my house, apartment. Whatever. Where I've been living. You know where it is, don't you?"

She looked up and met the accusation in his stormy eyes. She nodded slowly. "Yes, I've been there once, before you came home."

"Let's not call it home," he said bitterly. "It obviously hasn't been my home for a while."

She swallowed back the plea that she wished she had the courage to make to him. It could be his home again— it *had* been these past weeks. Why couldn't he just let them start afresh? She knew why. Xander was the kind of man who did nothing without weighing all the options, without being 100 percent certain of whatever he did. He didn't like surprises, and this morning had definitely been a very unwelcome one.

"Okay, let me know when you're ready."

"I'll be right down," he said and left the room.

Olivia took her mug to the sink and tipped out the congealed contents. Even thinking about the dash of milk she'd stirred into her coffee made her stomach lurch in protest.

The prospect of taking him back to his apartment terrified her. What if he remembered everything? The anger,
the lies…the grief?

She had to face the truth. He may not want to even
see her again after today. In fact, if he remembered the
rest of his lost memories, he very likely would get on
the phone to his lawyer and tell them to continue with
the proceedings she'd requested a halt to. There was nothing she could do about it, and the helplessness that invaded every cell in her body was all-consuming.

Olivia found her handbag and car keys and went to the
entrance hall to wait for him. The keys to his apartment
were in the bottom of her bag, exactly where she'd left
them the day she'd brought him home from the hospital.
It felt like a lifetime ago.

Xander was dressed in a smart pair of dress trousers
and a business shirt when he came back down. He'd obviously had a quick shower, and his hair was slicked back
from his face. He'd trimmed his beard to a designer stubble. Now he looked far more like the corporate Xander
who'd walked out on her two years ago.

"Ready?" she said, needing to fill the strained air between them with something, even something as inane as
the one word she'd used.

Of course he was ready. He was here, wasn't he? Impatience rolled off him in waves.

"Let's go," he grunted and held the door open for her.

Even in his fury he couldn't stop being the gentleman
he intrinsically had always been. His courtesy, however,
brought her little comfort.

The drive toward the harbor bridge and into the city
seemed to take forever in the frigid atmosphere in her
car. Once they hit Quay Street, Xander shifted in his seat.

"Where are we going?"

She could tell it frustrated him to have to ask. "Parnell. You have a place on the top floor of one the high-rises."

He nodded and looked straight ahead, as if he couldn't wait to get there.

By the time Olivia pulled into the underground parking garage and directed Xander to the bank of elevators nearby, her nerves were as taut as violin strings. She felt as if the slightest thing would see her snap and fray apart. The trip up to Xander's floor was all too swift, and suddenly they were at the front door.

She dug in her bag and drew out the keys, holding them up between them.

"Do you want to do the honors?" she asked.

Xander took them from her and looked at the key ring. "I don't know which one it is," he said, a deep frown pulling between his brows.

She pointed to the one that would lead them inside and held her breath as he turned it in the lock and pushed the door open. Olivia followed him as he stepped inside. The air was a little stale, and there was a fine layer of dust everywhere after a month with no cleaning service. She almost ran into Xander's back when he stopped abruptly and stared around the open-plan living area off the entrance hall.

"Do you…is it… Is anything familiar to you?" she tentatively asked.

Xander simply shook his head.

He hated the place. Sure, it was functional—beautiful, even, in its starkness—and heavily masculine. But it didn't feel like home. The lack of a feminine touch, with not even so much as a vase on display in the built-in shelving along one wall, confirmed that he lived here alone. Of course, if he'd had a new partner, she'd have been the one at his bedside after he woke up, not Olivia.

He walked around the spacious living area and clamped down on the growl that rose in his throat. This place should at least feel familiar in some way. These were his things. His recent life. Yet he didn't sense even the remotest connection to anything, not like he did to some of the things back at the house across the harbor.

The anger that had buoyed him along since he'd overheard Olivia on the phone left him in a rush, only a deep sense of defeat remained in its wake. He looked around one more time. Still nothing. A hallway beckoned, but he found he lacked the energy to even want to push himself down that corridor and see what lay beyond it. A bedroom, no doubt. It would almost certainly feel as foreign to him as the rest of the apartment already did.

Weariness pulled at him with unrelenting strength. He didn't belong here, either.

"Take me back," he said roughly. "Please. I've had enough."

Olivia came to stand at his side. Everything about her seemed to be offering refuge, from the expression on her face to the arms she gingerly curved around his waist.

"Maybe losing your memory wasn't the worst thing, Xander. Have you stopped to consider that? We've been good together. Happy. It's proof we can do better together—*be* better together. Can't we just take that and build something great with it now all over again?"

He wanted to say yes, but some unnamable thing held him back. They started toward the door, then stopped abruptly at the sound of the doorbell, swiftly followed by the sound of a key being inserted and the door being opened.

Olivia's eyes opened in shock as a petite young woman let herself into Xander's apartment. She recognized her instantly. The woman had been an intern at Xander's office shortly after their marriage. Olivia knew she'd worked her way up since then. But what was Rachelle doing here, and why did she have a key to Xander's apartment? Her shock at seeing the woman was nothing to what came next.

"Rachelle, how are you?" Xander asked with a smile on his face that had been missing for the better part of today.

Olivia couldn't help it. She felt an immediate pang of jealousy. There'd always been something about Rachelle that had grated on her—a familiarity with Xander even when their marriage was at its best that had made Olivia feel as if she was operating off her back foot around her all the time.

Rachelle came forward and gave Xander a welcoming hug and kiss on the cheek. Olivia wondered if her eyes were turning an unbecoming shade of green as a wave of possessiveness swept through her. It was all she could manage to stand and smile politely, especially when what she wanted most was to drag the other woman off her husband and push her out the door. She took in a steadying breath. That wasn't her. She'd never been the jealous type, but Rachelle brought out the feral in her, always had.

"Xander! It's so good to see you," Rachelle gushed, still hugging him. "We were all so shocked at your accident. I'd have come to see you at the hospital, but they restricted visitors to immediate family only. But I called the hospital regularly and stayed up-to-date with your progress. Until recently, that is."

Rachelle finally looked at Olivia, who bit her tongue to keep from replying. The obvious reproach was there in the younger woman's words. Olivia lifted her chin, accepting the challenge.

"I've been in touch with Ken to let him know Xander was recuperating at home," she said firmly.

"Of course you have," Rachelle said with a slight curve of her lips. She turned her attention back to Xander. "I just thought I'd call in to see how Xander was and to see if there was anything he needed. This is his home, after all, isn't it? I didn't realize he was staying at your house." She turned to face Xander. "So, are you returning soon?"

Olivia held her breath. Was he?

Xander shook his head. "I don't know. I don't think so. Not yet, anyway."

Olivia fought to hold herself upright. No easy feat when she wanted to sag in relief.

"In fact," Olivia said with a forced smile, "we were just leaving."

"Oh," Rachelle said, disappointment clear in her face. "That's a shame. I've been looking forward to catching up."

Before Xander could respond, Olivia spoke again. "Perhaps another time."

She maintained eye contact with Rachelle, neither woman backing down from the silent challenge that hovered between them. Rachelle was the first to break.

"Of course," she muttered.

Xander excused himself to use the bathroom, leaving the two women alone in the foyer. Rachelle waited until they heard the bathroom door close before wheeling to face Olivia.

"He doesn't know, does he?"

"Know?" Olivia remained deliberately evasive.

"About you two. About your divorce. About Park—"

"He knows that we're separated and we're working through that. The doctors have said not to try and force anything."

"Olivia…"

"No." Olivia put up a hand as if she could physically stop the younger woman from doing anything she wanted to. "If his memory comes back, it will do so in its own good time."

"But what about when he comes back to work? Everyone there knows about his past. People will talk to him."

"But he's not fit to return to work yet anyway, so that's a bridge Xander and I will cross when we get to it."

Rachelle looked at her in disbelief. "I can't believe you're lying to him like this."

"I'm not lying," Olivia replied emphatically. *But I know I'm not exactly telling him the truth, either.* "Look I think it would be best if you leave. I'll take care of the plants before we go. You can leave your key with me."

Rachelle shook her head. "No. Xander gave me this key and if I give it back to anyone, it'll be to him."

Olivia didn't say anything, not wanting to push the issue and definitely not wanting to explore the idea of why Xander would give one of his colleagues a key to his apartment.

"You're going to have to tell him sometime," Rachelle continued. "If you don't, I will. He deserves to know. You can't just reclaim him like a lost puppy. He left you, Olivia. He had his reasons."

A sound down the hallway made both women turn and look. Xander—something was wrong, Olivia thought and quickly headed in his direction.

Xander stood at the basin in the bathroom, his hands gripping the white porcelain edge in a white-knuckled grip. A headache assailed him in ever-increasing waves. He had to lie down, to sleep, but he couldn't do that here. This place was all wrong. As angry as he was with Olivia, he needed her right now—needed to go back to their home. He must have called out, made some noise or something, because she was suddenly at his side, concern pulling her brows into a straight line and clouding her eyes.

"Another headache? Here," she said, rummaging through her handbag. "I brought some of your painkillers, just in case."

She pressed two tablets into his palm and quickly filled the water glass on the vanity with water and handed it to him.

He knocked the pills back with a grimace. "Take me back to the house, please."

"You don't want to take a rest here?"

He shook his head and immediately regretted it as spears of pain pushed behind his eyes. "Just get me out of here."

She slid a slender arm around his waist and tucked herself under his shoulder to support him. Slowly they made their way out of the room and down the hall. Rachelle still stood in the living room. He caught a glimpse of the shock on her face.

"I have to take him home," Olivia said with a proprietary note in her voice that even he, in his incapacitated state, didn't miss. "Please make sure you lock up behind you."

"Do you need me to help?" the other woman asked, stepping to his other side.

"We can manage," Olivia replied firmly and guided him to the door.

"Xander, I hope you're better soon. We miss you at the office…I miss you," Rachelle called out as they left the apartment.

The door swung closed behind them, and Xander winced again as it slammed. They made it down to the car and Olivia adjusted his seat back a little so he could recline and close his eyes. Throughout the drive back to

Devonport his mind continued to whirl around the stabs of pain that continued to probe his skull.

He'd thought the apartment would bring him answers. Instead it had only brought him more questions. Nothing had felt familiar or right or as if it truly belonged to him. Not the furnishings, not the clothes in the wardrobe he'd gotten a glimpse of before heading into the bathroom—not even the cups and saucers he'd seen in the kitchen cupboards when he'd looked there.

And then there was Rachelle. She'd been so familiar with him, as if they were far more intimately acquainted than mere work colleagues. Had he moved on from his relationship with Olivia so quickly? It seemed almost impossible to believe. Yes, Rachelle was attractive—if you liked petite brunettes with perfect proportions. But he had a hankering for slender redheads, one in particular—even if she had been holding out on him about them living apart.

But Rachelle. He'd recognized her. She was a part of his past, although he couldn't remember all of it. She was deeply familiar to him, more so than could be accounted for with his memories from six years prior. Did that explain why, when she'd come into the apartment, she'd gone straightaway to hug him and kiss him? The fact that her kiss had landed on his cheek had been a result of him moving slightly at the last minute; otherwise he knew she'd have planted one right on his lips. Judging by Olivia's reaction to the other woman, he doubted very much that she'd have been pleased about that happening.

Still, it made him wonder what his relationship with Rachelle was. She was more than just a work acquaintance. He knew that much from her behavior, not to mention the fact she had a key to his apartment.

Had he gone from one failed whirlwind relationship into another? It didn't seem right, not likely somehow. If only he could remember!

Twelve

Olivia lifted Xander's feet up onto the sofa and drew the drapes in the sitting room to block out the afternoon sunlight. He hadn't even wanted to tackle the stairs when they'd arrived home. His headache must be bad, she thought, checking to see that his chest continued to rise and fall as he slipped deeper into sleep.

But she had him back here; that was the important thing. He could so easily have told her to leave him at the apartment. Maybe even leave him with Rachelle. The very thought painted a bitter taste on Olivia's tongue. She'd tried to like Rachelle on the occasions she'd met her at company functions, back before her marriage had ended. Had even attempted once or twice to be friendly. But the other woman had always carried herself with an air that implied she believed she was several notches above Olivia on the totem pole of life. How could she not be when Olivia had been, first, a schoolteacher, then, second, a stay-at-home mother while Rachelle was actively and successfully pursuing a high-flying career?

Rachelle had never made a secret of the fact she found Xander attractive, and Olivia had felt threatened by her confidence, not to mention the increasing number of hours in a week Rachelle spent with Olivia's husband. But Olivia had never once believed that Xander would embark on an affair. That simply had never been his style. But then, he'd changed so much after Parker's death. Maybe he *had* picked up with Rachelle after he'd moved out. Goodness only knew the woman hadn't been subtle about her attraction to him.

In the two years of their separation, Olivia had been working so hard just to keep herself from falling apart over the loss of both her son and her husband that she'd never stopped to consider that Xander might have gotten himself a girlfriend. Hadn't wanted to consider it, more like, she forced herself to admit. In fact, the idea hadn't even occurred to her when she'd brought him home from the hospital. Why should it, when the doctors had never mentioned Xander having any visitors other than his mother? Surely a girlfriend would have had some visiting rights?

She pushed the thought out of her head, preferring not to allow her mind to stray down that path. But she couldn't help it—she kept seeing Rachelle insert herself into Xander's arms and kiss him. And not only had Xander recognized Rachelle; he hadn't exactly pushed her away.

Olivia forced herself to do the math about just how far back in his memory Rachelle could be found. Rachelle had started at Xander's firm before Parker had been born. Did his memory loss stretch back that far or was he actually beginning to recall things and people from his missing years?

She checked on Xander one more time; then, satisfied he was deeply asleep, she went to the kitchen to make herself coffee. As she automatically started the machine and poured milk in a mug, her thoughts kept straying back to Rachelle and Xander—and how at home the woman had seemed in Xander's apartment. Just how large of a role did she play in Xander's life outside work, and how long had she been there? A year? Two years? Longer? Had she been hovering in the background even during Xander's marriage, just waiting to snatch him up as soon as he was free? And had Olivia herself furthered the woman's plans by not being the wife she should have been? Had her focus on her newborn son and then her developing little boy been so singular that it had driven her husband away from her and into the arms of another woman? It wouldn't be the first time in history that had happened.

But she hadn't been the only one wrapped up in Parker. While Xander hadn't initially been thrilled about the pregnancy, especially when he'd discovered it hadn't been a blessed accident but a decision she'd made without him, he'd been as besotted with their son on his birth as she'd been. Had they both gotten so caught up in being parents that they forgot to be partners? Was that something Rachelle had taught him how to be once more?

Fear and insecurity wended their way into Olivia's psyche like the persistent vines of a climbing weed. She couldn't lose him again—she simply couldn't. She hadn't fought when he'd left. And even though on the surface, at least, she'd looked as if she was coping, she'd still been too bruised, too grief-stricken, after Parker's death to have the energy. But she had energy now, and she knew she had to dig down deep and fight for her man. To consolidate her place in his life and in his heart so that they could work through everything together.

The second she'd seen him at the hospital, she'd known she'd do anything for him. She loved him as much now as she had when they'd first fallen headlong into love together.

Nothing, and no one, was going to get in the way of her repairing their broken marriage.

They deserved a new and better start together. She'd certainly learned from her past mistakes and accepted there had been many of them. She wasn't perfect by any standard, but, then again, neither was Xander. She loved him, imperfections and all. She'd grown as a person since he'd left. Deep in her heart Olivia knew that as long as Xander was willing, they could really make a go of things. They could build their marriage into the loving and lasting state of union she'd always wanted.

What if he wasn't willing? What if his recall, if it came, included every awful word she'd flung at him in grief and anger in the aftermath of Parker's death? What if he couldn't forgive her those things? She couldn't blame him if they were enough to make him leave. After all, they'd had that effect the first time around, hadn't they? She closed her eyes on the memory, and sucked in a deep breath. This time would be better. They had the cushion of time and distance now, and surely these past few weeks had shown him that they were far better together than apart?

So what could she do? There was only one thing that echoed in her mind. She had to give herself to him. Heart and soul, holding nothing back.

The afternoon passed in a blur. Xander locked himself in the office off her studio and told her quite emphatically he didn't want to be disturbed. She filled her afternoon packing her car with the paintings she needed to deliver to a gallery in the morning. With Christmas in only four weeks' time, she and her agent were hope-

ful for a high level of sales, especially now demand for
her work was growing.

By the time she prepared their evening meal, Xander
still hadn't come out of the office. Worried about him
now, especially in light of the severity of the headache
he'd suffered that morning, she risked knocking on the
office door and popping her head in without waiting for
him to respond.

"Xander? Are you hungry? Dinner's ready."

She'd gone to the bother of making one of his favor-
ites—steak Diane with fresh spears of asparagus and
baby potatoes. A pathetic peace offering given the day
they'd had, but in lieu of being able to talk this out with
him she'd felt she had to do something.

"I'm not hungry," he said without turning his head
from the computer screen on his desk.

She ventured into the room, looking to see what held
his attention so strongly. A ripple of unease went from
head to toe as she recognized the staff profile page from
Xander's firm. Up front and center was a photograph of
Rachelle. Olivia's hands curled into impotent fists as she
forced herself to breathe out the tension that gripped her.
One by one, she uncurled her fingers.

"It's steak Diane. Would you like me to bring a tray
out to you here?"

"Trying to butter me up?" he asked, finally turning to
look up at her. A cynical smile twisted his lips.

"No. Well, not entirely. I'm not sure that any food
could make up for the shock you had today. I'm sorry,
Xander. I meant to tell you sooner. I just…couldn't."

Xander rubbed at his eyes wearily. "I guess it's not
the kind of conversation you have on an everyday basis
with a convalescent husband, is it?"

Olivia felt the tight set of her shoulders ease a fraction.
It was an olive branch. One she'd grasp with both hands.

"Come, eat," she implored, gingerly putting a hand on his shoulder.

He lifted his hand and briefly laid it over hers. "I'll be through in a minute. Just let me shut everything down."

She wanted to stay and wait for him. To ask him if he'd discovered whatever it was he'd been looking for, but she knew she'd be pushing her luck. Slowly, she walked back to the kitchen and plated up their meal. All the while, the image of Rachelle's profile photo burned through her mind. Why was he looking at it? Was he remembering what they'd been to each other? Were his feelings for the other woman resurfacing? Thinking about losing Xander again just killed her inside.

The past weeks had taught her they belonged together, now more than ever. She loved him with every breath in her body, every movement, every thought. She just had to prove it.

Xander was surprised when Olivia went up to bed ahead of him. Then again, she hadn't slept half the afternoon away like he had. She'd been on tenterhooks all night, and he'd had the impression she'd been on the verge of saying or asking something several times, only to back down at the last minute.

Today had been a revelation for them both. He'd had the shock of learning about their separation, and Olivia had certainly looked stunned when Rachelle turned up at his apartment.

He thumbed the TV remote, coasting through the channels mindlessly as he turned over the things he'd discovered today. None of it made any sense to him, no matter how he approached it. He didn't feel as if he'd developed a romantic bond with Rachelle at all. Surely if they'd been a couple, he'd have experienced something when he'd seen her. He'd only felt mildly uncomfortable when she'd hugged and kissed him. Not like when he touched Olivia and certainly not at all like when they'd made love last night.

His fingers curled tight around the remote, making the plastic squeak. Even just thinking about his wife—and she was still his wife—was enough to awaken a hunger for her in him. How could things have gotten so bad between them that they'd separated? Why hadn't they been able to work things out?

With a harsh sigh, Xander switched off the TV and got up to turn off the light and head upstairs. He may as well lie awake in bed upstairs as sit here alone with the inanity of the TV clogging his brain.

He took the stairs confidently, but he hesitated when he reached the top. There was muted light coming from the bedroom, and a delicate scent wafted toward him. Vanilla maybe? His footfall was silent on the carpet runner that led down the hall toward their bedroom. He hesitated in the doorway, taking in the room and the setting Olivia had obviously gone to some lengths to create.

The drapes were drawn but billowed softly in the evening breeze. Dotted around the room—on top of the bureau, the bedside tables, the mantelpiece of the fireplace—were small groups of candles in glass jars. The scent in the room was stronger, and he felt his body respond to the seductive scene.

Olivia came through from the bathroom, wrapped only in a towel. His breath caught in his lungs as his eyes traveled hungrily over the smooth creamy set of her shoulders. His gaze lingered on the hollows of her collarbone before dropping lower to the shadowed valley of her breasts, exposed above the moss-green towel that was a perfect foil for her hair.

She'd clipped her hair up loosely, exposing the delicious curve of her neck, and silky strands tumbled to drift across her shoulders. He was struck with a sudden deep envy of those strands.

"Looks like you're trying to seduce me here," he said, his voice thick with desire.

"Is it working?" she said, her voice equally husky.

"I'm not sure. Maybe you need to keep going."

He watched as she slowly untucked the end of her towel. The material dropped away, revealing her beautiful body in one fell swoop. Xander's mouth dried. He swallowed, hard. Olivia reached a slender arm up and tugged a few pins loose, sending her hair cascading over her shoulders. Her nipples, normally a pale pink, had deepened in color and were tight buds on her full breasts— just begging for his touch, his lips, his tongue.

Xander's body felt taut and hot, his clothing restrictive as his erection hardened even more. She was so beautiful, and she was walking toward him. He forced himself to keep his hands by his sides as she stopped in front of him. Clearly she had an agenda—far be it from him to make any changes to whatever she had planned.

"How about now?" she asked.

She caressed one breast with her hand, stroking lightly across her nipple, and he watched, mesmerized, as her skin grew even tauter.

"Yeah," he answered, his voice gruff with the need that pulsed through him like a living thing. "It's working."

A tiny smile played around her lips. "Good," she whispered before going up on her toes and kissing his lips.

It was a tease, just the lightest of butterfly caresses, but it acted like a torch to volatile liquid. In that instant he was fully aflame—for her. She must have sensed it, because her fingers were at the buttons of his shirt, deftly plucking them open and pushing the garment off his shoulders to fall silently to the floor. Her hands spread

124 THE WIFE HE COULDN'T FORGET

like warm fans across his skin, rubbing and caressing him. He was hot for her, so very hot his blood all but boiled in his veins.

He reached up to touch her and pull her to him, but she grabbed his hands and held them at his sides.

"Let me," she whispered. "Let me love you."

She bent her head and kissed his chest, tracing tiny lines with her tongue and then kissing him again. And then her tongue was swirling in tight little circles around his nipple. He groaned out loud, couldn't help it, as a spear of need bolted through his entire body.

Olivia's hands were at his belt, undoing the buckle, and then at the button of his trousers, then—finally—at the zipper of his pants. She slid one hand inside the waistband of his briefs, her fingers like silk as they closed around his thickness. She stroked him slow and firm, and it was all he could do to remain a passive subject in this sensual onslaught on his body.

He felt her move before he fully understood her intentions, felt his trousers and his briefs disappear down the length of his legs, felt Olivia's hot breath against his thighs.

Felt her mouth close around his aching flesh.

"Livvy," he groaned, tangling his fingers in her hair as she used her tongue in wicked ways that fried his synapses.

And then he was beyond thought, locked only in sensation until even sensation became too much and he lost control, soaring on the wave of a climax that initially made his entire body rigid as pulse after pulse of pleasure rocketed through him then left him weak and shaking with its magnitude.

Xander pulled Olivia up and into his embrace, holding her close to him until his heart rate approximated that of a normal person's.

"Ready for round two?" Olivia asked softly.

"Round two?"

"Yeah. I have a lot of time and a lot of loving to make up."

"Don't we both," he agreed, pressing a kiss on to the top of her head.

He let her walk him backward toward the bed, where she pushed him onto the mattress and bent to remove his clothes from where they'd tangled at his feet. She rubbed her hands over his body, from the tips of his toes, up his legs and over his abdomen as she positioned herself on the bed over him.

"I've missed you, Xander," she said, her blue eyes staring straight into his—honestly burning there like an incandescent flame.

In the gilded light of the candles' glow she looked more beautiful than he'd ever seen her. Her hair was a tangle of gold-red waves that tumbled in glorious abandon over her shoulders to caress her skin. Her breasts were high and full, her nipples ripe for his touch—and touch them he did, taking them between thumb and forefinger and watching her face as he teased and tugged on them.

His body was quick to recover from his earlier climax, and he felt himself harden beneath the heat that poured from her. He slipped one hand between her legs, smiling as he discovered her readiness.

"Show me," he urged her. "Show me how much you missed me."

She reached for a condom she must have slipped under the pillow earlier and covered him, taking her time over it and turning the act into an art form of simultaneous seduction and torment. Then she positioned him at her entrance and slowly took him inside her body. Her thigh muscles trembled as she accepted him deep within.

"You feel so right inside me," she gasped with a strangled breath. "I never want to let you go."

Then she started to move, and all he could do was glory in the pleasure she gave him, holding on to her hips as she rocked and swayed and dragged them both toward a peak that arrived all too quickly and yet not fast enough at the same time. She melted onto his body, her curves fitting against him like a puzzle piece made only for him. He folded his arms around her and held her tight, lost in the perfection of the moment.

Much later, Olivia rose and disposed of the condom they'd used. He watched her through hooded lids as she extinguished one candle after another. The room softened into gray, then into darkness as she worked her way closer to the bed and climbed in next to him. He rolled her onto her side and curved his body around her back, marveling again at the perfection of how they fit together.

"Good night, Xander," she whispered in the darkness. "And...I'm sorry about today."

In response he squeezed her tight and pressed a kiss at her nape. He listened as she drifted into sleep.

As sorry as she truly seemed to be, he felt as though she still held something back. Something vital and just out of reach of his battered mind. Would he ever remember?

Thirteen

Olivia woke late the next morning feel both well used and well satisfied. She turned her head on the pillow and looked straight into Xander's clear gray eyes.

"I love you," she whispered. "So very much."

She pushed back his hair from his forehead and leaned over to kiss him before rolling over and getting out of bed. Xander caught her wrist, tugging her back down into his arms.

"Stay," he commanded, lifting her hair and nuzzling the back of her neck.

Goose bumps peppered her body. Oh, he knew all the right places, and he took his time exploring them over and over again. It was nearly eleven when they rose and Xander joined her in the shower.

"We should just spend the whole day naked," he said, slowly soaping up her body and sending her heart rate into overdrive all over again.

"I wish I could, but I have to take my work to the gallery. I'll be busy all afternoon and into the evening with the exhibition opening." She rinsed off, then pushed open the shower door. "I have to do this, Xander. It's my career now, my reputation as an artist."

"Then go do your thing. I'll find something to keep me occupied today."

"You could come, too," she offered, feeling a spark of hope light within her.

"Next time maybe, okay?"

Olivia bit back her disappointment. She knew it would probably be too much for Xander to be out most of the afternoon and evening, but she was reluctant to break the bubble of this new closeness they shared. She quickly dried herself then blow-dried her hair. Xander finished in the shower and then dried and dressed right next to her. Olivia tried to think back to the last time they'd been in the bathroom together like this. It was such a normal everyday part of life, and she'd missed it more than she realized as she teased him about hogging the mirror.

"You're taking your beard off?" she asked.

"Yeah," he said, lathering up with shaving foam. "I'm ready to be me again."

Olivia's brush tangled in her hair, making her wince. Ready to be him again? What exactly did he mean by that? She disentangled the bristles from her hair and put the brush and dryer on the bathroom vanity before sliding her arms around Xander's naked waist.

"I kind of like the person you are now," she said, pressing a kiss between his shoulders.

"You didn't like the old me?" he asked, halting mid-stroke with his razor, his eyes meeting hers in the mirror.

"I loved the old you, too, Xander. But we've both changed. I like the person I am now better, too. Maybe that was part of the problem before. I was always trying to be something or someone else. Maybe I need to take a leaf out of your book and just be me again."

She pulled away from him and finished her hair—the noise of the hair-dryer making further conversation difficult. The stress and worries of the day before still lingered too close to the surface for her. If she didn't have to be away from the house today, she most definitely wouldn't be. But she'd been telling the truth when she'd said that her career and her reputation rested on this show. The gallery was one of the most prestigious in Auckland, and she considered herself fortunate to receive an invitation to exhibit there. Of course the cut the gallery would get on any sale was substantial, she reflected, but the exposure her work would receive was worth more than money.

Later, after they'd had fluffy omelets with chopped fresh chives and bacon, hot coffee and toast, Xander helped her carry the last of her canvases out to her car.

"Thanks," Olivia said as she closed the back on her station wagon. "I'm not sure what time I'll be home, but I'll probably be late, after dinner anyway."

"I can look after myself."

"And you promise that if you get a headache, you'll take your pills and rest?"

"You don't need to babysit me, remember?"

"I know." She pressed her hand against his cheek. "But I worry about you."

"I'll take care, I promise," he said solemnly before turning his head to kiss the inside of her palm.

Across the street Olivia caught a glimpse of one of their neighbors putting Christmas lights up in the eaves of their house. It reminded her again that the holiday was less than four weeks away. It gave her an idea.

"Maybe when I get home—or if I'm too late, maybe tomorrow—we can put up the Christmas tree. I didn't bother when…" Her voice trailed off for a moment before she took a deep breath. She had to get over her reluctance to talk about the past. "When we were separated. It brought back too many memories of the fun we used to have. Anyway, I'll go up to the attic and get the stuff down for us when I get back, okay?"

"That sounds like a good idea," Xander agreed. "I'd like that. Now, you'd better get going. I thought you didn't want to be late?"

Olivia glanced at her wristwatch and exclaimed in shock. "Oh, is that the time already? You're such a distraction!"

He laughed and swooped in for another kiss, this time a lingering caress full of promise. "Hurry back—I'll be waiting."

Olivia drove away with a last glance in the rearview mirror. Xander stood in the driveway, hands resting on his hips, watching her go. He made it so hard to leave him behind, for more reasons than she cared to examine. The shadow of a passing cloud suddenly obscured the sun, darkening the road before her and making her push her sunglasses up onto her head. A shiver traveled down her spine. Olivia shook off the sensation, not wanting to examine the sudden sense of unease that gripped her.

It was just because she was leaving Xander for several hours on his own, she rationalized. Since he'd been home again, the longest she'd left him was a couple of hours while she ran errands or went shopping. It was natural to feel uneasy, but there was no cause for alarm. Nothing would go wrong.

Xander watched her car turn out the drive and the automatic gates swing shut behind it. The gate. There was something about the gate, some memory attached to it that was just out of reach. A sharp stab of pain made its presence felt behind his eye, and he closed his eyes and shook his head slightly to rid himself of the pain.

Take your pills. It was as if Olivia's voice were stuck in his head, he thought with a smile as he headed back into the house. Well, he'd promised her he'd look after himself. And, he had to admit, he had no desire for a repeat of the headache that had struck him yesterday. Inside, he found the painkillers and took the required dose, then retired to the hammock for a while until the nagging pain eased off. It didn't take long.

While he rested, he thought about what he should do to fill the hours until Olivia returned. The Christmas tree! Of course. He knew she'd mentioned putting it up together, but he also knew she'd love the surprise of seeing it decorated and lit in the large front bay window to welcome her home.

They'd always stored the tree in the attic, and, since she'd said she hadn't even put it up the past couple of years, he shouldn't have too much trouble finding it. Motivated by the idea of her pleasure in seeing the tree finished, he went inside and upstairs. The stairs to the attic were as narrow as he remembered them, and he fought back an odd sense of light-headedness as he placed his foot on the first tread.

At the top of the stairs, he pushed open the door into the attic, taking a bit of time to allow his eyes to adjust to the gloom. Light streamed in from the small diamond-paned windows at each end of the attic and dust motes danced on the beams. Xander sneezed and cursed under his breath.

Moving farther into the attic, he got his bearings and looked around at the boxes and shrouded pieces of furniture they'd stored there. He shifted a few cartons in an attempt to get to where he last remembered seeing the tree and decorations. If Olivia had told the truth, they'd be exactly where he himself had put them.

He straightened for a moment. *If* Olivia had told the

truth? Why would he think she'd lie about something like this? Why would she lie to him about anything? *Maybe because she lied to you about your separation*, a voice echoed in the back of his head. He pushed the thought down. She'd explained why she'd withheld that piece of information. Sure, he didn't agree with her choice, but if they were to move forward, he had to be willing to get past it. She'd accepted some of the blame for what had gone wrong between them. Considering what he knew of himself along with what she *had* told him, he could see how easily they could have drifted apart.

Born the youngest of two boys, he'd pretty much always been treated as an only child after his older brother died in a drowning accident when Xander was only about three years old. Looking back, he could see how his parents had each coped in their own ways. His mother by becoming a distant workaholic and his father, sadly, by retreating into himself and becoming unable to work at all.

Xander still remembered coming home from school and letting himself into their home, knowing his mother would still be at work and wondering if that particular day would be one where his father would be happy to come outside and kick a football with him or whether Xander would end up sitting on the floor outside his parents' bedroom, listening to his father sob quietly as he remained locked in grief for the son he'd never see grow up.

There was probably more of his mother's influence in him than his father's, Xander acknowledged. If nothing else, he'd always fought hard to live by his mother's example. Never letting life get him down, dealing with his grief privately and always striving hard for the future.

While he'd never seen his father as weak, because even as a child he'd understood what his father was going through had little to do with strength or weakness, he hadn't wanted to *feel* as overwhelmingly as his father had either. As a result, he'd always controlled his emotions strictly, keeping them on a tight rein. Xander hadn't dared to experience extreme highs or extreme lows in his personal life; he had, instead, poured himself into work and achievement. Now he wondered if that driven part of him had also been a part of what had put a wedge between him and Olivia? He couldn't remember, no matter how hard he tried.

What he did know was that he was prepared to give her the benefit of the doubt and to give their marriage another chance. Perhaps the accident and his amnesia were a good thing after all. He knew he could be stubborn and move on if he thought something wasn't working. Rather than work on their marriage, he would have rejected any overtures she'd made to work things out.

Even so, he couldn't deny the niggling feeling that there was more to their separation than the brief explanation she'd given him yesterday. And then there was the matter of Rachelle and the fact she had a key to his apartment. Something really didn't feel right about that, but he couldn't put his finger on it. He would, though. He felt so much better. Stronger both mentally and physically, except for these bloody headaches, he thought as he shifted a few more cartons, then squatted down to read the lettering on a box shoved to the back.

He recognized the writing—it was his own. The box was ignominiously labeled "Stuff." He tugged it toward him and opened the flaps. In it were framed certificates and some old photo albums. A surge of excitement filled him. Maybe the contents would cast some light over his lost years. He pulled out the first album and absently thumbed through it. It dated back to his years in university, before he'd met Olivia. No, there was nothing there that he didn't know well already.

He shoved the albums and certificates back in the box and pushed it back against the wall. With the digital age it was more than likely there were no physical albums of his more recent years. Maybe he needed to look harder at his computer files. See what was there that dated back from when he could last remember and up until now.

But before he could do that, he needed to find the Christmas decorations. Xander dug around a few more boxes but ended up with nothing more than a sneezing fit. He was just about to give up completely when he spotted two more boxes in a dark corner. Maybe this was what he'd been looking for.

He dragged the boxes under the remaining light. They weren't labeled like all the others were. Neither looked like the long narrow carton he knew had always stored the tree, but maybe one held the decorations. There was definitely something familiar about them.

A weird sensation swept through him, making him feel a little dizzy again as he rocked back on his heels. He shrugged it off, thinking that he probably just needed some fresh air. The tiny ventilation holes in the eaves near the windows weren't the most efficient. He'd been up there awhile already, and, with the sun beating down on the iron roof, it was getting pretty hot.

Xander tugged at the tape binding the first box with a grunt of determination. It came away with a satisfying sound. Once again that feeling of being off balance assailed him. Xander closed his eyes for a brief moment and waited for the sensation to pass. This one was worse than the last and left him sick to his stomach. He swallowed and forced his eyes open.

"Just this one," he said aloud as he lifted the flaps. "Then I'm heading back downstairs. What the—?"

His voice trailed off into silence as he pulled out the first of the items inside. A child's clothing, precisely folded in layers—a little boy's things, to be more precise. Xander put them to one side and reached in again. Toys this time. A teddy, a few die-cast trains and cars.

His stomach lurched, and Xander fought back the bile that crept up his throat. He *knew* these things. These pieces of another life, another time. The frustrating sense of limbo he'd been living in since waking up in the hospital began to peel away from him, layer after layer. The hairs on the back of his neck stood on full alert, and an icy shiver traced down his spine.

Without another thought he tore open the second box. Cold sweat drenched his body. More clothes, more toys and, near the bottom, photo albums. He lifted them from the box. Even in the muted light of the attic he could see the dates on the albums. He picked up the oldest of them and slowly opened the cover. There on the first page was a grainy sonogram picture. He traced the edges of the tiny blur on the picture with the tip of one finger as a powerful wave of déjà vu swept over him. And with it, a memory. A sense of excitement and fear and love, all in one massive bundle of emotion. And then loss. Aching, wrenching, tearing loss.

Xander turned the page of the album to a photo of Olivia, a younger and more carefree Olivia than the one he'd seen off today. There was a series of photos of her, first with a big smile and flat tummy, all the way through to a photo of her with her belly swollen with pregnancy and a finger pointing to a date circled on the calendar.

The next page saw him staring at himself, proudly holding a squalling newborn infant.

His son.

Fourteen

A sob tore from Xander's throat and his chest tightened, making every breath a struggle. *He remembered.* He remembered everything, all the way back to the day that Olivia told him she was pregnant—and the fight they'd had that night over her news.

He'd been furious with her for taking that step without his knowledge. It hadn't been an accident. It had been a calculated decision she'd made without him. He hadn't been ready. He could still recall the heady rush of their relationship, their haste to marry and build a life together. Hell, he'd barely come to terms with their closeness before she was telling him they had to make room for another person in their lives. A person who'd depend on them for everything.

Xander hadn't known if he had it in him to love even more than he already loved Olivia—at least not until he'd experienced the joy of Parker's birth. Tears ran unchecked down Xander's cheeks as he turned more pages, then reached for the next album and the next. Each one cataloguing their beautiful little boy's life, until there was no more. The last photos were of Parker's third birthday in the backyard. A pirate theme had been the order of the day, and even Xander had dressed in kind.

They'd been so happy. So complete. And then, with one stupid forgetful moment on his part, it had all ended.

The devastation of Parker's death, along with the certainty that he could have prevented it, had left Xander crushed by guilt. He wiped at his face, trying to stem the tears that wouldn't stop falling. This was what he'd forgotten. This was what he'd built walls around his heart and his mind for. To stem the searing, clawing pain that now threatened to tear him into tiny pieces.

Xander staggered to his feet, leaving the albums and the toys and clothes scattered around the cartons on the floor. He wobbled toward the doorway and stumbled down the stairs, as uncoordinated and clumsy as he'd been in those early days back in the hospital. At the bottom of the stairs he turned right and went straight to the bedroom next to his old home office.

Now he understood why his office had always been here. He'd hated every second he had to spend away from home when Parker had been alive. With this home office, he'd had the best of both worlds. Able to watch his son grow and learn every day, and meet the demands of his career and provide for his family at the same time.

His family. Their little unit of three. Xander could never have believed that the power of their triangle could ever have been torn apart. Hadn't understood that when you ripped away one edge of the triangle that the other two sides would collapse. Not together. No. But apart. In their grief, he and Olivia had inexorably turned away from each other.

He pushed open the bedroom door and looked around the bare walls and floor. The only thing that remained was a bureau that had stored Parker's clothes. Olivia had gotten rid of everything else. She'd wiped their son's existence from their home, in fact, from their very lives with clinical precision—just like his mother had when Xander's brother had died.

Xander dropped to his knees. Grief crashed over him with the power of a tidal wave. It felt as raw and as painfully fresh as if it had been only yesterday that he'd been forced to say goodbye to his son. The child of his body, of his heart. He roared in frustration and anger and sorrow, the sounds coming from deep inside him. Sounds he'd never allowed out, ever, but now it was as if he couldn't stop them.

He had no idea what the time was when he pulled himself back to his feet and made his way to his bedroom. No, not his bedroom anymore. Olivia's. He'd made his home elsewhere, and now he knew why. He went into the bathroom and showered again, all the while attempting to block out the memory of the last time, only hours ago, that he'd shared this same space with Olivia, and what they'd done.

The memory wouldn't be suppressed. His body, traitor that it was, stirred to life at the images running through his mind. He turned the mixer to cold, standing beneath the spray until the pain of the icy water was almost equal to the pain that pulsed in the region of his heart.

He leaned his forearms on the shower wall and let his head drop between his shoulders, allowing the water to pound on the back of his neck and down his back. Questions whirled in his mind. Why had she kept this from him? What had she been thinking? Why hadn't she told him everything when she'd had the chance yesterday?

By the time he turned off the water and stepped out of the shower to dry himself he was no closer to finding any answers. She'd tricked him into coming here and she'd tricked him into staying—just as she'd tricked him into parenthood. Why?

Xander studied his reflection in the mirror, hardly recognizing the man whose tortured gray eyes stared back at him. He couldn't stay here. He couldn't listen to another lie from Olivia's lips. The betrayal of what she'd done was as excruciatingly painful now as the words she'd flung at him after Parker had died had been.

They'd still been in the emergency room. Pushed to one side while the doctors and nurses had worked frantically to save Parker's life. Until they accepted that nothing they did made any difference. Until the frenetic busyness fell silent and Olivia had turned to him and said it was all his fault. He hadn't wanted Parker and now her precious child was gone. Oh, she'd apologized afterward, but once spoken, the words couldn't be unsaid. Their hurt had spread in him like a voracious disease. Eating away at him until he had nothing left to give.

She'd blamed him for their son's death, but no more than he'd blamed himself. It had driven a wedge between them, creating a void that might possibly have been repaired had he needed her less and she'd needed him more. And he had needed her. The depth of his grief terrified him, made him afraid he would sink into the abyss of misery that had claimed his father. So he'd made a tactical withdrawal from his emotions, and, along with that decision, Xander had pulled away from his wife. And she'd done nothing to pull him back again—not until she'd shown up at his hospital room with a smile and a lie.

Xander picked his clothes up from the floor and bundled them up into a ball. They stank of his fear for what he'd discovered upstairs in the attic and of his grief and anger. He never wanted to see them again. He grabbed clean clothes from the bureau and the wardrobe, then

yanked everything else he owned off its hanger and from
its drawer and piled it all onto the bed.

Rummaging in the hall cupboard unearthed a suitcase
that looked both new and familiar. He remembered buying it before a trip to Japan last year. Olivia must have
brought his things from his apartment in it. He squeezed
his clothing into the case and zipped it closed. Then he
picked it and the bundle of clothes he'd discarded up and
carried them downstairs. The case he left just inside the
sitting room. The other things he shoved in the trash bin
outside the back door.

He should just go, he thought. Leave now before she
came back. But some perverse masochistic impulse urged
him to stay. To face Olivia and to ask her what the hell
she'd been thinking. Masochistic? No, it wasn't masoch-
ism to want answers. He deserved the truth from her,
at last. No more subterfuge, no more lies or half truths.
Everything.

Olivia was on a high when she pulled her car into the
drive. The exhibition had been an enormous success.
The gallery owner had been thrilled not only with the
commissions they'd earned but also with the requests for
more of her work in the future. There was international
interest in her work, too. Sure, she knew better than to
think her success from this point out was guaranteed,
but tonight the world was her oyster. She couldn't wait
to share the news with Xander.

She looked up at the house as she rolled to a stop outside the garage. It hadn't been dark long, but no lights
were on inside. At least not at the front of the house.
Maybe he was around the back or even in his office in
the cottage.

Grabbing her bag and the bottle of champagne the
gallery owner had given her before she'd left the exhibi-

tion, she got out of the car, quickly walked up the front path and let herself inside.

"Xander?" she called, clicking on the hall light.

A sound in the sitting room made her halt in her tracks and change direction.

"Xander? Are you okay?" she asked, turning on the overhead light in the room as she entered it. "I hope you're up to celebrating. The exhibition was fab—"

Her voice broke off as she took in the appearance of the man sitting in one of the armchairs, dressed in what she thought of as his "new life" clothes and with an expression on his face that sent a spear of alarm straight to her heart.

His voice was cold. "How long did you plan to keep the truth about Parker from me?"

She sank into a chair behind her, her legs suddenly unable to hold her upright a second longer. "I...I didn't plan to keep it from you. I just couldn't talk about it. I didn't know where to begin, what to say...I still don't."

He cocked one eyebrow. "Seriously? Even now you can lie to me, Olivia? Yesterday didn't give you ample opportunity to fill me in? Hell, any time in the last nearly *two months* wasn't enough time for you?"

He stood, and she fought to find the words she should have said anytime before now. "Xander, please. Don't go."

"A little too late to be saying that, don't you think?" he replied, his voice as sharp as one of the chef's knives in her kitchen.

"I tried, Xander. Honestly, I wanted to tell you."

"But you didn't. You packed our son's entire life into boxes and shoved them in a dark corner. You already wiped Parker's existence from our home and our lives once before—why wouldn't you continue to do that given the opportunity? I don't know you anymore, Olivia. Maybe I never did."

She pushed herself to her feet. Even though her legs trembled beneath her, she sifted through the shock that near paralyzed her to find something to say.

"Didn't you do exactly the same thing? Wipe Parker from our lives when you walked out that door, when you walked away from me?"

"I left you because I couldn't pretend that the past had never happened, like you did. It happened. I know it did, and I've regretted that day every conscious moment of my life since. You seemed to find it so easy to just pick up and carry on. As if Parker had never been born," he accused.

"I couldn't hold on to the past." Olivia clutched at her blouse as if doing so could ease the tightness deep in her chest. "It was killing me, Xander. But you couldn't see that. Holding on to Parker's memories, seeing the reminders of his life every single day? It was killing me inside, destroying me. I had to move forward or die. I had to put everything away, or I knew I'd end up being buried with him."

"Even at the price of our marriage? At the expense of *us*?" Xander shook his head. "And you say I did the same thing as you? I didn't. I couldn't. I loved our son with every breath in my body."

"So did I!" she shouted at him. "And I loved you. I still love you. That's why I did what I did. I brought you home, and I hoped against hope that you wouldn't remember because then we could forget the past and the hurt and the awful things we said to each other back then. We could be together, like we're meant to be. The way we have been. But you, you're running away again, just like you did last time. Why stand and face our problems when you can just walk away, right?"

The bitterness in her words stained the air between them.

"You have the gall to accuse me of running away? You

didn't want me anymore. You made that patently clear when Parker died. Sometimes I wonder if you ever loved me or if I just conveniently fit into the plan you had for your future. You certainly didn't need *me*. It makes me wonder why you even bothered to lie to me all this time."

Her throat choked up—just like it had the last time he left her. Her words, her fears, all knotted into a tangled ball that lodged somewhere between her heart and her voice and made her too afraid to tell him how she really felt.

Her words, when they came, were nothing but a stifled whisper. "I did it for us. For our marriage. It, no, *we* deserved a second chance, but you wouldn't listen when I said the past didn't matter. That it was our future that was important."

"*I* wouldn't listen? You shut me out, Olivia. You shut me out from the truth. From our son's memory, from our past. No!" He waved his hand in a short cutting motion in front of him. "You don't get to do this again. You don't get to make my decisions for me."

"What about our decisions, Xander? The decisions we should be making for *us*?" she pleaded.

"Us? There is no us."

Outside, she heard a car pull up and the driver toot the horn. Xander bent and reached down for the bag she hadn't seen standing there before. She recognized the suitcase immediately—after all, it hadn't been that long ago she'd packed it herself.

"Goodbye, Olivia. You'll be hearing from my lawyer—and this time the divorce is going through."

He started to walk toward the door, and she followed him, her movements jerky as if she were some marionette being played by a demented puppet master.

"Xander, please, don't go. Don't leave me," she implored. "We've been happy together. Things have been good again since you've been home, and this is *our home*."

He kept walking. Olivia put on a burst of speed, passing him and getting to the door before him. She pressed her back to the solid wooden surface, barring him from dragging it open and walking away from her.

"Think about how well we worked together with your rehab and how close we've become again. This is our chance to rebuild our lives. We made mistakes before— I know that. But we can work past them. Please don't throw away this chance for us to make it all right again. To rebuild our marriage."

He put his hands on her shoulders and physically steered her away from the door. She lacked the strength to fight him and just watched as he turned the brass knob and opened the door wide.

"You're good at this, you know," she murmured, using the only weapon she had left. "Walking away. You blame me for lying, for withholding the truth from you, but you're equally to blame for the way things fell apart. You always walk away instead of accepting or asking for help. You're prepared to share your body, but you've never shared your deepest feelings or your thoughts with me. Ever.

"Please, Xander. I can be there for you. We can work through this. Let me help you come to terms with your grief. You say I put Parker's life away into boxes, but you did exactly the same with your feelings. You stopped working at home and you spent every hour you could at work. We never talked. We never admitted how much we needed each other. Help me, Xander. Let me help you."

Xander shook his head again, his face a taut mask devoid of expression, his eyes cold. "You are the last person I will ever ask for help."

He stepped through the open door and out onto the

porch. Past his shoulder, out on the street, Olivia saw Rachelle get out of the car and look toward the house. Xander raised a hand to Rachelle in acknowledgment and kept walking.

Olivia stayed there, frozen in the entrance hall of her home, as she watched her husband walk away from her for the second time in their marriage. His parting words echoed in her mind. As the sound of Rachelle's car driving away faded into the distance, Olivia slowly shut the door and rested her forehead against its surface.

Every part of her body hurt from the inside out. She'd thought it was bad the last time he'd left her, but she'd still been so numb with losing Parker that she hadn't had the capacity to think or to feel too much. But now—given all that had developed between them since he'd been back, given how much she still loved him—she hurt in ways she'd never dreamed possible.

Where did this leave them, exactly? Wherever it was, she knew she didn't like it. Hated it, in fact. Hated that once again she'd allowed the best thing that had ever happened to her to walk out that door.

And still she loved him.

Fifteen

Xander sat in the car as Rachelle drove away from the house, his eyes fixed forward. *Look to the future*, he told himself, *away from the past*. Away from the hurt, the anger, the betrayal. Anger still simmered beneath the surface. At Olivia, at himself.

"Did you want to stop somewhere for a meal or a drink?" Rachelle said as they entered the harbor bridge approach.

"No," he said abruptly. "Thanks," he added. "Just to my place would be fine."

She nodded, but he sensed her disappointment. He remembered now that before his accident they'd become closer than two people who simply worked together. Friends still, not lovers. But they'd been heading in a more romantic direction. Although, when he'd been honest with himself, he'd found it impossible to engage his emotions to the extent he needed to in order to embark on an intimate relationship with someone. He knew she was a lot more invested in developing their relationship than he'd been. At least she'd never hidden that from him, not the way Olivia had hidden so much.

His stomach tightened on an unexpectedly sharp pain. Why did it hurt so much to be leaving her again? He'd already done it once before—and now that he remembered why, he understood and agreed with the choice he'd made two years ago. This time shouldn't have been any different, and yet it felt as if he was leaving a vital part of himself behind.

Being a Friday night, traffic was quite heavy. The journey gave him far too much time to think and reflect. He was relieved when Rachelle pulled into the underground car park and drew to a halt in one of the parking spaces allocated to his apartment.

She turned off the engine and twisted in her seat to face him. The smile on her face didn't quite match the uncertainty he saw in her eyes.

"Xander? Are you okay? Do you want me to come up with you?"

"Look, thanks for the ride, but I'd prefer to be on my own right now."

Her smile faded. "You're not angry with me, are you? I wanted to say something to you when I saw you and Olivia at the apartment, but she wouldn't let me."

Xander sighed. He just bet Olivia didn't let Rachelle say anything. "Of course I'm not angry with you," he said and leaned forward to kiss her on the cheek. "I'll see you on Monday, okay? At the office."

"You've been cleared to come back to work? That's fabulous. We've missed you so much. *I've* missed you."

"Cleared or not, I'm coming back. Even if it's only for a few hours a day. I need to get back to normal." *Whatever normal is now*, he added silently. "Again, thanks for the ride. I appreciate you coming to get me at such short notice."

"Anytime, you just call me. I'm here for you. I could even get you some groceries now, if you like, and bring them back. It's pretty empty up there right now."

He shook his head emphatically. "No, that's fine. I'll get some things delivered in."

"On the weekend?"

"I'll deal with it," he said firmly and opened his door to get out of the car. "See you Monday."

She took the hint and nodded, but her disappointment was clear in her eyes. "Monday it is. Good night, Xander. I'm glad you're back to your old self."

After she'd driven off, he took the elevator to his floor and let himself into his apartment. The soullessness of the space was just what he needed right now. He didn't want memories or feelings or anything. Except maybe a shot of whisky. He walked over to the cabinet where he kept his liquor and grabbed a bottle of Scotland's finest before going to the kitchen, where he splashed two fingers of amber liquid in a crystal tumbler.

He walked over to the windows that looked out over the harbor and toward Devonport—toward Olivia—and took a sip of the spirit. It burned as it went down, not the deep satisfying burn he'd anticipated but something far less pleasant. Xander looked down at the glass in his hand and wondered what the hell he was doing seeking solace in alcohol. He'd never done it before, and he certainly shouldn't be starting now.

He strode to the kitchen and tipped out the contents of the tumbler into the sink. He needed a distraction, but whisky wasn't it. He stared at the large flat-screen TV mounted on the far wall of his sitting room. No, not even watching a movie or channel surfing appealed. Instead, Xander walked down the hallway toward his bedroom, stopping at the door to his office.

His hand was on the handle before he realized what he

was doing. Work had always been a panacea for him—why should that be any different now? He should still have some client notes here he could go over. He rued the fact his laptop had been destroyed in the crash. Not even its leather case had protected its harddrive from the impact. If he'd had the laptop, at least he could have looked forward to losing himself for a few hours by up-dating himself on his files and who had handled what in his absence.

The minute Xander stepped in his office he knew Olivia had been in there. The picture of Parker that he'd taken with him the first time he'd left her wasn't on his desk where he knew he'd left it. A roll of rage swelled inside him. Wiping their son's memory from their house had been one thing, but tampering with his apartment, as well? That was going too far.

He searched the office for the picture, his movements becoming more frantic the longer it took him to find it. The relief that coursed through his body when he found the frame, face down in a drawer, was enough to make him drop heavily into his chair. He looked at the beloved face of his only child. Felt anew the loss and grief that he usually kept locked inside. Relived the guilt.

Carefully he put the picture back on his desk where it belonged and stared at it for several minutes. Losing Parker was a reminder that he couldn't stray from the path he'd set himself. He didn't want to love again the way he'd loved Olivia and their little boy because when it all fell apart it hurt far too much.

He understood why his father had collapsed within himself the way he had. His grief and guilt over Xander's brother's death had been too much for him to handle, especially with the way Xander's mother had locked herself in a non-emotional cocoon and forged her way through the rest of her life. He hadn't had the support he needed. After losing his son and his marriage, Xander hadn't had any support to lean on, either. But he was tougher, more determined not to become a victim of his own dreadful mistake, and if that meant separating himself from emotion—the way his mother had—then that's what he would do.

It had been the longest two weeks of her life and Olivia felt decidedly ragged around the edges when she forced herself to get out of bed and embark on her new daily routine. Who was she kidding, she wondered as she padded downstairs in her dressing gown, her hair askew and her face unwashed. This tired, halfhearted attempt to continue on as though everything was normal was a step back into the past, hardly anything new.

The house felt empty without Xander there, and her heart echoed with loss. She'd spent the past fourteen days listlessly wandering around, feeling unmotivated and empty. Even a call from the gallery owner to say they'd just sold the last piece and had requests lining up for more of her work couldn't lift her spirits.

She'd screwed up. Again. So what now? She aimlessly went through the motions of making coffee and pouring it into a mug. As she lifted the brew to her lips to take a sip, the aroma filled her nostrils and turned her stomach. She'd been off and on different things for days now, and coffee was just another to add to the list. With a sigh she tipped the contents down the drain and turned instead to put the kettle on. Maybe a cup of peppermint tea would revive her flagging appetite.

As she pulled a teabag from the box in the pantry she forced herself to acknowledge that it would take more than a cup of herbal tea to make things better. There was only one thing—one man—who could make a difference in her life. The only one who had ever mattered. Xander.

She'd just finished brewing the tea when the phone rang. She recognized the number on the caller display with a sinking sensation that pulled at her stomach. Her lawyer wasted no time on pleasantries.

"Mrs. Jackson, we've been instructed by your husband's lawyers to expedite matters relating to your dissolution of marriage. Do you need us to forward new forms to you, or do you still have the ones we originally sent?"

So, he hasn't wasted time, Olivia thought as she acknowledged the lawyer's request. "No, I still have the originals."

"All you need to do is sign them, put them in the enclosed envelope and post them today. Or I could arrange a courier to collect them from you if you'd prefer. It seems Mr. Jackson is in somewhat of a hurry."

Olivia closed her eyes against the burn of tears. Her voice shook as she spoke. "I see. I'll get the papers back to you. There's no need to organize a courier."

There was a brief silence on the other end before she heard her lawyer clear his throat. "Thank you," he said. "And, Mrs. Jackson? I'm so very sorry things didn't work out for you."

"I am, too, Mr. Clement."

She hung up without saying goodbye, and the phone fell from her hands to the floor. She wrapped her arms around her waist and bent over as uncontrollable sobs racked her body. It was over and it was all her fault. If only she'd been up front with Xander from the beginning, he might have been receptive to starting again. But now, with the stupid decisions she'd made, with her inability to face the pain of the past, she'd ensured they had no future together at all.

Eventually she dragged herself back up the stairs and into her en suite. She pulled open the drawer where she'd stowed the papers and reached inside, her hand hesitating as it hovered over the sanitary products stored there. Something wasn't right. She reached into the drawer and grabbed the little pocket-size diary she kept a record of her cycle in and counted back the days. She was two days late. Nothing really to worry about. Unless you factored in the minor detail that her periods always came every twenty-eight days without fail.

Her hand trembled as she shoved the diary back in the drawer and slammed it shut—leaving the folded envelope exactly where she'd put it, forgotten now in light of what she was dealing with. She'd been under a lot of stress, hadn't been eating or sleeping properly. No wonder she was out of kilter, she tried to tell herself. But all the while she knew her excuses were a waste of time. She knew the signs as well as she knew her face in the mirror each morning. The lack of appetite, the need to nap at odd times of the day, not to mention her reaction to the coffee she'd made this morning. And then there was the metallic tang that had been in her mouth the past couple of days. A tang she remembered vividly from when she'd become pregnant with Parker. She'd been ignoring each and every sign. Choosing oblivion over reality—which was what had led her to this situation in the first place.

Pregnant. With Xander's child. What the hell was she going to do now?

Three days later Olivia had her confirmation. The nurse at her doctor's surgery had been filled with quiet excitement on her behalf. An excitement that Olivia was hard-pressed to feel. She had to tell Xander straightaway. This wasn't something she could, or would, withhold from him.

The minute she got home she called his cell phone. It rang only a couple of times before switching to his answering service. Olivia disconnected the call. He must have diverted her call the moment he'd seen her number on the caller display. The knowledge that he wasn't even willing to speak to her on the phone was a blow she hadn't expected. Not prepared to give up at the first hurdle, she dialed again. This time it went immediately to the service and she left him a message.

"Xander, I need to see you. It's urgent. Meet me tomorrow, please." She named a café in Devonport, a short ferry ride for him across the harbor, and stated what time she'd be there.

Now all she could do was wait.

Sixteen

Xander arrived before the time Olivia had indicated, but she had still gotten there ahead of him. She saw him the minute he came through the door, and he watched as her cheeks suffused with color and her eyes grew bright.

"I got your message," he said unnecessarily as he sat down opposite her at the table. "What do you want?"

"I'm glad you came. I didn't want to tell you this in a message."

"For two months you've held things back from me and *now* you want to tell me something? What is it?" he asked, not making any effort to keep the irritation out of his voice.

He wasn't prepared for what came next.

"I'm pregnant."

He stared at her in shock. *Pregnant?* Silence grew between them. A waitress came over to take their order, and he waved her away. Finally he found his tongue.

"What do you mean, pregnant?"

"What it usually means." Olivia gave him a smile, no

more than a twist of her lips really and certainly not the
fulsome smile he was used to seeing on her face. It made
him look at her more sharply and note the dark bruises
of sleeplessness beneath her eyes and the pale cast of her
skin. Concern for her swelled inside him, but he ruth-
lessly quashed it. It shouldn't matter to him if she slept
or ate or looked after herself. Unless what she'd just told
him was true.

"We're having a baby," she affirmed.

Every cell in his body rejected the words. *A baby. No.
Not again. Never again.* They'd used protection. Even in
his amnesiac state he'd followed the protocol he'd insti-
gated after Parker's birth.

"But how—?"

"The condoms we used were expired," she said by way
of explanation, her eyes not leaving his face for a second.

"Did you know that before we used them?"

"No! Of course I didn't. I'd forgotten all about them,
to be honest. You must have bought them well before…"
Her voice trailed off.

Before Parker died. And, yes, their purchase had been
made well before then. There had been little intimacy
between him and Olivia during Parker's last year. Their
son had been plagued with virtually every cold and flu
known to man after he began preschool and was exposed
to germs from the other children. Olivia had said his im-
mune system would strengthen eventually. However, it
had meant she'd spent more nights curled up in bed with
Parker, trying to soothe him back to sleep, than she had
with Xander. Their lovemaking had become sporadic
at best as she'd poured all her care into nursing Parker
to health.

Now she was pregnant again. An icy shaft of trepidation sliced through him. What on earth did she expect
from him? Was she trying to manipulate him again? She

said she hadn't known the condoms were expired, but could he believe her? Maybe she'd planned to become pregnant all along, making the decision without him just like she had the first time. Binding him to her through an innocent baby when everything else she'd tried had failed, perhaps?

"You're telling me you didn't do this deliberately?"

"Of course I am. I swear I'm telling you the truth," she said, her voice raising slightly and making heads turn toward them. She continued, "If you'll remember, you were the one to initiate things the first time we—"

"I remember," he said, cutting across the words she'd been about to say.

Words that all too easily painted vivid memories in his mind of every single exquisite moment they'd spent together. The sounds she'd made when they made love. The scent of her body. The feel of her as she climaxed around him and as he spent himself inside her. The intense sense of belonging as they came back down to earth and fell asleep in each other's arms. He didn't want to remember. He couldn't risk allowing himself to feel.

"Is this why you haven't signed the papers yet?" he demanded.

"No! To be honest with you, I forgot all about them."

"Honest? That's a novelty for you these days, isn't it?" At Olivia's shocked expression he huffed out a sigh. "I'm sorry—that was uncalled for."

His mind scattered in a hundred different directions, but everything that passed through his thoughts settled back on one thing. Olivia was pregnant, and, if she was to be believed, they were equally responsible for this situation. The knowledge was a bitter pill to swallow. Either way he looked at it, another child of his would be on this earth, which meant he had responsibilities to that child. Responsibilities he had promised himself he'd never bear again.

Xander abruptly pushed his chair back from the table and stood. "Thank you for the information," he said and turned to go.

He was forced to halt in his steps when he felt Olivia's hand catch him on the arm.

"Xander, stay—please. We have to talk about this." Her voice rose again, attracting the same attention as before.

"Don't make a scene, Olivia. You asked me to come here and I did. You've given me your news and now I'm going. In the meantime, perhaps you could complete your part of the dissolution document and return it to your lawyer as requested?"

He stared at her hand until she let go. The second she did so he started for the door. But the short walk to the ferry building or the ride across the harbor back to the office passed in a blur. All he could remember were Olivia's words. *I'm pregnant.* They echoed in his mind, over and over again.

He couldn't do this again—didn't want to ever face being a father again—but circumstance now forced it on him. There were choices to make. Tough ones. Xander reached for the phone and hit the speed dial for his lawyer's office.

Olivia was working in her studio when she heard a van pull up outside her house. She walked over to the driveway to see who it was and was surprised to see a courier there. She wasn't expecting anything. The courier handed her an envelope, got her to sign for it and went on his way. Olivia felt dread pull at her with ghostly fingers as she identified the source of the envelope. Xander's lawyer.

Slowly she walked to the patio at the back of the house

and sat down at the table. She stared at the envelope, wondering what lay inside. She couldn't bring herself to open the packet; she didn't want to see in black-and-white whatever demand or dictate Xander had dreamed up in response to the news he was going to be a father again. She was still having a hard enough time coming to terms with the way he'd behaved when she'd told him the news yesterday. She didn't know what she'd expected him to do or say, exactly, but it hadn't been to simply get up and walk away from her—again.

A blackbird flew down onto the lawn and cocked its head, staring at her with one eye before pecking at the ground, pulling out a worm and flying away. She felt very like that worm must feel right now, she realized. At the mercy of something bigger, stronger and darker than she was. Helpless. It wasn't a feeling she was comfortable with, and it reminded her of all the things in her life she'd never been able to control. Control had become everything to her. It kept her world turning on its axis when everything else fell apart.

She picked up the envelope and turned it over and over in her hands. Had she really thought for a minute that Xander would be pleased with the news that she was expecting another baby? Maybe, in a sudden rash of idealistic foolishness, she had. The news had obviously shocked him—it had shocked her, too. She hadn't anticipated his utter indifference. So where did that leave them?

The obvious answer lay right there, in her hands, but still she couldn't bring herself to tear the envelope open. Instead, she placed it squarely on the table and went inside and brewed a pot of chamomile tea—taking her time over each step. Only after she'd carried her tea tray back outside to the table, poured her first cup and taken a sip did she pick up the envelope again.

She placed one hand on her belly. "Okay, little one, let's see what your daddy has to say."

With a swift tear it was open, and she pulled the contents out. She scanned the letter quickly, then read it more slowly on a second pass-through. Olivia went numb from head to foot. Xander's feelings couldn't have been spelled out more clearly. While he was prepared to offer generous financial support toward the child, he wanted no contact with the baby or with her whatsoever. There was a contract enclosed, setting out his terms and the sums he was prepared to pay, but she didn't even look at it.

Slow burning anger lit inside her. How dare he dismiss their baby like that? It was one thing to be angry with her—to not want anything to do with her—but to reject their child? It was so clinical and callous.

Olivia tossed the letter onto the table and propelled herself to her feet. She paced the patio a few times and came to a halt outside her studio. Through the open door she could see the canvas she was working on—a commission she'd earned as a result of her exhibition. Painting had always been her refuge in the past—through sorrow, through loss—but she knew that she needed to work this anger out of her system before she picked up a brush again.

With a growl of frustration she closed and locked the studio doors before she took the tea tray and Xander's wretched communication inside. Then, after grabbing her keys and sliding her feet into an old pair of sneakers, she went out the front door and down to the beach. She powered along the sand, oblivious to the sparkle of light on the rise and fall of the sea and the growing heat of the sun as it approached its zenith in the sky.

By the time she'd made it to the end of the beach and turned back again, she had worked the worst of her anger and, yes, her indignation, off. Olivia sat down on a park bench in the shade and waited for her breathing and heart rate to return to normal.

What had driven Xander to such a decision? she asked herself as she tried to rationalize his stance. This cold distance he insisted on maintaining was not something she recognized from the man she loved. She knew he could be distant and independent. He could also be stubborn and insanely detailed at times. But he wasn't the kind of man who could reject a child. Even as angry as he was about her pregnancy with Parker, he'd loved their son with an intensity that had often taken her breath away. Surely he couldn't *not* love another child of his?

She watched a lone gull as it circled on the thermals in the air before changing its direction and swooping down to the water. Was it that he wanted to be free like that gull there? Answerable only to himself? Had her lies and losing Parker the way they had made him incapable of loving ever again?

The answer that repeated in her mind was an emphatic no. In the weeks before he'd regained his memory she knew to the depths of her soul that he'd loved her. But if he was capable of love, why then would he withhold it from this baby?

Fear.

The word—so small, so simple and yet so powerful— came to her with blinding insight. He was afraid to love again—certainly afraid to love their baby but maybe even afraid to love her, too. After all, wasn't love based on trust? And hadn't she destroyed his trust in her not once but several times over?

Had she given him her shoulder to lean on in the wretched dark days after Parker died? No, she'd been filled with recriminations and pain and projecting her own guilt onto him. Had she tried to stop him leaving that first time? No, she'd been too numbed by grief to do anything.

She knew a little of his family's circumstances, even though Xander had never discussed it much and Olivia had never been close with her mother-in-law. Knew how his father had so grieved the loss of his firstborn son that he'd completely withdrawn from the family he'd had left. Understood that Xander's mother had worked hard every day she could to support her surviving son and her husband. His mum may not have shown her love with hugs and kisses, but she'd done the best she could to ensure their family was secure.

Was it any wonder then that Xander hadn't known how to express his grief? Why had she never thought about that before? He'd grown up with two complete extremes of how to cope with loss. Had anyone ever asked him how *he'd* felt about losing his brother, let alone his son?

She knew she certainly hadn't.

Where to now? How was she going to break through the armor Xander now protected himself and his emotions within? She'd already lost his trust, so was it even possible for him to forgive her and allow her back into his heart?

There were no secrets left between them now. She could only try. They'd made a child together out of love; that had to count for something. She owed it to Xander, to their baby and to herself to fight for what was right— to fight for their love and the chance to start again.

It was late when Xander listened to the latest message from Olivia. He'd been putting it off most of the day. Once he was home, he knew he couldn't put it off any longer. She'd been blunt and to the point. She'd acknowledged receipt of the offer through his lawyer, but she wanted to discuss it with him face-to-face first. She said that if he agreed to meet with her again, she wouldn't delay any further. Everything he wanted signed would be signed and returned at that meeting.

He knew he should call her back. Instead he dropped his phone on the coffee table in front of him and stretched out on the wide sofa that faced the view over the harbor. Lights sparkled in the inky darkness, like the stars of a distant galaxy. *Distant*, now there was a word. It described exactly how he felt when it came to just about everything in his life. Distant was safe; distant didn't flay a man's heart into a thousand shreds, nor did it betray a man.

He'd thought that distance was what he needed, what he wanted, and he'd tried to throw himself back into his work to gain emotional distance the way he always had when faced with personal upheaval. But in unguarded moments thoughts of Olivia kept creeping in. Her image when she came to the hospital, and he saw the love and concern so stark and clear on her face. Her determination to see him through the physical therapy he needed to do each day to regain muscle tone and strength after his coma. The sweet, soft sigh she made as he entered her body, as if, in that moment, everything in their world was perfect. And it had been.

And then there were the memories that went further back, to when Parker was alive, to the cute little family they'd been and how happy they were together. A visceral pain scored deep inside and reminded him anew that he'd never see Parker grow up. Pain laced with guilt that he'd been the one to leave their front gate open and that he'd been the one to throw the ball Bozo had chased out onto the road. Only two small things, each taken on their own, but put together they'd led to a tragedy of inestimable proportions.

The bitter irony that his little family had faced the

same awful loss as his parents had hadn't escaped him. But he wasn't his father. He wouldn't give in and buckle under the grief he felt. Instead he'd locked his feelings down. He would not be weak or needy. He would not, above all things, need Olivia more than she needed him. When it had become clear to him that she didn't need him at all, that she'd moved past their tragedy without him, Xander had left.

He groaned out loud. This was doing his head in. He needed a distraction, but what? Or who? He picked up his phone again and scrolled through his contact list. He wasn't in the mood for testosterone-driven company. His finger hovered over Rachelle's number. She'd made it more than clear these past few weeks that she was interested in picking up where they'd left off before his accident. In fact, she'd also made it clear she was willing to jump a few steps on that particular ladder.

Was that what would finally dislodge Olivia's presence from his mind? He could only hope so.

Rachelle arrived within thirty minutes of his call, and she glided into his arms as if she belonged there.

"I'm so glad you called," she said with a sultry purr as she lifted her face to his.

He kissed her and tried to feel something, anything but indifference, and failed miserably. Maybe he was just out of practice, he thought. *But what about Olivia? You didn't need any practice there*, came the insidious voice in the back of his mind. He pushed the thought away and led Rachelle into his sitting room.

"Would you like a drink?" he offered.

"Sure, a pinot noir if you have it," she replied, settling herself on the couch and crossing her legs.

He couldn't help but notice the way her skirt rode up on her shapely thighs. She might be petite, but there was nothing about her that wasn't perfectly formed—and she knew how to dress to highlight those assets, he acknowledged wryly. Again he anticipated the surge of interest, of desire, that should be starting a slow pulse in his veins. Again, nothing.

Xander snagged a bottle of wine from the wine rack and went to the kitchen to pour them each a glass. He returned to where she sat and passed her the wine. They clinked glasses.

"To new beginnings," Rachelle said with a glow of hope in her dark brown eyes, flicking her glossy black hair back over her shoulder. "And happy endings," she finished with a smile.

Xander nodded his head and took a sip of wine. Even that didn't taste right. In fact, nothing about this evening felt right at all. Rachelle began to talk about work—she'd recently received a promotion and was excited about bringing new ideas to the table. Xander enjoyed her lively conversation and approved many of her ideas, but when she turned the conversation to more personal matters and placed one dainty hand on his thigh as she moved a little closer on the sofa, he knew he had to bring the evening to a premature end.

"Rachelle, look, I'm sorry, but—" he started.

Regret spread across her face, but she mustered up an attempt at a smile. She lifted her hand from his leg and placed her fingers across his lips. "It's okay," she said. "I can feel you're trying, but it's not working, is it? And, really, you shouldn't have to *try*. The problem is—you're still too married to Olivia. Maybe not on paper and maybe not in your mind, but—" she placed a hand on his chest "—you most definitely are still married to her here, in your heart."

She leaned forward, put her wineglass on the table and rose from the sofa. "Don't get up," she said as he started to rise, as well. "I can see myself out. Oh, and I guess I'd better leave this with you, too."

Rachelle pulled a key out of a side pocket of her handbag and put it on the table next to her glass.

After she'd gone, Xander stared at the key on the table. He'd given it to her about a week before his accident. They'd been scheduled to attend a client function together, and he'd offered his place for her to get ready since she lived fairly far away. As she'd finished work ahead of him, he'd given her the key so she could let herself in and they'd then traveled to the venue together. He hadn't asked for the key back that night, or the next day, either, thinking that they would be developing their relationship further. He couldn't have been more wrong about that—accident or no accident.

He played her parting words over in his head. Was he really still in love with his wife? He got up and took the wineglasses to the kitchen. After pouring their contents down the drain and leaving the glasses on the counter top, he headed to his bedroom.

The room felt empty. Hell, *he* felt empty. It was past time to be honest with himself. He missed Olivia. And, more, he missed their life together and the new closeness they'd developed during his recovery. But could he forgive her? Could he let himself care for her—and for the baby on the way—when he knew they had the potential to hurt him so deeply?

No easy answers came to him through yet another sleepless night. They didn't come through a particularly arduous time at work the next day. He was tired and more than a little bit cranky when he arrived back at the apartment at eight o'clock that evening. The last person he wanted, or expected, to see was Olivia standing at his door, waiting for him.

Seventeen

Olivia straightened the second she saw him come out of the elevator and walk toward his apartment. Her face was pale and drawn, and he fought to quell the expression of concern that sprang to his lips.

"Olivia," he said in acknowledgment.

"I...I couldn't wait for you to return my call. I needed to see you."

"You'd better come inside."

He opened the door wide and ushered her into the apartment. His nostrils flared at the trace of scent she left in her wake, and instantly his body began to react. Why couldn't it have been like this last night? he asked himself. Why was it only Olivia who drew this reaction from him?

"Take a seat—you look worn-out," he commented as he put his briefcase down and shrugged out of his jacket. "Have you eaten?"

"Yes, thank you. I had dinner before I drove over."

"Were you waiting long?"

"Awhile," she answered vaguely.

He stood and watched as she took a seat.

"Xander, is it really too late for us?" she suddenly blurted, her hands fluttering nervously in her lap. "Can you truly not find it in your heart to forgive me and allow us to start over?"

He pushed a hand through his hair and breathed out a sigh. He'd asked himself the same question over and over last night and still he had no answers. Sure, his heart told him to give in and find a way to make their way forward in their lives again, but his head and his experience emphatically told him to walk away while he still could.

The thing was, he still felt so much for her. Even now every nerve, every cell in his body was attuned to Olivia—to every nuance and expression on her face, to the gentle lines of her body, to the fact she was carrying his baby. Reality slammed into him with the subtlety of an ice bucket challenge. Except this was no challenge. This was his life. The thing was, did he want it? Could he risk everything again and start a new life with Olivia and a baby?

"Xander? Please, say something."

Olivia's voice held a wealth of pain and uncertainty. A part of him wanted to reassure her, to say they could work things out. But the other, darker, side remembered all too well the child he'd been, the one who'd come home from school to a house filled with sorrow and devoid of emotional warmth—remembered the void left by his brother that was too big for Xander to fill on his own. A void like that left by Parker's death. One too painful to imagine even attempting to fill again. Love hurt, no matter which way you looked at it, and he was done with hurting.

He sat down next to Olivia, his elbows resting on his thighs and his hands loosely clasped. His head dropped between his shoulders.

"I don't think so," he finally said.

"At least that's more promising than a flat-out no," Olivia commented, although her voice held no humor.

He turned his head to look at her. Her features were so familiar to him. This was the woman whose gentle touch and quiet encouragement had helped him to recuperate and grow strong again. The woman he'd fallen even more deeply in love with as they'd lived together and made love. If he only let himself, he would be completely vulnerable to her again and to their unborn child. But he couldn't let go. He had to make the break and make it clean and fast.

"You'd better go. We have nothing to talk about anymore, Olivia," he said wearily.

"Not until you've heard me out," she insisted. "I have a right to tell you how I feel. I love you, Xander. Not just a little bit, not even a lot. I love you with every single thing I am. Every breath I take, every choice I've made since I met you. It's all about you. I know that some of those choices were the wrong ones, and I'm deeply sorry for those, but I'm learning as I go here. We both were— *are*," she corrected herself emphatically.

"I never asked for anything from you," he replied and started to rise. She grabbed his arm and tugged him back down.

"I know you didn't. I know you probably don't even want to admit that you want me, us, in your life at all. It's why you're pushing me away now. Why we probably lived such a parallel life before." She drew in a deep breath, then let it all go on her next words. "I've talked to your mother. I know what it was like for you when you were little."

"You what? Why? You had no right to talk to her."

Anger boiled thick and fast deep inside. Anger at Olivia for contacting his mother over something that was between the two of them only, and anger at his mother for talking to Olivia when she never spoke to him about the past.

"I needed to know, Xander. I had to find out if we had a chance. When Parker died, I did what I do. What I've always done for the past twenty years of my life. I picked up the pieces and I carried on."

"You didn't just pick them up. You boxed them up and put them away for good. You treated Parker's memory as if it was something to be forgotten, something to be swept away as if it had never happened."

Her voice was quiet when she replied. "It was all I knew how to do. I couldn't talk about it, Xander. We didn't talk about emotions in our house, and I suspect your house was very similar. Your mum told me about your dad, about how unwell he was. His grief went far deeper than mourning, and eventually it broke him completely.

"I don't want that for you, Xander. I want you to be whole. I want us to be whole, together. We can't do this on our own, apart. But maybe we can pull the pieces back together if we work together. Please, Xander, tell me you'll try. Tell me we're worth it." She took his hand and pressed it on her still-flat belly and begged him, "Tell me all three of us are worth it."

He looked down at his hand, then up to her face, where her eyes shone with unshed tears. His own eyes burned in kind.

"I can't tell you what you need to hear."

He could see this wasn't the answer she'd hoped for, but she rallied enough for one more try. "Think about it a little longer, Xander. Please. For all our sakes. Neither of us is perfect, but together we can make a good attempt at it. I know I pushed you away. I was as guilty as anyone of not sharing how I felt.

"It's not that I didn't care—I cared too much. If I let any of it out, how would I function? How would I manage to keep putting one foot in front of the other day after day? I couldn't let that grief float to the surface and still care for you at the same time. If I let it out, it would consume me. The only way I knew how to get through was to work. To put away all the reminders. To lose myself in being busy. I never meant to push you away."

"You didn't just push me away, Livvy. You pushed away every last physical memory we had of Parker, too. I felt like once he was gone, he didn't matter to you anymore. You never talked about him. You barely even mentioned his name."

"I never meant for you to believe that I didn't think Parker's life mattered. He mattered. You matter. *We* matter, don't we?"

She got up and began to pace the floor.

"After Parker died and you left, I threw myself into my painting. The time I spent working was the only time I didn't feel the pain of losing you both. All I could do was work, day in, day out. I couldn't sleep, couldn't eat, but I could paint, so I did. I produced my most emotive work ever. I even scored an agent from the paintings I did at the time, and they became the platform for my current success. But you know what?" She stopped pacing and faced him, her face a mask of pain and remorse. "I can't take pride in that even now. I feel like I cashed in on Parker's death. I painted out my grief, my frustration, my anger—my guilt."

"Guilt? What do you mean?" Xander stood up, his body rigid with tension, his hands curled into tight fists of frustration. "It wasn't you that left the gate open, nor were you the one who threw the ball for Bozo toward the road. That was all my fault."

A single tear slipped down Olivia's cheek. He ached to wipe it away, but he daren't touch her.

"I know I said it was your fault, Xander. It was far easier for me to point the blame at you than to admit my own accountability for what happened. Parker had been happily playing in my studio that morning—don't you remember? But the sounds he was making with his train set got on my nerves, and I couldn't concentrate on my work.

"I told him to go outside. If I hadn't done that—" Her voice broke off on a gasp of pain, and she hugged her arms around herself tight.

When he said nothing more, she went over to the sofa and grabbed her handbag. "I'm sorry, Xander. More than you'll ever know. I'd hoped, that if we talked—properly this time—that maybe we could work things out. But I guess the river runs too deep between us now for that to happen."

Before he could stop her or form a coherent sentence, she was gone. Feeling more horribly alone than he'd ever felt in his life, Xander sank back down onto the sofa and stared out the window. The last rays of the evening sun caressed the peninsula across the harbor. The peninsula where his home lay and, if he was to be totally honest, where his heart lived, as well.

He replayed Olivia's words over and over, thinking hard about what she'd said and in particular about her admission of fault in what happened that awful day when their world stopped turning. Why had she never said anything about that before?

I did what I do. What I've always done for the past twenty years of my life. I picked up the pieces and I carried on.

Of course she did. It was the example her father had set her and it was what he'd clearly expected of her after her mother died. In so many ways it was a mirror to what Xander had gone through as a child. Keep putting each foot forward straight after the other—no time for regret, no time for emotion. Do what needs to be done at all times. And whatever you do, don't talk about it.

Could he have made more effort to salvage their marriage after Parker died? Of course he could have. But he'd been turned in too much on himself. Focused too hard on protecting that facade that he'd spent most of his lifetime building, as his mother had built hers. He'd never seen his mother show weakness, never seen her so much as shed a tear. When the going got tough, as it had so often as she struggled to keep everything together, she just worked harder. And wasn't that exactly what he'd done, too?

When Olivia had told him they were expecting a baby, he'd thrown himself into work. He'd distanced himself from her and from the impending birth by doing whatever he could to ensure their financial security. He'd earned a promotion along the way. Successes like that he could measure, he could take pride in. What the hell did he know about being a father? Heaven knew he hadn't had a good example of one to call upon. He hadn't had any time to research it, to even get his head into the idea—they'd had no discussion, nothing, before she'd sprung it on him. And then to his amazement, when Parker had been born, the bond and the love had been instant. Equally rewarding and terrifying in its own right.

Fatherhood had become an unexpected delight. He'd been amazed at how effortlessly Livvy had transitioned from high school teacher to homemaker and mother. She did everything with an air of efficiency and capability that was daunting. Did she never question her ability to be a good parent? Did she never question his? If she had, he'd never seen any sign of it.

Part of his original attraction to her had always been to her self-sufficiency, but that very thing was what had slowly driven a wedge between them. It shifted the balance. But what he realized now, weighing her words and the feelings she'd finally opened up to him about this evening, was that in trying not to become a victim of his past, in trying not to be like his father, he'd fallen in the trap of behaving like his mother.

Why hadn't he been able to see that he didn't need to be a part of a dysfunctional relationship? When had he lost sight of all that was good and right about life? He thought back to the joy and excitement of meeting Olivia, of falling in love with her. He'd met a lot of women over time—beautiful, strong and successful women—and none of them had touched his heart the way she did. Why should it be wrong to be vulnerable to the one person he wanted to be close to?

Had he, with his own determined aloofness, contributed to the demise of their marriage? Of course he had. He had to accept that he couldn't be all things to all people. Surely his own mother's example had shown him that. Then why had he followed her path in life instead of his own?

He'd been a fool. A complete and utter idiot. He'd pushed away the one person in the world who loved him unconditionally. A woman who was flawed in her own ways but who needed him as much as he needed her. Of course he wanted, no, *needed* to be close to her. And that was okay. It didn't weaken him; it didn't diminish him as a man. It made him stronger because he loved her.

He got up and walked over to the window, one hand resting on the glass as he looked toward the dark bump on the distant landscape—the hill on which their home stood. So she'd made some stupid choices—hadn't he made some equally dumb ones? More importantly, could he forgive her for manipulating him when he'd come out of hospital?

The last vestiges of anger that had filled and driven him these past weeks faded away. Of course he could. They both needed to work on this. And now there was another life to consider, as well. How on earth had he even imagined that he could cut that child from his life? Not be there to see him or her be born and grow and learn and develop. It hurt to even think about it, and instinctively he began to shut down that part of him that felt that pain. But then he stopped. Pain was okay. *Feeling* was okay.

He closed his eyes and turned away from the window. Was he man enough, strong enough, to do this? To take a leap of faith and let love rule him and his decisions rather than depending on distance and control? He had some big decisions to make, and he had to be certain he was making the right ones. More importantly, he had to be making them for the right reasons.

Eighteen

It was Christmas Eve. Just under a week since Olivia had last seen or heard from Xander. She'd decided to make some effort with the decorations that morning and had gone up to the attic to find them. But the decorations had been forgotten when she'd stumbled across Parker's things that Xander had left scattered on the attic floor. She'd tucked away the clothes and toys, then picked up the albums. She was about to put them back in the box and seal it up again, but she changed her mind and took them downstairs instead.

Putting them back on the bookcase in the living room felt right. So did putting the framed photos of Parker back where they belonged. She got the toys out of the attic and loaded them into a carton in the room that had been Parker's. The room that would now become this baby's. After she'd done all that, she realized that the house felt different. Lighter somehow. Right. All of these things had been missing and, with them, a giant piece of her heart and soul.

She would never stop missing her firstborn, but at least now she could remember him with less of the sorrow that she'd been trying to hide from these past two years. And she could begin to forgive herself for her choices that day, too.

It was time for a new beginning. If only that beginning could be with Xander by her side. She'd lost count of the times she'd checked the answering machine at the house or the display on her cell phone to see if he'd called. It was time to face the awful truth. There would be no future together.

The dissolution order and Xander's offer of financial maintenance for the baby sat on the kitchen table in front of her. She had a pen clutched in her hand.

"Just sign the damn things and get it over with," she said out loud. Her hand fluttered to her belly. "We'll manage, you and me."

Before she could put pen to paper, the front doorbell rang. With a sigh of exasperation, she dropped the pen to the table and got up to see who it was. She felt a physical shock of awareness when she saw Xander standing there with one arm leaning up on the doorjamb, wearing his old uni sweatshirt and a disreputable pair of Levi's. Her heart picked up double time as her eyes raked his face, taking in the gleam in his slate-gray eyes and the stubble growing back stubbornly on his chin.

"Are you here about the papers?" she said, rubbing her hands down the legs of her jeans.

"Not exactly," Xander replied. "I have something for you, for Christmas. For you and the baby, actually."

Olivia felt confused. "For…?"

"Come and see."

Xander spun on a sneaker-clad foot and went down the path to the front gate. Beyond him, Olivia could see a family-friendly SUV. Clearly he'd been cleared to drive again, but she knew he'd never be seen dead in something like this. She was the one who'd always had the practical station wagon while he'd had the sporty little two-door foreign import. Maybe he'd borrowed the vehicle from someone else? Maybe his present was bigger than would fit in his car?

"Are you coming?" he called from the gate.

"Sure," she said, slipping through the doorway and down the stairs to the path. "Is this yours?" she asked, gesturing to the SUV when she got nearer.

"Yeah, I decided it was time to leave the racing cars to the experts and grow up a little. Grow up a lot, actually."

The back of the SUV was open. Through the tinted glass on the side Olivia could see an animal crate. She came to a halt behind the car and gasped when she saw the beagle puppy inside. Xander opened the crate and lifted the puppy out, depositing it squirming in Olivia's arms.

"Merry Christmas, Livvy."

The puppy lifted her head and enthusiastically licked Olivia on the chin, making her laugh out loud.

"But why?"

"Every kid needs a dog, right?" He grabbed a bag filled with puppy toys and food, tugged the blanket from inside the crate, then went to the front of the car and grabbed a pet bed from off the seat. "You mind if I bring these inside for you?"

"Oh, sure," she said, completely flustered. "Come in— have a coffee. Does it have a name?"

"She, actually. And, no, she doesn't have a name yet. I thought you'd like to choose one."

As they walked into the house Olivia saw Xander notice the photos of Parker that had gone back up on the hallway wall.

"You've put them back?" he asked, pausing by one

of the three of them—their faces alight with happiness and fun.

She swallowed past the lump in her throat. "They belong there. I…I should never have hidden them away. It wasn't right or fair—to him or to us."

Xander said nothing, but she saw him nod slightly. Tension gripped her shoulders, and she wished she could ask him what he thought, hoping that he'd at least tell her she'd done the right thing, but he remained silent. In the kitchen he spied the papers Olivia had been agonizing over signing.

"You were going to sign them, today?" he asked.

"I still can't bring myself to do it," Olivia admitted with a rueful shake of her head. "But I guess, now you're here. You may as well take them with you."

His face looked grim. "We need to talk."

Olivia felt her stomach sink. The puppy squirmed and whined in her arms. "Shall we take her outside first?"

"It's as good a place to talk as any."

Xander deposited the puppy's things on the floor and then he followed Olivia out to the patio where the puppy gamboled about, oblivious to the tension that settled like a solid wall between the two adults, all her attention on sniffing the plants and trees before she squatted happily on the grass.

"She's gorgeous, Xander. But why did you buy her?" Olivia asked, barely able to take her eyes from the sweet animal and hardly daring to look at the man standing so close by her side.

"I never had any pets growing up. My mother said she always had enough on her plate, no matter how much I begged and pleaded and promised to look after one. I guess I forgot how much I'd always wanted one and reverted to acting like my mother when you brought Bozo home that day."

Olivia couldn't help herself; she rested one hand on his forearm and reached up to kiss Xander on the cheek. He turned his head at the last minute, his lips touching hers and sending a flame of need to lick along her veins. Startled, she pulled back.

"Thank you—I love her already. She's beautiful."

"No, *you're* the one who's beautiful. Inside and out. I just never really appreciated how beautiful before. Livvy, I've been doing a lot of thinking. I've come to understand that I only allowed myself to see the outside, the surface. I convinced myself that was enough, that we could make a life together based on the physical attraction and chemistry between us. As long as it was just the two of us, I didn't have to delve any deeper into how I felt. I knew I loved you—but I don't think I ever really understood how much, and I hadn't really counted on sharing you with anyone else, whether it be dog or child."

He lifted a hand, gently tucked back her hair and cupped her face.

"Livvy, I'm sorry. I was a fool. I don't think I ever really knew what love was, or what lengths it could lead a person to, until I met you. I didn't deserve you, or Parker, or any of what we shared. If I'd been a better husband, a better father, maybe none of what happened that day would have occurred."

Olivia bit back a sob. There was so much pain and regret in his words, and she knew that he had little to apologize for.

"Xander, no. You were a great dad, and Parker loved you so very much. Don't sell yourself short. You weren't the one to make important life decisions without including me. You weren't the one to cast blame without seeing where blame truly lay. Those faults were all mine."

Xander shook his head. "I was his father. I should

have been able to keep him safe. It was my duty to him and to you, and I failed."

Her heart wrenched when she saw the tears that shimmered in his eyes. "The only person to blame that day was the guy driving the car that hit Parker and Bozo. If he'd been paying attention instead of texting, if he'd been driving to the speed limit instead of racing along a suburban road—then he'd have seen them run into the street and been able to stop in time. But we can't keep plaguing ourselves with 'what if,' and we can't keep blaming ourselves or one another for what happened. It happened. We can't turn back time, as much as we wish we could.

"I would have done everything differently that day too, if I could have, but nothing I do now will change that. And it's the same for you. Surely you see that? Xander, you *have* to see that and accept it to move past it."

Xander swallowed and turned away to watch the dog as she continued to explore the garden. "It doesn't make it any easier, though, does it?"

"And it's no easier handling it alone, either."

"No, you're right there. I watched my mother handle everything on her own while I grew up. She became so adept at it, so automatic about it all, that she wouldn't even accept help from me once I was able to give it. She told you that my father suffered a complete breakdown after my brother died, didn't she?"

Olivia moved to stand beside Xander, slipping her hand inside his. "Yes, she did. Until then I never understood how tough it must have been for either you growing up or for your mother—or even your dad, for that matter."

"I didn't really know any different at home. Sure, I knew what other families had and I knew our household was odd by comparison and that I couldn't bring friends home, but it wasn't until Parker died that I fully understood what my father must have gone through. I didn't want to fall down into that dark hole. In fact, I did everything I could to prevent that from happening. I never let out any of it—not my fears, my sorrow." He shook his head. "I tried so hard not to be like him. He couldn't even function without my mother there he depended on her so much. She had to go to work each day because if she didn't, we'd have nothing to eat, no roof over our heads. But from the second she left the house each morning to go to work, he'd weep. I'd let myself out the door to go to school, with the sound of his sobbing echoing in my ears. Some days, he'd find the strength to pull himself together, but as I got older, more and more often when I got home, he would still be crying.

"You know, when he died, I felt relief rather than sadness or loss because for the first time in years I knew he finally had peace. He couldn't forgive himself for my brother's death, couldn't talk about it, nothing. Most days he could barely get out of bed. He needed my mother for everything. I couldn't let myself be like him—not even the slightest bit."

Olivia squeezed his hand, hard. "Your whole family should have had more help."

Xander nodded. "Mum is not the kind of person who accepts help. She soldiers on. Does what needs doing and keeps looking forward. She was strong and capable and solid as a rock through all of it, and I really thought that was something to aspire to. In fact, I saw a lot of that in you, too. I don't think I ever saw her shed a tear or admit she couldn't handle anything.

"After Parker died, you coped with everything that had to happen afterward with the funeral—even giving our victim impact statement at the sentencing for the driver who killed him. Your composure scared me. Made me look at myself and question why I couldn't do those things. Was I my father's son?"

Olivia hastened to reassure him. "No, you weren't. You were grieving, too. Everyone copes in their own way, Xander. You couldn't be anyone other than yourself or feel anything other than what you were feeling at the time. Me, I pushed all my feelings aside, the way I learned how to do when I was a kid. Life goes on and all that," she said bitterly. "It got to the point where everyone in my family turned to me when it came to making choices about their life, even my dad. It became second nature to me, and it made me who I am.

"I never thought twice about involving you in the big decisions I made because I was just so used to following my own plan. And when I met you and we fell in love and got married, I thought I'd be able to craft the plan for both of us—for our life together. It's no wonder we fell apart through the very happening that should have driven us closer together."

Xander sighed. "It wasn't all your fault. Through our marriage I let you take control of everything because it was so much easier that way. It left me free to do what I saw as my role, the role my father never had in my memory. I needed to compensate for all the things he didn't do, but it wasn't without its own cost, was it? Do you think we can make it work? Give ourselves another chance at this thing called love?" he asked, still staring out at the garden.

"Yes, I *know* we can. Not because I want to or because you want to, but because we owe it to ourselves, and to Parker's memory and to the life of this new child we created, to do so—to be happy." She reached up to stroke his face and smiled when he turned into the touch and planted a kiss on her fingers. "I've never stopped loving you, Xander. I never will. I just needed to learn that to make a marriage work it needed to be a joint proposition—from start to finish—and I'm totally not ready for us to be finished yet."

Xander nodded. "Nor am I. I guess neither of us had the ideal example growing up, did we? And yet, somehow we managed to find one another—love one another." He looped his arms around her waist and stared deep into her eyes. "Will you help me, Livvy? Will you help me to grieve for our son properly? Will you let me help you, too? Will you let me love you for the rest of your life and raise this new baby, and maybe even others, with you?"

"Oh, Xander, I would love nothing else. I love you so much. I don't want a life without you. I want to be there for you, always. I want us to be the family we both deserve."

"As do I with you. Together, I promise. We're going to do this together, and we'll get it right this time, in good times and in bad."

He bent his head to hers and sealed his vow with the tender caress of his lips against hers. His touch had never felt more right or more special. Olivia knew, as her heart rate increased and as warmth began to unfurl through her body, that her heart beat for this man with a passion and a love that was equally reciprocated and that, together, they could do anything.

Xander looked across the lawn at the puppy who was now sitting down, staring at them both. "So, what are you going to name her?"

Olivia looked up at her husband, the man of her heart and the key to her happiness. "I think the question should be, what are *we* going to call her, don't you?"

As Xander's laughter filled the air around them and he squeezed her tight, Olivia knew without a doubt that this time they'd make it. This time was forever.

* * * * *

"There's always a catch." Kalissa smiled.

Riley agreed with that. "Catch is—" he settled a hand on her bare hip "—I'm falling for you."

Her smile widened. "That's not a catch."

It was for him, and that was the hard truth. He was quickly coming to care for this woman, but he was destined to upset and disappoint her. There was no way around it.

But not now, he told himself, not today. They could be together for a little longer yet, before the real world crowded in.

* * *

Seduced by the CEO
is part of the Chicago Sons series:
Men who work hard, love harder and live
with their fathers' legacies…

SEDUCED BY THE CEO

BY
BARBARA DUNLOP

Published in Great Britain 2015
by Mills & Boon, an imprint of Harlequin (UK) Limited,
Eton House, 18-24 Paradise Road, Richmond, Surrey, TW9 1SR

© 2015 Barbara Dunlop

ISBN: 978-0-263-25266-8

51-0615

Harlequin (UK) Limited's policy is to use papers that are natural, renewable and recyclable products and made from wood grown in sustainable forests. The logging and manufacturing processes conform to the legal environmental regulations of the country of origin.

Printed and bound in Spain
by CPI, Barcelona

Barbara Dunlop writes romantic stories while curled up in a log cabin in Canada's far north, where bears outnumber people and it snows six months of the year. Fortunately she has a brawny husband and two teenage children to haul firewood and clear the driveway while she sips cocoa and muses about her upcoming chapters. Barbara loves to hear from readers. You can contact her through her website, barbaradunlop.com.

For my husband

One

Kalissa Smith stripped off a pair of dirt-streaked garden gloves and paced backward from the Newbergs' house, smiling with both pride and satisfaction. It had taken a full month, but the new lawn gleamed emerald under the August sun. Beyond its scalloped edges, fresh, black dirt was mounded in flower beds positioned against the brick walls of the two-story colonial. Evergreens and dwarf maples were clustered in one corner of the spacious yard, providing shade and privacy.

"The ornamental peppers definitely work," said Megan, crossing from their company pickup truck in the driveway.

"It's a bit of a twist," said Kalissa.

Megan drew a deep breath. "I think they'll be happy with the twist."

"They'd better be happy."

The Newbergs were not the easiest clients in the world, but at least the job was finally complete.

"Did we make any money on this one?" Megan asked.

"I sure hope we did. We were underwater on the turf, but we saved on labor."

"Only because we did most of it ourselves."

"Good thing we charge ourselves such reasonable prices."

Megan smiled at the joke. "It does look fantastic."

Kalissa couldn't help flexing her sore shoulders. Her calves were tight and her abs ached from so many days of physical work. On the bright side, she had absolutely no need to visit a gym, and she was developing a very nice tan.

"I'm going to take some pictures for the web site," she said.

Mosaic Landscaping had been in business for just under a year, starting when Kalissa and Megan had both earned college diplomas in landscape design.

"There were three more inquires on our voice mail this afternoon," said Megan.

"Can we at least grab dinner before we start a new project?"

Megan chuckled. "On top of everything else, you want *food*?"

"Call me high-maintenance."

"I could go for a burger."

"Benny's, here we come."

Benny's Burgers was a funky little restaurant tucked in an alleyway near their landscape shop on the west side of Chicago. They'd rented the aging storefront and warehouse space because of its generous size and reasonable rent. Esthetics had little to do with the decision—though they had painted and brightened the upstairs apartment, moving two single beds and some used furniture into the space.

Kalissa retrieved the camera from the front of their serviceable, blue pickup truck, making her way around the yard to take shots from various angles.

At the same time, Megan gathered up the last of the hand tools, stowing them in the pickup box. Then she perched herself on the tailgate, scrolling through pages on her tablet.

"Any new inquiries from the web site?" Kalissa called as she lined up for a picture of the flagstone walkway edged with pink and white peonies. The front porch and double doors filled in the background, and the sun was hitting the flowers at just the right angle.

"There are still a lot of people looking for maintenance."

Megan and Kalissa had talked about adding a yard maintenance service to their business. It wasn't where they wanted to focus, but if they could hire a decent crew, they might be able to make a little extra money. Their business was gradually increasing its customer base, but the margins were thin.

Kalissa clicked the final shots.

"What do you think about doing that?" she asked as she made her way back to the truck.

"Is there something you've neglected to tell me?" Megan was staring at the tablet screen.

Kalissa stopped in front of her. "About what?"

Megan turned the tablet so it was facing Kalissa.

Kalissa reached out to steady it.

She squinted against the bright sunshine, and a photo of a bride and groom came into focus. The man was handsome in his tux, and the woman's dress was gorgeous, highlighted by a huge, multi-colored bouquet of roses, tulips and lavender.

"See it?" asked Megan.

"The Ferdinand Pichard roses?" They were stunning. Kalissa had never seen them in such a deep magenta.

"The *bride*."

"What about the—" Then Kalissa saw it. She snapped her hand back in astonishment.

"It's you."

"It's not *me*." Kalissa peered at the woman's startlingly familiar face. It obviously couldn't be her.

"Photo-shopped?" she asked.

"That's what I thought," said Megan. "But there are a bunch more." She moved so they could both see the screen while she scrolled through other pictures.

"What on earth?" Kalissa took control of the tablet. "Is this a joke?" She looked at Megan. "Did you do this?"

Megan stood up for a better view. "I only found it two minutes ago."

Kalissa stopped on a picture of the bride and groom cutting the wedding cake.

"Nice," said Megan. "Seven tiers."

"I obviously have money in this alternate life." Kalissa took in each of the bride's poses and expressions. "Too bad I can't float us a loan."

She struggled to figure out where her head shots could have originated, guessing this was some kind of on-line game.

"My birthday's coming up," she ventured, trying to imagine who, other than Megan, would spend this much time on a joke gift.

"Nice groom," said Megan.

Kalissa took another look at the man. "He is pretty hot."

"It says here he's Shane Colborn."

"Why do I know that name?"

"Colborn Aerospace," said Megan, identifying a prominent Chicago company.

"So, it was obviously somebody from Chicago who did this."

"I mean, this is the real guy. He *owns* Colborn Aerospace."

"Uh, oh." Now Kalissa was worried. "He's not going to think this is funny. Can anybody see this page?"

"I got it from a Nighttime News link."

Kalissa's confusion grew. "The national site?"

Megan nodded.

"Why? How? We have to get them to take it down."

"I think it's legit."

"That's ridiculous."

"I think you have a doppelganger."

"That's not a real thing." Kalissa studied the bride's face. "And there's no way someone could possibly look this similar."

It was a joke. These had to be pictures of her that somebody had taken without her knowledge.

"Maybe you were part of a cloning experiment?"

"I doubt they had human cloning when I was born."

"I hope they still don't have it now," said Megan. "You know, there is one other possibility,"

Kalissa waited a moment. But when Megan didn't finish, she glanced up. "What?"

"You have an identical twin," said Megan.

Kalissa shook her head.

"You *were* adopted."

"I was nearly a year old when I was adopted. My mother would have known if I had a twin sister. She would have said something."

Gilda Smith hadn't been the most organized person in the world. She was fond of sherry, and her memory was never the greatest. But you didn't forget that your adopted daughter had a twin sister.

Megan looked pointedly down at the screen. "Maybe they split you up."

"Who would do that? And why keep it a secret?"

"It says she's Darci Rivers. Well, Darci Colborn now."

"My birth name was Thorp."

"And your legal name is Smith. Whoever adopted this Darci would have changed hers too."

"It can't be," said Kalissa, fighting the logic of Megan's assumption. "It just can't."

Megan shrugged her shoulders, clearly resting her case.

As Kalissa took in every inch of the woman's face, her chest tightened, and a strange buzzing sensation made its way along her limbs. She struggled to wrap her head around the information.

The resemblance was far too close to be a coincidence. Unless this was some elaborate photo-cropping joke, there was a real possibility she had a secret twin sister.

"You should call her," said Megan. "Maybe *she* can float us a loan."

Kalissa was appalled. "You didn't actually say that."

"The woman just married a billionaire."

"So what?" The Colborn money had absolutely nothing to do with Kalissa.

"The minute she gets a look at you—".

"I'm not about to let her get a look at me."

"Why not?"

"Because I'm not going to be that person."

"Really? What person is it you're not going to be?"

"The long-lost relative who pops up the minute there's money in play."

"You don't have to ask her for money."

Kalissa wasn't fooling around here. "It doesn't matter if I ask or not. They'll think I've been waiting in the wings all these years, and now I've decided to pounce."

"She'll probably just offer it up."

"*Stop* it."

"We'd pay her back."

"See?" said Kalissa. "*See*? Even you think I'm after her money. And you know me better than anyone."

"It's not like she'd miss a few thousand. *Temporarily*."

Kalissa closed the window and handed back the tablet. "No. No. And no."

"You can't just ignore this."

"Watch me."

Riley Ellis was both thrilled and terrified. He had a newly expanded aircraft factory, a significant new sales contract, a massive mortgage on the commercial building and a maxed out line of credit. Ellis Aviation was entering a whole new phase of existence.

"Flipping the switch now," he said to Wade Cormack on the other end of the cell phone in Seattle.

"Congratulations," said Wade. He was the owner of Zoom Tac, the company supplying most of the parts for the new E-22 short haul jet.

Riley twisted the switch, and the main overhead lights came on in sequence. Computers came to life, and robotic machines started their power-up sequence along the assembly line. The hundred staff members on the floor sent up a cheer.

He hadn't really turned everything on with a single switch. The supervisors and foremen at each station had simply taken the overhead lights as a signal to go live. It was eight a.m., August 16th, day one of the expanded operation.

From the interior walkway on the third level, Riley gave everyone a wave and a salute. "The clock is officially ticking," he said to Wade.

The cheering gradually died down, and everyone's attention turned to their tasks.

"Now you just need to get the glitches worked out of the supply chain," said Wade.

"The custom rivets finally arrived. Colorado's good on the sheet metal. How are your new parts certifications coming?" Riley moved along the walkway to his office, the spring-loaded door shutting out the noise behind him.

"My guys say they're on track."

"That's great." Riley plopped down on his desk chair.

The new office was compact and utilitarian, with big windows overlooking the factory floor. His production and sales managers had offices on either side of him, with the various unit supervisors near their staff's stations throughout the facility.

Out of habit from all the recent construction, he'd worn cargo pants and a t-shirt, his feet clad in steel toed boots. Part of him was itching to get down there on the floor and plunge in. But he realized he had to stay at the helm.

He had over a hundred and fifty workers now, operating on three shifts. They needed a leader, not a colleague. And he had to keep focused on the company's strategic direction.

"Good luck," said Wade.

"Talk to you in a few days." Riley ended the call.

As he settled back in his chair, his thoughts went fleetingly to his father, Dalton Colborn. The man had never once acknowledged Riley as his illegitimate son, and he'd certainly never given him any support or encouragement. Still, their lives had ended up following a similar path.

At the moment, Riley couldn't help but wonder if this was how Dalton had felt in the early days when his fledgling company had first started to grow. Had he experienced this same combination of exhilaration and flat-out fear? Dalton had gone from nothing to a billion dollar aerospace company before he'd died, so he must have taken chances along the way.

Shane Colborn had inherited that dynasty. Shane was the legitimate son, the golden child.

"Well, Shane," Riley said out loud to the empty office, wishing he had a shot of tequila or even a beer to use for a toast. "Let's find out if your illegitimate half-brother can give you a run for your money."

His phone pinged with a text message.

He set aside his thoughts and checked it. The text was from Ashton Watson, his high school friend. It was a photo tagged: Blew my mind.

Another text came immediately from Ashton. I've met the bride.

Curious, Riley tapped the photo. It expanded to show a

picture of Shane dressed in a tuxedo standing next to a gorgeous, auburn haired woman in white lace. She had a trim body, bright green eyes and flawless skin, a true ten on the hotness scale. Then again, a ten was exactly what Riley would have expected for Shane.

His office door opened, and Ashton strode right in. "She's a piece of work, that one. Nasty as they come."

"She doesn't look nasty," Riley couldn't help but observe. She looked classy and beautiful, and also very happy. Then again, she'd just married a billionaire in a lavish wedding that was reported to have cost several hundred thousand dollars. That would probably make the nastiest of women happy.

"Just don't tick her off," said Ashton.

"How do you know her?"

"She was Jennifer's roommate."

"Jennifer?"

Ashton gave an exasperated sigh, lowering himself into the single guest chair. "I dated her for four months."

"Did I meet her?"

"Yeah. At least once. I'm sure you met her. Blond hair, blue eyes, great legs."

"You just described every date you've had since freshman year."

"She was different. Anyway, it doesn't matter. It's going to go bad for Shane. I'd put money on it."

"Couldn't happen to a nicer guy," Riley drawled.

Ashton grinned and cocked his head toward the interior windows. "Looks really good out there."

"I can't believe we're finally up and running."

"I knew you'd do it."

"I haven't done it yet." Riley rose to gaze out at the factory himself. Machines were running. People were working. But it was a long, long road to any kind of profitability. He sure hoped he could make it.

Ashton stood beside him. "Yeah, you have. Before long, you'll have more contracts than you'll know what to do with."

"Believe it or not, I've been thinking about Dalton."

"Seriously?"

"I was thinking, he had to have started out like this, same risks, same fears, same hopes."

It took Ashton a second to respond. When he did, his tone was thoughtful. "You're more like him than Shane is, you know."

"That's not my ambition. Riley had no admiration or respect for his biological father. He hated the man."

"Shane had it handed to him on a silver platter. You had to fight for every inch to get where you are."

"Where I am is deep in debt and tip-toeing along a cliff of complete disaster."

"That's what makes it exciting," said Ashton. "No risk, no reward."

"Is that why you fly the way you do? The adrenaline rush?"

Ashton was a helicopter pilot, and he volunteered for search and rescue on his days off. He had a reputation for saying yes to the riskiest of flights.

"Sure," Ashton said with a shrug. "That and it impresses the girls."

"Like you've ever had trouble getting girls." For some reason, Riley took another look at the picture of Shane and his bride.

"Her name is Darci Rivers," said Ashton.

There was something compelling in the woman's emerald eyes, a secret in her lush smile. Riley suddenly pictured her shiny hair splayed across a white pillowcase.

He shifted and quickly banished the image.

"You think he made a mistake?" he asked Ashton.

"Oh, he made a mistake all right. That creature's got claws."

"Well, I hope she distracts him," said Riley.

He and Shane would be going after the same airline contracts from here on in. If Shane was newly married to a handful of a wife, it might give Riley an advantage.

Through the glass of the restaurant window, a good looking, neatly dressed man caught Kalissa's eye for a second time.

He was staring openly now as she wheeled a trio of azalea plants across the lighted patio garden.

It would be nice to think he was interested in her. He was extremely attractive, with dark eyes, a straight nose, and the kind of square chin that made a man seem powerful. But she was dressed in dirt streaked blue jeans, a faded green T-shirt and a pair of scuffed, serviceable work boots.

Her hair was pulled back in a ponytail. At least it had started the day that way. By now, it likely resembled a rat's nest. And the morning's fifteen second application of mascara would have long since rubbed off.

No. The thoughts running through his head were not about getting her phone number. Judging by his growing frown, he was probably offended by her dirty, disheveled state as he tried to enjoy a refined meal.

She kept right on walking, focusing on the uneven cobblestones in front of the wheelbarrow tire, finally stopping at the raised garden bed between two magnolia trees.

"Two foot intervals look right to me," said Megan, straightening from where she'd dug a trio of holes.

Kalissa focused her attention on the garden bed that stretched along the wrought iron fence. "As long as the evergreens stay properly trimmed, this is going to be stunning."

Someday, her budget permitting, Kalissa wouldn't mind dining out here, or even inside. Her gaze darted back to the bank of windows that revealed the elegance of the main dining room.

The man was still staring at her, and she quickly looked away. He was probably just curious about what they were doing—though it had to be obvious. It was also possible he was bored with his dining companion and seeking a distraction.

Despite herself, she covertly shifted her glance to take a look at his date. She was surprised to find he was sitting across from a man. The man looked serious, gesturing with his hands as he spoke. It could be a dull business meeting, she supposed. They were both wearing suits.

"Let's do it," said Megan, releasing the rope on the burlap sheet that surrounded the azalea's root ball.

Kalissa quickly took the other side of the plant, lifting it and then adjusting it to position it in the hole.

Suddenly, a male voice surprised her. "What are you doing out here?"

Megan looked up, and Kalissa turned her head.

It was the man from inside the restaurant, and he was obviously angry. Her first thought was that they had somehow disturbed his dinner. But they weren't making any noise. Surely planting azaleas wasn't that objectionable.

She straightened to face him.

"Are you spying on me?" he demanded.

The question took her completely by surprise. "Am I what?"

"You've been watching me."

"Only because you were watching me."

He gestured to the wheelbarrow and the plants. "What *is* all this?"

"Azaleas," said Megan from behind her.

"We're planting azaleas," said Kalissa, squaring her shoulders and folding her arms across her chest.

He scoffed a sound of disbelief. "Outside my window."

"You *own* the restaurant?" Her question was sarcastic. If he had anything to do with the management of the restaurant, he'd have known Mosaic Landscaping was working here all week.

"I meant the window next to my table."

"I have no idea who you are," said Kalissa. "What's more, I don't care who you are. If you'll excuse us, we have work to finish."

"You have no idea who I am?" There was a note of disbelief in his voice. He jammed his thumb over his shoulder. "And I'll bet you have *no idea* I'm having dinner with Pierre Charron?"

Kalissa reflexively glanced at the window. Then she looked straight into the stranger's eyes. "None whatsoever."

His steel gray eyes narrowed.

"I'm getting the manager," said Megan.

"No, you won't," said the man.

"Excuse me?" said Kalissa, widening her stance. "You think you can stop us from getting the manager?"

"You're bluffing," he told them with conviction. His critical gaze took in her outfit. "You're not going to want to explain this to any manager."

"Explain why we're planting flowers?"

"Explain why you're trespassing."

Kalissa searched her brain for an explanation. He'd accused her of spying. What was he doing worth spying on?

"Are you breaking the law?" Perhaps they'd inadvertently stumbled on something to do with a crime or maybe national security. Should she be frightened?

"I can't believe he sent you." Then a flash of confusion came into the man's eyes. His voice lost some of its edge. "*Why* did he send you? Why *would* he send you?"

Kalissa extracted a business card from her pocket and held it out. "Mosaic Landscaping," she said. "See, that's us."

Looking suspicious, the man took the card and read it.

"Nice level of detail," he said, sounding ever so slightly impressed. "But why you?"

She took a stab at answering the bizarre question. "Because I have a diploma in landscape design."

He drew back. "Are you serious?"

"Completely serious."

He took a long look at her clothes and her hair. "It still doesn't make sense."

"It makes perfect sense, when you think about it," said Kalissa.

Her apprehension began to moderate. The man was clearly more puzzled than angry.

He shook his head. "Why send his wife? He wouldn't send his wife."

"I'm not married," said Kalissa.

"Give me a break."

"Kalissa?" Megan interrupted.

"No, seriously," said Kalissa. She stripped the glove from her left hand and wiggled her fingers to show him.

"The diamond is probably in your safe."

"Kalissa."

"I don't have a safe."

Megan grasped her shoulder from behind, stepping closer. "Kalissa, he thinks you're *Darci*."

Kalissa twisted her neck to look at her friend. "What?"

"She *is* Darci," said the man.

"Darci," Megan repeated with a meaningful stare.

"Darci Colborn?" Kalissa asked, the lightbulb coming on inside her head.

"This is ridiculous," said the man.

Kalissa turned back to him, realizing there was a simple explanation. "I get it. I'm not Darci Colborn. I look a little bit like her."

"A *little bit*?" asked Megan.

"The jig is up," said the man.

"There is no jig, and it's not up. I'm Kalissa Smith. I can prove it. I have identification."

He peered at her, and the minutes stretched by. It was obvious his brain was piecing through the situation.

"What have you got against Darci Colborn?" she asked him.

"I've never even met her."

"Then, that's why you're confused. She's quite different than me in person."

"You know her?" he asked.

"I've seen videos."

"They're twins," said Megan.

"We don't know that," Kalissa said to Megan.

"You should contact her," said Megan.

"Shut up," said Kalissa, having no intention of getting into that debate again, now or in the future.

"This is going to keep happening," said Megan.

"It's a fluke."

"You're a landscape designer?" asked the man.

"Yes."

"Your name is Kalissa Smith."

"Says it right there on the card."

"And you don't know Darci Colborn?"

"Didn't even know she existed until last week. It's weird, but it's no big deal."

"I'm sorry," he said, looking like he probably was, even though he was still watching her intently.

"No problem."

The strength of his gaze sent a shimmer through her chest. He really was an incredibly good looking man. He was tall, fit, and somewhere around thirty. Too bad she was such a mess. And too bad his interest had nothing to do with her personally.

"Can I keep the card?" he asked.

"Do you own a house?" asked Megan, stepping up beside Darci. "Do you have a yard?"

He pocketed the card. "I do. Goodnight, ladies."

"Goodnight," Kalissa automatically echoed.

With a nod, he turned to walk back to the restaurant.

"He was hot," said Megan.

"He was strange," said Kalissa, watching his broad shoulders as the glass door opened and then swung closed behind him.

But she had to admit, he was also hot. There was something extraordinarily sexy in his deep voice. Part of her hoped he might actually call. Against all logic, that same part couldn't help but hope it would be about more than just landscaping.

Two

The next evening, sitting on his deck with Ashton, Riley was still trying to figure out Kalissa Smith.

His brother's wife had a sister. She had a sexy, feisty, *secret* twin sister. And nobody seemed to know she existed.

"Setting aside the 'how on earth' questions," said Ashton, helping himself to a slice of pizza from the carton on the wood slat table between them.

The sun was setting beyond the park, over the vast stretch of orderly rows of houses north west of Chicago. The lengthening shadows showed Riley's yard as plain and stark.

"Setting that aside," he said, though he'd pondered the very question in bed last night, then again at work today.

He'd also pondered Kalissa, her crystal green eyes, those deep red lips, and what looked like a perfect body, nearly but not quite camouflaged by her work clothes. He'd checked social media sites today, but there were no tagged photos of Kalissa Smith. Her name was on the Mosaic Landscaping site, but it didn't have her picture.

"Could she have been spying for her sister?" Ashton asked.

Riley had considered and discarded that theory. "If she was, she deserves an acting award."

"And it seems pretty elaborate," said Ashton, propping his feet up on one of the wooden stools.

Riley had to agree. "There's no way she overheard our conversation from out on the patio. All she could report was that I met with Pierre Charron, and maybe for how long. And why would you use a Darci clone to do that? There are far easier ways. Bribe a waiter, for example."

"So, what are you going to do?"

Riley reached for his cell phone. "I'm thinking about doing some landscaping."

Ashton smiled. "Keep your enemies close?"

Riley fished into his shirt pocket for the Mosaic Landscaping business card. "I don't think she's the enemy. I don't know what the heck this is all about."

"You think they're really twins?"

"They're absolutely identical."

"You sure it wasn't Darci?"

"I'm positive. I checked. Shane and Darci were at an art gallery last night, a charity event on the other side of town."

Ashton was silent for a few minutes. "Then why pursue it? What's in it for you?"

Riley dialed with his thumb. "I don't know yet."

Ashton shifted in his chair, turning sideways to face Riley. "You're attracted to her."

"She's attractive," Riley admitted.

"This isn't about wanting what Shane's already got."

Riley frowned. "I've been over that for a very long time."

"You sure?"

"Yes."

"Mosaic Landscaping," came Kalissa's breathy voice.

"Is this Kalissa?" He already knew the answer.

"Yes, it is." She sounded like she was slightly out of breath.

"This is Riley," he hesitated over his last name. "Have I called at a bad time?"

"Not at all. How can I help you?"

He pictured her pushing a wheelbarrow, flushed cheeks, a bead of sweat at her temple. "I was hoping to make an appointment with you."

"Okay. Are you looking for a site visit? Or do you want to come into the office?"

"The office. Is today a possibility?"

"Um." She blew out a breath. "We'll be back there in about an hour. Is that too late?"

"An hour is fine." He glanced at his watch and realized it was coming up on seven. "Long work day?" he couldn't help but ask.

"About normal," she said. "Riley...?"

"We met last night."

There was silence on the other end.

"You asked me if I had a yard."

"Megan asked you if you had a yard."

"Well, I do. Have a yard." He gazed out over it, knowing the front yard was just as neglected. "I've been thinking about it, and it could use some landscaping."

"Is this a joke?"

"No joke. I need some landscaping."

Ashton rolled his eyes and lifted his beer to take a swallow.

There was another pause before she continued. "What's the lot size?"

"Seventy by one-hundred and thirty. I have an oak tree."

"Bully for you."

"I mean that's all I have. It's a patchy lawn with a single oak tree. It's pathetic, really. I don't know how you'll save it."

"Maybe we should come out and take a look," she suggested.

"I'd rather talk first. You know, toss around some general ideas."

"Whatever you prefer. Seven forty-five? Mr..."

"Seven forty-five sounds good. I'll be there." He disconnected.

"Smooth," said Ashton.

Riley reached for his own beer. "I don't want to tell her my last name."

He didn't want her to know he was Shane's competitor. She might not know the Colborns yet, but Riley was willing to bet she'd meet them soon.

"Make one up," said Ashton.

"I don't want to lie to her either."

"Ha, there's a challenge. She's coming to your house, and you'll have to write her a check."

Riley had already thought of that. "The house is registered to Ellis Aviation's numbered holding company, and I can pay the bill in cash."

"Oh, that will allay her suspicions. She'll think you're a criminal."

"Or a conspiracy theorist." Riley took a thoughtful drink. "You know, that could work. I accused her of being a spy last night. If I behave like I'm generally paranoid, she'll think it's just my personality."

Ashton chuckled. "Can I come along? This sounds entertaining."

Kalissa couldn't decide if Riley was paranoid, a covert operative or maybe even in the witness protection program. He claimed to be a conspiracy theorist, but she wasn't buying it. Never mind that few conspiracy theorists would describe themselves that way, over the past week she'd found his most dominant characteristics to be intelligence and hard work.

He was far more normal and much more agreeable than he'd seemed at first, and she hated to think that somebody that great looking and sexy would be unbalanced. It wouldn't be fair to the women of Chicago.

After thinking it through, she was going with the witness protection program theory.

He'd offered to pay a premium, so they'd bumped him to the top of their list. After some initial work, mostly to level the ground and rip out the sickly lawn, the delivery service had dropped off a load of milled, Colorado flagstone. The installers were due on Thursday to lay the rock for the patio.

She was excited about the patio, and in particular that Riley had agreed to a spa and barbecue area. It was exactly how she'd do the yard if she was the owner. She knew the final photos were going to look great on their web site.

The sun was setting now as she made her way around to the back of his house.

"Thirsty?" Riley surprised her by calling down from the sundeck above her.

She looked toward the sound of his voice.

"Looks good." He nodded to the flat stones piled on wood pallets. Their tones were rich and varied in rust, browns and chalk. "Come on up."

"Sure." She crossed the raw dirt to the outdoor staircase and made her way up to join him.

"Iced tea?" he asked as she made it to the top. He gestured to a pitcher on a round wooden table that was bracketed by two wooden deck chairs.

"Love some."

She lowered herself into one of the chairs, taking the weight off her tired legs.

It had been a hot day, and her powder blue cotton shirt was clinging damply to her body. Her jeans were dusty, and her hair was sticky with sweat and garden dirt.

She pulled out her ponytail and ran a hand through it, discovering a twig and a couple of leaves. She couldn't help but sigh as she discarded them. It seemed Riley was never going to see her at her best.

He'd arrived home from work about an hour ago, just missing Megan who'd left for another jobsite. He was dressed in his suit pants and dress shirt, his tie loosened around his neck. His hair was neat, his face clean shaven, and his fingernails were spotless.

She glanced down at her own fingers and curled them into her palms. She'd worn gloves all day and kept them relatively clean, but she was in desperate need of a manicure. She couldn't remember the last time she'd worn nail polish or had her hair trimmed. She'd pretty much kill for a spa day.

He poured the iced tea. "Looks like you've made good progress."

"Your lawn is gone," she acknowledged.

"Wasn't much of a lawn to start with."

She didn't disagree. "There must have been a lot of annual ryegrass in the mix. Did you aerate, fertilize, re-seed?"

There was humor in his eyes. "Your lips are moving, and sounds are coming out, but…"

She found herself grinning in return. "Never mind. We'll take care of it."

"Where's Megan?"

"We're starting another job over in Oak Park."

"You seem busy."

She accepted a glass filled with sweet tea and plenty of ice-cubes. "We're getting there, slowly. We keep adding casual workers to our roster. But it's hard to be competitive and still make a profit."

"I hear you." He gave a sage nod as he sat down.

"You said you own your own business?" She'd come to understand that he was a private person, but she hoped he'd share a few more details.

"We manufacture parts, mostly for the transportation sector. Margins are tough in any business."

"How long have you been in business?"

"Ten years all told. I started small. You?"

"Just under a year. We've been working hard, and our customer base is gradually growing." She lifted her glass in a toast. "Thank you for adding to it."

"I'll tell my friends about you."

She took a sip.

"Anything you need me to do tonight?" he asked.

Though he rarely got home before seven, Riley had jumped in on several occasions, getting work done after the crews left, both to save money and to make things smoother the next day.

"We've leveled the ground." She rose to gaze over the rail. It was growing dark, but she could still make out the newly worked area in the yard. "Next step is for the installers to lay the stone."

Riley rose and moved to stand beside her. "Next step requires professional expertise?"

"It does."

"And I'm not an expert."

"Not unless there's something you're not telling me." She let the comment dangle, wondering if he'd decide to divulge something new.

A gust of a breeze came up, and she brushed her loose hair out of her face.

"There is something I'm not telling you," he said in an oblique tone than triggered a shimmer of sexual awareness.

"What is it?" She found herself holding her breath.

The silence stretched, so she looked up. He was closer than she'd realized. His gaze was warm and intimate.

The awareness increased, warming the surface of her skin while paradoxically raising goose bumps.

Without a word, he brushed a stray lock of hair back from her temple.

His callused fingertips seemed to hum against her skin. His touch felt good. It felt sexy.

"You're incredibly beautiful," he whispered, easing slightly closer.

The statement took her by surprise. "I'm mostly dusty."

He smiled. "I can't see any dust. But I can see your gorgeous eyes, and I can see your beautiful lips."

His smile disappeared, and he ran the pad of his thumb across her lower lip.

"Soft," he whispered, leaning in.

She drew in a breath and held it.

His palm slipped up, cradling her cheek, his fingertips easing into her hair. He bent his head.

She stilled, waiting.

The kiss started soft, but soon heated between them. Her fingers curled into her palms, and she stretched up. Her lips parted, and he firmed his own, bracing his free hand across the small of her back.

She opened wider, and his tongue flicked in. She met him with her own, angling her head. She raised her palms to his chest, sweeping them upward, marveling at the definition of his pecs, then the breadth and strength of his shoulders. Her arms wound themselves around his neck.

He pressed their bodies together, her breasts against his chest, his thighs hard against hers. The kiss was sexy and deep, oddly familiar. She wanted more from him, even as she acknowledged this was happening at lightning speed.

He seemed to sense her hesitation.

He broke the kiss, drawing back.

"Wow," she managed.

"Wow," he echoed, gazing into her eyes.

The sun was completely gone now, and soft darkness surrounded them, a shaft of yellow light coming from a small window in his house.

He kept his arm around her, still holding her close. "You should come out with me."

She hesitated, unsettled by the sudden shift between them. "I don't usually…"

"Kiss like that?"

"Date customers." Though she had to admit, she couldn't remember a kiss like that.

"You've only been in business a year," he said. "It can't have come up that often."

"I suppose," she was forced to agree.

"Has it ever come up?" he asked.

"Not really."

"So you don't have a rule against it."

"I don't have a rule for it either."

"Where do you want to go?" he asked.

She cocked her head. "I haven't said yes."

"I figure I'll increase my odds of a yes if you like where we're going."

The logic made her smile. "Take a stab."

He smoothed her hair again. "No help from the lady?"

She struggled not to react to the intimate touch. "No help."

"Navy Pier. Ferris wheel and a pretzel dog."

She was surprised, but also intrigued. "You're inviting me out for a *pretzel dog*?"

"I'll throw in some ice cream."

She put a note of astonishment in her voice. "You expect me to say yes to that?"

He didn't look worried. "You don't strike me as a symphony and Le Petit Soleil kind of girl."

She wrinkled her nose and gave a little sniff. "That's only because you've never seen me clean. It's an unfair bias if you ask me, and not worthy of you, Riley."

Uncertainty finally appeared in his eyes. "You'd prefer the symphony?"

She'd liked teasing him. "Your first instinct was right. Add the fireworks, and you've got yourself a deal."

He gave her a squeeze. "You're messin' with me."

"I am."

"I shouldn't like it so much."

"Probably not."

"Can I kiss you again?"

The amusement went out of her, replaced instantly by desire.

"Just once." It was a warning to herself more than to him.

"Just once," he agreed.

"Because…"

He dipped his head toward her, voice dropping to a whisper. "Because this is too fast."

"It's too fast," she whispered back.

"It's too hot."

"It's too hot."

His lips brushed hers. "It's too everything."

"Oh, yes."

He kissed her long and deep.

"It's not really a date," Kalissa said to Megan as they moved through the racks at Annabelle's Discount Boutique. They'd found a couple of hours to spare this morning, and it had been ages since Kalissa had bought any news clothes.

"Boy, girl, dinner, entertainment," said Megan. "What part of that is not a date?"

"I mean it's not a buy a new dress and get my hair and nails done kind of date." Kalissa held up a pair of dark blue, skinny jeans. "What do you think?"

"Cute. What's the price?"

"Thirty-nine ninety-nine, with fifty percent off."

"You can add my thirty percent off coupon."

"So, that's about fifteen bucks. I can afford fifteen bucks."

"They'll go with this," said Megan, holding up a white and silver tank top.

"I sure couldn't show up at work in that," said Kalissa.

A camera flash went off in her peripheral vision, and she turned to see two young women giggle as they looked at their phone screen then back at her.

"You like the top?" she asked them, holding it out. It was cute, but she'd give it up if they'd fallen in love with it.

They didn't answer, just gave her a thumb's up and backed away.

"What the heck?"

"It's the Darci thing," said Megan.

"What do you mean?"

"I mean, those two think they just saw the wife of a billionaire shopping at a discount store."

Kalissa glanced at the two retreating women. Suddenly self-conscious, she glanced around the store to see if anyone else was paying attention to her. They weren't, thank goodness.

"I wonder how they'd react to me using a coupon," she speculated.

"I think a lot of celebrities buy things on the cheap."

"Darci's not a celebrity."

But Kalissa now felt ridiculously conspicuous, and she glanced around the store again. Who else was out there covertly watching her? Who else might mistake her for Darci and think Darci was doing something inappropriate.

"Oh, crap." She tightened her grasp on the jeans.

"What?" Megan looked from side to side.

"Riley. The date. Me and him together at the Navy Pier."

"Those jeans will look great," said Megan. "And try on the top. I bet it works."

"What if somebody sees us? What if they think I'm Darci? What if they think she's cheating on Shane?" Kalissa had absolutely no desire to mess up anybody's life.

"It could happen," said Megan, looking thoughtful.

Kalissa put the jeans back. "Maybe I should cancel."

"You can't cancel. He seems like a great guy. And what are you going to do? Never go on a date again?"

"Maybe we could do something a little less public."

"There's always the symphony. It's dark in there."

"I have no interest in the symphony."

"Yeah." Megan nodded. "Besides, at a snooty event like that, everyone really would think you were Darci."

"This is a problem."

Megan lifted the jeans and handed them, along with the top to Kalissa. "It's not your problem."

"It's Darci's problem." Kalissa tried to work her way through the ethics of the situation. "I at least owe her something for being my sister. Don't I?"

"So, tell her."

"That I'm going on a date?"

"That you *exist*. Give her a heads up. That'll keep the reporters from blindsiding her with it."

"I could call her," said Kalissa. "Or drop her an e-mail." An e-mail sounded a lot less intimidating.

"She'll think you're a wing-nut."

"Maybe. Probably. I could send her a photo."

"She'll assume it's her, or that it's photo-shopped like you did."

Kalissa thought it through. "I could hold up today's newspaper, so she'll know that it's current."

"That would be a great way to meet her security team or maybe the Chicago Police."

"I'll phone her," said Kalissa, deciding it was the best option. "Do you suppose our voices are alike? Would she recognize it?"

"Just stop by her office," said Megan. "Colborn Aerospace has its own building down by the river. There's a huge sign."

"How do you know this?"

"I internet searched her, of course. Didn't you?"

"No. Not really. Okay, maybe a little bit. I found out she has the same birthday as me."

"Surprise, surprise."

"Just drop by her office," Kalissa pondered out loud. "Say, hi there. I'm your twin. If anyone asks you why you were on a date at the Navy Pier tomorrow, you can let them know it was me."

Megan chuckled. "Try on the jeans first. But, yeah, that's basically it."

"I could be in and out in five minutes."

"With the jeans?"

"With Darci." Kalissa couldn't quite shake the fear that any contact would be an intrusion on Darci's life. "If she doesn't want to talk. If she's too busy. I'm in, I'm out, she's warned, we're done."

"I'm guessing she might have a few questions for you."

Kalissa decided it was the best course of action. What Darci did with the information was entirely up to her. But it was colossally unfair to risk the press running with the story before Darci, and especially Shane, knew the truth.

"Shane Colborn is on line three for you," Emma Thatcher, the Ellis Aviation receptionist, announced through the inter-office phone line.

Riley moved the receiver from his ear and stared at it for a moment.

"Riley?" Emma's voice came through the tiny speaker.

"Are you sure?" he asked her.

"He claims to be Shane Colborn."

"Did he say what he wanted?"

"You want me to ask?"

"No. That's fine. I'll take it. Thanks, Emma."

"No problem."

Riley pulled his thoughts together, waiting a beat before pressing the blinking button. "Riley Ellis here."

"This is Shane Colborn."

"What can I do for you?" It was the first time Riley had spoken to his half-brother in more than a decade. They'd exchanged approximately three sentences their entire lives. And not one of them meaningful. Beyond that single moment when they were both teenagers, Shane ignored him. It was clear Shane preferred to live in denial.

"I understand you've put in a bid with Askeland Airlines."

"Where did you get that information?" Riley had no intention of either confirming or denying it.

"From Richard Price, the VP of purchasing." There was an edge of annoyance in Shane's tone. "He's hinting that your price is surprisingly low."

"You expect me to discuss my price with you? You expect me to discuss *anything* with you about a bid that may or may not exist? You have heard of collusion, right?"

The annoyance in Shane's tone ramped up. "I'm *not* asking you to collude."

"Good."

"This is a courtesy call."

Riley scoffed out a cold laugh. "So far, this seems real courteous, Colborn."

Shane's tone was a growl. "There are also laws against predatory pricing."

"Those laws are there to protect small companies. You're a billion dollar conglomerate. I'm not even a tenth of that."

"The law goes both ways."

"You'd be laughed out of court." Not that Riley was doing anything remotely illegal.

"You could be laughed into a jail cell."

"We're leaner than Colborn. That's just the way it is."

"We have a reputation for excellence."

"That and a tell-all book from your former mistress accusing you of collusion and corporate espionage. Are you spying on Ellis Aviation?"

"Don't be absurd."

"Marrying a pretty wife can't fix everything."

Shane's tone went hard. "Leave my wife out of this."

An image of Kalissa appeared in Riley's head, and guilt immediately slammed into him. Shane was right. This had nothing to do with Darci.

"You're right," he said. "I apologize."

It took Shane a moment to respond. "Everywhere I look, everywhere I turn, *you* seem to show up."

"We're in the same business," said Riley, wondering if Shane would finally acknowledge their family relationship. He lobbed him an opening. "It must be in the genes."

Again, there was a moment of silence. "Is that a crack?"

"Take it however you want."

"Inheriting something is only the first step. The place doesn't run itself."

"Inheriting is a big step," said Riley. He'd have been happy to inherit a dollar. He'd have been happy if Dalton had even once looked him in the eyes.

"I've been on my own for over six years." Shane sucked in an audible breath. "Forget it. I don't give a damn what you think."

"And I don't give a damn what you think. I bid the contracts I see fit. I've been independent since day one, and I'm planning to stay that way."

"This is strictly business?" asked Shane.

"Strictly business," said Riley.

"It feels." There was a searching tone to Shane's voice, and he paused again.

Riley hated that a mere phone call could unsettle him like this. He hated himself for hoping that Shane would acknowledge him. He'd been waiting for scraps from the Colborn table his entire life. He needed it to stop.

"Is that it?" he asked, anger crackling his tone.

"That's it," said Shane.

Riley slammed down the phone.

Three

In the lobby of the Colborn Aerospace building, Kalissa lost her nerve. She felt suddenly vulnerable in the cavernous space, phones ringing, dozens of footfalls echoing against the marble floor, men in expensive suits, women in tailored black and white. Halfway to the long, curved reception counter, she turned back.

"Mrs. Colborn," a woman approached her in a steel gray skirt and matching jacket. It was brightened by a teal blouse. "Did you get a chance to read the food services report?"

"I'm sorry," said Kalissa, her voice coming out raspy from her tight throat.

"What was that?" the woman asked. When Kalissa didn't respond, she kept on talking. "I can ride up with you on the elevator."

"Mrs. Colborn?" called another voice, a man this time.

The first woman put a hand on Kalissa's back, turning her. "Don't look up. Just keep walking and listening to me. Pretend I'm saying something absolutely riveting."

"Uh, what?" Kalissa glanced toward the voice.

"Don't look," the woman warned. She gave a nod to a security guard who moved forward to meet the man.

Another security guard held an elevator for them.

"Thank you, Bernie," said the woman as they stepped inside.

Kalissa nodded to the guard named Bernie, and he reached around to press the button for the twenty-first floor. Then he stood in front of the door until it closed. Kalissa guessed her sister and her husband didn't cram into the elevator with a dozen other people.

Her nerves ramped up even further.

"The food services report?" the woman asked.

"I'm sorry," Kalissa repeated, not knowing where else to

go with the question. She didn't want to tell some stranger she was Darci's twin before she told Darci herself. She was beginning to realize how poorly she'd thought this through.

"Not to worry," said the woman. "Give me a call when you get to it. It's all good news. The international stations are getting rave reviews, and we've had inquiries from two national food magazines about interviews. Can I tell them you'll be available?"

"Can I, uh, get back to you?" Kalissa asked weakly.

The woman peered at her. "Are you okay?"

"Just fine."

"You're not getting that flu are you?"

"I do have a bit of a headache," Kalissa replied honestly.

The elevator came to a halt, pinging at the twenty-first floor. The doors slid smoothly open.

Kalissa stepped out, not sure whether to go left or right. There was a small reception desk in the foyer, but she didn't want to ask which way it was to her office.

"Mrs. Colborn?" A woman came worriedly to her feet from behind the reception desk. She glanced down a hallway behind her, then she looked at Kalissa again. "I didn't see you leave."

Kalissa breathed a sigh of relief. At least she knew which direction to go.

"Your clothes," said the woman, bustling out from behind the desk. "Did something happen to the Farsen Kalick jacket? Do you need me to call the cleaners?"

"It's fine," said Kalissa, picking up her pace, heading for the hallway where the receptionist had looked. "I'm fine. I'll let you know."

She cleared the reception area, leaving the women behind her. She passed several closed doors. Two had nameplates on them, both belonging to vice-presidents.

At the end of the hall, she came to a set of double doors with brass handles, Shane Colborn, President. Her legs nearly gave way, and she put out a hand to brace herself against the wall. She did *not* want to run into Shane before she found Darci.

For a second, she considered turning back. But then she'd

have to face the receptionist again, and she couldn't see how she'd make it out of the building without being approached by other employees.

She straightened from the wall and took the right turn. A few moments later, she breathed a sigh of relief. She'd found it, her sister's office door: Darci Colborn, Director of Staff Services.

It was open about six inches, and she could hear Darci's voice inside. "I'll be down to the cafeteria later on."

Kalissa's stomach clenched hard, but she couldn't help a nervous smile. Darci sounded just like her.

"Okay," said Darci. "Yes, I can."

Kalissa gave a tentative knock, and the door swung further open.

Darci looked up from where she was still speaking on the phone. She leaned over for a better view, and her jaw snapped shut.

"I..." said Kalissa, not knowing where to start.

"I'll call you back," Darci said into the phone, replacing it on its cradle.

She moved around from behind the desk, taking several swift steps forward.

"I didn't mean to disturb you," said Kalissa.

"What on earth?" Darci stopped about ten feet away.

Voices sounded around the corner of the hallway, coming rapidly closer. Kalissa quickly stepped inside the office so they wouldn't see her.

"I'm so sorry," said Kalissa, regretting her decision to show up unannounced. "I thought this was the best way. But I didn't think...I didn't know...I realize this must be a bomb-shell for you."

"Who *are* you?" asked Darci.

"My name is Kalissa Smith. I saw your wedding pictures, and well...I guess you can figure out why I'm here."

"You look just like me."

"I know."

"I mean *exactly* like me."

"Weird, isn't it?"

Darci moved closer, peering at Kalissa.

Kalissa knew she was doing the same thing back.

Darci's eyes might be a slightly paler shade of green. But their mouths were identical, so were their chins, their noses, even their hairline. Kalissa had never come across anyone with that little swoop at their part, never mind the exact shade of auburn in their hair.

"Are we twins?" asked Darci.

"I think we must be. My birthday is October third."

Darci's eyes widened. "Holy cow."

"I didn't want to bother you," said Kalissa. "I wasn't going to say anything. I mean, I know you must be busy, being a newlywed, and with this huge company and all. But I'm going on a date tomorrow night, and there were these girls in Annabelle's Discount Boutique, and they thought I was you, and they took a photo, and I realized it could happen again, somewhere else, like the Navy Pier, while I was on a date, and people might think it was you." Kalissa clamped her mouth shut. "I'm rambling."

"We're twins," said Darci in obvious astonishment. "I don't understand. How did that happen? Were you raised by our mother? Why didn't she bring you back? And why didn't dad ever tell me that—" Darci smiled. "Now, who's rambling?"

"It's unbelievable," Kalissa whispered.

She hadn't expected to feel this way, this ache deep down in her heart. She wanted to grab Darci and pull her into a hug. She had a sister. Tears started to tingle at the backs of her eyes.

The door whooshed open behind her.

"Sweetheart," came a man's voice. "Tuck is asking if… Oh, I'm sorry."

Kalissa turned.

The man, obviously Shane, instantly froze in place.

"Darling," said Darci, a tremor in her voice. "It appears there's something more my father neglected to mention."

"What on earth?" Shane started to circle Kalissa.

"We have the same birthday," said Darci.

"Is this a con?"

Kalissa couldn't help but smile. She didn't blame Shane one bit for his suspicions. She'd have worried about him if he had accepted this at face value.

"Is she asking for money?" asked Shane.

"No," said Darci.

"I'm not," said Kalissa. "You couldn't get me to take money if you tried."

His eyes narrowed. "That's how all the best cons start off."

"Look at her," said Darci.

"We'll want DNA," said Shane.

"Take it, if you want it," said Kalissa. "But it's not necessary. I'm not going to hang around. I only wanted to warn you, well, warn Darci. Since your wedding, people have started to mistake me for her. I'm out in public. I shop at discount stores. Sometimes I swear, or get angry with a store clerk or, and this is the big one, go out on dates. I have a date tomorrow night, and I was worried I'd be mistaken for Darci. That might look bad on the two of you, and I didn't want to cause either of you any trouble."

Shane stared at her in silence.

"Thank you," said Darci. "That's very considerate of you. But seriously." She broke into a grin. Then, without warning, she rushed forward, opening her arms to pull Kalissa into a hug. "I have a twin sister."

Kalissa closed her eyes, unexplainable feelings coursing through her.

Darci drew back, cradling Kalissa's cheeks with her hands. "You are beautiful." Then she laughed. "Didn't that sound conceited."

Kalissa took in every contour of Darci's face, settling on her left cheekbone. "You have a freckle."

"You don't."

"I don't," Kalissa agreed.

Shane cleared his throat. "I'm cancelling everything for the rest of the day."

Kalissa turned to him. "Oh, no. Don't do that. I didn't plan to mess up your day."

"Of course I'm doing that. You two have a million things to talk about. We'll go to the penthouse, order some dinner. And wine. We'll need some really good wine."

"For a toast," said Darci.

Shane gave a disbelieving shake of his head. "A toast is the least of why we need the wine."

Riley could have happily done nothing but stare at Kalissa all night long. Her hair was full and shiny tonight, bouncing around her bare shoulders. Makeup brightened her beautiful face. While her tight jeans and the breezy little tank top were already giving him fantasies.

They'd snacked their way through the food kiosks and bought matching key chains with colorful, stylized letters on the fob. He'd held her hand while they navigated the crowds, waiting in a long lineup to get on the Ferris wheel. But it was worth the wait. The skies were clear, dotted with faint stars, while the skyline of Chicago was illuminated in the clear night air.

The bustle and noise of the crowds disappeared as they swept upward in the dangling car. The wind buffeted them, cooling the air temperature. Riley wrapped an arm around her, letting his fingertips brush her smooth, bare shoulder.

"I've never done this before," she told him. "Wow. Look at the city."

"You've never been up here at night?"

She shook her head. "I mean it's my first time on the Ferris wheel. I've never been to the Pier before."

"I thought you said you grew up in Chicago."

"My mom wasn't into things like this." They hit the outer apex of the curve and she grasped his arm. "This is fantastic."

Gratification swelled his chest. "No wonder you seem like a little kid."

She tilted her head to give him an unabashed grin. "Do you mind?"

"Not at all." He liked that about her. In fact, so far, he liked everything about her.

As they swung toward the top, he impulsively leaned in for a kiss. Her lips were warm and moist against his. She tasted like cotton candy, and he couldn't stop himself from taking the kiss deeper and deeper.

By the time he pulled back, they'd crested the top. Her eyes were shinning in the ride's bright lights, and her rosy cheeks had a new glow.

"I used to come here with my friends sometimes," he told her. "When I was a teenager."

It was a rare occurrence, since his childhood years hadn't held much in the way of amusement. His mother had been the runaway daughter of Irish immigrants. With only a tenth grade education, she'd worked as a housekeeper for Dalton Colborn for nearly twenty years before succumbing to a bout of pneumonia.

Determined to hold Kalissa even closer, he settled his free hand at her waist, finding a warm strip of skin at her stomach.

"Were you a wild teenager?" she asked.

"Occasionally," he admitted. "We used to street race, and we partied pretty hard. We once stole ethanol from the high school science lab. Made a killer punch that got about thirty kids blasted."

"Who's we?"

"My friend Ashton and I."

"I can picture that."

It occurred to Riley that if he wanted to impress her, he should probably change the subject from his teenage transgressions. "What about you? What were you like as a kid?"

She smoothed her hair in the wind and gave him an innocent smile. "I was good as gold."

"I don't believe you."

"It's true. I studied hard trying to get a scholarship, and I had a part time job from the time I was fourteen. I wanted to go to college, and I knew my mother could never afford it."

"So, you were the consummate good girl?"

"I was."

He moved in to playfully nuzzle her neck. "That's sexy. It makes me want to corrupt you."

She tapped him in the chest. "There's something wrong with you." But she was laughing as she said it.

"There's a whole lot wrong with me."

"Do tell."

"I don't think so."

The ground rushed up, and the car glided to a stop, giving him an easy way out of the conversation.

He exited first, then took her hand, keeping hold of it as they walked away.

"It's almost time for the fireworks," he said.

"I can't wait."

"The best view is at the far end of the pier."

"Let's go." She picked up the pace, leaning up against his arm.

He liked the feel of her against him.

The crowds had grown thinner as the evening wore on, with fewer kids darting from side to side on the walkway. They passed under strings of decorative, white lights and along yachts moored in the lake. Her hand felt good in his, but he gave in to the urge to wrap his arm around her shoulders again. She slipped hers across his back, and their thighs brushed together while they walked.

He didn't want the night to end. He wanted to take her home with him, make love to her, sure, but also hold her sleeping in his arms, talk to her over breakfast, maybe plan their Saturday together.

The vision prompted a wave of guilt. She was open and fresh and genuine, while he was a fraud, hiding the most basic of information from her.

Determined to get them on a better footing, he found a clear spot in the crowd. Then he urged her toward the rail, turning her there so they were face to face.

"What now?" Her smile was in place, but she was searching his expression with obvious confusion.

"It's Ellis," he said, ignoring his own hesitation. "My last name is Ellis."

Her smile faded, and she peered at him intently. "Are you in the witness protection program?"

"No." Where had that come from?

"I thought maybe you'd testified against a crime boss or something."

"I'm not a criminal."

"You said you were a thief."

"Ethanol. From an institution. Probably about ten bucks worth of the stuff."

Her smile came back, and her voice went sexy and low. "Riley Ellis."

Something shifted inside him.

She repeated his name.

He kissed her. It was fleeting at first, but then deeper and longer. He loved kissing her. But they were in public, so he forced himself to stop.

He rested his hands on the rails, arms around her, slowing his breathing down. "I promised you fireworks."

Her eyes were wide and clear, her lips dark red. "You meant in the sky, right? Not the ones going off inside my brain right now."

His hands twitched. "You have absolutely no sense of self-preservation."

"And you have no sense of humor."

"You are not a good girl."

"I said I was *once* a good girl." She planted a quick kiss on his mouth and then ducked under his arm.

He immediately caught her and wrapped his arm around her as they walked. "Okay, now you're taking all the fun out of the chase."

"There they go," she called out as the first red and yellow starbursts banged through the air and lit up the sky.

They quickened their pace, laughing as they went. Riley

found them a table at the beer garden, ordering beers and a savory platter.

He angled his chair toward her. He'd seen the fireworks before, but he'd never watched Kalissa watching them. The bright colors reflected off her skin and flashed in her shinning eyes. She was so much more beautiful than the display in the sky.

She caught his gaze and did a double take.

"Hey," he said softly.

"Hey."

"How do you like them so far?"

"They're stunning."

"Stunning," he agreed, his gaze fixed on her.

She glanced back at the sky, but then returned her attention to him.

"Want to know what I did yesterday?" she asked.

"Absolutely." He wanted to know everything about her.

She traced a line along her plastic beer cup. "I met Darci."

Everything went still inside Riley.

It took him a minute to respond. "Your sister?"

"Yes, my sister. Who else would I be talking about?"

He sat back in his chair.

He'd known this would happen. At one point, he'd even thought it might be good for him. He'd considered that Kalissa might give him some inside information on Shane.

But that was days ago. Now he didn't want Kalissa talking to the Colborns at all.

Riley definitely wanted to see her again.

But now that she'd met Darci, well, sisters talked, even estranged sisters were likely to talk eventually. And when they did, it was game over for him. Because the minute Shane knew Riley was in her life, he'd do everything in his power to turn her against him.

"How did it go?" he managed to ask.

"It went well, really well. They seem terrific, very down to earth, way more down to earth than I expected."

"Great," he said, covering his expression with a drink of his beer.

The fireworks popped and cracked in the distance, and the crowd oohed and aahed. Riley wanted to put his fist through the table.

Kalissa could tell something had changed. It was subtle, but Riley was quieter during the drive home, and he wasn't making any jokes. He drove directly to the Mosaic Landscaping storefront, swinging his sports car to the curb.

He hadn't suggested stopping at his place. Not that she'd wanted to stop at his place. Not that she would have said yes to stopping at his place. But there was something weird about him not even asking.

He pulled on the emergency brake, leaving the stick shift in neutral and the engine running as he exited the driver's door. He moved to her side of the car, opening the door and taking her hand while she stepped out.

"Thank you," she said, wishing this feeling of dread would go away, wishing he'd say or do something to reassure her. "I had a very nice time."

"I did too." His expression looked sincere.

What was she missing?

She took another stab. "I'm sorry I can't invite you upstairs. Megan's there and, well, it's a pretty small apartment."

The opening was a mile wide, but he didn't suggest an alternative to her place.

"I understand," he said instead, easing a little closer.

"Is something wrong?" she couldn't help asking.

"Everything's great. You're great." He tucked her hair behind one ear, sliding his palm to the back of her neck.

Anticipation warmed her skin and increased her pulse.

"Goodnight, Kalissa," he whispered. His lips came down on hers, soft and hot. But the kiss was slightly different. It didn't hold the burning passion of the ones on the Ferris wheel.

She slipped her arms around his waist, and he did the same with his free hand. Angling her body against his, she deepened the kiss. He followed suit, and she could feel his muscles hardening against her.

His hand slipped downward, splaying over her rear, pressing her into the vee of his thighs. He kissed her deeper, his tongue plunging into her mouth. She welcomed the passion, answering back, arousal growing in waves inside her.

Her imagination took flight. If not his place, maybe a hotel. His car didn't have a back seat. And she was too old for that anyway. But it had to be somewhere. He was a powerful, sexy, virile man, and the chemistry between them was all but combustible.

Then he broke the kiss, drawing back no more than an inch.

She waited for his suggestion, his solution. He had to be thinking the same thing as her.

"Goodnight, Kalissa."

As his words registered, she bit back the *yes* waiting on the tip of her tongue. She swallowed instead, letting her arms go loose around him.

"I'll see you next week?" he asked.

It was clear he meant when she came to work on his yard. "You will."

"Great." He gave her a nod. Then he stepped further back, and his gaze went meaningfully to the small door across the sidewalk.

It took her a minute to react. She opened her purse, fumbling for her keys, keeping her head down as she crossed the narrow sidewalk.

Beneath the streetlight, she pushed the key into the deadbolt lock, turning it full circle before twisting the knob and pushing the door open. As she worked up the strength to turn around, he gunned the engine, peeling away from the curb, accelerating down the empty block.

That was it. He was gone.

"Kalissa?" Megan called from the top of the stairs.

"On my way," Kalissa managed in return, swallowing her disappointment and confusion as she secured the door behind her.

Megan came down a couple of steps. "How did it go?"

"Good," said Kalissa, starting up the staircase. "Fine."

"What's wrong?"

"I don't know."

"Did he try something? Was he a jerk?"

"No, nothing like that." It was nothing even remotely like that.

Megan turned, and they filed into the one room apartment.

Kalissa tossed her purse on the table and plunked down on the worn sofa.

"We had a great time," she said, walking through it in her mind.

"And?"

"He kissed me. He kissed me on the Ferris wheel, then again while we walked on the pier, then he kissed me goodnight."

Megan took the other end of the sofa. "So, why do you look so bleak?"

Kalissa was starting to question herself. "Okay, it's not like I wanted to fight him off with a stick. But he didn't make a move."

"You just said he kissed you."

"He didn't try to get me back to his place."

Megan grinned. "Let me get this straight. You're upset because he was too much of a gentleman?"

Now, Kalissa was starting to feel embarrassed. "It's always nice to be asked."

"But you would have said no."

"Yes." Kalissa paused. "Maybe. Probably. *Yes*. I would have said no. But he seemed really into me, and then pfft, this little kiss goodnight."

Megan peered at her. "Your lips are red and swollen."

Kalissa's fingertips went to her mouth. They were hot to the touch, and they did still tingle.

"He might just be a nice guy," said Megan.

"Even nice guys want sex."

"You're funny. And you're making too much of it. Did he say he'd call you?"

"He said he'd see me at his place."

"Which, he will."

"Not until Monday. Well, maybe Sunday afternoon."

Megan pulled her legs beneath her. "Ah yes, the sleepover."

"Do you think that's weird?" Kalissa asked.

"Darci wanting you to spend the night at her mansion?"

"It's less than two hours away."

"You're not going to want to drive home Saturday night. But the answer is yes. There's nothing about you going to stay at your secret, billionaire, twin sister's mansion that's not a little weird. You don't have to work at all on Sunday, you know."

"We're so busy," said Kalissa. She wasn't about to stick Megan with extra work. And she wanted to see Riley. She needed to talk to him again, to look him in the eyes and figure out exactly what had happened between them.

Four

Sunday afternoon, Riley was planted on his front steps while a dump truck noisily deposited a load of topsoil at the front of his yard. Megan appeared, caught a glimpse of him and altered her course. She trotted up the concrete staircase and sat down beside him at the top.

"How's it going?" she opened.

"It's fine." It was quite a bit below fine, but he wasn't about to share his worry with Megan.

Earlier, she'd mentioned that Kalissa had spent last night at the Colborn mansion, and Riley had been stewing ever since. He kept playing an imaginary conversation in his head, one where Kalissa told Darci she'd been on a date with Riley Ellis, and Shane reacted like a madman, warning her off, demanding she never see him again.

Maybe he shouldn't have been so quick to walk away Friday night. He sure hadn't wanted to walk away, and Kalissa had sent some pretty unmistakable signals. He should have acted on them. He should have taken her to his place to see where things would lead.

He'd worried that getting closer was a mistake. The closer he got, the more likely it was she'd mention him to Darci. But maybe that was a backward strategy. Maybe he'd blown the only chance he'd ever have to get closer to her. It might have been better if they'd spend the night together before Shane had a chance to turn her against him.

"You waiting for her?" asked Megan.

Riley fidgeted, getting the uneasy feeling Megan was reading his mind.

She glanced at her watch. "She said she'd be here around four."

A denial seemed pointless. "You've talked to her?"

"A couple of hours ago."

He swallowed, fighting his curiosity but immediately losing. "How did it go for her last night?"

"I think it went okay."

"She's in a good mood?" If Shane had told her the truth about Riley, surely she'd be angry.

Megan stood up and waved her arms to attract the attention of one of the gardeners. "The maples go in the back!" she called.

The guy nodded and strode toward a pickup truck where the workers appeared to be unloading the trees at the front of the driveway.

Megan sat back down. "You'd think they could take a minute to read the plans."

Riley couldn't care less about the yard layout. The maples could go on the roof for all he cared. He wanted to know about Kalissa.

He clenched his jaw to keep from repeating the question. He didn't want to draw attention to his curiosity.

"A good mood?" Megan asked, re-opening the topic.

"Happy?" he elaborated, feeling like he was back in high school.

"With visiting her sister?"

He gave her a sidelong glance to see if she was messing with him. What was with the third degree? "Yes, happy with visiting her sister."

"They had barbecued quail and toured some huge, dungeonesque wine cellar. Who barbecues quail? Brauts and burgers, sure. Maybe a steak. But quail? What were they trying to prove?"

"That he has more money than God."

"Shane?"

"Yes, Shane."

"I'm not even sure he was there. She sat up half the night talking with Darci."

A raw feeling of dread invaded Riley's stomach. "But she sounded okay?"

"A little tired."

This was like pulling teeth. "But not upset?"

She shifted her butt on the porch, curiosity coming into her tone. "Riley?"

"Yeah?"

She was silent until he looked her way.

"What are you doing?" she asked.

He played dumb. "What?"

"You're practically obsessing."

"I'm making conversation."

Megan tipped her chin toward the road. "There she is."

Riley's immediate reaction was relief. But it was followed quickly by trepidation.

Kalissa had parked down the block, out of the fray, and he watched her expression carefully as she approached. She was smiling. That was good, wasn't it? It had to mean he hadn't been caught.

But how long could he reasonably expect that to last? He was already operating on borrowed time. He needed to get to know her. She needed to get to know him before the bombshell was dropped.

"Do you need her here right now?" Riley asked Megan.

"What?"

"Kalissa. Can you live without her today?"

"Today's almost over."

"Is that a yes?" He came to his feet.

Kalissa was at the driveway.

"I guess, why?"

He tried to look blasé. "I wanted to take her out."

"Again? Now?"

"Yes to both."

"Where?"

"I don't know yet. Can I steal her?"

Megan gave a shrug. "If she wants. But I don't understand. She said you were a bit standoffish there at the end."

He looked Megan straight in the eyes. "That was a mistake. I've changed my mind."

A knowing smile grew on her face. "Then go for it."

Thank goodness.

He gave her a nod. "Thanks."

"No problem. Oh, good grief." She jumped up, her attention back on the gardeners. "They can't just eyeball it."

Riley's attention was solidly on Kalissa. He was walking fast, and he met her halfway up the driveway.

Her smile was tentative, definitely uncertain.

He could have kicked himself for making the wrong call Friday night. He took her hand, turning her in one smooth motion, keeping his momentum up as he headed for his car.

"What are you doing?" she asked, glancing back over shoulder.

"Let's get out of here."

She tugged on his arm. "I can't leave."

He urged her along. "Sure, you can. I checked with Megan."

"We have a bunch of work to do."

"I want to show you something."

"What?"

He had no idea. He figured he'd come up with something along the way. "It's a surprise."

He pulled out his key fob and hit the unlock button for his car door. Then he opened the passenger door, yawning it wide. "Hop in."

"This is crazy."

He smiled at her. "We'll grab something to eat."

"I can't abandon Megan."

"I told you, I already talked to Megan. Look." He nodded across the yard.

Megan, good on her, was grinning and waving goodbye.

"What's this about?" Kalissa asked, bracing her hand on the open door.

"You're not much for surprises, are you?"

"I'm not."

He scrambled for a quick answer. "I know a great little place near Lake Forest."

"Lake Forest?"

"Yes."

"We're going all the way to Lake Forest to grab something to eat."

He liked being this close to her. It didn't matter where they went. He could happily stand here on the sidewalk with her all evening long. "It'll only take an hour. And it's a nice day for a drive."

Her expression softened. "You better hope there's no traffic."

"Get in the car, Kalissa."

A light of amusement came into her eyes. "Aren't you demanding?"

He brushed the backs of his fingers along the curve of her chin. "Only when you're stubborn."

"I'm not stubborn."

"Good. Then hop in."

She looked like she was about to argue, but then she turned and settled herself in the low-slung seat.

"Thank you," he said.

"You've got me curious." She crossed her legs. They were covered in cropped black pants that were topped with a black and white checkerboard T-shirt.

He liked her shoes, black with open toes and a wedge heel. He particularly liked the wink of her toes, her slim ankles, and those toned, tanned calves.

"Riley?"

He quickly straightened, shaking off his wayward thoughts. He closed the door and crossed to the driver's side.

"I hope this is another casual spot," she said.

He started the engine, putting it into first and pulling the sports car away from the curb. Then he reached into the centre console and extracted his sun glasses.

"It's nicer than the food court," he said.

"Waiters and everything?"

"I'm hoping to redeem myself."

"I had a lot of fun at the pier."

"I know. I'm talking about the way I behaved after the pier." He figured there was no point in letting it simmer.

"Did something go wrong?" she asked, canting herself in the seat so she was looking directly at him.

He pulled the car to a stop at the light leading onto Hamilton, flipping on his left signal. "I didn't want to push you."

It was true. It might not be the whole truth, but it was definitely true.

"You'd rather I pushed you."

He turned his head to take in her forthright expression. "I promise you, that'll never happen again."

"I can't see your eyes."

He pulled off his glasses to make his intentions crystal clear. "That'll *never* happen again."

"Good to know." Her gaze flicked out the windshield. "Light's green."

A horn sounded behind him.

It was pretty clear to Kalissa that the drive was going to take more than an hour. Riley had chosen the scenic route, taking secondary roads that meandered along the lakeshore.

"How did it go with Darci last night?" he asked her as they made their way past a beach. The strip of park was quiet except for the wind blowing through the oak trees and the whitecaps crashing on shore.

"How did you know about last night?"

"Megan mentioned it. She said you went to the mansion."

Kalissa smiled at the memory. "That's some house they've got out there."

"Big?" asked Riley.

"Humongous."

"I guess that's what you can buy when you're a billionaire."

"Shane doesn't seem like a billionaire."

Sure, he had nice clothes and expensive real estate, and she was pretty sure Darci had said something last night about a private jet. But if you'd met him at a shopping mall or on the street, you'd never know.

Riley looked skeptical "How does he not seem like a billionaire?"

"He's pretty down to earth."

"He's trying to impress you."

"I don't see why he'd care."

"Maybe because you're Darci's twin sister?"

"He seems genuine."

"I doubt that."

The flip remark annoyed her. "How would you know? You've never even met him."

"I met him once," said Riley, an edge to his voice. "In passing. A long time ago." He paused. "I'm sure he's changed."

"Why are you doing that?"

"Doing what?"

"Giving in with your teeth clenched. If you want to fight with me, fight with me."

"I don't want to fight with you."

"You've obviously got something against Shane. Or are you jealous of his money?"

"He's just one more rich guy in Chicago."

"Well, I'm a little jealous of his money." Not that Kalissa had any interest in a mansion. But she'd love to pay down Mosaic's line of credit. And she could sure get used to that wine cellar.

"He'll probably give you some of it," said Riley.

"I should sock you for that one."

"Not while I'm driving. But later, if you like."

"I wouldn't take his money if he forced it on me. Just because there's some random, genetic connection between me and Darci—"

"She's your identical twin."

"I know that."

"That's hardly random."

"My point is, being related to her doesn't give me any call on their wealth. That's one of the reasons I tried to stay away from her. I knew everybody would think I was after her money. I'm incredibly grateful that Darci and Shane at least don't think I'm a gold digger."

"I don't think you're a gold digger."

"Then why are we arguing about it?"

"You're the one who brought it up."

"I did not."

"You said you were jealous of his money."

She realized Riley was right. "I didn't mean it that way."

"Okay."

"I meant it in a theoretical, fantasy-like way. Who wouldn't want a little extra money to toss around?"

"I'd take a little extra money." Riley slowed the car and pulled off the road into a wide parking lot.

"What are you doing?"

"I'm thirsty."

He maneuvered the car into an empty parking stall close to a grassy, tree lined area of the park. The branches swayed in the wind, and there was a strip of sandy beach on the far side of the lawn, with big foaming waves rushing up onto it.

"We could take a walk on the beach," he suggested.

She couldn't help but smile at that. "Have you been brushing up on dating?"

"Huh?"

"Long walks on the beach. I'm pretty sure that's the number one documented female dating fantasy. We expect you to pour out your heart and soul to us, while holding our hands, scampering in the waves, and looking like a guy in a hair products' commercial."

His brows went up. "Scamper?"

"Yes."

"I did not know any of that."

She gave him a smirk. "Are you afraid to scamper?"

He reached down to untie the laces of his hikers, heaving a long-suffering sigh. "I'll do what I have to do."

She realized he was serious about walking. "I've never seen it done during a gale force wind."

He glanced out the windshield. "It doesn't look so bad."

She retrieved her purse from beside her feet, opening it to search for a stray ponytail elastic. "Probably no more than sixty knots. But I am thirsty."

"That's the spirit. I'd say forty-five knots, tops."

While he peeled off his boots, Kalissa fastened her hair and kicked off her sandals.

They got out of the car into the breeze. Luckily, it was warm. In fact, it was kind of refreshing.

She tipped her chin and let the sunshine caress her face.

Riley slipped his hand into hers, and they started across the thick grass to the concession stand.

Halfway there, a black lab bounded toward them. It dropped a stick at their feet and wagged its tail, brown eyes looking eagerly up.

Riley let go of Kalissa's hand and picked up the stick. He gave it a mighty throw, sending it spiraling in a high arc to land on an empty stretch of sand.

"That's some arm," she told him.

"I was a pitcher for a while in high school."

"Were you good?"

"Not bad. There were other guys who were better."

She found her sympathies engaging. "Did you get cut from the team?"

"No." He gave her a playful shove with his hip. "I did not get cut from the team. I had too much studying to do senior year, so I didn't try out."

"What were you studying? Where did you go to college?"

"I stayed in Illinois. IIT Armour College."

"Nice. I went to community college, got a diploma not a degree. I was pretty much on my own for money. Well, I was completely on my own for money."

The dog loped toward them again, returning the stick.

Riley threw it once more.

"You like dogs?" Kalissa asked.

"I do."

"Did you have them growing up?"

He shook his head. "Pets were not one of my mother's priorities."

"What about your dad? Brothers and sisters?"

His gaze was on the dog as it picked up the stick. "Just me and my mom. It wasn't Norman Rockwell."

"Same with me," she said. "Which isn't unusual for adopted kids."

"Was it lonely for you?" he asked, taking her hand again.

"It was. She, uh…" Kalissa hesitated. She didn't like to broadcast her past. But it sounded like Riley had been there himself.

"My adopted dad died when I was five. My mother never really recovered. She drank after that. Quite a lot. So I pretty much raised myself."

He gave her hand a small squeeze. "My mother worked. She didn't have the skills to make much money, so she was gone for long hours. I hear you on raising yourself."

"How could you afford IIT?"

"I was lucky enough to get a scholarship."

"So, quitting baseball worked for you."

"It did."

"I wasn't smart enough to get more than a community college scholarship." She wasn't indulging in self-pity. It was just a fact.

"Don't sell yourself short. Your intellect gives me a run for my money."

She appreciated the sentiment. "I'm beginning to doubt that."

"It wasn't brilliance that got me there. I studied my butt off in senior year. I had my head in textbooks every waking minute."

"I worked weekends and most evenings in high school."

If she hadn't, they never would have made the rent on their modest basement suite. By that time, her mother was drunk every day, and welfare checks alone would never have covered their living expenses.

The dog was back again, dropping the stick.

"He knows you're a soft touch," said Kalissa.

Riley hurled the stick. "He'll wear out eventually."

"Thank goodness you can throw so far."

"If you'd had time to study," said Riley, "You could have won any scholarship you wanted."

She didn't buy it for a second.

"I can tell," he said.

"You cannot."

"How were your grades?"

"Fine. I guess they were good."

"How good?"

"A's and B's," she admitted.

She'd been lucky enough to have a knack for most subjects. It made up for her lack of time to study around her part time job. But high school coursework was nothing compared to college.

"I rest my case," he said. "Soda good for you?"

They had arrived at the little concession stand set amongst a dozen wooden picnic tables.

"You have no case. Soda sounds great."

Riley stepped up and placed their order.

"You think you'll ever get a dog?" Kalissa asked while they waited.

"I will someday. Maybe when I'm settled, when the business is running well, and I have a family."

"You want a family?"

"Yes, I do. I want a wife, a couple of kids, and a white picket fence. I want to create what I never had growing up."

"Norman Rockwell?"

"A modern version."

The young man behind the counter handed them two cardboard cups filled with ice and cola.

"If you need any landscaping," Kalissa joked as they strolled away.

"You'll be my first call."

"Unless you're planning to stay in the house you've got. It's going to look great. Well, from the outside." She hadn't seen much of the inside, only the basement.

His tone turned intimate. "You'll have to come and see the rest of it."

She looked up, meeting his dark eyes, and her heart gave a couple of quick beats. "You think?"

"I know."

The dog dropped the stick beside Riley's feet, and Kalissa's phone rang in her pocket.

He quickly got rid of the stick again.

"It's Megan," said Kalissa.

He surprised her by whisking the phone out of her hand.

"Hey," she protested.

He put it to his ear. "Megan? Yeah. Can this wait?"

"Give that back," said Kalissa.

"Uh-huh," he said into the phone.

Kalissa leaned in to call out. "Megan? Megan, I'm here."

"Don't be melodramatic," Riley said to Kalissa. "She is," he said into the phone. Then he gave a mischievous grin. "No, we're not."

"What's she asking?" Kalissa stage whispered.

"What do you think?" he asked her.

Kalissa called into the phone again. "We're in public, on the beach."

"How would you feel about Kalissa turning this thing off for a while?" Riley asked Megan.

"I'm not turning my phone off," said Kalissa.

"Okay," said Riley.

"Good," said Kalissa.

"I was talking to Megan."

"I'm not turning it off."

"Great," said Riley. "Thanks." He ended the call.

"Hey!"

"She's fine with you turning it off."

"I'm not turning it off."

Megan's calls were probably the only ones that might be important, but she could get other calls. Her sister, for example.

"I will if you will," said Riley.

"No."

"Let's pretend we're out of tower range."

"Like if we were hiking the Adirondacks?"

He handed her phone back then drew his own out of his pocket. He moved his way through the screens.

"There," he said. "Mine's off." He waited.

"I didn't agree to this."

"This is a lot like hiking the Adirondacks. Except there'll be plumbing, fine china, and a Maitre-de."

A Maitre-de? "Where, exactly are you taking me?"

"Turn off your phone. You can do it, Kalissa."

Something was making her hesitate. But there was no reason to refuse. If Megan knew she was out of touch, nobody would worry if they couldn't reach her. "If I turn it off, you'll tell me where we're going?"

"Absolutely."

She gauged his expression. "Tell me first."

"You don't trust me?"

"I don't."

He gave a long suffering sigh. "It's a restaurant called the Trestle Tree. It's in a historic building on the lakeshore. It used to belong to a railway baron."

"I've never heard of it."

"You think I'm making it up?"

"I think I don't know much more than I did two minutes ago."

"Maybe, but I kept my side of the bargain."

He had her there.

She gave in and shut down her phone.

Five

"I'm not going in there," said Kalissa, one hand resting on the dashboard.

Riley didn't understand. "I ate there once a couple of years ago. It's really nice inside."

As far as he was concerned, it was nice outside too, a four-story, red brick, historic building, lined with arched windows and decorated with a narrow wrought iron balcony along the second floor. It was illuminated by pot lights and spotlessly maintained, with a gleaming white concrete staircase and trimmed plants bracketing a green and glass double door.

"I'm talking about the people," she said.

"What's wrong with the people?"

A man in a neat business suit was escorting two women up the short staircase. He looked to be in his fifties. One woman was about the same age. The other looked to be in her twenties. A daughter, Riley guessed. He didn't see a single thing wrong with them.

"Are you blind?"

He assumed it was a rhetorical question, but he answered anyway. "No."

"The dresses, Riley. Look at their dresses."

"What about them?"

One woman was in royal blue, the other in black.

"Now, look at me." She gestured to herself.

"You look fantastic."

She did. The simple black slacks clung to the curve of her hips, and the white top showed off her tan. Her hair was only slightly windswept. Her green eyes sparkled beneath the streetlight, and her face seemed to get more beautiful by the minute.

"I'm wearing jeans."

"Those aren't jeans."

"They're black, but they are jeans. And look at you?"

He glanced down at his khaki pants. Okay, they weren't exactly formal, but they were clean.

"You look like you walked off a shop floor."

"I did."

"Exactly. Let's go somewhere else, maybe a café or a drive-through."

"You want me to take you to a drive-through?"

Like he was going to trump Shane by taking her to a drive-through. No way. Tonight was about impressing her, showing her his better qualities before Shane could enumerate his failings.

"We could grab a burger and find a nice park for a picnic."

"We're not going to a drive-through. Look at those people." He pointed to a party of four on the sidewalk. "They're more casually dressed."

"Nice try."

Okay, so maybe it was a stretch. The men were both wearing blazers, but the women's dresses were much shorter and less formal.

He glanced around for a solution.

Then he saw it.

"If I change?" he asked.

She frowned. "Into what?"

He pointed two doors down the street to a clothing store.

She chuckled, obviously assuming it was a joke. "You're going to buy new clothes?"

"Why not?"

"Because that's a crazy idea."

He opened the door. "Let's at least go look."

"You're a crazy person," she called from behind him.

But she climbed out of the car.

He waited for her and held out his hand.

"I don't know why I humor you," she muttered.

"Lighten up."

"I am light. At least I'm usually light." She paused. "Fine.

Okay. I'll stop complaining. What's the worst that can happen?"

He raised her hand and kissed it while they walked. "That's the spirit."

"You're mocking me."

"You're pretty easy to mock."

When they made it to the store, he pushed the door open.

Inside, it was long and narrow, done in grey tones with muted lighting. It featured men's dress shirts, slacks and sport coats down one side, with ladies skirts, blazers and classic blouses down the other.

"The women's wear looks a bit conservative," he whispered in her ear. "But see what they've got."

"I'm not going to—"

He shot her a mock scowl. "If I'm going to look dressier, you have to make an effort too."

She held up her hands in surrender. "Okay, okay. I'm not complaining."

"Glad to hear it."

A woman approached them. "Can I help you?"

"Do you have any dresses?" Riley asked her.

"We do," she answered brightly. "It's a small collection. They're closer to the back. This way."

It didn't take Riley long to find slacks, a shirt and a jacket that would fit him. He left the new things on and dropped the tags and his old clothes at the checkout counter. Then he headed to the back of the store to find Kalissa.

She was emerging from a changing cubical in a simple, short black dress. It looked nice, mostly because it was Kalissa inside. But it seemed a bit boring.

"My shoes will work with this," she said to the clerk.

"Do you have anything with some color?" asked Riley, glancing at the racks beside him.

"You don't like it?" asked Kalissa. "It's very versatile."

He lifted a frothy, bright blue dress with a single, jeweled shoulder strap. "What about this?"

She looked aghast. "I'm not buying that."

"You're not buying anything. I am. Try it on."

The clerk grinned at the exchange.

Kalissa opened her mouth, but he beat her to the punch.

"What else do you have?" he asked the clerk. "She needs something pretty. We're going to a very important dinner."

"You're nuts," said Kalissa.

"You promised you wouldn't complain," he countered.

"You want me to stand here and shut up while you spend a fortune on a dress I'm only going to wear once?"

"Now you're catching on."

The clerk's grin grew wider, and she put a hand on Kalissa's arm, her voice reflecting a wise tone. "Honey, there are times when you simply keep quiet and let a man have his way. This is one of them."

Kalissa hit Riley with a stern stare. "Is that truly what you want me to do?"

"Absolutely." He couldn't stop a smile. He might not be Shane, but he wasn't impoverished either. He could indulge her in whatever fancy dress she wanted. "Feel free to accessorize."

She rolled her eyes, but held out her hand for the blue dress.

"I'll see what else we have," the clerk cheerfully added.

Riley waited while Kalissa changed.

When she emerged, he gave a low whistle. The fabric gathered softly across her breasts, with a weave of jewels swooping under the bodice, up to the single shoulder strap, leaving plenty of bare skin. Man, he loved her shoulders.

Beneath the bodice, soft, translucent fabric fell to a scalloped hem at mid-thigh, revealing her smooth, toned legs.

"That's the one," he said.

The clerk arrived and glanced down at an armful of dresses.

"You've decided?" she asked.

"What do you think?" he asked Kalissa.

"It kind of works." There was a glow to her expression.

"We'll take it," he said.

"I have some silver shoes," said the clerk. "The black is rather jarring."

"I don't—" said Kalissa.

"Sure," said Riley.

"I'll be right back," said the clerk.

Kalissa pursed her lips.

"No complaints," Riley warned.

"I'm not saying a word."

She turned to look in a three way mirror, and Riley's knees almost gave way. Her back was very nearly bare, a large diamond shape was cut out between the bodice and the skirt. It was the sexiest thing he'd ever seen.

The clerk returned with the shoes, and Kalissa sat down to try them on. Even before she stood up, he knew they were perfect, slim, high heels, a silver sheen, and little straps around her ankles. Forget dinner, he wanted to carry her off to the nearest bedroom.

She rose, and he joined her in front of the big mirror, deciding she looked perfect next to him.

"Do you think they'll let us in the restaurant now?" he asked.

"Where are you going?" asked the clerk.

"The Trestle Tree."

"Oh, you've hit it just right."

"He wanted me to wear jeans." Kalissa told the woman.

"Buying new clothes was my idea," Riley pointed out.

Kalissa just smiled at her reflection, swaying ever so slightly so that the hem brushed her legs.

The clerk frowned. "You can't wear jeans to the Trestle Tree."

"Noted," said Riley.

"It seems we make a good team," Kalissa teased.

"You're strategic direction, and I'm implementation."

"That sounds about right."

It was right. They were right together. And he wanted to keep the togetherness going for a long, long time.

The wind had died down, and after they'd finished eating, Kalissa had moved with Riley to the patio overlooking the lake. They were standing at the rail under a starry sky, sipping coffees laced with brandy, sugar and whipped cream.

It felt decadent. She felt decadent. Everything about the evening felt decadent, from the wild mushroom and goat cheese appetizer to the cedar planked salmon. And the dress, she loved her new dress. She especially loved the way Riley's fingertips now brushed her bare back.

"This was nice," she told him. "Thanks for talking me into it."

"Thanks for coming along." His lips brushed her temple.

It was the simplest of kisses, but it sent a reaction skittering over her skin. She was intensely attracted to him. She liked his looks, his voice, and his scent. She particularly liked his mind, his intelligence and agile wit.

He held his own against her sarcasm and challenges. Most men either backed off or became genuinely angry. As a teenager, she'd tried to temper that facet of her personality, having been told by friends and often by her mother that she'd frighten boys off. But she didn't want to change. She wanted to be strong.

But then, sometimes she wanted to be soft. She set her coffee down on the stand-up table beside them and leaned her head against his chest.

He followed suit, getting rid of his own cup.

"No pressure," he said. "Believe me, the last thing I want to do is make you uncomfortable."

She smiled to herself. "Okay."

"But, up there."

She looked, and found him gazing at the three stories above them. Lights shone from some of the windows.

"They have guest rooms," he continued. "I saw a sign with a picture on the way in, and they look very nice."

"You're suggesting something?" Already her pulse had jumped. Her skin warmed and a thrill of arousal swirled inside her.

He looked down, meeting her eyes in the darkness. "I'm not going to leave it to you this time."

"To push?"

"I'm pushing," he said, his head dipping toward her. "You can say no, but I'm definitely the one pushing tonight."

He kissed her, and her desire ramped up. She didn't want to say no. She wasn't going to say no. Riley was amazing, and she was dying to spend the night in his arms.

She drew back. "Let's see if they have a room."

A glow came into his dark eyes. His hand closed over hers, and he led her from the rail, back through the restaurant and into the lobby of the inn.

"Checking in?" asked the man behind the reception counter.

"We don't have a reservation," said Riley.

The man hit a few keys on the terminal in front of him. "Let's see what we have available."

"With a view if that's possible," said Riley.

"We have a junior suite with a king sized bed, a connected seating area, and floor to ceiling windows overlooking the lake."

"We'll take it," said Riley, giving her hand a squeeze.

Her heart kicked up, her chest tightening with exhilaration and just a touch of anxiety.

After checking in, they took a creaking, ancient elevator to the fourth floor. Then they followed a scuffed and uneven hardwood floor hallway to the end before finding their room.

"The rooms looked nice on the lobby poster," said Riley, a touch of worry in his tone as he wiggled the metal key into the deadbolt lock and turned.

The heavy door squealed as it swung open.

He fumbled for the light switch, found it, and the big room came into view.

It didn't disappoint.

"It's gorgeous," Kalissa breathed, stepping inside to look around the airy space.

The carpet was plush beneath her feet. A pristine, blue and gold striped Victorian sofa was bracketed by two matching armchairs, the arrangement set in front of a marble fireplace with a hearth that stretched to the high ceiling. A huge brass bed was positioned in an alcove, the head decorated by rich fabric, draped on the wall. In the center of the room, the ceiling was domed, carved and painted white, matching the scrolls of the crown molding above abstract blue and copper wallpaper.

Throw pillows were everywhere, including on a bay window bench seat that overlooked the dark lake. Heavy curtains hung from brass rings above six massive windows. The colorful pillows all but buried a thick quilt on the bed.

She turned a lever on one of the windows, and the catch came free.

"Look at this," she said, pushing the window wide to let in the fresh air.

"Look at this," said Riley in a low, reverent tone.

She turned.

He was gazing intently at her. The expression in his eyes was passionate and possessive.

"You don't want to check out the room?" she asked.

"Not really." He moved forward.

"You want to check out the bed?"

"I do."

She snuck past him to the mound of pillows that buried the white quilt. "You think we can *find* the bed?"

In answer, he scooped her into his arms.

"Hey."

Before she knew what was happening, he'd placed her in the middle of the pillow pile.

"I found it," he said, lowering himself to the edge of the bed.

"I don't think I can move in all this."

"You don't have to move."

His hand skimmed down her calf, coming to the buckle on her new shoe. "I love these."

"I think I'm getting blisters."

"Poor you." He released the strap, easing off the shoe.

"Oh, that feels *good.*"

"So, I'm off to a promising start?" He switched to the other shoe.

"You're off to a fantastic start."

"Glad to hear it."

He lifted her bare foot, bending her knee, then leaned forward to place a kiss on her ankle. "Better?"

"Better."

He worked his way up her calf, making small circles with his thumb. Her skin warmed under his touch, the warmth turning to arousal as he massaged the back of her knee. When his hand moved up her thigh, the arousal turned to need.

"Riley," she breathed.

He stretched out beside her, his palm moving to her rear, cupping her silk panties. He smoothed her hair back from her face, coming closer.

"You're amazing," he whispered.

"I'm not doing anything."

"Yes, you are."

She touched his shoulder, marveling at its strength, moving her hand down his arm, memorizing the definition of his muscles. She cupped the hand that was at her cheek, loving the textured skin, the wide palm, the strong, blunt fingers.

She turned her head and kissed his palm, tasting it with the tip of her tongue.

He groaned.

Then he kissed her exposed neck, slowly making his way to her shoulder with a pattern of hot kisses.

She let her head fall back, clinging tight to his hand, letting the arousing sensations wash over her.

He drew back, gazing into her eyes. Then he zeroed in on her mouth, and passion overtook her. Her arms went around his neck, holding him tight. His kisses were long and deep. His hand stopped on her rear, then it fisted around her panties, dragging them down.

She kicked them off.

He slipped her single shoulder strap down, kissing behind it and nudging the dress aside to expose her breasts. Her nipples went taut beneath his kiss. They tingled, sending bands of want straight to her abdomen.

She blindly reached for the buttons on his shirt, awkwardly popping them from their holes, pushing his shirt off, and pressing her skin to his.

He hugged her tight, rolling so that she was sprawled over his chest, her hair dangling in a curtain around his face. He kissed her mouth again, pulling up on her dress, breaking the kiss just long enough to remove it and toss it aside.

She was naked then, and he was hot and so incredibly sexy.

She pushed herself up, sitting astride him.

"You are incredible," he whispered reverently, cupping her breasts.

She tipped back her head, and her toes curled in.

"You have a condom," she managed.

"I do."

Relieved, she popped the button on his slacks. She drew down the zipper. He bracketed her hips, holding her firmly against him as his hips rotated beneath her.

She didn't think she'd ever been this aroused.

Then his hands moved to her thighs, stroking their way up. She cried out when they met, buckling with the sensation.

She dragged down his pants, and he kicked them off, donning the condom.

"Like this?" she asked, positioning herself on top again.

"Like anything," he groaned, grasping her hips and pulling her home.

Energy raced through her body. She rocked against him, over and over again.

"This is incredible," he ground out. "*You* are incredible. I'm not. I can't."

She leaned in to kiss him, capturing his tongue and returning with hers. His hands roamed her body, finding secret places that made her twitch and buck with reaction.

Finally, he flipped them over, bracing the small of her back, pulling her into him as he thrust forward harder and harder, increasing their speed. Warmth glowed in the base of her brain, getting hotter and brighter.

The world disappeared. Nothing existed but Riley, his

breath in her ear, the scent of his skin, the feel of his body as he pulled hers to unimaginable heights.

She groaned as she hovered for a long, long moment.

"Kalissa," he cried, his body convulsing within her.

She crashed over the edge, spiraling downward in pure ecstasy.

"Riley," she gasped, hoping he'd catch her, knowing he'd catch her.

His arms were solid steel around her, and slowly the freefall ended, the soft pillows cushioning her.

Her heartbeat was wild. His heart thudded in return.

They both breathed deeply.

His body was a hot weight on top of her. It felt good. She felt safe. She never wanted him to leave.

"Wow," he said, smoothing back her hair. "Just…wow."

"I'm not going to argue with that."

"Well, that's a switch." There was a clear smile in his voice.

"You are *so* brave to tease me."

He lifted his head. "Am I too heavy?"

"No." She looked into his eyes. "I like it."

"Oh, man. Kalissa." He kissed her.

Then he kissed her again, and again, each one longer and deeper.

His hand covered her breast again, and her nipple hardened to a peak.

"Can we?" he asked in a strained voice.

"Yes," she answered. "Oh, yes."

In the early morning sunrays, Riley watched through half closed eyes as Kalissa eased up on her elbow beside him. Her hair was tousled, and the pure white pillow and comforter billowed around her. She gazed at him in silence.

"What are you thinking?" he asked.

"You're awake." Her voice was husky with sleep.

"I am."

"Did I wake you?"

"No. What are you thinking?"

She paused. "I was thinking it never happens this way."

He loved the sound of her voice. The words didn't even have to make sense. "What never happens which way?"

She cracked an obviously self-conscious smile. "You meet a guy. He's smart, funny, good looking, and then…" A delightful touch of pink flushed her cheeks.

"Sometimes it happens that way." And he was beyond thrilled that it had.

"There's always a catch."

He agreed with that. "Catch is." He settled a hand on her bare hip. "I'm falling for you."

Her smile widened. "That's not a catch."

It was for him, and that was the hard truth. He was quickly coming to care for her, but he was destined to upset and disappoint her. There was no way around it.

But not now, he told himself, not today. There was still some more time before the real world crowded in.

She glanced behind him and her expression sobered. "We're late."

He realized she'd glimpsed the bedside clock. "I disagree. We're right on time."

"I'm late for work." She gave a longing glance around the picturesque room. "I'm late for my real life."

He slipped an arm beneath her, determined to hold her in place. "Real life's over-rated."

"Maybe so, but mine's out there waiting for me."

"Let it wait." Deep down, he knew he'd never have another chance like this.

She sat up, giving him a lovely profile view of her breasts and the indentation of her stomach.

"I can't abandon Megan."

He rose beside her, searching for the words that would change her mind. Then he spotted her cell phone on the bedside table. He reached for it and swiftly opened her contacts. There was Megan.

He connected a call and put it to his ear.

Kalissa obviously heard something, and she turned to look at him. Her brows knitted in confusion.

"Hey, you," came Megan's sing-song voice. "How'd it go?"

"It's Riley," he said.

Megan's tone immediately changed. "What's wrong?"

"Nothing's wrong. Kalissa's right here."

"Who are you talking to?" asked Kalissa, her confusion obviously growing.

"Where's here?" asked Megan.

"Lake Forest."

"What are you doing way out there?"

"Hey," Kalissa called. "That's *my* phone."

"Tell her hi," said Megan.

"Megan says hi," Riley told Kalissa.

"Give it back." Kalissa lunged forward.

He leaned away from the bed, reaching for her shoulder to hold her at arm's length.

"I was hoping to keep her for a while," he said to Megan.

"I'm taking a shower, then we're coming home." Kalissa called out so that Megan would hear. She was obviously trying to glower at him, but the amusement in her eyes was giving her away.

"She's taking a shower?" asked Megan.

"No." Riley hesitated, wondering how much he ought to reveal. "I, uh, just came in and woke her up."

"Oh, good grief," said Kalissa. "She's not going to buy that. Give me the phone."

"Do you need her right away?" asked Riley.

"Tell her to have fun," said Megan.

"Give me that phone," said Kalissa, punctuating her words by bopping him in the shoulder with the heel of her hand. Her lips twitched as she clearly fought a smile.

"Megan says to have fun."

"I am *not* going to have fun."

He grinned in triumph. "You're already having fun."

"You should probably let her talk to me," said Megan.

"Okay," Riley agreed. "But you're my wing-man in this."

Megan laughed.

Riley handed the phone to Kalissa.

"Hey," Kalissa said into it, giving Riley a stern glare.

He pulled her close, folding her against his chest.

To his delight, she didn't fight him.

"It was nice," she said to Megan.

"Nice?" Riley growled in an undertone.

She elbowed him in the ribs.

"That's nuts," she said to Megan. "We'll head back right away."

"Tell her I'll have you home by tonight," said Riley.

"She can hear you," said Kalissa.

"Is she agreeing?" asked Riley.

"She's not the person you have to convince," said Kalissa.

Then she took the phone from her ear.

Megan's voice was tinny but audible. "Do you two even need me in this conversation?"

"Yes," said Kalissa.

"No," said Riley.

Megan gave a spurt of laughter. "Take the day. You sure deserve it."

"So do you," said Kalissa.

"I'll take one later."

There was hesitation in Kalissa's expression. She looked up at Riley.

He gave her an encouraging smile and ran his fingertips from the tip of her smooth shoulder, over her collarbone and up her neck.

Her head tipped ever so slightly, and her eyes closed.

"Fine," she breathed in capitulation.

"Thank you, Megan," Riley called.

"You can't have her forever," warned Megan.

"We'll see you tonight," he answered, lifting the phone from Kalissa's unresisting hand and ending the call.

As he gazed at her creamy skin, her gorgeous hair and those full luscious lips, he thought forever sounded about right.

Six

In an open air art market, in a historical section of Lake Forest, they found some dramatic metal sculptures. Kalissa knew they'd be perfect for Riley's patio. After a brief protest, he agreed to buy them. He was now lugging the two unwieldy pieces toward his car.

His phone rang, and he glanced down at his pants pocket.

"You want me to?" Kalissa asked, tentatively reaching.

"Can you just tell me who it is?" He shifted the sculptures to give her access.

She reached into the pocket, taking a moment to get her hands on the phone.

His eyes twinkled. "Keep looking."

"You have a one track mind."

"I do around you."

She managed to extract the phone, lifting it to check the display.

"Wade Cormack?" she told him.

Riley blew out a sigh. "I'd better take that." He glanced around, spotting a bench under a tree. "It's a business associate. Can you tell him to hang on?"

"Sure." Kalissa pressed the answer button. "This is Riley Ellis's phone," she answered as she followed him toward the bench.

"And who is this?" The man's voice was smooth and professional.

"This is Kalissa Smith. He'll just be a moment."

"Are you his new secretary?" asked Wade Cormack.

Kalissa hesitated, wondering how exactly she would describe herself. "Something like that. I'm on contract."

Riley set down the sculptures and gave her a look of confusion.

"What kind of a contract?" asked Wade.

"Mr. Ellis is ready for you now," she said in a very proper voice, grinning as she handed over the phone.

Riley listened for a moment. "She's none of your business, that's who she is."

Kalissa chuckled as she plopped down on the bench next to the sculptures. His gardener? His date? His one night stand? All were true one way or another.

"No," said Riley, his voice rising. "Of course not. Give me a break."

His expression sobered. He glanced at Kalissa, then he turned and took a couple of steps away.

She tried not to listen to what was obviously a confidential call, but his voice carried.

"How did you find that out?" asked Riley, bracing his feet apart.

Kalissa focused her attention on the clusters of people walking past, couples, families, some with strollers, many of them carrying paintings and other packages.

"Crap," Riley spat in a tone of disgust.

Kalissa found herself sitting up straight, taking in his tense posture. Whatever had happened, it obviously wasn't good, and it seemed like their stolen day away was about to end.

She was disappointed by that. Having worked through her guilt at leaving Megan on her own, she'd started to hope Riley would suggest stopping for dinner on the way back to Chicago.

"As soon as I can," said Riley. "Maybe somewhere over-seas?"

His head nodded. "I know. He'll have thought that through too. Damn-it."

Kalissa's emotions wavered between pity and curiosity.

"I'll let you know," said Riley.

He turned back, shoving his phone into his pocket.

She came to her feet. "Do we need to go back?"

"What?" He was obviously distracted.

"Do we need to go back? Are you in a hurry?"

"It's all right," he said, gathering up the sculptures.

"It's okay if you do," she told him. "It wouldn't hurt for me to check up on—"

"There's a guy," said Riley as they started their way back down the pedestrian street. "He's a competitor. He paid a 'rush' premium to buy up all the stock on a particular part that he doesn't really need from three different suppliers. So they've back-ordered on me."

"Why would he do that?"

"To shut down my assembly line and destroy my company."

"That's appalling."

Riley stared straight ahead, his pace increasing as he talked. "He's a very competitive man."

"He sounds like a bona-fide jerk."

Riley's jaw clenched tight, and they walked in silence for the next block.

"What are you going to do?" she asked.

"Try to find another source for the part."

"Can you do anything to him? Take him to court maybe. Is it illegal?"

"It's not illegal. It's ruthless, and it's definitely smart."

She was surprised that Riley would have anything positive to say about the man.

"Smart?" she asked.

"Brilliant, actually. I didn't see it coming."

"Who is he?" she asked.

Riley's expression relaxed. "Nobody important. Definitely nobody you need to worry about."

"If he can destroy your company…" How could that fail to make him important?

"If a competitor can destroy my company that easily, I don't deserve to succeed."

"Seriously?"

"Seriously. Tell me, what would you do if another landscaping company bought up all of the, say, Boxwood?"

She came up with a quick solution. "I'd substitute Privet."

"If you couldn't substitute? What if every customer you had demanded a Boxwood hedge as part of the garden design?"

"I'd order from out of state."

"And if there was none available out of state?"

She thought about it for another moment. "Well, it would take a while, but I could start a nursery and grow my own."

It took her a second to realize that Riley had stopped walking. She turned back. "What?"

"You'd grow your own," he said, a calculating look in his eyes.

"It would take a while. And I'm assuming I could get my hands on some seed."

"I can get seed," he said.

She wondered if she'd lost sight of the overall metaphor. "Are you saying you want a Boxwood hedge?"

His attention moved back to her. "What?"

"We're not seriously talking about a hedge?"

His brow furrowed. "No."

"I thought maybe I'd missed a left turn in the conversation. We're still talking about you. The seeds aren't literally seeds."

"They're not seeds." He began walking again.

She trotted a couple of steps. "So, what are they?"

"A titanium alloy, C-110M."

She rolled that one over in her mind. "What exactly is it you do, Riley?"

"It's not as complicated as it sounds. It's just a type of metal. If we have approved specs, we can contract someone to make the part. It'll be expensive, and it'll take some time, but it's not impossible."

They'd arrived at the car, and he popped the small truck. "Well, this is going to be a tight fit."

She took in the space and the shape of the sculptures.

"Turn that one sideways, big end that way." She pointed.

He set it inside.

"The other should nestle with the sunburst part in the space that's—"

It was clear, he was way ahead of her, and he set the second one down. They fit perfectly, and he stepped back.

"We're going to have to restrain ourselves for the rest of the afternoon," he said.

"I thought we were done."

"We only made it halfway through the art fair."

"Don't you have to get back to work?"

It was pretty obvious he had problems to solve.

"We've got some time." He shut the lid of the trunk. "I wanted to buy you a painting, or a vase, or maybe some earrings."

Her fingertips rose reflexively to her earlobe. "You can't buy me jewelry on our second date."

He stepped closer. "Why not?"

"It's too…too…" She struggled for the right word. "Intimate."

He took one of her hands, twining his fingers with hers, pulling her closer, his voice going low. "Too intimate? You were there last night, right?"

"That's not the same thing."

"Physical intimacy is not the same as emotional intimacy?"

"It's not." It wasn't.

He gave her what looked like a tolerant smile. "Okay."

"I'll take a vase," she said.

"Sure." He stepped closer, brushing up against her. "Unless you happen to fall madly in love with a pair of earrings."

His touch brought back memories of last night, and fresh desire swept through her. "I won't."

He gave her a warm smile. "Never say never."

She waited for his kiss, eyes closing, lips parting, her chin tipping toward him.

He didn't disappoint.

His lips were hot, his kiss thorough, and his arms wound tight around her. She wished they weren't on a public street. She wished they were back at the inn, wrapped in the cocoon of that soft bed. She desperately wished she could rewind and have last night start all over again.

Riley spoke to Ashton across a hewn wood table at The Copper Tavern. Rock music came from the speaker above them, while a muted Cubs game played out on the screen above the bar.

"We can have the engine mounting bracket custom made," said Riley. "But it's going to be tough on the bottom line. It's a structural part, so we'll need permits and certification. And if he does something like that again, it could sink us."

"Can you stop him?" asked Ashton, as the waitress set two frosted mugs of beer in front of them.

"We're going through the E-22 specs part by part to see where we're vulnerable."

"Can you retaliate? Buy up all the stock of something he needs?"

"His pockets are way deeper than mine," said Riley.

He was ticked off at Shane, but he had to reluctantly admire the play. Now he needed a play of his own.

"What about the girl?" asked Ashton.

"The girl?"

"The twin. Can you use her against Shane?"

"You mean Kalissa?"

"Yeah. Is there a way to parlay that into something—"

"I'm not dragging Kalissa into this." She wasn't a pawn in their battle.

Ashton drew back. "I don't get it. I thought that's why you were dating her."

"That's not why I'm dating her."

"Then why are you dating your rival half-brother's sister-in-law?"

"I like her."

"Sure," Ashton said with a shrug. "I've seen pictures. What's not to like?"

"I mean, I like her. I'm not going to use her to get to Shane."

Ashton stared at him in obvious confusion. "You can't truly fall for Darci's sister."

"I'm not falling for her." But even Riley could hear the lie in that statement.

"I'm serious," said Ashton.

"I've seen her a couple of times, a couple of dates."

Ashton's eyes narrowed further. "And, have you…"

"None of your business."

"Oh, this is great." Ashton threw up his hands. "You're sleeping with her, and you don't want me to know about it?"

"It's none of your—"

"Yeah, yeah. I get it. And when was the last time you were discreet about your sex life?"

Never, was the last time Riley had kept his sex life secret from Ashton. It had never much mattered. It had always been casual, a fleeting good time with women who made no bones about telling their own friends about him.

Riley took a swig of his beer. It was satisfying going down. Though he now wished he had something stronger. He probably should have gone with a boilermaker.

"You can't think this is going to work," said Ashton.

"I don't expect anything to work. I know exactly what's going to happen."

"What's that?"

"As soon as Shane hears my name, he's going to out me as his rival, then he's going to undermine me, and then Kalissa's going to walk away."

Ashton was nodding. "At least it won't come as a surprise."

"It won't come as a surprise. I can handle it."

A beat went past in silence.

"Why don't I believe you?" asked Ashton.

"Because I'm lying." Riley signaled the waitress for a shot.

Ashton held up two fingers. "To me or to yourself?"

"To both of us. I spent half the night trying to figure out a way this doesn't blow up in my face. I mean, why can't I have a chance? Why is it automatically impossible that this gorgeous, bright, enchanting woman can be mine?"

"Do you need an answer to that question?"

"No," said Riley. "I need a plan."

"That's a whole lot harder than an answer."

"Isn't it?"

The waitress dropped off two shots of whiskey.

Both men downed them and took long swallows of their beer.

"You have to tell her," said Ashton.

"I know." That was the only part of the plan that was clear to Riley.

"Before he tells her."

"He doesn't know I'm seeing her."

"He will."

"He will," Riley agreed. "I was thinking one more date. We've had two, three if you count Monday. And they went great. It all went great."

"So, be honest with her."

"I need a little bit more, first." Riley made a space with his finger and thumb. "One more date. If she knows me better, she'll have some perspective. Maybe, just maybe, she'll question some of the negative things he'll tell her."

Ashton gave a sarcastic chuckle. "You really are cynical."

"I prefer to think of it as realistic."

The Cubs hit a two run homer to take the lead in the bottom of the eight, and a cheer went up in the bar.

"I wish I could stay and help you," Ashton said as the noise died down.

The words surprised Riley. "You going somewhere?"

Ashton nodded, his attention on his glass. "I took a search and rescue job in Alaska."

"You *what*?"

"I gotta get away for a while."

Riley was astonished. "From what? Sunshine and civilization?"

Ashton looked up. "I told you about Jennifer."

"Jennifer? You mean the woman who was once Darci's roommate?"

"I need to clear my head."

"You said you two broke up."

"She dumped me."

"So?"

Ashton normally went through multiple girlfriends a

month. Sometimes he walked away, sometimes they did. In the past, it had never bothered him which way it went.

"I don't get the connection to Alaska," said Riley.

"I keep wanting to call her." Ashton signaled for another round of shots.

"So, call her," There was no harm in trying.

"She was pretty definitive last time we talked."

"So instead you want to forget her." Riley thought he got the logic. "I doubt there are a lot of women in Alaska to help with that. Maybe try California."

Ashton chuckled. "I wish it were that easy. I don't want another woman."

"You don't?"

"I haven't been with anyone since Jennifer." Ashton spun his mug. "That was five months ago."

Riley's jaw went lax. "Say, what?"

"I need to clear my head. I don't exactly know what the deal is. I mean, she's great." Ashton paused. "I guess that's it. She's great. Full stop. And I blew it. And I need to get her out of my head before I can move on."

The waitress breezed over with their shots, setting them efficiently on the table. She seemed to gauge the mood of the table and didn't linger for any chit-chat.

"Why didn't you say something?" Riley asked Ashton.

He could have helped. At least, he thought he could have helped. He'd have tried, even though he wasn't exactly a relationship expert.

"I thought I could walk it off. I *am* going to walk it off. But not here. Not in Chicago."

"Is there anything I can do?"

Ashton held up his shot in a toast.

Riley followed suit.

They clicked the glasses together and downed the whisky.

"Don't fall for Kalissa," said Ashton. "It's not going to end well."

"Gotcha." But Riley knew that train was already barreling out of the station.

"Tell her the truth," said Ashton.

"I will."

"I mean now. Right now. Women need to trust you. If Shane beats you to it, you won't be able to dial it back."

Kalissa had lingered in Riley's yard after work was done on Tuesday, but by eight o'clock, he still hadn't come home. She'd told herself he was obviously dealing with his business problems. She mostly believed herself, but she couldn't quite banish the worry that he'd purposely stayed away.

On Wednesday, she was needed on another job site. She briefly considered making an excuse to go to Riley's again, hoping to run into him, but, thankfully, reason overrode emotion. She wasn't going to go chasing after him as if they were in high school.

She spent the day in Oak Park. It was a big, Tudor style house with peaked roof lines and stone facings. The front yard was sleek and modern. It was a corner lot with a three foot stone retaining wall. The owners wanted the front gardens expanded and the yard re-turfed.

By contrast, the backyard was a traditional English garden. It was terribly overgrown, but it had enormous potential, and they'd be working there with plants that were exotic in Chicago.

It's where Kalissa had focused for the day, wandering through trellises and stepping stones, a burbling pond, creeping vines and a profusion of wildflowers.

She heard her name called and popped her head up from a bed of lavender. The sound was coming from the driveway gate.

"Hello?" she called back.

"Kalissa?"

She recognized her sister's voice. She rose to her feet, peeling off her gloves, delighted with the surprise.

"Hey, Darci. What are you doing here?"

"Right now, I'm trying to find you."

"It's a bit overgrown. Follow the sound of my voice."

"I'm trying."

"Can you see the pond?" Kalissa asked. "The stone pathway leads you right there."

"Oh, yes. Here I am, at the pond."

"Take the right hand path. I'll meet you."

"Got it. Shane," Darci called out. "Take a right at the pond."

"What pond?" came Shane's voice from a greater distance.

Darci came into view, and the two women met under a vine covered pergola that shaded them from the sun.

"This is amazing," said Darci, looking around.

"Don't you love it?"

"I want one."

"Maybe for your birthday," Shane joked, emerging along the path.

"It's charming," said Darci.

"Can you build us one of these?" Shane asked Kalissa.

"Sure," Kalissa joked in return. "Just let me know where on your hundred acres you'd like me to put it."

"Anywhere you want," said Shane. "My mother was very particular about the grounds. Me, not so much. You can do whatever you like."

"You should," said Darci, enthusiasm in her voice. "You should re-do the whole place."

Kalissa laughed. "That would take a few years."

Shane shrugged. "It's a good idea."

Kalissa waved him off. "Right."

"I'm serious," he said, looking like he was. "Take over the grounds."

She felt the need to inject some reality into the conversation. "It would be a full time job."

"For more than one person," he said. "How do you think Megan would feel about it?"

"We are not having this conversation," said Kalissa.

"It's not the most outlandish idea in the world," said Darci. "Your work is terrific. And you'd never have to worry about advertising, finding new clients, dealing with difficult people."

"You're not riding in here on your white, billionaire charger and plucking me out of poverty."

"You're in poverty?" asked Shane.

"I'm exaggerating for effect," said Kalissa. Though compared to them, she was certainly impoverished.

She hadn't told them she and Megan lived above the landscaping shop. She'd feared they'd feel compelled to save her from her frugal circumstances.

"Give it some thought," said Shane. "The offer's out there."

"Sure," Kalissa lied. "I'll think about it."

Shane looked at Darci. "She's not going to think about it."

"She might," said Darci.

"She's too proud. Not that I blame her."

"You two can see me standing here, right?" Kalissa laughed.

"You're going to have to get used to us," said Shane.

"I'm trying," she answered honestly. "But I need to manage my own life."

"I understand," said Shane. "And I admire you for it. But at some point, it gets ridiculous."

Kalissa felt her guard go up. "Earning my own living is not ridiculous."

"You're Darci's sister, Ian's daughter, he—"

"Shane," Darci's tone was unusually sharp. "It can wait."

"It can," Shane agree. "I apologize, Kalissa." He glanced around the yard. "Why don't you tell us what you're doing here?"

Kalissa knew they hadn't stopped by to hear about her landscaping job. "What's going on?" she asked her sister.

"I really want to hear about the garden," said Darci.

"No, you don't."

"Yes, I do."

"You two sound like a couple of eight year olds," said Shane, a trace of laughter in his voice.

"That's because we missed being eight year olds together," said Darci. "Tell me," she said to Kalissa.

Kalissa gave in. "We'll have to cut a lot of it back, and re-do a bunch of the woodwork. You saw the pond? We're going to expand it and create a recirculating creak, with a little water-fall to aerate it. I love the wildflowers. They attract dragon-flies, bumble bees, butterflies. When we're—"

A figure appeared in Kalissa's peripheral vision, standing at the edge of the pergola, silhouetted against the sun.

Kalissa shaded her eyes to see. "Riley?"

A glow of pleasure grew in her chest. She was frighten-ingly glad to see him.

"Hi, Kalissa." His tone was soft, intimate, his focus intent on her. "Megan said you'd be here."

Shane swiftly looked over his shoulder. "*Ellis*?" His voice was incredulous.

Riley's expression froze, his gaze darting to Shane and sticking.

"What are you doing here?" Shane demanded.

Kalissa's chest went hollow. "You two know each other?"

"Yes, I know him," said Shane, turning fully and plant-ing his feet apart. "He's Ellis Aviation, the guy who's been a thorn in my side."

Kalissa didn't understand. "Riley?"

"I need to talk to you," Riley said to Kalissa.

Kalissa took in Darci's tense expression. "What's going on?"

"He's not a good man," Darci said to Kalissa. She looked quite upset.

"He's the scheming competition," Shane barked. "Tell me how you know him."

Kalissa recoiled from the anger in Shane's voice. "We met a couple of weeks ago."

She scrambled her thoughts back to the restaurant that night, trying to remember how it had played out. Riley had though she was Darci. And he'd confronted her, accused her of spying on him.

"By chance," said Riley.

"I just bet it was," said Shane. He shifted, putting himself between Kalissa and Riley.

"We need to talk," Riley said to Kalissa, moving so he could see her.

"I don't think so," said Shane.

"You knew them," she said to Riley, assailed by a feeling of betrayal. "You knew them all along."

"Not the way you think," said Riley.

"What way do I think?"

No wonder Shane was angry. Riley had played her, and she'd fallen for it hook, line and sinker. She'd dated him. She'd slept with him.

"What did you tell him?" asked Shane, his voice bitter.

She hadn't told him anything. What could she tell him? She didn't know anything.

"Leave her alone," demanded Riley.

Darci moved closer to Kalissa, linking their arms.

"*Me* leave her alone?" Shane spat out.

"It's not her fault," said Riley.

Shane's voice lowered, sounding more controlled. "What's your game?"

"*My* game?" Riley scoffed.

Kalissa's throat went tight. She felt a tremor start deep inside her. She couldn't listen to this. She couldn't stand to know she might have compromised Darci and Shane.

Riley had pretended to like her in a bid to undermine her family. Mortification washed over her as she remembered the things they'd done together.

"Do you want to get out of here?" Darci whispered in her ear.

Kalissa gave a jerky nod.

"Let's go." Darci urged her to the side of the pergola, skirting Riley.

"Don't go," he called to her.

"Who *are* you?" she managed, her voice quaking. "Why would you *do* that to me?"

"I came to tell you," he said. "The reason I'm here right now is to tell you the truth."

"You expect me to believe that?" She was through being naive.

"Don't talk to her," said Shane. "Talk to me."

Riley shot him a glare.

Darci urged her forward, and Kalissa went willingly.

Seven

Riley moved to go after Kalissa, but Shane was on him in a second, blocking his path.

"Don't talk to her," Shane growled. "Don't touch her. Don't go near her *ever* again."

"Back off," said Riley, voice tight, sorely tempted to take a swing.

"No, you back off, you son-of-a-bitch."

Riley saw red. He stepped up, only inches from Shane's face. "Are you *out of your mind*? My mother was one of the sweetest, most gentle, hardest working people who ever lived. I don't give a damn what you say to me or about me, but don't you ever, dare—"

"Whoa," Shane drew back, looking shocked. "It's an expression."

"Yeah, right," Riley spat with disgust. "It's just an expression."

"It is."

"Nothing to do with you and me."

It shouldn't have surprised Riley that Shane was feigning ignorance of their relationship. It was all he'd ever done.

Shane's expression hardened again. "*Kalissa* is what has to do with you and me."

Riley's anger warred with regret. He didn't want to cause her any grief. "She didn't tell me a thing. She didn't have to. Your moves are pretty obvious."

"My moves? *My* moves?"

"The engine mounting bracket."

"What engine mounting bracket?"

"You're going to lie about it, too? Come on, Colborn, at least be man enough to admit it when you undermine me."

Shane looked confused. "You're the one who headhunted my guys."

"I did that. And I was up front about it."

"You failed."

"I got a couple of them," said Riley.

"Not the best."

"Not yet."

Shane's tone seemed to moderate. "You're still trying to sink me?"

"You're trying to sink me. Every Bradley lower front engine mounting bracket from every distributor? Not a lot of finesse to that move."

"Somebody bought up *just* the lower fronts?"

"Yeah, you did."

"It wasn't me."

Shane looked so sincere that it gave Riley pause.

"Are you that good at lying?" asked Riley.

"What would be the point of lying?"

"That's what I'm trying to figure out." Riley knew it was going to be fairly easy to confirm.

Shane drew an exasperated sigh. "Stay away from Kalissa. She's got nothing to do with this."

"Agreed." Riley didn't want Kalissa to have anything to do with the feud between him and Shane. "But I'm not staying away from her."

"Oh, yes you are."

Riley sputtered a ragged laugh. "Not happening."

Anger flooded back into Shane's eyes. "Are you looking for a fight?"

"No. But I'm not backing down from one either."

Shane would try to sway Kalissa. Riley couldn't stop that. But he had a side to this story, too.

He wasn't going to tuck his tail between his legs and walk away from what he wanted because his golden-child half-brother demanded it.

Not this time.

"I can protect her," said Shane.

"You don't have to protect her. Not from me." Something

compelled Riley to be honest. "I'm not going to do a thing to hurt her."

"You already have."

"I wish I hadn't. That wasn't my intent. When I take you on, Shane, I'll do it straight up. I'm not hiding behind a woman."

"Again, you already have."

"I was trying to figure out how to tell her."

"That you were plotting against her family? Yeah, I can see how that's a hard subject to bring up."

Riley had been trying to figure out how to tell Kalissa that Shane was his *brother*. There was a root cause to this bad blood. Could they not at least be upfront about that when they were alone?

What exactly was Shane's problem? Was he afraid he was being quoted or recorded, that Riley would defame their father's name or go after the inheritance? Did he resent Riley so much that he couldn't even bring himself to say the words?

Riley knew it was probably all of that.

"This conversation is pointless," he said. He turned to walk away.

He made it only a few steps.

"Was it working?" Shane asked from behind.

Riley stopped. "Was what working?"

"Were you getting to her?"

Riley considered his answer. He turned back. "She likes me."

Shane scowled at him, jaw set. "You hurt her, and I'll annihilate you."

"You're already trying to annihilate me. But my beef is with you. I won't use her as a pawn."

This time, Riley did walk away, out of the yard and around the big house.

He slammed the door of his car and peeled away from the curb, bringing up the revs and increasing his speed until a traffic light forced him to brake. Then he smacked his hand down on the steering wheel.

He didn't doubt for a second that Shane would protect

Kalissa. He had the resources to put an impenetrable wall around her.

Riley had to talk to her. He had to convince her that what they'd shared was real. Yes, he'd stayed silent about Shane. But it wasn't so he could use her. It was so she'd give them a chance to get to know each other.

A chance was all he'd wanted, all he still wanted. A chance to hear the sound of her voice, feel the silk of her skin, and taste the sweetness of her lips all over again.

The driver behind him honked his horn, and Riley hit the gas.

Kalissa was *not* going to dissolve into a puddle of emotion.

"It's no big deal," she said to Darci across the table in the garden tearoom.

Barely five blocks from the Oak Park house, her sister had directed her into a restaurant parking lot. The place was unnaturally serene, with piped flute music, a burbling fountain, white wrought iron furniture and dozens if not hundreds of potted plants decorating the terra cotta brick floor.

"We only met a couple of weeks ago," she said.

Darci waited, and Kalissa recognized the technique.

It was one she used herself when one of her friends was upset. Let them talk their way through it and get it straight in their own head before you offered any advice.

"I know what you're doing," she said to Darci.

Darci smiled. "What am I doing?"

"You're letting me think this through."

"Is that a bad thing?"

"No, it's a strange thing. It's what I usually do with other people."

"Are you getting anywhere?" asked Darci.

"Not really. I wish I was. I mean, he seemed so great. Yeah, it was weird when we first met. He actually thought I was you. And he accused me of spying on him. I guess I pushed the significance of that to the side when I started to like him. I told myself he must have seen your picture in the media, because he said he'd never met you."

"He hasn't."

"But he knows Shane."

"Not really. He's Shane's competition, but I don't think they'd met in person."

Kalissa digested the information. "At least he wasn't lying. Well, about that much, anyway."

The waitress brought them hot tea and scones. Kalissa would have preferred something stronger than Earl Gray, but she didn't want to seem crass.

"Did he lie about other things?" asked Darci, spooning sugar into her tea.

"There's no way to know. Man, it felt like such a whirlwind. I thought...I mean...Okay, this is so embarrassing."

Darci reached out and touched her hand. "We're sisters."

Some of the tension eased in Kalissa. "We are. Not that I know how to be a sister."

"We'll make it up as we go along."

"We can, can't we? It's not like you'll be able to call me on doing it wrong."

Darci smiled into her cup.

Kalissa braced herself, rotating her own cup in its delicate saucer. "I thought I finally knew what it was like to be falling in love. There. I said it. I feel like an idiot."

"I'm so sorry," said Darci.

"It's not your fault."

"For any part Shane's relationship with Riley might have played in messing this up."

"It was messed up to start with. Shane was the only reason Riley gave me a second look."

"I don't believe that for a second." Darci gave a small laugh. "It's weird, trying to compliment someone who looks exactly like you. I was about to tell you, you were beautiful. But that's like complimenting myself."

"You *are* beautiful," said Kalissa.

"Shane thinks so. So, we've got him on our side."

"I read that he was named the most eligible bachelor in Chicago."

"And *he* picked *us*."

"He picked *you*." Kalissa sobered. "You don't suppose the two of them are fighting back there?"

"Maybe," said Darci.

"I meant a fistfight. They both seemed really upset. Maybe we shouldn't have left."

"Quick, gut reaction, don't think about it, who do you want to win?"

Riley.

Kalissa closed her eyes and a sense of longing over-whelmed her. She missed him. She'd started missing him the minute he dropped her off on Monday night.

She'd been so ridiculously happy to see him today. In the split second before Shane had spoken, she'd already imagined Riley's arms around her, holding her tight against his strong body. It had felt so, so good.

"I slept with him," she blurted out.

Darci's brow went up.

"In Lake Forest. We had dinner at this cute little inn. Then we got a room. It was fantastic. Best sex I've ever had."

Darci's mouth twitched in a smile. "Wow. I like being sisters." Then, she grew serious. "I mean, oh, I'm so sorry."

"I don't usually do it that fast. That is…" Kalissa groaned. "I feel like I should defend my morals. I don't sleep around."

"Good to know. Not that I care. I slept with Shane while I was spying on him. That's not exactly admirable."

"You spied on Shane?"

"Long story. I'll tell you about it sometime." Darci tore off a bite of her scone.

"Thank you," Kalissa said softly. "For being here and listening."

"I'm sorry you got hurt."

"I'll get over it." Kalissa hoped this annoying, empty ache would disappear soon. "Darci, he was so good at seduction. I bought into everything he said."

"You weren't expecting him to lie."

"No, I guess not. Did he think I'd have insider information on Colborn Aerospace?"

"You might. You could have. You probably will someday."

"No." Kalissa held up her palm. "You are never, *ever* to tell me anything about Shane's company. Clearly, I'm the weak link."

Darci gave what looked like an amused smile. "We'll see."

"What do you mean, we'll see. Just agree to keep quiet."

"You might need to know someday. And what are the odds someone else will target you to get to Colborn?"

"Small, I suppose." Kalissa's thoughts returned to Riley.

"Zero," said Darci.

"Do you suppose he wanted something specific?"

"He's been undercutting Shane on international contracts. And he tried to hire away some of the Colborn staff."

"He didn't seem underhanded." She sipped her tea and discovered it was now lukewarm. "Then again, I guess he showed me what he wanted me to see."

"A harmless, trustworthy guy."

Memories were coming back to Kalissa. "It took him the longest time to give me his last name. For a while there, I thought he was in the witness protection program, because something seemed off. He told me he was a conspiracy theorist, but it didn't ring true. Then again, I suppose he was the one plotting the conspiracy. And he really downplayed his business. Though, I guess telling me the details would give away his secret. He made it sound small, nothing like Colborn."

"It's a lot smaller than Colborn," said Darci.

"He's ambitious," said Kalissa, guessing he must be jealous of Shane's success.

"He's ruthless and scheming."

Kalissa agreed.

He was also sexy and witty, astute and charming. But she had to forget those qualities. If she didn't, it would be impossible to forget him.

* * *

Riley hated approaching Kalissa out on the street, but he couldn't take the chance of waiting until tomorrow. Shane was sure to put some kind of protection around her. He might even move her behind the walls of his mansion.

Riley was certain she'd never show up at his house to work again. He expected Mosaic to simply walk away from the job, leaving his yard half done.

So he was waiting in the alcove next to the Mosaic shop, under an awning to keep out of the drizzling rain. Megan had gone inside about an hour ago. But she'd been walking, and their pickup wasn't parked out front, so Riley had hope that he hadn't missed Kalissa.

He still wasn't sure what he was going to say. Apologize, sure. But he also had to convince her to give him another chance. He knew it was a long shot, but he had to take it.

A pair of headlights rounded the corner, the beams flashing off the dim building of the narrow street. Water splashed beneath the tires. It was a pickup, and it was the right color.

It pulled into a vacant spot. The driver's door opened, and he tensed as he recognized her, auburn hair cascading forward as she climbed out. He gazed at her slim shoulders and long legs, that pretty profile he'd watched so many times.

She slung a big purse over her shoulder. Then she locked the door and scooted across the street, avoiding puddles along the way.

"Kalissa?" He wanted her to hear his voice and know it was him before she saw a man lurking in the shadows.

She stopped five feet from the curb.

"It's Riley," he said.

She glanced up and down the darkened street. "What are you doing here?"

"I need to talk to you."

"I have nothing to say."

"Please just listen."

She walked determinedly forward. "No."

"Kalissa."

She halted beside him. "What? You're going to tell me some more lies?"

"I want to explain."

"That's pointless. I don't trust you."

"I understand."

Her tone dripped with sarcasm. "How magnanimous of you, to understand why I might not trust a lying jerk who lured me into his bed."

"I didn't—"

"Come on, Riley. You're going to tell me you didn't have sex with me?"

"I meant I didn't lure you."

She lifted her chin. "You're right. I came willingly. What's your point?"

"My point is I'm sorry."

Her voice was brittle. "For having sex with me?"

"No. *No. Never.* I'd have sex with you a thousand times more." He knew the words were wrong, but he couldn't seem to stop them. "I wanted to tell you about Ellis Aviation, about Shane, about everything."

"What stopped you?"

"I knew you'd walk away."

"I *would* have walked away."

"And I didn't want that. You meant too much to me. You *mean* too much to me."

"I meant nothing to you."

The light rain was dampening her hair, glistening when it misted her cheeks.

He reached for her hand, but she jerked it away, hiding it behind her back.

"If you meant nothing to me," he said. "I wouldn't be here."

Instead of responding, she clamped her jaw shut.

"Think about it, Kalissa. My cover's blown. From a business perspective, I'm sunk. There's only one reason for me to be here."

She seemed to ponder his words for a few moments. Then

she spoke. "Just because I can't see the scheme, doesn't mean you're not hatching one."

"Sometimes it does."

"You're too smart for me, Riley. You know things I don't know. You want things I can't understand."

"I want you."

She shook her head. "You already played that card."

"It wasn't a game. Everything between us was true."

"You mean there were no other lies? Only the ones I caught you in? Do I look stupid? Do I act stupid?"

He battled an urge to reach for her. "I was going to tell you. I was trying to figure out the right time and the right way."

"I don't believe that for a second."

"I thought if you got to know me, if I could make you like me, if I had a chance before Shane turned you against me, you might listen to my side of the story."

"You can't make me trust you by lying to me."

Ashton's words echoed inside Riley's head.

"I know that. If I could go back, I'd have told you that first day." He hesitated. "Maybe."

She folded her arms across her chest and pursed her lips with obvious impatience.

"I'm trying to be honest here," he said. "If I could go back, it would be hard. If I told you up front, you'd have never agreed to go out with me."

She gave a sharp nod of agreement.

"And we wouldn't have had that night on the pier, or that drive up the coast, or the night in—"

"Stop it, Riley."

"I can't stop thinking about it."

"You have to stop thinking about it."

"Can you?"

Her slight hesitation told him there was a chance. A very, very small chance he could get through to her.

"Yes," she said in a small voice.

"Now who's lying?"

She opened her mouth.

He reached out and put his finger across it. "Don't lie to me, Kalissa. I've done enough of that for the both of us."

He couldn't stop himself. He stepped forward.

"I can't," she said, a catch in her voice.

"I'm not asking you to trust me."

Her eyes were wide and luminous in the pale streetlights. She looked frightened and uncertain. He hated himself for doing that to her.

"All I ask is a chance," he said, struggling to control his own emotions. "Don't walk away."

She blinked rapidly, and he drew her into his arms.

"I'm so sorry, Kalissa. I'd give anything to start over, to make circumstances different."

Her voice was muffled against him. "We can't."

"I want to figure this out."

"She's my sister, Riley." But her body had molded against his.

"I know."

"I've only just found her."

"I know that too." He tightened his hold.

"You're trying to harm them."

He wasn't. Then again, he was. He was trying to harm Colborn Aerospace. "That has nothing to do with you."

She drew back to look up at him. "You can't put me in the middle."

"I won't," he pledged.

"You are."

"Kalissa." He brought his palm to her cheek.

Her skin was so smooth, so soft, warming beneath his touch.

His gaze moved to her lips.

It might be the last time. He couldn't let it be the last time. He simply couldn't let this be the last time he kissed her.

He brought his mouth to hers, and he pulled her tight. Her lips were hot and soft and sweet. They parted beneath his, and he kissed her deeply, arousal coming to life within him.

He longed to be back in Lake Forest. He wished they'd never come home.

"Ms. Smith?" came a deep officious male voice.

Footsteps beat toward them.

Kalissa jerked back, obviously alarmed.

"Don't worry," said Riley, knowing exactly what was going on. "He'll be from Shane."

Riley straightened to glare at the man, keeping one arm around Kalissa. "Are you trying to scare her to death?"

"I'm paid to protect her."

Kalissa turned to the tall, angular man. "Protect me from what? Who are you?"

"Your brother-in-law Shane Colborn asked me to make sure you're safe at all times." The man eyed Riley up and down.

"No way," said Kalissa.

"She doesn't want you around," said Riley.

"My name is Patrick Garrison, ma'am. I'm with West Shore Security Services."

Kalissa retrieved her phone. "Please tell me you're not armed."

"You don't need to worry about that, ma'am."

She dialed her phone.

Riley met the man's steady gaze. He got that the guy was a professional bodyguard, but he wasn't about to be intimidated.

"Darci?" said Kalissa. "I'm standing outside my apartment looking at a guy from West Shore Security."

She glanced at Riley.

"I don't think he would," she said into the phone.

Patrick Garrison's phone rang.

He answered. "Yes, sir?" There was a pause. "She is." Another pause, and Garrison's gaze went to Riley. "I'm assuming it's him."

"It's me," said Riley.

"This is ludicrous," Kalissa said to Darci.

"I will, sir," said Garrison. "Absolutely." He ended the call.

Riley's phone rang.

Kalissa carried on with Darci. "Tell Shane to, I don't know, fire him, I guess."

Garrison smirked.

Riley checked the screen on his phone. The number was blocked.

He put it to his ear. "Yeah?"

"It's Shane."

"No kidding."

"What are you doing?"

"I'm talking to Kalissa. What are *you* doing?"

"I'm protecting Kalissa."

"So am I," said Riley.

"From you."

"She doesn't need it. She doesn't want it."

Kalissa was gaping at Riley while she spoke to Darci. "Tell me that's not Shane talking to Riley."

Riley gave her a nod of affirmation.

"*Darci.*"

Garrison stepped back, and Riley could swear he looked amused.

Kalissa held up a hand. "This is *ludicrous*!"

"Tell her to come stay with us," said Shane.

"I'm not going to—" But then Riley realized Shane was talking to Darci.

"Don't to it," Riley said to Kalissa.

"What?" Kalissa said into the phone. "No." Her gaze darted to Garrison. "I'm sure he will, but—"

"She's staying here," Riley said to Shane.

"It's none of your business," replied Shane.

"Riley's not going to hurt me," Kalissa insisted.

"They think I'll *hurt* you?" Riley couldn't believe they'd even suggest it. "Quit messing with her mind," he said to Shane.

"No," Kalissa repeated into the phone.

"What are you saying to her?" Riley asked Shane. He immediately realized it was a stupid question. "What are they saying?" he asked Kalissa instead.

"They want me to have Garrison drive me to the mansion."

"You already told them no." Then Riley looked at his phone and realized he didn't need to be talking to Shane. He hung up.

"We need to talk," he told Kalissa with conviction. Then he glared at Garrison. "She's perfectly safe."

The man crossed his arms over his chest. "Oh, I know she's going to be safe."

"Say goodbye to Darci," said Riley.

"I have to go," Kalissa said into the phone. "I have to talk to Riley." She paused. "Five minutes." She silently nodded. "I will. Bye."

Thankfully, she ended the call.

"Back off," Riley said to Garrison.

Garrison looked to Kalissa.

"This is foolish," she said.

"No argument from me, ma'am."

"Can you." She made a shooing motion with her hands. "Just back off a bit?"

"Whatever you say, ma'am."

"Clearly, that's not going to be the case," Kalissa mumbled.

Despite everything, Riley's mouth twitched at the comical situation.

"You think this is funny?" she demanded.

"No. Sorry."

"It's not funny."

"I know."

"Stop laughing."

"I did."

She stared at him, her chest rising and falling with deep breaths.

"Can we talk?" he asked, sobering completely. "Just the two of us? Somewhere…not here?"

She didn't answer. Uncertainty flicked through her beautiful eyes.

He knew he had to convince her. "We need to talk."

"I can't trust you."

"I know. I understand. But you were there, Kalissa. This isn't nothing. We can't just walk away."

She still didn't answer.

He reached out and took her hand.

She looked down. It took her a long time to speak. "It can't be tonight."

He was disappointed in that, but he could live with it. "When?"

"Can I call you?"

"*Will* you call me?"

She frowned.

"If you don't, I'm calling you."

She squeezed her eyes shut. "Okay."

He eased in. "I want to kiss you."

"You can't."

"I want it bad."

She opened her eyes. "Garrison might shoot you."

"He won't risk hitting you."

"I think he's probably a good shot."

Garrison was likely an excellent shot. Riley couldn't imagine Shane hiring anyone but the best.

But he didn't want to kiss her in front of her bodyguard. He wanted to kiss her all alone, preferably in a bedroom, his bedroom. He bit back a curse.

"I'll miss you every second," he told her instead.

"I'm not making any promises."

"I know."

He had to accept her hesitation. He had a long way to go before she'd trust him again. And Shane would be working against him. Shane would do everything in his power to make sure Riley failed.

Eight

In the morning, Patrick Garrison was waiting on the sidewalk outside Mosaic Landscaping.

Kalissa's surprise was quickly overtaken by concern. "Please tell me you haven't been here all night."

"Hello?" said Megan. "This is the guy?"

"This is the guy," said Kalissa. "Did you stay here?" she asked Garrison.

"I'm Megan." Megan held out her hand.

"I just came on shift, ma'am," Garrison said to Kalissa, briefly shaking Megan's hand.

"Ma'am?" asked Megan. "He calls you ma'am."

"For some reason," said Kalissa. "So, how does this work? Are you actually planning to follow me around all day long?"

There was the faintest of smirks on Garrison's face. "It helps if I stay close to you."

"You know this is unnecessary, right?" She realized he was being paid by Shane, and he had to do his job, but he had to have seen last night that Riley was no real threat.

She couldn't figure out Riley's angle. It was pretty obvious he'd romanced her in the hope she'd get him information on Colborn Aerospace. But he was caught now, so there was no way that was ever happening.

So, why did he persist? Why the pretty words last night? And why had she, even for a moment, considered he might be sincere?

"You're actually her bodyguard," said Megan, peering at Garrison as if he was from another planet.

Garrison stared back, his expression inscrutable. He didn't answer.

"Are you armed?" asked Megan.

"He doesn't like to talk about that," said Kalissa. "Should I drive slow so you can keep up?"

Garrison's smirk was back. "Not necessary. But it'll be easier if you ride with me."

Megan's expression brightened. "Like our chauffeur?"

Garrison frowned at her. "I was referring to Ms. Smith."

Megan linked her arm with Kalissa's. "I'm with her. You can drive us both."

"He's not driving us anywhere."

Kalissa could put up with Garrison following her around. He seemed quiet and well-behaved. She didn't think he'd get in the way. And, quite frankly, she didn't have the energy to fight Shane. She needed all her brain power to work through the situation with Riley.

"We can stop for canned pomerinis on the way home," said Megan. "He'd be our designated driver."

"Canned pomerinis?" asked Garrison.

"Pomegranate and candy apple martinis," said Megan.

Garrison shuddered. "Is that a joke?"

Kalissa started for their pickup truck. "I'll try not to lose you," she said.

Garrison immediately turned his back on Megan and fell into step beside Kalissa. "I'd prefer it if you'd come with me," he said.

"We need the tools in the back of the truck."

"I can drive the truck."

"The gearshift is a bit tricky."

He stifled a cough. "I think I can manage."

"Oh, let him drive," said Megan. "I was serious about the canned pomerinis."

"I wouldn't advise excessive amounts of alcohol," said Garrison, stopping as Kalissa stopped next to the truck.

"You're not going to be a buzz kill, are you?" asked Megan.

Garrison looked down at her. "Do you *have* to be part of this conversation?"

"Hey, buddy. I'm on your side."

Megan raised a playful fist to sock him on the arm. Kalissa had seen her do it a thousand times.

Garrison's hand moved like lightning, grabbing her wrist.

"Whoa," said Megan, taking a half step back.

"That was impressive," said Kalissa.

Garrison immediately let Megan go. "I'm not trying to be impressive. I'm just trying to do my job." His attention was on Kalissa. "And that job will be a whole lot easier if you let me drive. So, what do you say?"

Since it was by far the longest speech she'd heard him make, she decided to take it seriously.

She had no reason to make Garrison's life difficult. She could argue this out with Shane, or she could make the best of it. A couple of days, a week max, it should all blow over. Riley would give up, Shane would stop worrying, and Garrison could go back to guarding people who were in some kind of real danger.

"Fine," she agreed, digging into the pocket of her blue jeans. "The brakes are spongy, there's a shudder when you take a hard left, and if you hit a bump, it'll jump out of second."

Megan pulled open the passenger door and climbed to the middle of the bench seat.

Kalissa was happy to take the window.

"I'm calling Riley," she told Garrison as he slammed the driver's door shut. "You might want to get another job lined up, because this'll be over soon."

"To the Oak Park jobsite," said Megan in a theatrical voice. "It's nine-thirty-seven—"

"I know where it is," said Garrison.

"How do you know that?"

He shot Megan a look of disbelief.

"You investigated us?"

Kalissa found Riley's number in her contact list.

"I broke into your computer," said Garrison.

"No way," said Megan.

Kalissa put the phone to her ear.

"Saw everything," said Garrison.

"Not the—" Megan clamped her jaw shut, clearly trying to figure out it Garrison was messing with her.

"Kalissa?" Riley answered.

"Hi," she said, her chest going warm at the sound of his voice.

She angled herself toward the window as the truck gained speed down the street. She realized Garrison could still hear her, but she didn't want him to see her expression on top of everything else.

"How are you?" asked Riley.

"I'm okay." She drew a breath, telling herself to get a grip.

This wasn't a budding romance. It was a failed attempt at espionage. Her next move wasn't to swoon in Riley's arms. It was to convince him she was a lost cause. He'd have to find some other advantage over Shane.

"When can I see you?" he asked.

"The sooner the better."

His voice brightened. "Yeah?"

"Not for that."

"I'm not making any assumptions."

"You said we had to talk."

"We do."

"I agree." She glanced at Megan and Garrison.

Both were silent and focused out the windshield. But she knew they had to be listening to every word. Megan, because she knew Kalissa was still attracted to Riley, and Garrison because he'd want a heads-up regarding her plans.

"I'll come to you," said Riley. "Are you at home?"

"We're on our way to Oak Park."

"We?"

"Me, Megan and Garrison."

Riley chuckled, sounding more amused than worried. "I gotta hand it to Shane."

The words puzzled her. "What do you mean?"

"I'd have done exactly the same thing. If I was him, I wouldn't let you anywhere near me."

"Should I be staying away?"

"No way. I'm not him, I'm me, and I want to get as close to you as possible."

"I don't even know how to take that."

"What's he saying?" asked Garrison.

Kalissa gave the man a warning glare.

"This isn't what you think, Kalissa," said Riley.

"What do I think?"

"I'm heading for the car. I'm on my way. Let's talk when I get there."

"I'm only going to tell you this can't happen." For some reason, her stomach cramped over the words.

"I know that."

"I can't trust you."

"I know that too."

Her mind went to last night, and their kiss, and his words. And she couldn't help having second thoughts about the wisdom of seeing him in person. He seemed to know exactly what to say to throw her off.

There was no possible way this was a coincidence. He was using her, and she needed to end it quickly and completely.

"I'll see you there." She quit the call before he could answer.

"What are you going to say to him?" asked Megan, giving Kalissa's shoulder a rub.

"I'm going to tell him to go away and never bother me again."

"Works for me," said Garrison.

"Works for me too," said Kalissa, mentally crossing her fingers.

She had to stick to her guns. She couldn't let herself get lost in Riley's sexy voice or look too deeply into his dark eyes, because then she'd start wondering, she'd start hoping—

"Do you think there's any chance at all it's a coincidence?" she said out loud.

"No," said Garrison.

"That what's a coincidence?" asked Megan.

"Riley falling for me, me falling for him, completely independent of anything between him and Shane."

"No," Garrison repeated.

"How do you mean?" asked Megan.

Garrison frowned at Megan. "Don't encourage her."

"What encourage her? I'm asking a simple question."

"To which the answer is no. He's Colborn's business rival. He lied about who he was. He romanced and seduced her. That's one impossible coincidence." Garrison downshifted to take a tight corner.

"I'm not saying it was." Megan's voice rose. "I'm just asking what she means." She turned to Kalissa. "What do you mean?"

"I mean…" Kalissa wasn't exactly sure what she meant.

She was grasping at straws. She wanted to believe Riley liked her, that he was attracted to her, that he'd somehow fallen for her in record time. Because the alternative was that he was cruel and she was foolish. She didn't want either of those things to be true.

Riley caught the grim expression on Garrison's face as Kalissa opened the passenger door of his sports car.

"If you get in, it'll give us some privacy," he told her.

She gave a nod of agreement and sat down.

Garrison took a step toward them, then another.

Kalissa shut the door.

Riley gave a half second's hesitation, then he let his instincts kick in. He turned the key, shoved it into first and peeled away from the curb.

"What are you *doing*?" Kalissa demanded.

"Giving us some privacy," he said as he glanced in the rear view mirror.

Garrison was sprinting back to Kalissa's truck, leaping into the driver's seat.

"Riley!"

"Do up your seatbelt."

"Stop."

He swung the sports car around a tight corner, barely slowing for the stop sign. "I can't stop. We need a few minutes alone."

"So, you're *kidnapping* me."

"Technically, yeah, I guess." He glanced in the rear view mirror.

"You *guess*?"

There was no way the pickup truck could outrace him, but he didn't dare hit a stoplight. "I had to get you away from him."

"Why? He was only going to stand there and watch."

A red light loomed up, and Riley switched to the right lane, pausing for a truck to go by before swinging in front of a minivan. The driver hit the horn.

"Riley!"

"I didn't want him to stand there and watch."

"This is dangerous."

"There's nothing to be afraid of."

"You mean, other than death in a fiery crash?"

There was a distinct edge of sarcasm to her tone. He couldn't tell if she was frightened or angry.

"We're not going to crash. I'll slow down in a minute."

He wove his way through traffic, gaining speed on a straight stretch.

Her cell phone rang.

"Damn." He knew there was no way to stop her from answering.

She pulled it out, shaking her head at him in annoyance as she put it to her ear. "Hello?"

She paused a moment. "You don't think I already *told* him to stop?"

"Is it Garrison or Shane," asked Riley, re-evaluating his rash plan.

This may have been a mistake. He could have been more subtle, gaining Kalissa's and maybe even Garrison's trust before trying to get her alone. But he'd known this might be his last chance.

"No," Kalissa said into the phone. "Don't call the police. He's stopping. He told me he'd let me out."

Riley glanced at her in surprise, trying to guess what she was doing, afraid to hope it could be in his favor. But he was too busy driving to look at her for long.

"I'll call you back," she said into the phone. Then she disconnected. "You've got Garrison completely freaked out."

They came up on the river, and he swung off the main road, onto the forest road that he knew led to a small parking lot.

"I swear I just want to talk."

"You think this will make me *listen*?"

"I don't know what I'm thinking," he confessed. "This was spur of the moment."

He slowed the vehicle as they drove into the near empty parking lot. His heart rate calmed and the adrenaline stopped pumping.

"I can't stand the thought of Shane keeping you away from me," he said. "I can't stand it, Kalissa. If it's your choice, fine. If you can't get past my secrets, and you want me gone, I'm gone. But it's not going to be *him*. It's not going to be *his* choice."

He swung into a spot on the far side of a parking lot that bordered an oak and aspen forest. Then he shut off the engine and silence rose around them.

"What do you think you can say that could possibly make a difference?" she asked.

He turned in his seat, struggling to compose something in his mind.

"I can only tell you the truth. And I'll admit it, for a moment, *only* a moment, the day when I called to hire you, I thought about how I could use you against Shane."

"You can't."

"I never tried. It was for a few seconds, max. But then I realized why I was really calling you. I liked you. I was attracted to you. I wanted to get to know you."

"We'd had a five minute conversation on the restaurant patio. And you were mostly yelling at me."

"I know. But there was something there." Again, he searched for the words. "It was an instantaneous attraction."

"How convenient for you."

He'd known this wasn't going to be easy, and he struggled to stay calm. "Did I ask about Shane? In all the time we were together, did I ever once bring up Colborn Aerospace?"

"I'm sure you were leading up to that."

"I wasn't. I knew you'd eventually tell them my name. And I knew when you did all hell would break loose."

"So, why didn't you tell me?"

"I was planning to—"

"I mean, before you slept with me. That would have been a nice thing to do, Riley."

"I didn't plan to sleep with you."

She scoffed out an exclamation of disbelief. "We just happened to have dinner at a romantic little inn up the coast?"

"I didn't even think of that place until we were halfway there. I was winging it at that point."

"And I should believe this, why?"

Her phone rang again.

"Don't answer it."

She lifted the phone. "He'll only zero in on my GPS."

"That's in the movies."

"I think it's real." She raised the phone to her ear.

"I'm fine," she said.

Riley wondered if it was still Garrison, or if Shane had joined the party.

Then she held the phone out to him.

"Which one?" he mouthed.

That earned him a flash of a grin. "It's Garrison."

Riley figured he had little to lose. He accepted the phone. "Yeah?"

Garrison's tone was rigid. "Whatever it is you're doing, stop."

"We're talking."

"Where are you?"

"Yeah, right."

"Listen, I'm the most reasonable guy you get to deal with on this. And if you harm one hair on her head."

"What is *with* that? I don't care what my— I don't care what Shane told you, I am *not* going to hurt Kalissa."

Riley took in her flushed cheeks, her slightly mussed hair, the worn T-shirt and those faded jeans atop well used leather work boots. He'd do anything for her, anything, he realized—including let her go.

He looked straight into her eyes, still talking into the phone. "I've said my piece. I'm done. We're in the river parking lot, across from the pond."

The line went dead.

Kalissa blinked at him in obvious confusion.

He handed back her phone. "There's nothing more I can say. The ball's in your court."

He levered out of the car and walked to the passenger side, opening her door to wait for Garrison.

As she stepped out, he tried to muster up a smile. "I do still want to kiss you."

She was close, just a foot away. The sunshine reflected off her creamy skin and glowed in her deep, green eyes.

"I don't know what to think."

"I can't help you there." He smoothed his palm across her cheek, maybe for the last time. "I know what I think, and I know I'm being honest. But you're going to have to make up your own mind."

He heard a vehicle turn the corner beyond the trees.

Her voice was soft. "I'm scared."

"Don't be scared. It's just a relationship. You can break it off any old time you want."

"I don't want to hurt Darci."

"Do you think Darci wants to hurt you? We can make this work, Kalissa. You and me can just be you and me. We never have to talk about them. We don't even have to mention their names. There's no way for me to use you against Shane if we never even mention their names."

The truck pulled into the parking lot.

She swallowed. She opened her mouth, then she closed it again. "I'll call you."

He gave a self-deprecating smile. "That's what you said last time."

"And, I did."

He had to admit, it was true.

"And, I will," she said. "I need to talk to Darci, but then I'll call you."

The vehicle drew closer, tires crunching on the gravel.

"Can I kiss you?"

She nodded.

He leaned in, knowing he had only seconds before Garrison broke them apart.

It was a sweet kiss, an encouraging kiss. It wasn't anywhere near to the kiss he wanted from her, but it told him there was hope. She wasn't yet walking away.

The truck door slammed shut, and she drew back.

Riley stepped aside, watching as she turned and made her way to Garrison.

Once she was safely inside the truck, Garrison advanced on Riley.

Riley braced himself.

"That was gutsy," said Garrison, a note of what sounded like admiration in his tone as he came to a halt a few feet away.

The remark took Riley by surprise, and he didn't know how to answer.

Garrison's voice hardened. "Do it again, and I'll take your head off."

Riley knew how to answer that one. "Not necessary. Though I would like to see you try."

Garrison gave a brief glance to the truck, and his expression relaxed a fraction. "She didn't tell you to get lost?"

"She didn't."

Garrison nodded thoughtfully, and he turned back to Riley. "I've got my job to do. And I'm a professional. And I report to Shane Colborn." He paused. "But I gotta tell you. I think I'm pullin' for you."

With that, he walked away, leaving Riley momentarily stunned.

Garrison climbed into the driver's seat, reversing and heading for the exit.

Riley's gaze followed Kalissa's profile through the window. He hoped she'd call soon. He didn't think he could stand to wait.

"We agreed not to talk about you," Kalissa told her sister. "Either of you." She glanced to Shane who was glowering in the corner of the great room's alcove.

It was hard not to be intimidated by the castle-like size of the mansion, not to mention the stone work and the hundreds of antiques.

"How exactly is that going to work?" asked Darci.

"I'm not sure," Kalissa admitted. "There are some bugs we have to work out."

Darci looked uncomfortable. It was clear she was choosing her words carefully. "You know he's got some kind of vendetta against Shane."

"I don't want to hurt or upset you," said Kalissa.

"This isn't about me."

"I'm upset," said Shane, striding closer.

"No, you're not," said Darci. "You're ticked off."

"Oh, yes, I'm ticked off. He's an opportunistic lowlife. He's taking advantage of your sister."

"I know what I'm getting into," said Kalissa.

"Do you?" asked Shane. "He's doing this because of me. I can't stand by and—"

"It's not up to you," said Darci.

"I'm talking about a date," said Kalissa. "A simple date."

"She's not going to give away corporate secrets," said Darci.

"I'm not worried about corporate secrets," said Shane. "I'm worried about Kalissa. How are you going to feel when he breaks her heart?"

"My eyes are wide open," said Kalissa.

Shane clamped his jaw.

"If you like him," Darci said to Kalissa. "Then, you like him. It's not up to us to decide."

"I didn't mean for this to happen." Kalissa felt compelled to explain to her sister. "But there's something about him."

She wasn't ready to walk away from Riley. She figured it was a fifty-fifty chance he was conning her. But she was on alert now. She wouldn't accept anything he said at face value.

"Garrison stays," said Shane.

"Well, that's going to put a damper on the evening," said Darci.

"I'm in absolutely no danger from Riley," said Kalissa.

"It's beyond Riley," said Shane. "You're my sister-in-law. Somebody might mistake you for Darci. Riley or no Riley, you're vulnerable."

Kalissa came to her feet. "Now you're just making things up. You and Darci don't have any protection."

There was a beat of silence.

"We do," said Darci. "It's discreet. But we have a security staff."

"Seriously?"

Darci nodded.

Kalissa sat back down. "Are you in any danger?"

"No more or less than anyone else with family wealth."

"Am *I* in danger?" Kalissa had never thought through the implications of being a carbon copy of Darci.

"It's nothing we can't handle," said Shane. "And it's definitely nothing specific. If there's ever anything specific, we'll tell you up front."

Kalissa struggled to wrap her head around the situation. She couldn't.

She swallowed. "Is Garrison going to be my BFF?"

Darci cracked a smile.

"Is there a problem with Garrison?" asked Shane. "We can assign someone else to you."

Kalissa waved away the suggestion. "Garrison is fine. I kind of like him. He argues with Megan a lot, but it's rather entertaining."

"When are you going out with Riley?" Darci asked.

A warm feeling pulsed through Kalissa when she thought

about having another date. She couldn't help a soft smile. "I'm guessing as soon as I call him."

Darci and Shane exchanged a look.

"See what I mean," said Shane, conviction in his tone.

Kalissa looked to Darci in confusion.

"He thinks you've fallen head over heels and you're not thinking straight."

"I always think straight." And right now Kalissa's thoughts were moving straight to Riley. She couldn't wait to call him.

"Get him to come here," said Shane.

Kalissa couldn't believe she'd heard right. "That would be a colossally bad idea."

"You can't chaperone them, darling," said Darci.

"You should stay the night," said Shane. "Better yet, move in."

Kalissa couldn't help but laugh.

"Or we can get you a suite in the building in town. It's centrally located, and security is great."

"You'd *get* me a suite?" Kalissa couldn't believe she'd heard him right.

"Yes. In the same building we're in."

"On the waterfront? In downtown Chicago?" The real estate values there were astronomical.

"You could visit Darci anytime you wanted, without even going outside in the winter."

"I can't get used to this," Kalissa said to Darci.

"It is a bit disorienting," Darci agreed. "We'd let you pay rent."

"You're on *his* side?"

"It's a nice building. We'd get two bedrooms. Megan could stay there with you."

Kalissa stood again, pacing toward the corner fireplace. "This is so wrong."

"It's an apartment," said Darci. "Sure, maybe a bit bigger and a bit better location than most. But it's still just a rental apartment."

"No way," said Kalissa.

"I'm going to browse around," said Darci.

"Good idea, sweetheart."

"You two are ganging up on me?" There was no way Kalissa could go along with this.

Darci gave a shrug. "What can I say? I'm sleeping with him. He'll always be on my side."

"*You're* the one on *his* side."

"Same difference."

"No, it's not."

"If it makes you feel any better," said Darci. "I want you to be my neighbor just as much as Shane does."

"It's a bad idea to rent from family." Kalissa was sure she'd read that somewhere.

"What could go wrong?" asked Darci. "No matter what happens, you'll still be my sister."

"We'll do it through a management company," said Shane. "You'll never even know Colborn owns the place."

Kalissa braced herself on the brick fireplace hearth. "What part of *no* are you not hearing?"

Darci looked at Shane. "No? Did she say no? I'm not sure I'm familiar with that concept."

Shane looked amused. "People don't say no to us, Kalissa."

"That's because you're filthy rich and can fire everybody around you."

"Sure. That and we donate to a lot of charities."

"I am *not* a charity."

"And this isn't a donation. It's the purchase of a capital asset, which you will rent from us."

"We're paying three-hundred and fifty dollars a month for the suite above the store."

"Deal," said Shane, and he held out his hand, walking toward her.

"Nice try."

"Deal, Kalissa," he repeated. "I'm going to do whatever it takes to make your sister happy."

Kalissa clasped her own hands firmly behind her back, refusing to shake on it. "In this instance, I am not helping you out one bit."

Nine

Riley couldn't help but smile at Kalissa's curiosity as she gazed out the window of his car at the darkening city.

"It would be easier," she said. "If I could just tell Garrison where we're going."

"Why should I make things easy for Garrison?"

Riley had nothing against Garrison. He really did seem like a decent guy. But who wanted a bodyguard on a date?

She glanced in the passenger side rear view mirror. "He's stuck at the last traffic light."

"I'm sure he's got a tracking device on you."

"What?" Kalissa glanced down at herself. "Really? Where?"

"Probably your phone."

"This is weird," she said.

"No kidding. It's a whole different world when you have their kind of wealth."

"It sounds like you're no slouch either, Mr. Ellis Aviation." There was an accusation in her tone.

"I'm slowly getting there."

"Not as slowly as me. So, where are we going, money-bags? Some swanky, five-star restaurant? Maybe a champagne harbor cruise?"

"We're heading away from the lake."

"So, not a cruise." She peered out the windows on all sides. "Not a lot of restaurants around here either. By the way, I can't believe you took me out for a pretzel dog on our first date."

"You liked the pretzel dog."

"Sure, but you could have done something a bit more impressive."

"It wasn't impressive?"

"Not really."

"Then I don't think you're going to be too impressed to-night either."

She straightened in her seat. "Well, this doesn't sound promising for you."

"Problem is, you come across as being so down to earth."

She cocked her head. "That's a problem?"

"I don't want to spoil you."

"How incredibly considerate."

"We can't have you turning into a princess."

"I don't know about that. Maybe I'd be a good princess."

"Then let your brother-in-law buy you a penthouse."

"You have to pretend you don't know about that. I shouldn't have said anything. I promised you and I wouldn't talk about them." Her voice was pure worry.

"But he seemed okay that we're going out?"

"Not particularly. But I'm an adult, and he can't exactly hold me prisoner."

Riley glanced in his mirror, seeing Garrison's headlights coming up fast. "He's giving it an awfully good shot."

"He claims it's safety, that him and Darci also—" Kalissa clamped her mouth shut.

"I don't think it's a state secret that the Colborns have se-curity," said Riley.

"It's safer if I don't talk about them at all."

"That's a bit impractical. Are you going to talk to them about me?"

"Depends."

"On what?"

She gave him a saucy smile. "On what you do."

"You mean on what *we* do. Do women share that kind of thing with their sisters?"

"I don't know. Maybe. Probably. I've never been a sister before."

"Then I'll be sure to give you something to talk about."

He steered the car into a huge, arena parking lot.

"What is this?"

Then she obviously spotted the sign. "The Fall Home and Garden Show?"

He grinned. "I thought you might like to check out the competition."

A smile grew on her face. "This could be fun."

"And only fifteen bucks apiece to get in."

She feigned shock. "You're spending a whole thirty dollars?"

"I might even spring for some pizza."

"Be still my beating heart."

"And an ice-cream bar," he added, finding an empty spot three rows from the entrance.

They left the car and crossed to the main door. There, Riley purchased their tickets, and Kalissa went first through the turnstile.

"Dude," hissed a voice from behind him. It was Garrison, gesturing to the pop-up banners. "Are you *sure* about this?"

"Completely," said Riley.

"Do you need me to float you a loan?"

"No, I don't need a loan. She's going to love it."

"Have you *seen* her sister's house?"

"Once," said Riley, hating the memory he recalled. "But I don't think Kalissa is like that."

"They're *all* like that."

"I'm taking my chances." Riley moved through the turnstile.

He shook off the memory of his teenage trip to the mansion, and Dalton's disdainful face. Instead, he focused on Kalissa, coming up behind her and putting his hand on the small of her back.

"What first?" he asked.

"The outdoors section," she said. "I'm thinking we should put a pond in your yard."

"I'd go for a gas fire pit." He wasn't crazy about ponds.

"You don't want a waterfall, maybe some ceramic frogs?" She started walking along the wide, crowded aisle.

"I liked that gazebo thing in Oak Park."

She slowed to look at a rock pond display.

"I'm not putting in a pond," he stated.

"But it's adorable," she sing-songed. "Look at the birds, and the little train."

"Maybe if I was seven."

"I thought you wanted kids someday."

"That means I have to buy a train?"

"No. But you should put in a pond."

"Look at this?" he tightened the arm around her waist and propelled her to the fireplace display on the opposite side of the aisle. "Toasty warm, and all that comfy furniture."

"I do like the stonework," she said.

"Could you put a cover over it?" he asked, serious about the question. "Maybe set it up next to the spa?"

She considered the display piece. "With some kind of a chimney, sure."

"I'm thinking of cool, rainy nights. A naked dip in the hot tub, then wrapping up in cozy, white robes, a mug of hot chocolate laced with brandy while we snuggle on a cushy, outdoor sofa."

"Forget about the train," she said, her voice breathless. "You're getting a fireplace."

He tightened his hold and gave her a kiss on the temple. "Who cares about the kids."

"They'd love a waterfall and a pool."

"For that, I'd need a bigger yard."

"It's your fantasy. Fantasize a bigger yard."

"I'm serious."

"About what?"

"The fire pit."

She pulled away to look up at him. "Really?"

"Would you like it?"

"Sure. Who wouldn't? But they're pretty expensive."

He glanced at the nearby displays. "There are more over there. Tell me what you like. What would suit my yard?"

"Okay." She nodded, her expression growing serious as she walked toward the other backyard mock-ups.

He paused to take in the view from behind, her long legs and those cute, spike heeled sandals, the way her bright blue skirt flowed over her hips, the little geometric cut-outs near her shoulder blades, and the smooth, tanned length of her arms.

His gaze settled on her profile, and the way her shiny hair curled around her cheeks and the nape of her neck. She was a cut above everyone else in the room.

And then it hit him dead center of his brain. Garrison was right. Riley had screwed up.

This was definitely not the way a woman dressed to wander the home and garden show.

He caught up to her and put an arm around her shoulders. "Let's get out of here."

She looked up. "Huh?"

"Let's go."

"But I like this one." She pointed to a fireplace.

"This isn't much of a date."

"It's a fine date."

Fine? Yeah, that's what he was going for. *Fine*.

She pointed. "Look at those colors in the ashlar stone."

He didn't bother. "Let's go find some dinner."

"We should at least pick up a brochure."

He pulled out his phone and snapped the barcode. "Got it. I know a great place."

"Last time you said that, we ended up in a hotel room."

"No hotel. Just a restaurant."

Her forehead furrowed.

"Unless, that is, you want a hotel. Then I'm all in. We can do room service if you'd like."

She looked around the cavernous show. "We've barely seen anything here. What changed your mind?"

"You."

"How did I do that?"

"You're not dressed for a trade show."

"Well, I didn't expect to be going to a trade show."

"What did you expect?"

"I don't know."

He took her hand in his, holding it between them, moving up close and lowering his voice. "You picked that particular dress to wear tonight. What did you expect, Kalissa?"

Her eyes were luminous as she gazed up at him. "Honestly, that I wouldn't have it on for long."

Riley's brain flat-lined. Then it restarted, and the breath whooshed into his lungs. He moved for the exit, pulling her with him.

"Hello?" She quickly sorted her feet out beneath her.

"When I'm not meeting your expectations," he said. "You should speak up."

She laughed. "The trade show was fun."

"This date is obviously not reaching its potential."

"Are we going for dinner now?" she asked with mock innocence.

"Yeah, right." They breezed through the exit.

"What about Garrison?"

"Garrison can take care of himself."

"I mean, what's he going to think?"

"He'll think we're leaving."

"Where are we going?" she asked.

"My place. I will feed you. Eventually. But you can't toss something like that out on the table and not expect me to react."

"I expected you to react."

"Good."

"I'm not naïve, Riley."

"Good again." Every minute he was with her, he liked her better and better.

The wind was rushing through the parking lot. The smell of rain was in the air, and thunder rumbled in the distance as they quickly made their way to the car. He opened the passenger door.

She paused and placed the palm of her hand against his chest. "I really did like the trade show."

He covered her hand as the first fat raindrops hit the windshield. "You're going to like my place a lot better."

She smiled. "I like confidence in a man."

"Good. Get in."

She sat down, and he pushed the door shut, all but trotting around to the driver's side.

Lightning flashed in the distance, thunder catching up as he started the engine.

The rain opened up on top of them.

"Nice timing," she said.

He checked out the flashes above them and put the wipers on high. "We're driving straight into it."

"Better than running straight into it. Boy, did I pick the wrong shoes."

He stopped to look down at her feet. "I'll carry you. I love those shoes."

She wiggled her foot back and forth. "Bit of a change from the work boots."

"Bit of a change," he agreed, putting the car into reverse, telling himself he could wait the twenty minutes it took to get home. But then he was definitely peeling those shoes from her feet.

A puddle was already forming at the exit to the arena parking lot. He splashed through it, and took a left onto the four lane road, heading for the lineup of traffic lights, hoping for as many greens as possible.

"I was daydreaming about a spa day," she said. "A new pedicure, maybe a facial."

The first light was green, and he silently celebrated. "Why not do it?"

"It's expensive. But someday…"

"Someday when your company hits it big."

"Exactly."

He wanted to tell her he'd pay for a spa day. He'd happily pay for a dozen of them to make her smile like that. But Shane was busy trying to throw material things her way, and Riley didn't want to be like Shane.

The second light was green, and there was little traffic. He knew if he kept to the speed limit, the lights were fairly well synchronized along this stretch.

"It'll happen for you," he told her.

"We had to hire three more casual guys. Word of mouth seems to be making a difference for us."

"You do very nice work."

An air horn blasted through the dark.

Riley instantly spotted the bright headlights bearing down on Kalisssa's side of the car. Then he saw the skid of the on-coming truck's tires as they hydroplaned over the water, jack-knifing the trailer under the red light and into the intersection. It was headed right for them.

He slammed on his brakes and cranked the steering wheel. "Hang on!"

He turned them on a dime. The huge truck grill took out the driver's door mirror, and the car bounced against the angle of the trailer. It barely registered that they hadn't been crushed, when Riley's back tire hit a curb, flipping the car onto its roof, spinning them twice around on the median.

The first things that registered in Kalissa's mind were the strange voices above her head. For a second, she thought it was a television, then she wondered why there was a party going on in her bedroom.

She tried to open her eyes, but the light was too bright.

"Kalissa?" It was Darci's voice. "Honey, can you hear me?"

"Darci?" Kalissa's throat was parched and sore, and her voice came out as a croak.

"It's me."

Kalissa felt a cool hand smooth across her forehead. "What are you doing here?"

Could she be having a dream?

"There was an accident," said Darci. "You're in a hospital."

Kalissa opened, her eyes, recoiling and blinking rapidly against the bright light. She quickly turned her face to the side. There were half a dozen people beside her bed, more beyond the glass windows of the room. Most wore hospital uniforms, many were moving around. Machines beeped and carts rolled along the corridor.

"How—" And then she spotted Riley in the small crowd. He had bandages on his hand and forehead, and his shirt was torn.

It all came back to her, the bright lights, the loud horn. She'd thought for sure she was about to die.

"Riley?" she managed.

"He's here," said Darci. "He only has scrapes and bruises."

"He could have killed her," came Shane's distinct voice.

Kalissa shook her head. "He saved me. The truck, it was—" She stopped talking to swallow. Why did her throat hurt so bad?

"You got hit on the head," said Darci. "But they took x-rays, nothing is broken."

"My throat hurts."

A nurse appeared. "Would you like some water?"

Kalissa nodded.

The nurse quickly produced a plastic glass with a straw.

"Can I sit up?" Kalissa's body ached, but nothing was acutely painful. She felt a little silly lying here while everyone stood around her.

The nurse nodded, and Shane pressed the button at the foot of the bed, cranking her up.

She took a sip of the water. It was cool and soothing.

"I don't understand why my throat hurts."

"You screamed," said Riley from a few feet away. "Pretty long and loud when we flipped over."

"Haven't you done enough?" Shane demanded.

"We flipped over?" Kalissa asked Riley, struggling to remember.

He moved forward, giving Shane a glare on the way past. "How much do you remember?"

"The big truck. The lights. The horn." She stopped to take a shuddering breath. "It was coming straight for me."

"His tires were hydroplaning," said Riley. "The driver couldn't stop for the light. He's pretty shaken up."

"Does he know we're okay?"

"He does."

"If you hadn't turned so fast." Kalissa tried to keep the tremor from her voice.

Riley took her hand. "I turned," he said.

She nodded. There wasn't a doubt in her mind that he'd saved her life.

"You're coming home with us," said Shane.

"No." She didn't want to go home with Darci and Shane. She still wanted to go home with Riley.

"It's not a choice," said Shane.

"I'm—"

Riley gently squeezed her hand. "Let them take care of you."

"I don't need to be taken care of. I'm fine. Nothing's broken."

"You're not fine. Not yet."

"I am."

"Try to move something, anything."

She frowned at him. But then she braced her hand on the rail and shifted on the bed. Pain shot through her lower back, radiating down her arms and legs and up her neck.

"Ouch," she admitted.

Darci patted her knee. "Just for a day or two. Let us pamper you."

"Megan needs me."

"Not like this, she doesn't," said Shane.

Kalissa looked up at Riley. She might be in pain, but she still wanted to be with him.

The look in his eyes told her he understood. He leaned down to whisper in her ear. "I'm not going anywhere. You heal. I'll be waiting."

She wanted to wrap her arms around his neck and hold him close, but it was too painful to move.

"You about done, Ellis?" asked Shane, voice hard.

Riley straightened. "Not nearly. But she needs her rest. Take her home."

The two men glared at each other.

She wanted to tell them to stop, to please stop, but she didn't have the energy.

Then Riley's expression became gentle. He leaned down and gave her a kiss. "Call me when you feel like it."

"I already feel like it."

He smiled at her. "Sleep first, eat something, maybe take a long bath. I'm sending you a gift card for a spa."

She opened her mouth to protest, but he put his finger across her lips.

"Don't bother," he said. And then he was gone.

Darci and a nurse helped her into her clothes. She felt even more silly riding in a wheelchair. Then again, she really didn't feel like walking all the way to the parking lot.

Garrison was in the hallway standing next to Shane, and he gave her an encouraging smile as they wheeled her out.

"Next time," Shane told Garrison in an undertone. "She rides with you."

"I'll try," said Garrison. "But, for what it's worth, the guy's got skills. He knows what he's doing."

"You said he was reckless."

"I said he was fast. I don't know how he avoided the semi. I thought she was dead."

Shane swore.

"That's enough," said Darci. "We're not going to keep re-hashing it. Kalissa is fine."

"I'm fine," Kalissa said from the wheelchair.

Or she would be fine. She'd be fine after something to eat and a good night's sleep.

The elevator doors slid open, and Shane took over from the nurse, pushing her over the sill.

"Do you think we could stop for a burger?" she asked. "Benny's on Ponderosa has a drive through."

"We're not going anywhere near Ponderosa," said Shane.

"We can go past Ponderosa," said Darci.

"We're going downtown," said Shane. "There's a deli, a pizza place, or steak and seafood all on the same block as the penthouse."

"I'll take anything on rye," said Kalissa, "with Dijon and tomatoes. Maybe some fries."

"That sounds pretty heavy," said Darci. "Would you rather have soup?"

"I hit my head, not my stomach. And I'm starving."

"We'll get you anything you want," said Shane. For the first time since Kalissa had woken up, his voice was sympathetic.

They descended to the admitting area, waiting while Garrison retrieved an SUV. She and Darci took the back seat, while Shane sat up front. Garrison drove.

She dozed off in the car, and it seemed like only seconds later that Shane was helping her to the penthouse.

Garrison did the sandwich run, and Darci lent her a pair of pajamas. Soon she was tucked in their penthouse guest bedroom in a comfy, king sized, four poster bed.

Darci arrived in the dim room with bags of sandwiches.

"Does Megan know what happened?" Kalissa asked.

Her purse and phone were on the other side of the room, and she really didn't feel like getting up again.

"Riley called her from the hospital."

"That was nice of him."

"You smile when you say that." Darci took a seat at the foot of the bed, leaning back against one of the posts.

"Did I?"

"You smiled when you saw him at the hospital too."

"I like him," said Kalissa.

Darci dug into the bags, extracting a wrapped sandwich. She leaned forward to hand it to Kalissa.

"Thank you," said Kalissa. "I'm really hungry."

Darci opened a second bag, this one brown instead of white. And Kalissa noticed two different logos on the outsides.

"He went to two places?" she asked.

"They don't have fries at the deli."

Kalissa was embarrassed. "He didn't have to hunt down fries for me."

"You wanted fries, Garrison got you fries."

"I can see I'm going to have to be careful what I ask for around here."

"You had a bad night. It's the least we could do."

"No," Kalissa disagreed, even as she accepted a carton of fries. "This is the *most* you could do. You're treating me like a princess."

"You are a princess."

Kalissa smiled, remembering Riley's comment.

"What?" asked Darci.

"Something Riley said."

Darci waited.

"He said he didn't want me to turn into a princess."

Darci munched down a fry. "Is he worried about that?"

"I told him you wanted to get me an apartment. I'm sorry. I know I promised I wouldn't talk to him about you. But that seemed innocuous. And I was rattled by the offer."

"You can talk to him about us," said Darci. "It seems overly complicated not to."

"I don't want to give anything away."

Darci's expression was serious. "Do you trust him?"

"I don't know. I like him. I'm attracted to him. I want to trust him. But I really don't know him."

Darci nodded. "It could still be a con. He's got a lot of motivation to get into your good graces." She took a bite of her sandwich.

"It doesn't seem like a con. At least, not when I'm with him. I was going to sleep with him again tonight."

Darci appeared at ease with the revelation. "You're over twenty-one."

Kalissa bit down on the stack of ham and turkey. It was tasty and supremely satisfying.

"What are you going to do now?" asked Darci.

"Eat then sleep."

"We should invite him over here."

"Him?"

"Riley."

Kalissa didn't think she could be hearing right. "We?"

"Shane and me. And you, of course."

Kalissa shook her head. "Bad idea. Very bad idea. I didn't take you for an idealist."

"I'm not," said Darci. "But it's pretty obvious there's something building between the two of you, and—"

"And it might die a quick death. Maybe my memory of the sex is skewed. He might not be that good."

"Did you drink a lot that night?"

"Some wine, nothing out of the ordinary."

"Then he was probably that good."

"I was about to find out." Kalissa grinned self-consciously. "If not for that stupid semi."

Fear came over Darci's expression. "When Garrison called, I was so scared. I thought I'd found you only to lose you."

Kalissa's heart contracted. She leaned forward and reached for her sister.

Darci's hand met hers halfway, and they held tight.

"You're not going to lose me," Kalissa promised.

"And you're not going to lose me. Not over Riley or Colborn Aerospace or anything else. Shane will come around."

"You *are* an idealist."

"Maybe." Darci's eyes twinkled with mischief as she smiled. "But I can pretty much get Shane to do whatever I want."

Ten

"I nearly killed her," Riley said to Ashton.

"The truck driver nearly killed her," Ashton responded. "You got her out of the way."

It was after five, but the afternoon shift was humming outside Riley's office at Ellis Aviation. They'd just won another European contract, and Riley was in talks with a Canadian airline for ten E-22s. The prospect of the Canadian contract should have been a relief. But it would only exacerbate the problem with the engine mounting bracket shortage.

"I'm not going to stay away from her," he told Ashton.

"Who's saying you should?"

The door suddenly opened, startling them both.

Shane stood there, his shoulders stiff, jaw clenched.

Riley came to his feet.

Shane spared a fleeting glance at Ashton.

"I wanted to tell you man to man," said Shane.

"I've said everything I'm going to say to you about Kalissa. Do your worst." Riley narrowed his gaze. "And then I'll do mine."

Shane took three paces into the room. "This isn't about Kalissa."

The statement took Riley by surprise.

Shane kept talking. "It's about the engine mounting brackets."

Riley narrowed in on Shane's expression. "What about them?"

"You were right."

"I know." Riley hadn't guessed about Shane's involvement, he knew it for certain.

"One of my department heads," said Shane. "He thought he was helping."

"He was helping. Helping you, at least."

Shane shook his head. "It wasn't on my orders."

Riley didn't believe it for a second. "Are you here to throw him under the bus?"

"I had no idea."

"You got caught, Shane. Own up to it."

"Are you calling me a liar?"

"Yes."

Shane's complexion turned ruddy.

Ashton stood.

Shane looked Ashton up and down. "I don't want any trouble."

"You look like you do," said Ashton.

"It's fine," said Riley. He wasn't afraid of Shane.

"I fired him for it," said Shane. "But you go ahead and believe whatever you want."

"I generally do."

"I don't do business that way. I don't have to."

Riley hated to admit it, but Shane's words had a ring of sincerity to them. Shane might resent the hell out of Riley but, aside from that ludicrous tell-all book by the ex-girlfriend, Riley had never heard talk of Shane being dishonest.

Then again, there was one way to find out for sure.

"Then I guess you'd be willing to walk it back?" Riley asked. "Sell them to me at wholesale?"

It was clear Shane hadn't anticipated the request. "You haven't found another source?" Then he gave a harsh laugh. "You obviously haven't found another source, or else you'd force me to keep my capital tied up."

"I found another source," said Riley. "But at a higher cost."

"So you're suggesting we help each other?"

"I'm suggesting we don't harm each other."

"That'll be novel," said Shane.

"Won't it just?"

They both stood their ground, until Shane gave a sharp nod.

Riley's opinion of him went up the smallest of notches. "You actually fired him?"

Shane's nod was grim. "There are lines you don't cross."

Riley tried to square Shane's apparent moral framework with a man who continued to shun him as a half-brother. He couldn't.

Shane stared out the office window to the plant floor. "It's bigger than I expected."

"We're growing," said Riley.

"Tetralast robotics?" asked Shane.

"Maybe."

Shane turned and gave him a knowing smirk. "We've got them too."

"You going to give me a tour of Colborn?"

"Nope."

"Then stop checking out my shop."

Shane put his back to the window. "You can talk to David Gorman about the engine mounting brackets."

"And Kalissa?" asked Riley, hoping this might be an opportunity to clear the air.

"She says she's going home tomorrow."

"I know."

"Garrison's staying with her."

"I know that too. For the record, I don't disagree."

"That's *such* a relief," Shane drawled.

Riley considered his brother. "I think it's our destiny to duke it out. And I wouldn't care about that, except neither of us can stay away from Kalissa."

"You can stay away from her."

"No." Riley shook his head. "I can't."

Shane seemed to think for a minute. "We could ignore each other," he offered.

The suggestion struck Riley as elegantly ironic. "I guess it's worked well enough for the last thirty years."

Shane's gaze narrowed in what looked like puzzlement but had to be irritation. He was obviously intent on keeping up the façade through thick and thin.

Fine with Riley. Right now, he was only interested in Kalissa.

* * *

A hurricane lamp flickered in the center of the hewn, polished table, and the perimeter lighting glowed orange against rustic walls of the steakhouse. Kalissa's big, leather chair was soft and comfortable, the music was pleasant and the conversation from the other diners was muted in the distance.

"I'm not trying to be clever this time," said Riley from across the table. "I'm not trying to be richer or poorer than I really am."

"Were you trying to be clever before?" she asked.

"I thought the garden show was clever. And I thought the pier would prove to you that I was a regular guy."

"And when you slapped down your credit card for a one-use, designer dress?"

"I was trying to impress you."

"And now?"

"Now." He reached across the table and took her hands in his. He had sexy hands, square, strong, smooth to the touch.

"Now I only want you to be comfortable."

"I am comfortable. These chairs are great."

"You're not sore?"

"I'm back to normal." She was at the job site most of the day with Megan, and she still felt fine. "I suppose I'm a little spoiled from staying at the penthouse. There's a chance I've turned into a princess."

He gave her hands a squeeze. "Whatever will we do about that?"

"My single bed and the bare light bulb above the Mosaic shop should cure me."

"Is that where you're planning to sleep?"

"Did you think I'd go back to Darci's?" She was surprised that he'd assume that about her.

"No." He drew out the word, putting a wealth of meaning into his tone as he smoothed the pad of his finger across her knuckles.

"Ahhh, you have a third option."

"I have a third option."

Kalissa had a feeling she was going to like the third option.

"You two ought to be ashamed of yourselves!" The strident voice of a woman interrupted them.

Kalissa's glance shot up to see a rotund, neatly dressed, fifty something woman bearing down on their table.

"Excuse me?" she asked in surprise.

"Ma'am, this is a private dinner," said Riley.

"Shameless," said the woman, smacking their joined hands. "Utterly shameless."

Riley jumped to his feet. "I'm going to ask you politely to—"

"What do you think you're doing?" a male voice boomed.

This time it was a man, likely in his thirties. He was tall, burly, wearing an expensive suit with a silk tie encircling his thick neck. He grasped Riley's arm.

Riley wrenched away. "Back off."

"Don't touch my mother," boomed the man.

"Tell your mother this is a private dinner."

"I'm telling your husband," the woman barked at Kalissa.

"I don't have a husband," Kalissa responded.

Another large man joined the first, boxing Riley against the table.

A waiter rushed over. "Is there a problem here?"

"Shane Colborn is a good man," said the woman. "He donated to the animal shelter." She suddenly grabbed Kalissa's wine glass, tossing the merlot, splashing Kalissa in the chest.

Riley jerked forward, and the two men lunged, one of them hitting him square in the stomach.

"Riley," Kalissa yelled.

Next thing she knew, a strong arm was around her shoulders.

"Take her," Riley yelled above her head. "Get her out of here." He returned the man's punch, then he ducked as the second man aimed a shot at his head.

Kalissa struggled against the arm.

"It's me," Garrison rumbled in her ear. "Come on."

"No." She wasn't abandoning Riley.

"I need you safe."

"No!"

"Then I can help him."

Reality hit Kalissa, and she started to move willingly away from the table. "Go," she said to Garrison. "Go back."

He banged open a black, swinging door that led to the kitchen.

"Keep her in here," he ordered a man in a chef's uniform.

The man nodded, and Garrison disappeared back through the door.

Kalissa couldn't believe it. How could it be happening? This was a classy place. How could a misunderstanding degenerate into a fist fight?

Shouts came through the door. Glass broke and something thudded against a wall.

The chef was on the phone, talking to the police, asking for immediate assistance. Kalissa was terrified for Riley and Garrison. She was desperate to see what was going on, but she was afraid the sight of her would only make things worse.

Then the two of them all but exploded through the doorway. Sweaty and disheveled, they each grasped one of her arms.

"Nearest exit?" Riley shouted to the chef.

"Fire exit." He pointed with his thumb. "But you'll set off the alarm."

"Okay by me," said Garrison, and the two of them pulled Kalissa along, her feet barely touching the floor.

"Are you guys okay?" she asked breathlessly as they wound their way around counters, grills and produce bins.

The entire staff had stopped working and gaped at them as they passed.

"We're fine," said Riley. "Keep going."

"Here," said Garrison, pointing to a door.

Riley pushed on the crash bar and shoved it open. An alarm sounded, and a light flashed above.

They rushed down a flight of wooden stairs, ending up in an alleyway.

"My car's right there," said Garrison.

"You parked in the alley?" Kalissa asked.

"I always park in the alley. It makes for a quick exit."

"This has happened before?" She had a hard time wrapping her head around that.

"Mostly with rock stars," said Garrison.

He opened a back door, and Riley pushed Kalissa inside. He followed her.

Garrison jumped in up front.

Riley turned to her, while Garrison started the engine.

"Are you hurt?" he asked.

"I'm fine. But I don't think my dress survived." The pale blue fabric was stained with red wine.

Riley cracked a smile, while Garrison glanced in the rear view mirror, a sparkle in his eyes.

"That woman was nasty," said Kalissa. "Not to mention judgmental."

Then both men coughed out a laugh.

"It wasn't funny," said Kalissa. "That was embarrassing."

"You didn't do anything to be embarrassed about," said Riley.

"Do we need to talk to the police?" she asked.

It felt as if they were fleeing the scene of a crime.

"I'll take care of it," said Garrison. "I know a bunch of guys at the precinct."

"Thanks for your help in there," said Riley.

"Thanks for yours," Garrison returned. "It caught me off guard. I wasn't expecting trouble in a place like that." He paused. "Lesson learned."

"I should have worn black," said Kalissa. "Lesson learned."

"The dress is replaceable," said Riley.

"What am I supposed to do, stay locked inside my house?" It wasn't like she could stop looking like Darci.

"I'm going to recommend you two do an interview," said Garrison. "Something on network television. We'll get the story out there, with your picture together, so people know there's two of you. That way this kind of thing will stop happening." He changed lanes and then retrieved his cell phone.

Riley leaned in and squeezed Kalissa's hand. "Are you sure you're okay?"

"I'm peachy. Hungry, but peachy. Any chance we're going by a drive-through?"

"We are *not* getting fast food tonight."

Garrison spoke into his phone. "There was a disturbance at the restaurant."

"You'd rather I starve?" asked Kalissa.

"She's fine," said Garrison. "She's with me. We're in the car."

"We'll go someplace else," said Riley. "Someplace quiet and discreet."

"That place was quiet and discreet."

"Got it," said Garrison, and he ended the call. He pocketed his phone. "Shane wants me to bring her to the penthouse."

"No," said Riley with a definitive shake of his head. "Our last date ended with her at Shane's penthouse. It's not happening again."

"Maybe I should just go home," said Kalissa, trying not to sound self-pitying.

"Take us to the Emerald Hotel," said Riley. "It has a secure floor, and we can order room service."

Garrison answered with a nod. Then he gave a wry smile. "Well, that'll be a fun conversation for me to have with Shane."

"Tell him I insisted," said Riley.

"Tell him *I* insisted," said Kalissa. She'd only seen the Emerald Hotel from the outside, but it was stately and elegant. She had high hopes for the room service menu.

Maybe they could salvage this date after all.

Riley checked in while Garrison waited.

Kalissa had taken a seat in the corner of the lobby. She was hunched over, clearly self-conscious about her stained dress. It was probably just as well she was keeping a low profile, Riley decided. She looked like an extra from a low budget horror flick—an adorable extra, for sure. But at first glance, somebody might dial 911.

"She's not going home tomorrow," Riley said to Garrison as they walked away from the counter.

"She's never going home," said Garrison.

Riley agreed on that. Making her relationship to Darci public would solve one set of problems, but it would create another. The sister-in-law of a prominent city billionaire couldn't live above a landscaping shop in a sketchy part of town.

"Tell Shane to arrange whatever it takes," said Riley. "I won't fight him on it."

"I doubt I'll have to tell Shane anything."

"True enough," said Riley as they left the check-in counter. This was one instance where Shane's take-charge attitude was a plus. "Can you let Megan know she won't be home tonight?"

"Will do."

Kalissa saw them approaching and came to her feet.

"I'll call you in the morning," Riley said to Garrison.

"Stay put until we talk."

"No problem." Riley would happily keep Kalissa safe and cloistered inside a hotel room for as long as it took.

Garrison peeled off with a wave, and Riley took her hand. "Elevator's this way."

"My life is completely out of control," she said as she fell into step with him.

"For tonight, it's completely under control."

"I'm in a five star hotel, in a stained dress, with no luggage and a vigilante grandmother after me."

A uniformed attendant checked the key card before allowing Riley to swipe it and open the secure floor elevator.

"Is he armed?" Kalissa whispered, glancing back as they walked through the doorway into the cherry paneled, gilded mirror elevator.

"I have no idea."

There was a single button on the panel for the thirty-second floor.

"Even if he's not," she said. "I bet he can keep the rogue grandmothers out."

"I'm betting he can too. You're not nervous are you?"

"I'm annoyed, and I'm sticky, but I'm not nervous."

He took in the big stain. "We really are going to have to replace that dress."

"Do you suppose the room will have bathrobes?"

"I'm sure it will."

The elevator came to a stop, the doors gliding open.

"Because I'd really love to take a shower and change."

"Go for it."

The suite was a very short walk, and Riley swiped the key.

The door opened to a big, bright living room with peach and gold sofas, an oak dining table for six, and a gas fireplace with a pale, fieldstone hearth. There were paintings on the walls and decorator touches in the lamps and knickknacks. A set of double doors at the far end led to the bedroom.

Kalissa stopped in the foyer and stared around the place. "Why didn't you just get a regular room?"

He latched the door behind them. "There are no regular rooms on this floor."

"This is enormous."

"I doubt we'll get lost."

"How much—"

"Don't worry about it."

"But—"

"You're safe here. That's all that matters. And nobody is going to bother us." He shrugged out of his jacket and tossed it on the arm chair. Then he loosened his tie. "We're going to relax and enjoy the rest of the evening."

She looked down at her ruined dress. "I'm definitely getting out of this."

He pointed to the bedroom doors. "Try in there."

She drew a resigned sigh, then she gave him a brave smile and headed into the bedroom.

Riley eased down on the sofa, shaking out his skinned knuckles and checking his phone for messages.

"They have robes," she called from the depths of the bedroom. She sounded excited.

Riley chuckled to himself. In a place like this, he could probably have an entire wardrobe sent up for her. But she was going to look great in the simple white bathrobe.

He heard the water go on, and he couldn't help picturing her in the shower, water glistening on her skin, soap suds coursing over her breasts, down her stomach, lower...

He shook his head, telling himself to focus on something else. There were a few messages from work, and he opened one of them, hitting a link to a financial report.

"Riley?" she called.

"Yeah?"

"You've got to come and see—"

He was on his feet halfway across the room before she finished the sentence.

"—the shower heads in here. Oh, hi."

Her smile was bright, and she was completely naked, standing inside the oversize, tiled cubicle.

"They shoot out from everywhere." She pointed to the half dozen spray nozzles.

He stripped off his tie and started on the shirt buttons.

"You're coming in?" she asked sweetly, her eyes dancing with mischief as she backed under the spray.

"I hope you're not too hungry," he told her, tugging off his pants.

She gave a mock pout. "It's happening a lot lately. I'm getting used to it."

"Here's a tip." He stepped into the hot spray. "Don't get naked and wet." He slid his arms around her hot, dripping body. "And don't be so incredibly gorgeous if you want me to focus on food."

She grinned and wound her arms around his neck. "Who says I'm hungry for food?"

She was hot and slick and soft against him, all curves and sweet spots. He ran his hands from her shoulders, to her back, over the curve of her rear, down the tops of her thighs.

"I've missed you," she whispered.

He hugged her tight, cradling her head against his chest, desperate to absorb and memorize everything, her scent, her touch, her taste. He blocked the spray with his back, tipping her chin, kissing her deeply.

Her tongue tangled with his, while her hands slid down his body, kneading his thighs, moving between them while the water rushed along his skin.

"Oh, sweetheart," he groaned. "Don't—"

"Don't?" There was a smile in her voice, and her grip tightened. "Are you sure? Don't?"

He groaned, gritting his teeth against the avalanche of sensations. "You're playing with fire."

"So, burn me."

He drew back to look at her.

Her eyes were opaque, her pupils dilated. Her skin was flushed, her lips dark red and parted, and her hair was mussed in a damp halo around her face.

"Do it now," she whispered. "Right now."

He lifted her, stepping forward so that her back was braced against the tile wall, wrapping her legs around his hips. Waiting was no longer an option, and he entered her in one smooth stroke.

"Riley," she moaned, clinging to him as he moved. "Yes. Oh, so yes."

"You have no idea how much I've missed you."

He kissed her neck, tasting its sweetness with the hot water droplets. He braced her firmly, increasing his pace, desire singing through his bloodstream, pushing him forward, blocking out everything but Kalissa.

"Faster," she told him. "Harder. Just…Oh…"

He increased their pace, the water pounding on his back, her breath in his ear, her scent surrounding him.

And then she cried out, her entire body convulsing around him.

He followed her over the edge, clinging tight as wave after

wave of ecstasy nearly buckled his knees. The pulses gradually subsided, and he realized his grip on her was too tight.

He eased back. "Sorry."

"For *what*?"

"It felt like I was crushing you."

"I didn't notice."

He smiled into her face and smoothed back her wet hair. "You are amazing."

"You're no slouch yourself."

"That was fast."

Her grin widened. "That was great. And I figure we've got all night."

"You figure right." He gave her a kiss.

"Do you think a girl could get a steak around here? Or maybe some chicken or pasta?"

He backed up so they were both under the spray again. "I'd say this girl could get pretty much anything she wanted."

Kalissa sat next to Riley on the king sized bed. They were both wrapped in hotel robes, finishing their wine while she flipped through news channels on the flat screen.

"Who do you think would want to interview us?" she asked.

She understood Garrison's plan, but she wasn't sure there'd be that much public interest in her and Darci.

"Any of the talk shows in Chicago," said Riley.

"I don't much like talk shows."

"You don't have to like them to be on one."

She continued flipping channels, through a couple of sitcoms and some sports games. "I like garden shows."

"No surprise there."

"And the ones with people buying real estate. That looks like a lot of fun."

"You want to buy some real estate?"

"It's not in my immediate future. But the people always seem really happy on those shows. It's usually a couple, sometimes some kids. They're embarking on a new chapter of their lives. I don't know, there's an energy to it all."

"Maybe you and Darci should go real estate shopping together. You could bring along a camera crew."

"Oh, sure. They could show the pathetic, impoverished relative being rescued by her benevolent, wealthy sister."

"That's not what I meant."

She knew it wasn't. And she was trying not to be sensitive. But she valued her independence, and it felt like it was eroding away.

He reached over and touched the bottom of her chin, gently urging her to look at him. "Hey."

"I know it's not what you meant." She regretted her reaction.

"Darci doesn't want to upset you. Even Shane doesn't want to upset you."

It wasn't what they did, it was who they were that was messing with her life.

"I'll handle it," she said with determination. "I am handling it."

"I've no doubt you will," he said. Then his tone changed. "But you do understand that your life has changed."

She focused her gaze on her lap, rolling the robe's flat belt into a spiral. "It doesn't have to change that much."

"It already has."

She fought a growing panic in the pit of her stomach. "I don't care about their money. I don't want their money."

"I think they know you're not a gold-digger."

"I can take care of myself."

"Under normal circumstances, yes. But these are not normal circumstances."

She didn't answer. She wanted to argue that tonight was an anomaly. What were the chances she'd run into another rabid Shane Colborn fan who felt it their duty to protect his marriage?

But she still remembered the day at the discount store. It was going to happen again, probably not every day, and probably not so dramatically, but there were going to be mix-ups. And she might find herself in embarrassing or dangerous circumstances again.

Riley tucked her hair behind one ear, giving him a better view of her profile. "You have to let Shane protect you."

"You hate Shane."

"I don't hate Shane. I don't like him. Okay, maybe I hate him. But that doesn't make him wrong."

"He wants me to landscape his mansion."

"That doesn't surprise me."

She unrolled the belt and started over. "He wants that to be my full time job."

"If I had a mansion," said Riley. "I'd want you to landscape it too."

"Would you try to buy me an apartment?"

"I'd buy you anything you wanted."

"Then thank goodness you're not a billionaire. I'd be a spoiled princess in no time."

Riley was silent for a long time, and for some reason, the silence felt tense.

She let go of the belt and rolled up on her knees, facing him. "If you had a mansion, I'd definitely landscape it for you."

He gave what looked like a weak smile. "Glad to hear it."

She wiggled in, cupping his face in her hands. It was rough with stubble, and his hair had dried in a mess. His eyes were soft gray. She loved his eyes. She loved his mouth. It was so incredibly kissable.

"Again?" he asked in a tone of surprise.

"I was only going to kiss you."

"You're trying to distract me."

That wasn't true. She'd wanted to look at him, touch him, breathe him in. But she wasn't ready to admit how badly she was falling for him.

So, she smiled and pretended it was only about sex. "Is it working?"

He glanced meaningfully down at her gaping robe. "What do you think?"

"I think you turn me on." She kissed his mouth.

He pulled her into his lap. "I think we need to have this conversation."

"You want to talk about sex?"

"I want you to be safe."

"I am safe." She turned so that she was straddling him.

He took a long look at her body through the parted robe.

But then he pulled the two lapels together and held them there. "I want you to go with Garrison tomorrow and then do whatever Shane tells you."

"And if he tells me to stay away from you?"

"Ignore that part."

"He'll move me into his building." It felt fundamentally wrong to let Shane and Darci do that.

"You know you can't stay where you are."

She put her hands over his, easing them from the robe until it fell open again. "I'm staying exactly where I am right now."

"You are shameless."

She leaned forward. "Can we talk about this tomorrow?"

His lips brushed hers. "Say yes."

"Yes."

"Yes, what?"

"Yes, I'll do what I'm told."

His hands moved to bracket her hips. "Do you know how incredibly sexy that sounds?"

"I'm half naked in your bed, and we've been apart for two weeks. Everything I say sounds incredibly sexy."

She kissed him, shifting so that their bodies pressed together.

He spoke softly against her lips. "You are also incredibly right."

Then he enfolded her in his arms, and she let reality slip away.

Eleven

Kalissa knew she had well and truly fallen through the looking glass. She stood next to Megan gaping at the two bedroom apartment.

"It's only a temporary rental," said Darci. "It would be nice, when we buy, to get something on a higher floor."

"I can see the lake clearly from here," said Megan, gesturing out one of the bay windows in the spacious living room.

The apartment was fully furnished, with a forest green sectional sofa, coordinating green and white striped armchairs, glass and brass tables dotting the living area, with a big, round glass topped table in the dining alcove. In the middle of it all, was a round, gas fireplace with beach rocks and a see-through chimney.

The kitchen was decked out with state of the art, stainless steel appliances, a massive island and pure, white countertops. The hallways led to two big bedrooms, each with its own en suite bathroom, and each of which led onto the wrap-around deck.

"We have a right of first refusal on anything that comes up for sale in the building," said Darci. "There are two units expected to be listed next month."

"I know I keep saying this," said Kalissa. "But this is too much. It's too big. It's too opulent."

"It's what was available," said Darci.

"When you buy, can it be something smaller?"

Darci exchanged a glance with Garrison who was standing in the doorway. He was either guarding it or giving the three women a wide berth.

Megan obviously noticed their look. "I don't think they come any smaller," she said to Kalissa.

"I'm not going to be able to get used to this."

"Well, I am," said Megan. "Never mind a bedroom, we each get our own bathroom."

"Which one do you want?" Kalissa asked.

Megan laughed. "Yeah, I think you get the master."

"Not necessarily."

"I'm just along for the ride."

"So am I," said Kalissa.

Darci looked to Garrison again.

He stepped forward. "Megan, I think we should go get some of your things together."

His words seemed to take Megan by surprise. "My things?"

"From the old place. Yours and Kalissa's."

"I'll come help," said Kalissa.

"Stay here with me," said Darci.

"*You're* going to help me pack boxes?" Megan asked Garrison with obvious disbelief.

"They'll need me," said Kalissa.

"I'm going to help you talk to the movers," Garrison said to Megan. "They'll pack the boxes."

"Stay," Darci said to Kalissa. "We've got some things to discuss."

"But…" Kalissa couldn't let everyone else do her work.

"They're professional movers," said Darci. "They won't break anything."

"I'm not worried about breakage."

Garrison opened the door and gestured to Megan.

"I can take a hint," Megan breezily told him as she strode for the door.

"Are you thirsty?" asked Darci.

Kalissa watched the door close behind the pair, feeling like she'd missed something important.

"Thirsty?" she asked.

"There's a wine cooler in the pantry." Darci made her way to the kitchen.

"It has wine in it?" Kalissa asked.

It was early afternoon, but it was one of the strangest days of her life. Wine wouldn't be the worst thing in the world.

"Shane had them move some bottles from the cellar last night."

"These are from the mansion?"

"They are," said Darci, selecting a bottle.

"Not the good stuff."

Darci laughed. "Don't let Shane hear you say that. He'll tell you it's all the good stuff."

Kalissa supposed that was true.

She moved closer to Darci. "You have to slow down. It's making me horribly uncomfortable."

"We should chat," said Darci, pressing the button on an electric corkscrew. "There are glasses hanging above the island."

"How does this place have wine glasses?" Appliances, Kalissa could understand, even furniture and the odd painting. But dishes?

"Sometimes people only rent it for a weekend. It's nice if it has all the amenities."

Kalissa wanted to ask how much they were paying, but she was afraid of the answer. Instead, she retrieved two wine glasses.

Darci crossed to the table. "We'll let it breathe for a minute." She sat down at one end.

Kalissa took the chair next to Darci's. They were padded and upholstered, and ridiculously comfortable for dining chairs.

"I haven't told you much about our father," said Darci.

"That's okay." Kalissa knew that Ian Rivers had been unhappy with his life and not particularly successful.

"No, it's not okay. There are things you need to understand. The first one is that our dad was once very close to Dalton Colborn."

"Really?" The revelation surprised Kalissa. "I thought you only met Shane in the spring."

"I did. Dad and Dalton went to school together. They opened a company together. They invented a turbine together. But then it all fell apart."

"What happened?"

"They fought. Dalton stole the turbine designs, and for some reason our father never went after him. I think he tried at first but gave up."

"So our dad was an engineer?" That was impressive.

"A good one, it turns out. When he died, well, I told you I spied on Shane."

Kalissa nodded.

"I did it to prove Dalton was a criminal, and that Shane's fortune was based on the theft of our father's intellectual property."

Now Kalissa was intrigued. "And that's how you met Shane?"

"He caught me spying."

Kalissa couldn't help but smile. She knew enough about Shane's temper to guess it hadn't been pretty.

"But he fell for you anyway?"

Darci smirked. "I guess I'm irresistible." She lifted the bottle of wine. "But, here's the thing. I had the last laugh. I proved our dad had invented the turbine."

Kalissa sat back in amazement. She had no idea what to say.

Darci started to pour. "You know I own half of Colborn?"

Kalissa didn't know the details, but Shane had made a few jokes about Darci's ownership. "Okay."

"That's not because I married Shane. It's because I could have sued him and won."

"You were going to *sue* Shane?"

Darci set down the bottle. "Here's the thing and, by the way, this is a very fine bottle of wine."

Kalissa glanced reflexively at the label.

"Our dad, your birth father, should rightly have owned half of Colborn." Darci lifted one of the glasses.

Kalissa quickly picked up the other.

"Congratulations, Kalissa Smith. Twenty-five percent of Colborn Aerospace belongs to you."

Kalissa nearly dropped the glass.

She couldn't form a word. She couldn't ask a question. Her vocal cords had frozen completely stiff.

Darci grinned as she touched her glass to Kalissa's.

"*What*?" Kalissa finally managed to sputter.

Darci drank. "We're in this together, sister. Take a drink."

"What? No. *No*."

"Yes," said Darci. "Drink."

Kalissa sat with her jaw hanging open.

Darci pushed the glass toward her. "It's not official until you take a drink."

"It's not official at all."

"Ah, but it is."

Kalissa did take a swallow of her wine. A big one.

Darci set down her glass. "Okay, that was fun."

"Fun? You think that was *fun*?"

"I know it's a bit freaky right at first. But you'll get used to it."

Kalissa came to her feet. "I'll get *used* to being a billionaire? It's not like a new haircut."

"It is, in a way."

Kalissa blinked at her sister in complete stupefaction.

"Well, a radical haircut. You have to start thinking of yourself in a new way. I'm glad you like Garrison, because he's not going away. From now on you won't have to worry about money. You can pay off whatever business debts you have, and grow your business a lot faster than you'd planned. That's all good, right?"

Kalissa dropped back into the chair.

"I'd have another drink if I was you," said Darci.

Kalissa took her advice. "This is insane."

"Yeah." The teasing look went out of Darci's eyes, and she topped up their glasses. "But I've been through it myself, and I'm here to help."

"Could you wake me up?"

That would be the most helpful thing Darci could do at the moment.

"You don't have to do anything right away," said Darci. "Settle in here. There are some papers to sign."

Kalissa felt a ray of hope. "What if I don't sign them?"

Darci shrugged. "It won't help. Shane has very good lawyers. We'll get you one way or the other." Her gaze went soft, eyes almost teary. "Our father would be so thrilled, *so thrilled* by this. We're together. And he's been exonerated. I know it's a lot to take in. But it feels so right. I've never been happier."

Kalissa squeezed her eyes shut. "A billionaire."

"Technically, only a quarter billionaire. But I'm sure you'll find a way to scrape by. First off, there are the clothes. And you'll never have to fly coach again."

Kalissa was too overwhelmed to laugh at the joke. "Who else knows?"

"So far, just me, Shane and a couple of lawyers."

"Can we keep it a secret?"

"For as long as you want. Well, you know, within reason. You don't have to be scared of this, Kalissa."

"Really? Because right now I'm terrified."

"We also told Garrison. It's not a good idea to keep secrets from your security people."

Kalissa could live with that.

"I just want to be normal," she said. Then she did laugh. "All right, as normal as I can be right now. Just for a little while longer."

For some reason, she dreaded telling Riley. He might not care. It might not change things between them. But she wasn't ready to take that chance.

Riley wasn't going to let Shane keep him away from Kalissa. Ellis aviation had just won the Canadian contract, and Shane was going to be massively annoyed. But that wasn't stopping Riley from showing up at her door.

The security desk had his name and let him straight through. So he headed up in the elevator. He'd brought along a large pizza and a six pack of imported beer, guessing Megan would be around on a Sunday night.

It was Megan who opened the door, but there were other voices behind her.

"Hi, Riley." She greeted him with a smile, pulling the door open. "Come on in."

Garrison was also in the room, as were Shane and Darci. Perfect.

"It's Riley," Megan called out, relieving him of the pizza box.

"Yum," she said to him.

Kalissa gave him a smile and rose to her feet, crossing to meet him. Behind her back, Shane scowled. Riley assumed he'd either heard about the new contract or about him and Kalissa having spent the night together. Either way, they'd agreed to ignore each other, and that was exactly what Riley intended to do.

He gave Kalissa a hug and a quick kiss. "Settling in?" he asked her.

"Getting thoroughly spoiled. Did you know The Range Club delivers steak and crab?"

Riley couldn't help but glance at the simple pizza box Megan had set on the dining table. Maybe he should have added the morel mushrooms.

"Didn't know that," he said.

"They were amazing."

"So, you're off corndogs, then?"

She gave him an odd look, and he realized there'd been a defensive edge to his voice.

"Nice place," he said to change the subject.

She glanced around. "It seemed huge at first. But I'm getting used to it."

Riley couldn't help but think that had happened fast. He shot another quick glance in Shane's direction, encountering his hostile stare. Was that his plan? Make her want the good life, knowing that he could give her more than Riley?

"Come on," said Kalissa. "Sit down."

She kept hold of his arm, leading them to one of the sofas.

Directly in front of him were the fireplace and a bay window overlooking the lake. Closer still was Shane's glare.

"I'll give you the tour later," said Kalissa. "But the other rooms are full of boxes."

"That's why we didn't cook," said Megan. "Anybody want pizza?"

Nobody took her up on the offer. Riley was hungry, but he'd wait.

"We don't end up doing a lot of cooking," said Darci.

Unlike Shane, she didn't seem irked with Riley. He hoped that was a good sign.

"I had the best of intentions," she said. While she spoke, Shane took her hand. "But everything is so close and so convenient. It was easy to get lazy."

"You're not lazy," said Shane.

"Well, Kalissa and I are still on a budget," said Megan.

Darci and Kalissa seemed to exchange a look.

"Good thing Colborn has accounts at the nearby restaurants," Shane casually tossed out. "Just give them our name."

Riley couldn't help smirking at that offer. Shane was playing this well.

"We can't do that," said Megan.

She looked at Kalissa, who was gazing at Darci.

"Thanks, Shane," said Kalissa. "That's very nice of you."

Riley felt himself stiffen.

"Are you *kidding*?" asked Megan. "We have carte blanche at five star restaurant takeout?"

"Only if we start using the stairs to wear off the calories," Kalissa said with a laugh that sounded slightly strained.

"Do we need more wine?" Darci asked brightly, coming to her feet.

Shane stood. "I can—"

"No, darling. Kalissa? Can you give me a hand?"

"If you don't need me anymore tonight, Mr. Colborn," Garrison said, rising.

"We're fine," said Shane. "Thanks."

Garrison gave him a nod. Then he turned to Megan. "Do you want me to move that box before I go?"

Megan's brow went up. "Box? Oh, yes please, the box. I'd forgotten about it." She unfolded her legs and pulled herself out of the deep armchair.

Kalissa and Darci went to the kitchen, while Garrison and Megan headed down the hall.

"You think you can keep up the pace?" Shane asked.

"I can afford all the steak and crab she wants."

Shane looked momentarily confused. "I meant the Canadian jet deal."

Riley gave himself a mental shake. "You heard?"

"Of course, I heard. You're spreading yourself pretty thin."

Riley wasn't worried. Well, he wasn't too worried. Maxing out capacity wasn't without its risks. "Maybe I'll hire some of your staff."

"Maybe I'll back out of the Dubai, Britain and California bids. I left myself an out clause. I'm betting you didn't. If you get every contract, it'll force you into late delivery penalties."

"No, you won't." Riley might not like Shane, but it seemed Shane stuck to his own moral code. "If you were going to fight dirty, you'd have kept hold of the engine mounting brackets. Or at least charged me a mark-up."

"It's not the same thing."

"Yeah, it kinda is."

"I'm not backing off," said Shane.

"I'm going to keep growing," said Riley.

"Then we're going to keep fighting."

"I thought we'd agreed to ignore each other."

"You want to sit here and scowl at each other instead?"

"Sure."

"We found a Chateau de Fontaines," Darci called out, breezing back into the room. "Kalissa's bringing you a glass," she said to Riley.

"We should take off," said Shane.

Darci glanced between the two men. She obviously understood the undercurrents, but she was doing her best to keep things light and cheerful.

"Early morning," Shane said to her, his tone implacable.

"You're right," she agreed easily.

"I think the corkscrew ran out of batteries," Kalissa said laughingly as she re-entered the room.

"We're going to say goodnight," Darci told her, moving to give her a quick hug.

Shane followed suit, hugging Kalissa tightly.

Riley found himself rising to his feet. He knew he had no cause to be jealous, but he hated watching another man touch her.

They finally made it out the door, and Kalissa returned her attention to the wine bottle, her tone still chirpy. "I'm not sure how we're going to break into this."

"*What are you doing*?" he asked.

"Huh?" she looked up.

"Is that all it takes? Expensive wine, free steak and crab?" Her expression fell. "What's the matter with you?"

"You can see what he's doing, can't you?" Riley advanced on her.

"Helping me out?"

"Throwing luxury in your face and hoping you'll like it."

"You want me to hate Chateau de Fontaines?"

"I brought beer. You used to like beer."

"Who says I don't like beer?"

Voices sounded down the hallway, and Riley remembered Megan and Garrison were still there.

"I also brought pizza, ordinary, normal, inexpensive pizza."

"Are you hungry?" she asked.

"I am."

"Then eat some pizza, and quit yelling at me."

"I'm not yelling at you." He stopped and lowered his voice. "I'm not yelling at you."

"You told me to come live here, Riley. You told me to do whatever Shane said."

"He's trying to steal you from me."

"No, he's not. He's already got my sister."

"Not like that."

"Then, like what?"

"He can't stand me."

"Well, you are trying to steal all his customers."

"It's more than that. He can't stand the fact that I'm breathing."

Kalissa set down the wine bottle.

"Grab the beer," she told him, reaching for the top button on her blouse.

"What are you—"

"Bring the pizza," she said, popping another button and another.

Riley glanced down the hall, worried about Garrison reappearing.

"Let's go be ordinary." She shrugged out of her blouse and let it drop to the floor.

"Stop it." He rushed forward.

She reached back to unclip her bra.

He grabbed her hand. "Seriously. Stop it."

"You want to fight with me?"

"No."

"Then bring the beer and the pizza." She tugged her hand away and sauntered down the hall to the first door. She opened it, slipped off her bra, and dropped the lacy garment on the hall floor, turning into the room.

Riley couldn't decide whether to be angry or amused. He was definitely aroused. Wasting no time, he balanced the beer and pizza in one hand, scooped up her blouse, then grabbed her bra and closed the bedroom door behind him.

"It locks," she told him, standing there in nothing but her panties.

"That's good." He quickly emptied his hands.

"This whole thing is confusing for me." She looked incredibly vulnerable standing nearly naked in the soft light.

"It must be," he said, moving instinctively toward her.

"I don't know how I'm supposed to act, what I'm supposed to feel."

"I want to help," he told her honestly.

"It's funny," she said, half to herself. "Right now, you're the most normal thing in my world."

He unbuttoned his shirt, tossing it away as he drew to a stop in front of her. "You're the most precious thing in mine."

She gave him a little smile. "You still want pizza?"

He kicked off his shoes. "Pizza can wait."

"It'll get cold."

"I'm getting hot."

Her smile grew. "I'm hot, too."

"You are definitely that." He reached out to cradle her head, stepping in.

"Riley?"

"Yeah?"

Their bodies met, meshing together as if they belonged like that.

"I didn't realize I was yours to steal."

"Surprised me, too." He leaned down to kiss her. "But I know that you are."

Twelve

Kalissa was slowly accepting that her life no longer had a normal.

"I'm clipping the transmitter to the back of your dress," the female technician told her. "It'll feel a bit clunky, but we'll keep it out of the camera angles."

"Have you ever done this before?" Kalissa asked Darci.

"Once," said Darci. "Under much more stressful circumstances."

"You don't find this stressful?"

They'd spent an hour in hair and makeup, had their black dresses fussed over by wardrobe, and now at least a dozen sound technicians, camera operators and assorted television crew were rushing around them on the stage.

Marion Ward, the local talk show anchor had briefly introduced herself, and then rushed off for her own preparations. Shane was standing in the wings, while Garrison and his cohorts were prowling around the studio, presumably checking for hidden dangers. The only thing frightening Kalissa at the moment was the idea of live television.

"It's better doing it live," said Darci. "That way, they can't selectively edit and make you sound stupid."

"I was hoping they could selectively edit to make me sound smart."

The technician smiled as she attached the mic to Kalissa's neckline.

"You're going to do fine," she told her.

"I'm going to freeze up."

"Then I'll do the talking," said Darci.

"Maybe we should have dressed exactly the same," said Kalissa. "That way, you could play both parts."

The technician chuckled.

Kalissa was wearing a form fitting black dress with cap

sleeves and a sweetheart neckline. Darci had also gone with black, but hers had spaghetti straps, beading on the bodice, and a short, pleated crepe skirt. Kalissa's hair was swirled up in a casual, messy knot, while Darci's was neatly braided above her forehead, flowing long down her back.

"Two minutes," called the producer.

Marion Ward rushed in, taking the high seat in between the two women. She sat straight, squared her shoulders, shifted at a slight angle to the camera, braced one foot on the cross bar and crossed her legs.

Kalissa watched carefully, emulating the pose, trying desperately to look relaxed.

"Let your shoulders drop," the sound tech whispered.

Then someone from hair and makeup rushed across the stage, fixing the hair at Kalissa's temple.

"Sixty seconds."

"First question is about your father," Marion said to Darci.

Darci nodded. She looked poised and confident.

Kalissa was starting to sweat.

The producer counted down, and everyone on the stage went still and quiet. The red lights came on for each of the three cameras.

"Three, two, one."

"Good evening, Chicago," Marion sang out. "And Welcome to City Shore Beat. With me tonight is Colborn Aerospace billionaire, Darci Colborn."

Kalissa's mouth twitched for a second. She felt an urge to correct the statement and say that Darci was now only a quarter billionaire.

"You'll remember her from this summer's grand wedding to Shane Colborn." Marion turned to Darci. "Welcome to the show."

"Happy to be here," Darci said with an easy smile.

"And joining us, to the shock and surprise of everyone in Chicago, including Darci Colborn, is Darci's identical twin sister, Kalissa Smith."

Two of the cameras swung to Kalissa. She fixed a smile on her face.

"Welcome to the show, Kalissa."

"Thank you," Kalissa managed.

"This is a tale of scandal, betrayal and long-lost sisters reunited."

Kalissa glanced to Shane while she struggled to keep her expression neutral. This didn't sound promising.

He gave her a thumb's up.

Marion canted her body toward Darci. "Darci, I understand you were raised by your father."

"I was. Ian Rivers was a brilliant if underappreciated engineer and innovator."

Marion turned to Kalissa. "You were separated at birth. Put up for adoption. You never knew your parents or your twin sister."

Kalissa wasn't sure there was a question in there. "Yes," she said.

"As far as we can tell," Darci jumped in. "Our parents separated, each planning to raise one of us. Unfortunately, our birth mother passed away when Kalissa was just a toddler."

Marion returned to Darci, obviously deciding she was going to be the better guest.

Kalissa wanted to apologize. But more than that, she wanted to run off the stage. Instead, she did her best to smile, knowing one of the cameras had stayed focused on her.

"But Kalissa wasn't returned to her father?"

"We don't know all the details," Darci said smoothly. "We do know our father was a business partner with Dalton Colborn. That's how Shane and I met. We've also learned, unbeknownst to my husband, that our father, Ian Rivers, was pivotal in creating the technology used by Colborn Aerospace today as a leading producer of commercial jets."

Kalissa cracked her first real smile. Shane had bet Darci she wouldn't find a way to plug the company.

"Shane and I were thrilled to meet Kalissa. She only learned of my existence because of our recent wedding. As

I'm sure has happened with many families, we were reunited because of pictures broadcast on the Internet."

Marion turned back to Kalissa. "What was your first reaction? How did you feel when you saw Darci for the first time?"

"I thought it was a joke," Kalissa answered honestly. "I thought somebody had photo shopped my face into her wedding pictures."

"And when you found out it was true? That your birth sister was one of the richest people in the country?"

Kalissa hesitated again. There was a calculating look in Marion's eyes. She was definitely setting up for the gold-digger angle, and Kalissa didn't know how to deflect it.

Darci spoke up. "My sister did the most honorable and unexpected thing."

A fleeting look of frustration crossed Marion's face. But then she smiled, and switched to Darci. "Which was?"

"She came to warn me. She had a date that night, and she was afraid people would mistake her for me, and that I'd be embarrassed by it. Shane and I were grateful."

"Grateful in a monetary sense?" asked Marion.

Kalissa was getting concerned. This was supposed to be a friendly interview.

"Are you asking if I've taken any of their money?" asked Kalissa.

Marion swung toward her. "Have you?"

"We've tried very hard to support Kalissa," said Darci. "But she's incredibly independent. The important thing for us is that we've found each other again and reunited as a family."

"That's the important thing," agreed Kalissa.

"But it's vastly changed your circumstances in life," Marion prompted, gesturing toward Kalissa.

"Vastly," Kalissa admitted. "But I imagine that's the case for everyone who finds a long lost relative, whether they're rich or not. I want people to know that I'm not Darci, and Darci's not me. There are two of us, and we look alike." Kalissa stared directly into the camera. "So, if you come across one of us, and we're doing something undignified or inappropriate, assume that it's me. As you can probably tell from this interview, my sister is much more sophisticated than I am. I'm about five minutes out of thrift stores and burger joints."

"Did I mention she has a terrific sense of humor?" asked Darci. Then she unexpectedly came out of her chair, crossing the stage in front of Marion.

Her move seemed to cause a flurry of activity behind the cameras, and Marion appeared quite horrified.

But, Darci kept walking, opening her arms to Kalissa. "Thank goodness you found us." Then she pulled her into a tight hug.

Ducking around Darci, Marion found a new camera angle. "And, uh, we'll be right back."

Darci drew back and gave Marion a withering look. "We're done." She unclipped her mic.

Shane was with them in seconds, followed by the security team.

"Clear the stage," ordered the producer.

A sound technician helped Darci scramble out of the microphone set up, and she quickly followed Shane and Darci out of the studio. Garrison walked beside her.

"What happened?" she asked. She realized it hadn't gone as they'd expected, but she wasn't sure why Darci was angry.

"You didn't need to say all that about yourself," said Garrison.

Kalissa didn't see it that way. "I just told the truth. That woman wasn't letting us say what we came to say."

"There was nothing in particular you needed to say. You only needed to be seen together. That host boxed you into a corner. It made Darci mad."

"I want the world to know it's me and not Darci out there making mistakes."

"You're not making mistakes, ma'am."

"You can call me Kalissa, you know."

"Not on the job."

"You call Megan by her first name."

There was a split second's hesitation before he spoke. "I'm not assigned to protect Megan."

They passed through the exterior door into the studio parking lot. Kalissa's eyes adjusted to the sunlight, and she immediately spotted Riley. He was thirty yards away, leaning against his sports car.

"Riley?" she said out loud. "What is he—" She stepped away from the group, walking toward him.

He straightened to meet her and smiled.

"What are you doing here?" she asked.

"I wanted to make sure it went okay."

"Why didn't you come inside?"

His gaze moved beyond her to Darci and the rest of the group. "It seemed like a family thing."

"It didn't go so well," she told him.

"I saw. I watched the broadcast on-line."

Kalissa nodded. "Garrison says I should have kept my mouth shut and just sat there."

"In those exact words?" Riley asked.

"Not exactly. But Darci cut it off because I was blowing it."

He took her hand. "You want to walk?" He nodded toward a walkway and an open green space along the curve of the river.

Kalissa glanced back at the group. "Garrison will have to come with us."

"Don't worry about Garrison. It's his job to worry about you."

"I don't want to make his job harder."

"You won't. It's not. Stop worrying about everyone else." He called out to the others. "We'll meet you back at the penthouse."

Kalissa decided some fresh air would do her good. She'd been cooped up in the apartment for four days now, and she needed to clear her head.

She walked beside Riley, putting the interview from her mind, forgetting about Garrison and everyone else. Trains and traffic echoed against skyscrapers across the water, boats chugged past, and they joined the steady stream of pedestrians taking in the afternoon.

Part of her wanted to tell him about her father and the inheritance. But another part wanted to keep the secret inside. It felt like, once she told him, the last barrier to her new reality would be gone. She wasn't ready yet.

They turned to walk along the black railing. A breeze swirled up from the water, chilling the air.

Riley shrugged out of his jacket and draped it around her shoulders.

"I've been thinking," she said.

"That's good."

"About taking Shane up on his offer."

"What offer is that?" She could hear the hesitation in Riley's words.

"Landscaping the mansion. Me and Megan. It would keep us working, keep our regular crews busy, but it would keep me out of the public eye."

Once it became known she was a shareholder in Colborn Aerospace, Kalissa knew her days of wheeling bark mulch and azalea shrubs would have to end. But she couldn't imagine being qualified to do anything for Colborn Aerospace.

"I'm sure Shane would like that." There was an edge to Riley's voice. "The place is a fortress."

"Garrison would like that," Kalissa joked, not wanting the conversation to get negative.

She glanced behind them to see where he was.

"I told you not to worry about Garrison. He knows his job. He seems good at it. You just have to live your life."

Kalissa couldn't help but laugh at that statement. She didn't even understand her life, never mind know how to live it anymore. She stopped walking, turning to lean on the rail and gaze out.

"What do you like about me?" she asked him.

He linked his arm with hers. "Everything."

"I mean specifically."

"Specifically, I like everything about you."

She sighed. "I feel like I'm caught between two worlds. One I know, and in it I'm doing okay. The other is unfamiliar and kind of scary, and I don't know if I can succeed."

"You'll be fine," he said, but she knew he didn't understand the magnitude of the problem.

"I'm going to change. I'll have to change. But I was thinking. If I knew the best parts of me, I could make sure I kept them."

He faced her and smiled. "You're not going to lose the best parts of you. They're you. They'll go anywhere and everywhere you go."

"I can't do my job anymore. I can't dig up people's front yards, lay stone and push wheelbarrow loads of manure."

"You can still do the planning. That's mostly your part anyway. Have you ever actually laid any stone? And when's the last time you dumped manure?"

"You know what I mean."

"I do," he said, putting his hand over hers. "Tell me what I can do to help?"

"This," she said. "Today. One more day. Can we go back to the pier, buy ourselves a corndog and be incredibly ordinary for a while?"

He brought her hand to his lips and gave her knuckles a tender kiss. "We can do anything you want."

To Riley, the Colborn mansion felt like the lion's den.

He followed a butler through what he knew to be the grand hall. Used mostly for entertaining, it had soaring, twenty foot ceilings, marble pillars and gleaming white archways. Around the perimeter were antique style lampposts, with an ostentatious wrought iron chandelier hanging in the center of the room.

Riley could only imagine who they were trying to impress. In the center of the room, a bronze stallion statue was perched on a massive, hewn wood table. Oil paintings hung on the walls, Dalton, Shane's mother, Shane himself.

Riley slowed down to look at them.

"If you'd care to wait here," said the butler, gesturing to a grouping of walnut and red velvet armchairs. "I'll find Ms. Smith."

Riley wasn't sure if it was a question or a command, so he nodded. One room in this place was as bad as another.

The butler's footfalls faded slowly away on the hardwood floor while Riley gazed at the paintings. He took in a suit of armor and some bronze statuettes placed on heavy, wooden tables. He couldn't help but wonder how often his mother had polished the pieces. They looked like they'd been there for decades.

He gazed around the huge room, mentally comparing it to their small, basement apartment twenty miles away. His mother had ridden two buses every day to get here. She'd cleaned up after Dalton Colborn, his wife and their guests, growing tired and ill while Dalton had looked down his nose at her, never caring that she'd once shared his bed.

The sound of footsteps echoed behind him, and he turned, expecting Kalissa.

It was Shane, who stopped short, obviously surprised to see Riley.

The two stared at each other, while resentment churned in Riley's gut.

Then Shane walked forward. "I didn't know you were here."

"I didn't expect you either."

It was midday Thursday, and Riley had guessed Shane would still be in the city.

"Starting the weekend early," said Shane. "You?"

"I'm here to see Kalissa." Riley stated the obvious.

"She's outside."

"Your butler told me to wait here."

Shane gave an absent nod, his gaze going to the large portrait of Dalton directly above them. Riley couldn't help but wonder if Shane was also considering the irony.

"I bet he'd turn over in his grave," said Riley.

Shane's gaze narrowed, but Riley wasn't in the mood to back off.

"Seeing you and me, here, together."

"Why?" asked Shane.

"Please don't," said Riley, his stomach cramping, his tone going hard. "Not here. Not now. Not when it's just you and me."

"Don't ask a question?"

"Don't play dumb," Riley spat out.

But Shane wouldn't let up. "He'd hate Ellis Aviation?"

"Yeah, right. Ellis Aviation is what would tick him off."

"Okay," said Shane, evidently willing to let it drop.

Well Riley wasn't, not this time, not if he was going to continue to see Kalissa and keep running into Shane. Not next to the antiques his mother hand polished, under Dalton's roof, with Shane standing there as the new lord of the manor.

"I'm talking about me," said Riley. "He'd hate *me*." He waited for Shane's reaction.

"Are you saying he knew you?"

Now they were getting somewhere.

"My mother brought me here once. I was thirteen. I was just old enough to get it. Do you know what he said? Do you know what he said to his own son?"

Shane went still.

Yeah, Riley had said it. He'd spoken the forbidden words the mighty Colborn family had hidden for so long. "He said, 'servants use the back door, and they don't wear dirty shoes in the hall'."

Shane reached out and braced himself on a table.

"That was it," said Riley. "The only words our old man ever uttered to me, and the only time he ever looked at me."

"He didn't—"

"Don't make excuses for him," Riley ground out. "You resent Ellis Aviation? You don't like me touching your sister-in-law? You think you can keep the Colborn family untainted by the illegitimate son of a *servant*?" Once rolling, Riley barely stopped for breath.

"I know you're poisoning Kalissa against me," he ground out. "And it's not going to work. I won't let it work. I grew up tough, Shane, a whole lot tougher than you. I was on the outside, and it was cold out there. I watched him dote on you. I watched him tutor you. Then I watched him hand you his world on a silver platter. All the while, I was fighting down there in the dirt. You might hate me, but that's nothing compared to how I feel about you."

The color had drained from Shane's face, and his chest rapidly rose and fell.

"Riley?" Kalissa shocked voice was directly behind them.

Riley pivoted, his stomach bottoming out, while Shane stood frozen.

"Riley?" she repeated. "*What* is going on?"

He cursed a streak inside his brain.

She swallowed. "Is it true? It's true," she laughed a little hysterically.

"I'm sorry," he blurted out, moving toward her.

She recoiled, taking a step back.

"I wanted to tell you." He kicked himself for letting his temper get away from him.

"That you're Shane's brother? His *brother*?" The pitch of her voice went higher. Her hand went to her forehead as if she had a sudden pain. "That you hate and resent him?"

"This is bad," said Riley. "I never would have—"

"Bad doesn't begin to describe it." She took another backward step. "I see it now. It's been about this all along."

He moved, trying to keep the distance small between them. "I shouldn't have come here. It was stupid for me to come here. I thought I could handle…"

"The lies?" she asked.

"I didn't lie."

"You did *nothing* but lie."

"Ellis," said Shane.

"Not now," Riley barked over his shoulder.

Kalissa let out a whimper and turned on her heel.

Riley followed, but she began to run.

"Ellis," Shane called behind him.

Riley ignored him. He had to get to Kalissa.

He caught up to her in the main reception room. She was heading for a staircase.

"Kalissa, *stop*."

She stopped. But she didn't turn around.

He slowed his pace, coming up behind her. "I know this must be a shock. I didn't say anything, because—"

"I'm only stopping because I want this to be final. I know I've been an easy mark. I don't know why, but I was attracted to you." She gave an unsteady laugh. Still, she kept her back to him. "You obviously know I was attracted to you. But I know how you operate, solidify your position before revealing the truth. It's not going to work a second time. I can't help you compete with your brother. I can't help you be a Colborn."

Riley was horrified by the statement. "That's not what I want."

She turned, finally. "Yes, it is." Her eyes glistened with tears.

"You and me, we have nothing to do with the Colborns."

"We have *everything* to do with the Colborns. Shane's the reason you want me. Dalton's the reason you're here. Your past drives you. From what I can see, it's always driven you." She swallowed and seemed to force herself to moderate her voice. "At least now I know why. I understand you, Riley."

"No, you don't."

She didn't understand him. If she understood him, she'd know he was in love with her.

"Leave," she said. "Just leave."

"I can't."

"You don't have a choice."

"Let's go somewhere, anywhere but here. Let's talk this through. I never, *ever* meant for any of this to hurt you."

She gave a weak smile. "So you can lie to me some more."

"I'm not going to lie. There's nothing left. You know everything."

She paused. "Yes, I do. I know everything. Goodbye, Riley."

"Kalissa, no."

But she was mounting the stairs.

He could see Garrison out of the corner of his eye. Riley wanted to chase her. But he knew he'd never get there. Garrison wouldn't let him get near her.

He tried to reason with her. "How can talking hurt?"

But she didn't stop, she didn't even look, she just disappeared around the corner of the staircase.

Riley's heart was pumping. It took every last ounce of control that he had to remain at the bottom of those stairs. There had to be something he could do. He needed a next move. But he couldn't for the life of him come up with one.

"Riley," Shane called out, passing Garrison to approach him.

"Not now," said Riley. "*Not…now*."

He knew leaving was his only move. Leaving and regrouping, then coming back, coming at this from another angle. Because there was no way this was the end for him and Kalissa.

Kalissa made her way across the mansion on the second floor. She took the service stairs and left through the back exit. There, she found Megan in the rose garden.

"I know it's a few weeks before we can start," said Megan, smiling with what looked like pure joy. "But I can't help wandering around out here and salivating. There's so much we can do with these grounds."

Kalissa forced her own smile. "Do you know where you want to start?"

"Not yet. Maybe the pond. How fun would it be to expand and get some pure white swans."

"Sure. Swans."

"I'm joking, of course." Megan peered at her. "Kalissa? What's wrong?"

"Nothing. Well. I just broke up with Riley." Kalissa's legs suddenly lost all their strength, and she sat down on the grass.

"You what?" Megan crouched down beside her. "Why? What happened?"

"Kalissa?" Darci called from the lawn beyond the garden.

"Over here," Megan answered, sitting down next to Kalissa. "Does she know?"

Kalissa nodded, her chest heavy and aching. "Shane was there."

Darci rushed past the Pink Flamingo bushes. "Are you all right?" she asked, dropping down beside Kalissa and giving her shoulders a squeeze. "I'm so, so sorry."

"What happened?" asked Megan.

"Riley lied again. Or is it still. I think it's still."

"Shane had no idea," said Darci. "He's stunned."

"What did he lie about?" asked Megan, glancing from one woman to the other.

"He's Shane's brother," said Kalissa. She reached out and grasped Megan's arm. She was coming clean, here and now. "And I'm inheriting—" She looked to Darci. "Is that the right way to say it? Inheriting?"

"Say it however you want."

"Part of Colborn Aerospace," Kalissa finished.

"What?" Megan looked confused.

"I'm not keeping any more secrets. I was trying to wrap my head around it, but you need to know. I tried to stop it, but I couldn't. It looks like I'm going to be crazy rich."

"What does that have to do with Riley?" asked Megan.

"Nothing," said Kalissa. "He doesn't know." Then it dawned on her. "I guess I'm keeping secrets from him, too." It was comically ironic.

"It's not the same thing," said Darci.

"Am I wrong?" asked Kalissa. "Was I wrong to keep quiet?"

"You broke up with him?" asked Megan. "Or the other way around?"

"It was me," said Kalissa. "He was talking to Shane, yelling at Shane really. He's spent his entire life wanting what Shane has, maybe even wanting to *be* Shane."

"So, Dalton was his father?" Megan asked. "He had a different mother?"

"She worked here," said Darci. "Apparently she was one of the housekeepers."

"Riley said she was young and didn't want to lose her job," said Kalissa, battling against instinctive sympathy for Riley. "That was before I knew he was talking about Dalton Colborn and this particular mansion."

"Shane didn't know," said Darci. "Riley thinks Shane shunned him all these years. But he didn't know."

"That had to be tough on Riley," said Megan.

"I can't help feeling sorry for him," said Kalissa.

She wanted to stay angry, but she couldn't help picturing him as a young boy, a teenager. He was hurt, wounded, and it seemed to have impacted his entire life.

"Maybe it's too soon to ask," said Darci. "Could you ever forgive Riley?"

Kalissa wanted it to be that simple. Her throat closed over again. "It's not about that. It's about Shane. Whatever Shane has, Riley wants, too. He's not thinking clearly. He's not seeing me clearly. It's all emotion and dark history." Darci's face twisted in a grimace. "He wanted me before he came anywhere close to knowing me." Kalissa looked to Megan for confirmation.

Megan didn't disagree.

"He had tunnel vision the whole time," said Kalissa. "And I was flattered. It was hard not to be flattered."

"But you like him, too," said Darci.

"Are you on his side?" Megan asked.

"I don't want there to be sides."

"Because he's Shane's brother," Kalissa finished for her. It was a terrible situation for Darci and Shane. Kalissa started to rise. "Listen, I'm going to get out of the way—"

"You're not going *anywhere*," said Darci, grasping Kalissa's elbow.

"This is a disaster." A tear crept from Kalissa's eye.

"And we're going to figure it out together," said Darci.

"I can't see him. I won't see him."

"You don't have to see anyone. I'm on your side, now and always. You're my family."

"Riley is Shane's family."

"It's not the same thing," said Darci.

"How is it different?"

"I don't know, but it is."

"I'm going to hate him," said Kalissa, trying, but failing to be strong.

The upright posture lasted about twenty seconds before she slumped. "Maybe tomorrow. I can start hating him tomorrow."

Darci slipped her arm around Kalissa's shoulders. "We just have to make it to tomorrow."

Kalissa gave a gloomy nod. Tomorrow seemed incredibly far away.

"We'll do something fun," Darci said with encouragement.

Kalissa knew she was reaching. She was trying to be a good sister, and come up with a distraction.

"Like what?" asked Megan, gamely buying in.

"Dinner out, somewhere nice?"

"I'm not going out in public," said Kalissa. That was the last thing she wanted to do.

"A tour of the wine cellar?" Darci suggested.

Getting drunk was tempting, but Kalissa knew she'd only feel worse in the morning. "Pass."

"Well, that's disappointing," said Megan with a mock pout.

Darci shrugged. "Wine cellar's not going anywhere. We'll do that another day." Then she snapped her fingers. "I've got it. Spa day. Well spa night. Night and day. There's no rush to get back."

"No, thanks," said Kalissa. "I don't want to run into anyone who saw the broadcast."

"We won't." Darci's voice held a lot of conviction. "Not in upstate New York."

Both Kalissa and Megan gaped at her in confusion.

"I've got a jet," explained Darci, pulling out her phone.

It took Megan a moment to speak. "You mean a private jet?"

"There's a place called Glimmer Mist Falls. Massage, facial, pedicure, mineral springs. They'll send a limo to meet the plane."

Kalissa shook her head. She just wanted to bury herself under the covers and wait for unconsciousness.

Megan stuck her hand in the air. "I'm in."

"We're not taking no for an answer," said Darci. "Garrison will help."

Kalissa had no desire to go along. Then again, she wasn't sure she had the energy to fight them off either.

"Sweetheart?" Darci said into the phone. "We want to take the jet to Glimmer Mist Falls." Her gaze went to Kalissa, turning sympathetic. "I think so, too." She paused. "We will. Thanks, honey."

Thirteen

For the next three days, Riley focused on two things, work at Ellis Aviation and coming up with a strategy to win back Kalissa. The work part was easy. All he needed there was energy and an edge. His frustration gave him both.

Getting Kalissa back seemed impossible. As long as she was out at the mansion, he couldn't get near her. He knew Shane would keep the place locked down tight. And Garrison was loyal to Shane. He might sympathize with Riley, but he would definitely do his job.

Even if Riley could find a way to see her, he didn't know what he'd say. She was right to accuse him of lying. He hadn't told her about Shane. And that made it look like Shane mattered. He didn't.

He cracked open a bottle of whisky in his kitchen, pouring a couple of ounces over ice. Liquor might not be the answer. But he was tired, and it was late, and he was sick of dreaming about Kalissa.

The dreams were spectacular, but waking up was a nightmare.

A knock sounded on his front door.

He double checked the clock. It was coming up on ten. While Ashton might drop in this late, Ashton was on his way to Alaska today. He'd invited Riley along. Riley had to admit, he'd been tempted.

He crossed to the foyer and opened the door, shocked to find Shane on the front porch.

"Is Kalissa all right?" The question was out before Riley could censor it.

"She's fine," said Shane. "She's in New York."

For some reason, the answer struck Riley as absurd. "Why is she in New York?"

All this time, he'd been picturing her at the mansion. It

annoyed him to be wrong. It annoyed him more that it was Shane who had the information.

"Darci took her to a spa. Garrison's with them."

"She's been wanting a spa day," said Riley, wondering why he was bothering to make small talk.

"You mind if I come in?" asked Shane.

The answer was yes. But fighting with Shane seemed like a reasonable distraction. So he stepped back. "Why not."

Shane entered, and Riley closed the door behind him.

"Drink?" asked Riley, holding up his glass.

"Yeah."

Riley headed for the kitchen, and Shane followed.

He poured another whisky, not particularly caring if it was Shane's preference or not. Then he handed Shane the glass.

"Why are you here?"

"Right to the point," said Shane. He took a swallow.

"No reason to beat around the bush. Do you want me to close my company? Leave the state? Have you changed your mind about fighting dirty?"

"I didn't know," said Shane.

"Didn't know what?"

"That Dalton was your father. That you were my brother."

"The hell you didn't," said Riley. "We talked about it."

Shane drew back, showing an admirable display of amazement. "When?"

"Freshman year, high school baseball tournament. We were on opposite teams."

Shane's gaze went off into space. "I have no recollection of anything like that."

"I called you brother and said we should talk. You called me a loser and a twerp and told me to get lost."

Shane seemed speechless.

Riley finished his drink and poured another.

"I couldn't have understood," said Shane.

"Right," said Riley. "It's your story. Tell it however you want."

"Honestly," said Shane. "I didn't understand. I didn't know. You think I'd *ignore* that all these years?"

"You did."

Shane paced across the kitchen. "I didn't. I don't know what else to say. Did my dad know?"

Riley set the bottle down with a crack. "She begged him to help her. He agreed not to fire her."

Shane swore angrily. He swallowed the whisky then marched over and poured himself another. "That's why Ellis Aviation."

Riley didn't argue the point.

"I can't say I blame you," said Shane. "Have you done DNA? Why didn't you come after some of his money? Even Darci came after his money."

"I'm not Darci."

"Fair enough. So, what do you want?"

Riley didn't even have to think about that. "Kalissa."

"I mean from me."

"You've got her right now."

Shane seemed to ponder. "I don't see that happening."

"I don't see me giving up."

"I don't think I can let you hurt her anymore."

Riley set down the new drink. He really wasn't thirsty anymore. "I never wanted to hurt her."

"So you keep claiming. Yet, it keeps on happening." Shane snagged a kitchen chair, setting it backward and straddling it. "I have a proposition for you."

Riley folded his arms over his chest and braced himself against the counter.

"Half," said Shane. "Right down the middle. The DNA checks out, you get half of my interest in Colborn Aerospace, half ownership of the mansion. I'm keeping the penthouse, but I'm sure you can afford your own. And I'll publicly acknowledge you, tell the world you're Dalton's son."

"Very funny," said Riley, battling to keep his emotions in check. He couldn't afford to take Shane seriously on this.

"It's not a joke," said Shane.

"What's the catch?"

"Catch is…"

Riley waited for it.

"You leave Kalissa alone."

"No." The word all but leapt from Riley's soul.

"That's my condition."

"The answer is no."

Shane rested his arm on the back of the chair. "Whether you mean to or not, you hurt her. Hurting her, hurts Darci, and I will do anything to protect Darci."

"Including buying off your illegitimate brother?"

Riley's emotions settled to normal levels. Yeah, this was Shane's idea of a joke all right, toss him an offer he couldn't accept.

"Including that," said Shane.

"Forget it."

"You're saying no to a quarter billion?"

"The price is too high."

Shane came to his feet. "For Kalissa."

"I want her back."

Shane returned the chair and moved to stand in front of Riley. "I'll hire an army."

"I know you will."

The two men stared at each other.

"You know," said Shane. "You look a little like him."

"I don't take that as a compliment."

Shane squinted. "I think we both know what the DNA is going to say."

"It's irrelevant."

"Maybe." Shane stepped back and started out of the kitchen. In the doorway, he turned back. "For the record, that was a good answer."

"For the record," Riley called to Shane's retreating back. "I couldn't give a crap what any Colborn thinks of me."

He reached for the glass and polished off the second drink.

Kalissa followed Darci up the compact staircase into the Colborn jet. They'd spent four days at the Glimmer Mist Falls spa, and she told herself she felt better. Megan had returned to Chicago after the first day to finish up Mosaic's final jobs, but Darci had insisted Kalissa stay.

Kalissa hadn't been inclined to argue. She was missing Riley every minute, and she hadn't been able to bear the thought of returning to the mansion or the penthouse. She wasn't sure she could do it now, but she knew she couldn't stay away forever.

The co-pilot greeted them in the doorway, cheerfully welcoming them on board. Despite several massages and dips in the mineral pool, Kalissa's muscles felt stiff and sore. She was trying to snap out of it, but her body felt heavy, and her head felt like it was packed in cotton.

"Darling?" said Darci as she entered the plane, a note of surprise in her voice.

Kalissa passed by the co-pilot to see Shane standing between the seats in the front row.

"I came along for the ride," he said, kissing Darci and giving her a quick squeeze. "Hi, Kalissa."

Kalissa mustered a smile. "Hi, Shane."

"How are you doing?" he asked, gesturing for Darci to take the window in a grouping of four seats around a small table.

"I'm fine," Kalissa automatically answered, moving to the seat facing Darci.

Shane looked to Darci for confirmation.

Darci made a rocking motion with the flat of her hand.

"I'm better than I was," Kalissa insisted.

"Marginally," said Darci. "I seriously thought about staying another day."

"We can't," said Kalissa.

"You can if you want," said Shane. He looked to Darci.

"I want to get back," said Kalissa, telling herself she meant it.

She'd sat around long enough wallowing in self-pity. People got through heartbreak all the time. She'd do it, too.

"Are you ready, sir?" asked the co-pilot.

"We're ready," said Shane.

The co-pilot secured the door, and they all buckled up.

"Thank you for doing this," Kalissa told Darci. Then her gaze took in Shane as well. "To both of you."

"You don't have to thank us," said Shane. "The money, this plane, even the mansion are yours now as much as they are ours."

She'd heard it from Darci a dozen times. But this time, Kalissa didn't let herself argue. It was time to accept her new life. In fact, it was time to embrace her new life.

"I want to know how to help," she said to Shane. "I can't just renovate the grounds forever. I want to contribute to the company."

Shane smiled. "Good for you."

As the plane taxied toward the runway, Kalissa squared her shoulders, feeling ever so slightly lighter.

"What about interior design?" asked Darci. "You've got a flair for color and pattern, and you definitely have an eye for utility."

"You mean, pick out upholstery colors and carpets?" asked Kalissa.

"She means head up the interior design division," said Shane.

"She could job shadow Agnes for a few months," Darci said to Shane. Then she switched to Kalissa. "Agnes is retiring at the beginning of next year. We have to find her a replacement."

"Maybe," said Kalissa, wondering how she could possibly be qualified.

The engines revved up to full power, and the captain released the brakes, sending them rushing down the runway. The jet was light and powerful, and it took off quickly, climbing up over the small town and banking along the river.

"I went to see Riley yesterday," said Shane as they leveled off.

Darci looked at Shane in surprise, while Kalissa stilled. Her chest tightened up again.

"Do we need to talk about that right now, sweetheart?" Darci put a wealth of meaning into her tone.

Shane seemed to ignore his wife. "I have to ask you, Kalissa."

"No, you don't," said Darci. "You don't have to ask her anything right now."

"What?" asked Kalissa. She was angry and heartsick, but she still found herself thirsty for news of Riley. She was in love with an illusion, and it was pathetic.

"I made him an offer," said Shane.

"Of what?" asked Darci, starting to sound exasperated.

Shane kept his focus on Kalissa. "Public acknowledgement that he's my brother and half of my interest in Colborn Aerospace. Plus, rights to the mansion."

"*What*?" Darci all but jumped out of her seat. "Why would you *make him part of our lives*?"

Kalissa had the same question, but it was none of her business, and she wasn't sure she could speak right now anyway. Riley tied up with Colborn? Riley coming and going from the mansion? There was no way she could cope with it.

But where could she go? Maybe leave Chicago?

"There was one condition," said Shane, his voice calm and steady. "He walks away from Kalissa. He doesn't hurt her by trying to get her back."

"You bought him off?" asked Darci. She glanced worriedly at Kalissa.

If possible, Kalissa felt even sicker. By lying to her and breaking her heart, Riley had convinced Shane to give him everything he ever wanted.

He'd won, and she'd lost her heart.

"He turned it down," said Shane.

"What part?" asked Darci, clearly confused.

"All parts," said Shane. "Everything. He refused to give up Kalissa. He said his birthright and a quarter billion weren't enough."

Darci's mouth opened, but she didn't say anything.

There was a roaring sound in Kalissa's ears. It seemed like the jet engine was getting louder and louder and louder.

"Kalissa?" Darci prompted, reaching to take her hand.

"I don't—" was all Kalissa managed.

"He picked you over me. He picked you over Colborn." Shane broke into a smile and gave what looked like an astonished shake of his head.

"Did he not understand the offer?"

"He understood," said Shane.

"Then why?" She couldn't form the right question. But she also couldn't stop a stubborn glimmer of hope.

"There's only one reason he'd do that," said Shane.

"Don't tell me you trust him," said Darci.

Kalissa found herself holding her breath.

"I don't know if I'd go that far," said Shane. "But I do know that he's in love with Kalissa."

"You're on *his* side?" asked Darci.

Shane gave an unabashed shrug. "He is my brother."

Kalissa's chest buzzed with a mixture of excitement and trepidation. She knew better than to hope, but she simply couldn't stop herself.

Riley stayed at the Ellis plant on Sunday until the walls started to close in. Then he headed to the gym, working out until he was exhausted, going home to a very long, hot shower.

He slipped on a pair of worn, gray sweats and padded barefoot into the kitchen, sticking his head in the fridge. He needed comfort food, maybe pizza or nachos or chocolate cake. He'd get lost in an action flick or three, then fall into bed and try very hard not to dream.

He knew he had to pick up the pieces of his life, but it wasn't going to happen tonight.

His front doorbell rang, and he swung the fridge door shut. He was torn between ignoring the sound and wishing it was something to distract him—maybe one of his neighbors was having a party or a flood.

It rang again, and he crossed through the living room to the foyer, opening the door.

His brain staggered to a stop.

Kalissa stood on his porch in a sophisticated, gold dress

with cap sleeves and a short skirt. Her hair was done up in a braid, and her makeup was heavier than usual.

"I bought this in New York," she said apologetically. "I'm a princess now, truly part of the Colborn empire."

"No. You're not." He didn't know what point she was making, but he knew it wasn't true.

"I've changed." There was a challenge in her voice.

"Not on the inside." He could see past anything she wore, any hairdo, any amount of makeup. "You'll always be you."

She moved through the doorway. Her expression seemed to relax, and she took in his damp hair, his bare chest and his bare feet.

He wanted to hope, but he didn't dare. Past her, he could see Garrison in the driveway. "Kalissa, what are you doing here?"

"We need to talk." She put a cool palm on his chest.

"Sure." He'd never refuse her, but he could already feel himself careening toward fresh heartbreak.

"But I don't want to talk." She tipped her chin, gazing up at him with the most blatantly sensual expression in her eyes.

"Kalissa." He was only going to be able to stand this for about five seconds.

"If you say the wrong thing." She brushed her body against his. "Then I'm going to have to walk out."

He wouldn't say the wrong thing. He *couldn't* say the wrong thing. He swung the door shut behind her.

"But if this is going to end," she said.

If? She'd said if. He clung to the word.

"Then I want to make love one more time."

She was talking nonsense. But he didn't care.

He scooped her into his arms, heading immediately for the bedroom. It was an outrageous suggestion. But he wasn't about to argue.

He set her on her feet next to his bed.

"Kalissa—"

"Don't," she whispered. She stretched up, pressing forward for a kiss.

He settled his lips on hers, raking his hand through her hair. But before it could get interesting, she broke away.

His heart sank.

But she stripped off her panties, tossing them aside. Then she yanked off his sweats and pressed down on his shoulders.

He sat on the bed. She slipped onto his lap, straddling his hips.

"Once fast," she told him. "Then again, really, really slow."

"Oh, yeah," he whispered, putting reason on hold and taking control of their kiss.

He made love to her twice over, communicating with nothing but touches, sighs and moans. Then when they were covered in sweat, and neither of them could move, he tucked her head against his shoulder and relaxed in complete satisfaction.

This had to be good. This couldn't be bad. Maybe they'd talk now, or maybe they'd wait until morning. Whichever it was, he had to get it right.

His phone rang.

He reached out and checked the number. "It's Garrison."

Kalissa smiled.

Riley answered. "Yeah?"

"Over to you?" Garrison asked.

"You can pick her up in the morning."

Kalissa stretched her arms above her head to grip the brass rails on his headboard.

Riley let his gaze scan her tempting body. "Maybe," he said to Garrison.

"Talk to you then," said Garrison.

"Yeah." Riley ended the call.

"This is a nice room," said Kalissa, gazing around at his furniture.

"You look very good in it." He wondered, if he barricaded the doors, how long it would take for someone to break in and rescue her.

"It's so normal," she said with a sigh. "Do you think we could stay here?"

"Yes." If he had his way, she was staying here forever.

She grinned, then sobered. "There's something I didn't tell you. And I'm sorry I didn't."

The statement surprised him. "You have a secret?"

She nodded. "It's about Colborn."

His phone rang again.

He swore.

"It could be Garrison."

"Don't move a muscle," said Riley. "You look perfect exactly the way you are."

He put one hand on her smooth stomach and used the other to pick up his phone. The number was blocked.

"Yeah?" His tone was impatient.

"Is Kalissa still with you?"

"Shane?"

"She's still there?"

"Absolutely," said Riley.

"Okay, so here's my new deal."

"Seriously? Do we have to do this *now*?"

"You keep Kalissa."

Riley stilled. He was listening.

"I publicly acknowledge you as my brother." Shane continued. "We merge Colborn and Ellis Aviation. We split the proceeds. We share the mansion. I'm still keeping the penthouse, but I figure you can share Kalissa's."

Riley wanted to scream the word *yes*! "Kalissa says she wants to stay here."

"Oh." Shane's tone turned cautious. "Well, I guess we can arrange something."

"Good."

"Have you proposed yet?"

"Goodbye, Shane."

"As your big brother, I feel it's my duty to—"

"You're a whole two months older than me."

"And a whole two months more married. Lock down the deal, bro. Do it now."

"I will," said Riley. He hesitated to ask the next question. "You think I have a chance?"

"A quarter billion is a lot of money. She knows you gave it up for her."

"Yes, I gave it— Oh. I get it." That was why she came back. "Thanks, man."

"No problem."

"I gotta go."

"Go."

Riley hit disconnect.

He moved close to her, putting his head on the pillow to whisper in her ear. "How can I make it work? What do you need me to say?"

She took his hand, holding it in front of her face, studying his palm. "Darci gave me half of Colborn. Wait, it's half of her half."

It struck Riley as an odd move for Darci to make. "Why?"

"Apparently, it should have belonged to my dad. I really am one of them, Riley. It's more than just being Darci's sister."

That was interesting. But Riley didn't want to talk about their families anymore.

He cut to the chase. "I love you, Kalissa."

She shifted to face him, her features close up and crystal clear. "I figured you must."

He chuckled gently and smoothed her hair, brushed her ear, stroked her cheek, then he kissed her lips.

"Shane told me you turned down his offer," she said.

"I only want you."

"I think it was a test. I think he did it for me. So I'd know for sure."

"Shane's pretty shrewd that way."

She gathered his hand and drew it to her chest. "I love you, Riley."

"Oh, sweetheart."

"I missed you so much."

"You don't have to miss me anymore. I wish I had a ring. I

wish we had champagne. It would be better if we were dressed. This isn't the kind of story you can tell the grandchildren."

"We can do all that later," said Kalissa.

"Marry me," said Riley.

"Yes. Oh, yes."

* * * * *

MILLS & BOON®

The Thirty List

At thirty, Rachel has slid down every ladder she has
ever climbed. Jobless, broke and ditched by her
husband, she has to move in with grumpy
Patrick and his four-year-old son.

Patrick is also getting divorced, so to cheer themselves up the two decide to draw up bucket lists.
Soon they are learning to tango, abseiling, trying
stand-up comedy and more. But, as she gets
closer to Patrick, Rachel wonders if their
relationship is too good to be true…

**Order yours today at
www.millsandboon.co.uk/Thethirtylist**

MILLS & BOON®

The Chatsfield Collection!

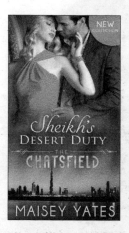

Style, spectacle, scandal...!

With the eight Chatsfield siblings happily married and settling down, it's time for a new generation of Chatsfields to shine, in this brand-new 8-book collection! The prospect of a merger with the Harrington family's boutique hotels will shape the future forever. But who will come out on top?

**Find out at
www.millsandboon.co.uk/TheChatsfield2**

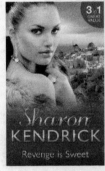

MILLS & BOON®

Desire™

PASSIONATE AND DRAMATIC LOVE STORIES

A sneak peek at next month's titles...

In stores from 19th June 2015:

- **Claiming His Secret Son** – Olivia Gates
  and **Seduced by the Spare Heir** – Andrea Laurence

- **Pregnant by the Cowboy CEO** – Catherine Mann
  and **Lone Star Baby Bombshell** – Lauren Canan

- **The Billionaire's Daddy Test** – Charlene Sands
  and **A Royal Amnesia Scandal** – Jules Bennett

Available at WHSmith, Tesco, Asda, Eason, Amazon and Apple

Just can't wait?
Buy our books online a month before they hit the shops!
visit www.millsandboon.co.uk

These books are also available in eBook format!